This novel is entirely a work of [illegible]
incidents portrayed in it are the [illegible]
Any resemblance to actual per[illegible]nts or
localities is entire[illegible]

Written by Shakira 'Scotty Unfamous' Scott

Proof read by Monica Rahman

Published by Quirky Culture LTD, UK, 2013

Unfamous@peppergrain.com

Cover art by Media Sharks | info@mediasharks.com

www.theunfamousseries.com

ISBN 978-1-62890-553-3

About the Author

Born and raised in London, England, Shakira 'Scotty Unfamous' Scott burst onto the scene in 2009 with her candid, loud and proud YouTube show 'SDTV'.

In 2010, Scotty posted 'Unfamous' on Facebook, and later on that year it was adapted into a stage play by the Flourish Drama Company. The Unfamous play went on to become the first stage production in history to sell out London's Lost Theatre.

In 2012, Unfamous secured Scotty the BYA Literary Arts Award, and in 2013 it was turned into a web series. Scotty received multiple award nominations from the BEFFTA and Screen Nation awards including Best Author, Best Web Series, Favourite Web Series and Favourite Web Series Ensemble.

Along with Unfamous and SDTV, Scotty also has also had her own radio show, hosted events, been featured in various blogs, magazines and much more.

Scotty is currently signed to Peppergrain, and is managed by Deb McKoy.

UNFAMOUS

VISIT THE OFFICIAL UNFAMOUS WEBSITE
www.theunfamousseries.com

TWITTER: @THE_UNFAMOUS
JOIN THE CONVERSATION: #UNFAMOUS

Love Scotty x

"And in the end we're all just humans...drunk on the idea that love, only love, can heal our brokenness."

-F. Scott Fitzgerald

*

This book is dedicated to all of you; my family, my friends, those I've worked with, those I've loved, those I've lost, but most of all; this is dedicated to my fans for their tremendous love and support.

You've all contributed in making Unfamous what it is today, and I am forever grateful for all of the blessings and lessons you have brought into my life.

I love you all 'to the moon and back'.
Thank you.

Scotty
x

Book One.

What do you do when your hero turns into the villain?
When the one who is meant to save you, puts you in harm's way?
My Superman, stripped of his cape
Unable to fly, so he falls from grace
And pulls me down with him then uses me to break his fall
Then claims he's sorry for it all
He dusts himself off and gets back on his feet
He walks away whilst I remain on the ground with no heartbeat
You broke me.
"I'm sorry."

-Lois Lane
Scotty Unfamous
From the 'Smoking in Cursive' poetry collection

1

Starbucks.

I want it all; designer labels I'll have to sacrifice feeding myself for, the finest weaves money can buy, streams of endless events where I'll be rubbing shoulders with some of the best of young urban London, making friends with certified underground celebrities who have connections to the real ones, living away from home being able to do what I want, when I want. Fortnightly mani/pedi's accompanied by fabulous cocktails and the latest gossip with my new girlfriends 'just because'. Sexy, young, eligible bachelors with great prospects, who drive nice cars, lusting after me and showering me with expensive gifts and becoming part of an untouchable 'power couple', like a mini Beyoncé and Jay-Z! Everyone knowing my name -Rio Antoinette Greene -and it holding the kind of weight that can open doors and break hearts.

This is it; the first day of the rest of my new life, the day I begin my mission to become one of the Unfamous.

It's the age of the non-celebrity, where the social networks have become an easy access platform to make any and everybody a star in their own right –without really making them a star –taking being popular to a whole new level. It's no longer enough just to be known amongst your peers; people are now striving to be known worldwide. With the drop of an entertaining YouTube video, a collection of eye-catching photographs plastered across Tumblr and Instagram, and a daily selection of candid tweets, you can become a star in a matter of weeks. It really is that easy; all you have to do is get people to take notice of you and you are on your way to being a sensation. That's what being an Unfamous is about; being sensational, being the kind of person that causes a stir. Admired by many and secretly hated by more, knowing a lot of people and a lot of people craving to say they know you.

This is the dream I am preparing to make my reality, starting now.

From the outside looking in, being one of the Unfamous looks so delicious, and I will make sure that I get a taste of it. I know it must seem strange to want something so superficial so badly, but I'm not alone. Secretly, everyone wants it, but only a few are actually willing to go after it, and out of that few, only a handful make it.

There's a difference between being popular and being an Unfamous. Being popular is being well known and generally quite likeable. Being an Unfamous is that, plus adopting the unspoken status of underground royalty. It doesn't matter if people like you or not, they respect you.

For what I want, popularity is simply not enough. Why? I'm tired of being insignificant! Honestly, that is my reason. You may think it's a pretty pathetic thing for someone to say about themselves, but it's the truth. I am insignificant and I've had enough of it. It's time for them to notice me; all of them.

Over the summer holiday I concocted various strategies to become one of the Unfamous. You see, my whole secondary school and college career consisted of me being that girl in the back of the class that didn't matter. I wasn't invited to any of the 'right' parties, I never got to hang out in the places where 'they' did because I wasn't important enough to warrant an invitation - and even if I did decide to turn mad one day and show up, I'd either be ignored due to my irrelevance, or stick out like a sore thumb and risk being ridiculed.

I sure as hell didn't have that whole 'swagger' thing down either. I was stuck in my drab look of a bushy low ponytail, dressed in my no nonsense leggings, jeans, hoodies and cardigans in muted tones. I was just a regular girl; a real plain Jane. No muss, no fuss; that was me.

I wasn't one of those weird clichés of the wallflower with no friends -I have a friend; Tyson James. Ty is my best friend. We grew up together in a modest part of south London, living only a few doors down from each other. Our mothers are best friends too, and living so close together means that Ty and I get to see a lot of each other. We are practically like family! We did go through that weird stage in secondary school where our bodies matured and I realised that he was...well, a guy, and he realised that I was a girl. Our relationship lasted one whole month before we decided that we'd had enough of each other and went back to being friends. I think it is definitely better this way, but when we first broke up Tyson didn't agree. He was hurt and wouldn't speak to me for weeks. That was the first time I realised how lonely I am without him.

It took a lot of persistence and shunning of my pride to finally get him to come back around. We're good now.

As many of you friends turned lovers may know, the dynamics of your relationship changes as the person that was once just your friend now holds more value as your partner. Things you used to be able to overlook before now matter more than you thought they would. You can't hold all the same conversations you did prior to your relationship because now you have someone else feelings to consider. That was a huge issue for me because Tyson is the only person I really speak to about everything, so when I realised that I was going to have to keep some things to myself in order to keep him from going into a strop, it bothered me. Tyson is likeable, he can make friends with almost anyone, so if he needed to vent, he had his boys to talk to - I only had him. How do you complain to someone about themself? Also, I have a tendency to overthink everything, a habit that is very hard to break even now. Overthinking Tyson just felt wrong.

Today is the first day of Fresher's Week at the one and only Brompton University in Westchurch. To say that I am keen to begin my fabulous new life as a Bromptonian is a gross understatement! Getting my acceptance letter was God answering my profuse prayers; I wanted to attend Brompton more than I wanted a pair of red bottoms…and believe me when I say I want those highly sought after shoes a hell of a lot!

There are several universities that are notorious for harbouring the Unfamous; Langford, Herring and Brompton. I chose Brompton because it is the original birthplace of the Unfamous university culture, and we all know nothing has a stronger influence than the source. If you are on top at Brompton, you are on top everywhere!

Brompton University is set on the outskirts of London near the very end of a tube line. Usually places this far out are a world away from the twinkling excitement of the city, but somehow Brompton has managed to turn the campus into a mini student friendly version, with clubs, restaurants, gyms, a supermarket, expansive library, our own little HSBC bank and more. It's a home away from home, with the added bonus of student liberation.

The campus is made up of clean lines, steely greys, authoritarian blues, glass and bright lights. Everything is pristine and perfect, with enough of a modern edge to make it one of the slickest looking universities around.

The beauty of Brompton is that it is one of the few universities that have a richly diverse student body, and to get accepted here you have to have top grades. Because of this, attending Brompton ensures that you will mix with ethnic excellence, which is probably why a lot of Unfamous 'somebodies' stem from here.

As studious as everyone is, Brompton built its infamous reputation on its infectious nightlife -their raves and ravers are a pretty hot commodity. When the Brompton stall popped up at the University Fair at my college, one of the most popular questions to the student ambassadors was "Are the raves live, yeah?", which would be met with a smug smile and a stern nod. The term 'work hard, play harder' can definitely be applied to this uni. I've heard many exciting tales of how Brompton students would attend coach raves in places as far as Coventry and still dominate the dance floor, yelling their arrogant chant "Brom-what? Brompton!" to the beat of whatever song was playing. I can't wait to scream it out with pride with all my new friends…and Tyson.

Today I am going to make my first official mark on the Brompton student body and put myself in the running for the 'Queen' of the first years.

Being my other half, Tyson is in on my plan as well but I have a strong feeling that he doesn't really care about being an Unfamous –after all, why would you care if people took to you naturally anyway -and is just going along with it to please me.

We are going to Starbucks for breakfast around 10am to go over the ground rules one last time, though I have a niggling feeling that I will have to keep reminding Ty throughout the day.

My brand new iPhone -which I had to BEG my mother for - vibrates erratically and dings on my no nonsense desk, which is long enough to hold my TV, books, laptop (a Macbook…naturally), a photo of my mum, my printer and a small amount of my shiny new luxury cosmetics –the rest were arranged on the shelves with my accessories, more books (more for leisurely reading than the thick text books on my desk that I'd been instructed to purchase for my lectures) and snacks that I see no need to keep in the communal kitchen in fear of them being nibbled by someone else.

I skip across my new campus room to see why Ty is bothering me already –it is not lost on me how sad it is that I know it is Tyson, due to the fact that he's basically the only person who ever contacts me…aside from my Mum. Whenever it's not them, I am always pleasantly stunned for a little while before answering.

It's a Whatsapp message. It reads:

Ri, have u got my Obviously sweater? I can't find it.

I look down at the light grey Obviously 'Good Vibes' sweater I have paired with my favourite black leggings (they're my favourite because they give my bum an eye-catching lift) and tan Timberland boots. I look across the room to the full length mirror that is glued to the inside of my wardrobe door and smirk, loving what I see.

This is our first day of uni and as far as I'm concerned, you only get one chance to make an impact, so I nicked Ty's Obviously sweater. This piece of clothing is an important part of my plan as the designer of the brand, Manny Nang, actually attends Brompton, so I figure, what better way to grab his attention than swagging it out around campus in his clothing line? 'Obviously' has been going strong amongst the Unfamous scene for just over a year now and with the release of his 'Good Vibes' range, which incorporated the multi-coloured lotus flower on the breast pocket area, Manny's popularity and the popularity of the brand showed no signs of slowing down. Last I heard, Manny had cut an exclusive deal with a popular UK urban platform U-Link TV to sell his new 'Good Vibes' hats. I want the hat, and I want Manny to be one of my friends.

Along with nicking Tyson's Obviously sweater and getting an iPhone, I finally relaxed my bushy black hair and added a few tracks of 1b weave to the back to make it a little longer and fuller. I ditched my pocketsize blue and white tin of Vaseline for my new collection of M.A.C lipsticks, purchased a tote bag from River Island and got my nails done stiletto style and painted them nude. Image wise, I feel that I'm off to a good start and though Ty had to suffer for my vanity I told myself that he'd get over it because it was for a good cause.

I message him back:

I stole it fair and square lol. Wear somethin else :p

I can picture him kissing his teeth and calling me a few foul names for stealing his stuff but I am too elated to care.

This day can go either way; we can show up at the Fresher's Fair and have people look at us and think 'Who are they?', or the usual could happen; people will glance at us and carry on with their business because our presence doesn't make enough of a statement. I am so over being overlooked.

My phone buzzes and dings with Tyson's reply:

Stop stealin my stuff!

I giggle, not bothered by his irritation. I am forever nicking Tyson's things; he should be used to it by now.

I chuck the phone into my bag, grab my keys off the shelf and double check my makeup before heading out to meet Tyson in the car park.

"Stop gobbling your food like that you tramp!" I snap shoving a napkin into Ty's strawberry jam and croissant caked hands.

We are having breakfast in the local Starbucks, and while I sat here demurely with my legs crossed, sipping my delicious, too expensive, hazelnut latte, Tyson is attacking his pastry as if it is his last meal.

I suggested that we come to Starbucks (instead of McDonald's as Tyson originally suggested) because all of the hipster wannabes are obsessed with it. I used to sit in envy watching them post photos of their branded Styrofoam cups and any add-ons on their Tumblr and Instagram pages, or expressing how much they couldn't wait to get their coffee fix on Twitter every morning, whilst other pretentious franchise coffee drinkers agreed with them. I couldn't wait to experience the magic of Starbucks myself, and here Tyson is munching away like a peasant! He is making us look as if we didn't belong in such an establishment.

Tyson rolls his eyes and scrubs the sticky flakes off of his fingers whilst his tongue sweeps over his full lips in search of any stray crumbs to nibble on.

"Happy now?" he asks once he is sure he has removed the offensive mess. I look down at his top, glaring at the impressive collection of croissant flakes that cover it.

I scowl and lean across the table to dust him off, "Honestly, I can't take you anywhere! Don't you think that other students are in here watching us…*judging* us?"

I know I'm going a little overboard with the whole first impression thing, but for my plan to work, Ty and I have to be on point EVERY step of the way. I'm not just trying to make us into the Unfamous, I want us to be part of the clique who run the Unfamous; the cream of the crop, the top dogs, the big cojones!

"You should have taken me to McDonalds like I wanted in the first place. I wouldn't have made half as much mess with a Double Sausage Egg McMuffin, or spent half as much!" Tyson retorts.

"We're Bromptonians Ty_"

He raises his hand to cut me off, "It's a university, not Lord of the Rings. Never refer to us as that again!"

I fan him off and continue, "We're *beyond* McDonald's!" I stress, "We belong in places like Starbucks where we can flaunt how fabulous the life of a young, hip, adult is via pictures of overpriced food on Instagram!"

Tyson makes a face.

"In the 90s, a value meal at McDonald's was £2.99; now they charge the same price as Burger King and have made their portions smaller, that counts as overpriced! This 1 dead croissant cost me damn near £3! It's just flaky sweet bread! I could've bought 6 in a pack from Asda for the same price!"

"Quality over quantity Tyson," I drone whipping out my phone and positioning my latte on the polished oak table.

Tyson watches in amusement as I snap my first Starbucks coffee cup picture.

"I can't believe you're doing this, you sheep! No one even follows you on Instagram, so who exactly are you showing off to?"

I narrow my eyes at him, "I'll hashtag it!"

"Yeah, that'll work!" he scoffs, dampening my dreams of Instagram fame with his blatant sarcasm.

"It will!" I snap changing the photo filter to give it more of a vintage feel.

Pleased with the shot, I upload it to my profile and hashtag it #Coffee #Starbucks #Breakfast and throw in #FoodPorn for good measure. Tyson cocks his head to the side making his long blacks braids swish as he does so, and smiles his tauntingly handsome crooked smile.

"You want this bad init?" he chuckles throwing his sticky napkin in my face. I narrow my eyes at him, trying not to return the smile, and fling the napkin back at him. He dodges it.

"Shut up!"

"No but really though -you over want this! Ri, you relaxed your hair AND put in weave; you're supposed to work up to weave. How you gonna jump from naps to tracks in one day!" He laughs.

Self-consciously, I smooth down my hair and scowl at him, fighting the urge to stick my tongue out like a 5 year old. As if he can read my mind, Tyson grins and pokes his tongue out at me. Oh the sweet satisfaction it would give me to dump the rest of my hot latte across the crotch area of his True Religions right now, but I know that I need him to look presentable for this plan to work so I pop him upside his head instead. There, that stopped him laughing!

"How you gonna hit me in public! You better behave yourself before I tell everyone you're a loser with no friends," he threatens playfully, rubbing the spot I just hit.

I arch a newly shaped brow at him, "Ty, if I'm a loser with no friends, then what does that make you, 'cause your friend count is looking kind of non-existent right about now."

"I'm not you; I've got friends. You just don't see them 'cause one person pitying you so much that they felt obliged to tolerate you is enough," he smiles leaning in and blowing me a cheeky air kiss.

The girls over at the next table look at us, trying to figure out the depth of our relationship; are we friends or more than that? I smile to myself enjoying the fact that they could possibly be jealous of me and Ty. I know Tyson is hot, but I don't care enough to revel in it.

I revert back to a scowl.

"You're an idiot! Seriously though Ty, I will kill you if you mess this up for us!"

Tyson rolls his eyes at me, "What makes you think that I will mess this up and not you?"

"Well, because I'm a genius and you…not so much!" I joke.

"I don't need to be a genius; I'm pretty!" He smirks, adjusting his snapback with a playful arrogance; now it is my turn to roll my eyes.

As much as I would love to burst his bubble, Ty is good looking and everyone knows it. At 18 years of age he stands at 5"11 with heavily lashed light brown eyes and a very kissable mouth embedded in his rich earthy brown skin that is practically void of any spots or blemishes (one of the many reasons I sometimes envy him). Better still, when he flashes his signature sexy crooked smile, the one dimple hidden in his left cheek appears. To sum him up perfectly, Ty is a walking cup of creamy hot chocolate that you would snuggle up to by the fire place with on a cold winter night. One indulgent sip warms you from the inside out, leaving you with that lovely concoction of feeling comfortable and sexy. He is a very easy person to be around, yet his looks have the ability to throw a girl off every now and then.

"Thank God for that! Hurry up and finish, we've got to get back to campus to sign up for stuff and then you've got to help me pick an outfit for tonight," I tell him before draining the remaining contents of my latte.

Ty furrows his brow, "Why do you want my help? I'm a guy!"

"That's precisely why! I need you to pick an outfit for me that will make even YOU want to do dirty things to me," I wink with exaggerated flirtation.

Ty responds with his crooked smile, "What you're wearing now isn't doing a bad job."

I feel myself blush but I make sure to appear unfazed.

"No homo dude, now hurry up!"

After much prompting (and a few kicks to his shin under the table), Tyson finishes his breakfast and we are ready for world *cough* Uni *cough* domination.

We make it as far as the exit when I have my first melt down. Heading our way is Georgia Daniels, one of the few people on this earth I can honestly say I truly hate.

My eyes widen and I grip Tyson's arm as if my life depends on it. What is she doing here? How did she get in to Brompton, she's not even that smart! Fuck! She's going to ruin everything!

"Ri ease up man, what the_ fuck me! What is Georgia doing here?" Ty finally spots her too and stops trying to loosen my death grip on his arm as understanding washes over him. "Rio, you didn't tell me she was coming here!" he hisses, keeping a trained eye on her as she and her gang of dolled up cronies get closer.

"Well I didn't fucking know, did I! All those weeks of planning...I thought I'd seen the last of her when we left college." I sigh in a defeated tone.

Ty pulls me off to the side out of her line of sight and spins me around to face him. He takes my face in his hands gently and forces me to look up at him.

"Are you giving up already?" he asks, his pretty brown eyes searching mine. I look away, already feeling the defeat beginning to consume me. If she is here there is no point to any of this; she knows too much.

Ty sighs and jerks my face back, "Are you being serious Rio?"

"Tyson, what do you expect me to do? She knows who I am, not to mention the fact that she also has some vendetta against me because of the whole Nathaniel thing; what's the point? The moment I step into the spotlight, she'll out me. This is her world; she's already one of them. I'm just some wannabe!"

Tyson huffs and lets me go.

"This is so dumb," he mutters under his breath. Sighing again, he takes my hand. "Rio, I want you to continue with your stupid plan! If this is what it's gonna take for you to realise that you're not beneath anyone, do it. Fuck what happened in college…you're a Bromptonian now yeah! Make sure she knows that!"

Without giving me a chance to reply or smile at the use of the word Bromptonian, Tyson grips my hand tighter and drags me right into the line of fire.

I am now right in front of her and the look on her face when she sees me sends a cold chill down my back. Her green eyes flicker between me and Tyson. She looks at him approvingly, obviously liking what she sees, seeing as he now looks even hotter than he did in college, but when she looks at me she releases the snide laugh that I know all too well.

"Hello Tyson," she smiles sweetly, choosing to completely disregard me, and then just like that she struts into Starbucks with her glam squad on her heels, snickering and muttering insults about me.

Bitch.

"Can you believe the cheek of that skank?" I scream for the umpteenth time as Tyson pulls into a campus parking space. He turns off the ignition and removes the keys so fast it is as if the whole drive back he has been anticipating getting away from me and my fluent ranting.

"Yes Rio, yes I can. Georgia is a bitch and has been for as long as we've known her, now shut up about it. Shit!" he cusses getting out of the car. I narrow my eyes and follow suit, slamming his door once I am outside. Ty's head snaps in my direction and he gives me a grim look that tells me I'd better not slam his door again if I know what is good for me. I jut out my jaw stubbornly and stomp all the way over to the entrance of his dorm building.

Tyson waves the small black electronic square that the university had given students to get through the main entrance to each dorm building over the black pad underneath the bells for the flat numbers. The little red light changes from red to green and the grey steel and glass door clicks open. Tyson pulls it open then looks back to roll his eyes at me.

"Hurry up!"

I poke my tongue out at him and jog the last couple of feet. I open my mouth to continue complaining, which Tyson promptly stops by clamping his hand over it.

"I know. Please, stop moaning, I'm begging you!" he pleads with mock exasperation.

I tug his hand off, "Fine!" I huff. Listening to 20 minutes of nonstop bitching about the same person I've been bitching about for over almost 2 years would wear on anyone's nerves.

I look up at my best friend and give him an apologetic half smile. He gives my arm a gentle squeeze in return, and then we head up to his flat.

We have an hour to kill until the Fresher's Fair begins, and with Tyson seemingly engrossed in the new Kendrick Lamar album I have nothing but time to sit lotus style on his student standard single bed and replay seeing Georgia disregard me in front of Starbucks over and over again.

It just isn't fair! I have put so much thought, work and money into making myself over to be this fabulous upgraded version of plain Jane Rio; I am dressed to perfection, living it up in Starbucks with my iPhone, student loan and my best friend, and just the sight of her shatters my carefully crafted delusions of grandeur.

I sigh heavily, wanting to complain some more, but Tyson has now moved on to singing (badly) along to the hook of his new favourite song. I want to scrutinize every minuscule detail of her 'mean girl' behaviour, then compare it to past situations in college where she has left me feeling like dirt under her fire engine red manicured nails.

I have a powerful desire to scratch her eyes out so that her physical beauty is no more and people can finally realise that she isn't a 'bad bitch' -she is just a bitch!

Where was all of this fire when Georgia was demonstrating how little she thought of me? I was too busy being 'College Rio' to stand up to her, stupidly giving her the upper hand. I should've said something, anything; anything that would show her that I'm not the same girl she used to giggle in the back of the class about with her friends, something that would let her know that she isn't allowed to make me feel like my relationship with the only boy that I ever truly loved was destined to fail because, in her eyes, I'm not half the girl she is. Well 'shoulda, coulda, woulda' never helped anyone get anywhere; the next time we cross paths I will be ready for her as 'Uni Rio'.

Although I won't tell him outright -because he'll get that stupid 'I told you so' smirk on his face -Ty is right; if I really want to do this, I am going to have to show Georgia that we aren't in college anymore.

I know that my transformation from nothing to something is going to be a little bit of a struggle, but it wasn't so daunting pre-Georgia, because I was meant to be convincing people who didn't know me from Adam, that I am the one to watch. Now I have to add Georgia to that group, and she will see right through my façade. If I don't get a handle on the new me now, she will be my shitty kryptonite and put an end to my Unfamous dreams.

With strengthened resolve, I sit straighter on Tyson bed. I know what I have to do; faking it until I make it is no longer an option. I'm going to have to be it.

2

Mixtape.

Music is playing, students are chattering, chanting and dancing, an array of bright colours taking the form of various banners, posters and balloons loom welcomingly overhead to signify the different societies, companies and events; we've just arrived at the Brompton Fresher's Fair. The excitement is palatable as the entire strip is overtaken by casually overdressed Brompton first years.

"All right, so what am I signing up for again?" Tyson whispers as we approach the diverse Brompton student community. I kiss my teeth -you wouldn't believe that I told him this information when we were in his dorm room all of 5 minutes ago!

"The Afro-Caribbean Society and the basketball team, dummy!" I reply, nudging him with my elbow.

Tyson furrows his eyebrows, "And why do I have to play basketball again?"

I stop in my tracks, fighting back the urge to pop him upside his head again. He is starting to irritate me now. Sometimes explaining things to Tyson is like talking to a 5 year old who has to know everything about nothing!

"Because," I snarl through gritted teeth "you are tall and pretty, and girls like tall, pretty boys who play basketball! Plus it is a very easy way for you to make guy friends. Now shut up and don't ask me anything else!" I continue walking.

As we make it into the thick of the crowd, the stares and curious glances began to travel our way, quickly eliminating any animosity that I had left in my body –I'm a sucker for admiration! I don't know what takes over me, but suddenly I am switching my hips as subtly as I can so that my walk has more of a sexy slink to it, knowing what the smooth swaying motions is make my bum look like in these oh so tight leggings. I make sure to stand a friendly distance away from whom the female student body are most likely labelling as 'Mr Tall, Dark and Handsome', so that people don't get the wrong idea. We can't look like we are *together* because that will only give the many female *frenemies* that I intend to make yet another reason to hate me. At the same time, I can't stand too far away because if the boys on campus assume that Tyson and I are an item, then it will send them sniffing over here a lot faster; after all (as the saying goes), nobody wants somebody that no one else wants.

I look over at Tyson to see if he is noticing the 'he/she would GET IT' looks, but it is as if he is oblivious to the attention. I am throwing around my best sugar and spice smile and Tyson has decided that instead of actually catching anyone's eye, he is going to play with his phone...

Oh my God, this boy is actually a genius! Of course he should be playing with his iPhone; practically all of the Unfamous have one, so by walking with it in his hand he is subconsciously projecting the calibre of person he is to his peers.

I pull mine out, look at the screen and roll my eyes -I want everyone to think that I am reading a message from one of my many admirers who just can't take the hint. In reality I am scrolling through my music playlist and typing in song names to make it seem as if I am replying. God, I'm sad!

"Good thinking," I giggle, nudging Tyson gently. He looks up from his phone as if he has forgotten I am there.

"Huh?"

"I said, good thinking...y'know...with the unveiling of the mighty iPhone," I say doing my geeky jazz hand gesture as I say iPhone. Clearly I have forgotten that I am smack bang in the middle of the Brompton University Fresher's Fair trying to pretend I am one of the cool kids. Cool kids don't do bloody jazz hands…do they?

"They'll definitely think we're one of them now," I grin. Tyson replies with a goofy grin and mimics my jazz hands back to me. I elbow him.

"Give me a break! This is all new to me, remember!"

As I say that, I spot the muscle bound frame of a legitimate member of the Unfamous clan, D-Man, walking towards us.

D-Man is an up and coming UK Hip Hop artist signed to London Underground Records (they're like the UK underground version of GOOD Music). He is one of the most rapidly growing

MC's since Kano in his early days, and here he is, clad in a black t-shirt and Ray Bans, walking straight in my direction.

I feel my right knee give way. Luckily Tyson is there to steady me before I make things any worse.

Tyson looks down at me and raises his eyebrow, "You all right?" I nod and straighten up.

I can feel D-Man's eyes on me. I don't have to look up see the expression I already know is be there, 'What is wrong with this girl?' I cringe inwardly; why did I do that? More importantly, WHY did I do that in front of D-Man? Shit!

"Is he looking?" I whisper to Tyson.

"Is who looking?"

"D-Man; is he looking at me?"

"Yo, swear down D-Man's here?"

"YES!" I hiss sharply, "He's right in front of you in the Jordan's. Is he looking at me?"

There is a pause.

"Uhh nah, not anymore. He's giving his mixtape to one girl."

Oh.

I don't want D-Man to stare at me as if I am some loser, but at the same time, I don't like going unnoticed either.

I run my fingers through the ends of my weave and straighten up with purpose.

Come, we're going to get a mixtape!"

"You don't even like D-Man's music," Tyson points out.

"So? He doesn't know that. Look I just wanna introduce myself okay! The mixtape's an excuse."

I slink towards my target while Tyson lags behind, pre-occupied with his phone once again. I glance over my shoulder at him to see him smiling at the screen.

"Who are you talking to?" I ask curiously.

"Some boom ting that lives on the floor above me," he smirks. I frown.

"You've already swapped contact details with someone?"

"Three someone's actually -all female, all in the running to 'get it'!" His grin picks up what mine lacks. How has he made new friends (I use the term loosely) already and yet I haven't so much as waved hello at the little Asian girl who lives next door to me?

"Shut up you slag!" I spit bitterly.

I know this sounds childish, but it's not bloody fair! Why do I have to put so much effort into socialising, when all Ty has to do is flash that stupid crooked smile and suddenly he's Mr Popularity? I'm attractive enough (now), and I have a pretty good physique that would make even Kim Kardashian do a double take, but for all it's worth, it doesn't even matter because I don't quite have that aura of Unfamous-ness going for me…yet. Tyson doesn't have the Unfamous aura either, but frankly he doesn't need it; he never did –he's a cute guy.

The difference between boys and girls when socialising is this; a guy can accumulate female friends that may want to get with him, but even if he doesn't want to take it there they'll hang around in the 'friend zone' just to say that the insanely hot guy is their friend.

A boy that attracts loads of girls will also attract more male friends as it never hurts to have a good looking friend to bring the birds flocking to their group, or as a wing man to assist them in 'securing a babes'.

Girls on the on the other hand, can accumulate guy friends because it's more than likely that the guy wants to get down and dirty with them, but if the girl isn't trying to make the relationship go in that direction then it's like 'Forget this, you're long!', and you never hear from them again until they're ready to make another attempt.

That's just the problem with guys; it's more complicated when it comes to girls as there seems to be this constant underlying rivalry- even if we won't admit to it –because we all want to be the 'Beyonce' of our group. There's a lot of bitchiness, gossiping and fake smiles between females, especially when men are in the picture, so it's harder to stay friends with them. Of course those scenarios aren't always the case, but they're common enough.

"Someone's got the jealousies," Tyson taunts me in a sing song voice. I want to smack his iPhone out of his hand and watch it smash to a million un-repairable pieces and see who has the' jealousies' then. Stupid boy!

"Why should I be jealous when I'm about to make one of the hottest upcoming UK rappers my first uni contact?" I retort confidently.

Tyson laughs, "Oh are you? Well go on then, he's coming your way."

I whip my head around to see D-Man directly in front of me, brandishing his new mixtape 'Nameless'. I roll my eyes inwardly; he thinks himself to be one of those conscious artsy rappers, who is constantly praised for being 'the truth'.

"Yo babes, my name's D-Man, I'm a new artist signed to London Underground records. What kind of music are you into?"

Say something relevant so he thinks you're 'down'!

"I love neo-soul." There; that is safe and true enough.

D-Man smiles at me, "Is it? Who's your favourite artist?"

Quick, Rio!

"Uh, Lauryn Hill. The Mis-Education is one of the greatest albums of all time!" I gush honestly.

D-Man nods approvingly, "Yeah I like Lauryn too. What's your name darling?"

I flutter my eyelashes, "Rio."

"Nice to meet you, Rio. Now there's no pressure to say yes, but I guarantee if you like Lauryn, you'll like my mixtape. Would you like to purchase it?"

He expects me to pay for this?

I hear Tyson snort behind me. I ignore him and smile sweetly at D-Man.

"Sure, why not! My friend listens to you all the time, you're really good. I basically know all your songs anyway and I'm happy to support great UK talent, so yeah -on one condition though…"

D-Man raises his eyebrow curiously, "And what's that babe?"

"I want you to sign it for me. When you blow I wanna show everyone I got a legitimate signed copy from the superstar himself!" I giggle.

He looks away, embarrassed, "Yeah, sure!"

I pull a pen out of my tote bag and hand it to him.

"To Rio…" I dictate. He smiles and scribbles on the cover.

I go to fetch my purse when he stops me.

"Nah, don't worry about the money babes," he hands the CD to me with a knowing smile, "I'll see you around yeah, Rio."

And just like that, D-Man is on his way and I feel myself physically relax. I look down at the free mixtape and release a small triumphant squeal; he wrote his number on the sleeve. I HAVE <u>THE</u> D-MAN'S NUMBER! Once I am sure I am out of his sight I wave the free mixtape in Tyson's face victoriously.

"Booyah! Suck on that!"

Tyson stares at the CD in disbelief then shoots a wary look after D-Man.

"You better not call him! You can't trust these industry guys." He warns protectively. I roll my eyes.

"You can't trust guys, period, but that's never stopped me. Look there's the ACS table. Let's go," I grin shoving him towards the ACS stall.

I take out my iPhone and key in D-Man's number then look up to see if anyone is watching me key in his number, and to my utter joy a few more guys are giving me the eye. Score!

I swing my 14 inches of 1B Yaki weave over my shoulder and switch my hips a little more, suddenly full of myself. THE D-Man gave me his number; achievement or what!

As Tyson and I approach the ACS stand I'm smiling and thinking to myself 'Nothing can ruin this high!' and then…

"Hey, welcome to Brompton ACS; you thinking of signing up?"

At the sound of that all too familiar velvety baritone, I freeze.I'd know that voice anywhere -it's the same voice that used to leak through my phone at 2am just to tell me that they were thinking of me, the same sweet, sweet voice that told me how much they loved me endlessly, the very same voice that had turned even huskier as they groaned, "Do you like that?" into my ear, knowing that what they were doing to me at the time left me incapable of forming actual words. It was the voice that broke my heart when they asked for my forgiveness of something that they knew I could never forgive.

My heart falters and the palms of my hands become damp. I suck in a deep breath, preparing myself to look up from my iPhone screen to confirm my suspicion. Thank God I look good, because if I looked like shit this moment would be even more gut-wrenching.

My almost black/brown eyes travel along his strong butterscotch arms, savouring the way his prominent veins weave intricately up them, disappearing underneath the sleeves of his black Ralph Lauren polo shirt. His golden skin reappears near the base of his kissable throat and my eyes locate the sexy cursive tattoo that graces his neck. It reads *'Love.'* Oh how I loved that tattoo. I continue along his chiselled jaw line to his soft lips that were notorious for making me become religious at the times when I was far from it, framed by a full 5 o'clock shadow of a beard. I stop there for a minute knowing, that once we make eye contact that I will have to try my hardest to keep it together.

I set my face into an unreadable expression then proceed to look into those dreamlike grey eyes.

"Hello Nathaniel," I breathe.

July 2011

"Rio...please, say something."

Nathaniel reaches out his hand to touch my shoulder -I retract from him like he has the plague. What does he expect me to say? I refuse to run through the routine drivel that people tend to do when they become victims of adultery. What will any of those overused questions gain me? Nothing! It isn't like they can rewind time and fix what happened to make it so that we wouldn't be having this conversation, so what's the point?

I want to slap him in the face so hard that his eyes go crooked and scream out 'How could you do this to me?', but I can't bring myself to do it. I love him too much.

My pride keeps my lips pursed together so tightly that they form a flat line where my mouth should be. I can hear him breathing heavily, trying to fight back his tears. He is sorry; that I am sure of.

Looking up from the spot on the ground that I have been staring at since he broke the news of his indiscretion, I unclasp my lips and exhale, unaware that I have been holding my breath. I meet his tear-glazed grey eyes with the darkest of glares and the voice that comes out of my mouth sounds alien, even to me. It sounds as if I lack the ability to feel anything at all.

"I hate you!" I hiss icily.

Nathaniel breaks my stare and looks at the ground as shame consumes him.

"Rio; I'm so sorry. I never meant for this to happen. I_"

"BULLSHIT!" I roar. The calm has passed.

"Rio_"

"SHUT UP!" I clamp my hands over my ears knowing that it won't stop me from hearing him completely, but hoping that maybe I can block him out enough so that I don't have to sit through another useless apology.

I'm not gonna cry, I'm not gonna cry. Just keep taking deep breaths Ri, you'll be fine. I'm not gonna cry.

"The last thing I would ever want to do is hurt you Ri. If I could take it back, I would. I messed up and I am so, so sorry; you have to believe me baby," he pleads as the tears keep filling his eyes almost to the brim, threatening to spill.

I snatch my hands away from my ears, "WELL YOU CAN'T!"

"Rio..." he takes a determined step towards me.

"STAY WHERE YOU ARE!" I scream. Just keep breathing. Do not cry!

"Why would you take it back, huh? Wasn't it worth it?"

"Rio..."

"ANSWER ME!"

"BECAUSE I LOVE YOU!"

I want to believe him, a part of me needs to, but you don't do this to someone you love. You're not meant to intentionally do something that you know will break their heart; that's not love.

A part of me is tempted to accept that Nathaniel is a guy, and that him cheating on me doesn't mean anything because this is just what guys do -but that sounds idiotic and desperate. My mother had been idiotic and desperate with my father and look where that got her. I was not about to make the same mistake.

"No you don't," I croak, closing my eyes as I feel my tears surfacing. Why did he have to say that? I was doing so well and then those three little words sent me crashing down.

"Nathaniel, you have no idea what love is! I would never even consider doing something like this to you because I love you. I would never have gone behind you back and slept with someone you hated because I love you. I would never be standing where you are right now breaking the heart of the person that loves me, because I LOVE YOU! You may think you do, but this shows that you don't really love me, and because of that, I don't want to love you anymore. We're done."

The tears begin to fall on both sides of the battlefield, and just like that, it is over -we are over.

As he edges towards my bedroom door to leave, I feel the threads that I never knew existed begin to unravel in my chest to reveal what I know will be a gaping hole once the process of losing my heart is complete. Nathaniel is my heart, but because of what he's done, I have to let him go and it hurts, it hurts like hell.

Why did he accept defeat so easily? Is that all the fight he has in him, or am I just not worth fighting for? I know I ended it and right now I can't bring myself to hear him out, but I'm sure that all my ladies know that when you are put in situations like this, you have to stick it out with a special kind of stubborn anger so that they don't think that they can just get away with it.

I hate to admit it, but I still want to be with him. I want to pretend this never happened and I want him to hold me and tell me that everything's gonna be okay…but he didn't.

We didn't even make it to love's autumn, so why are we already experiencing winter when love's summer was becoming so epic? He's ruined everything.

"Can I ask you one thing?" I sniff. Nathaniel swings around to face me with a look that says 'anything', "Why did it have to be Georgia?"

I tense, preparing for the worst, knowing that I don't really want to hear the answer, but it will irk me if I don't know what drove my boyfriend into the arms of another woman.

Nathaniel looks down and shrugs solemnly, "I dunno, she was just there, init. It didn't mean anything baby, I swear."

That's his reason?

"I can't even look at you," I sneer, "Just go."

The sound of my bedroom door closing behind him sends a chill through me. The book had been closed on an incomplete chapter and all I can do is cry as the realisation of the end sets in deeper.

I crawl into my bed and I cry, and cry and even when I think that I can't possibly cry anymore, more tears find their way down my face.

I don't know how long I've been laying here sobbing, but by the time that I calm down enough to focus, the sun has gone down. Perfect.

I stretch over to my bedside table and let my hand fumble over various objects until I find my Blackberry. I hold down the number '2' button and wait until the speed dial connects to Ty's number.

He picks up on the fourth ring.

"Yo!" he says lazily. I can hear determined, fast paced clicking in the background and what sounds like a football crowd cheering incoherently. I bet this boy is playing Pro Evolution on his X Box Live with his idiot friends as usual.

"Why are you forever playing that stupid game, you loser? Go find a girl and play with her instead!" I smirk despite my current mood. I don't know what it is about Tyson, but he just makes me feel better by doing nothing at all.

"Are you offering?"

"You wish!"

"Well shut up then. Throwing shade 'cause you ain't got no friends to play games with, loner! What d'you want anyway big head? You're distracting me from my game."

I remember why I called him and suddenly all of my sarcasm is dissipates.

"Nathaniel cheated on me…with…with Georgia," I say in a hushed voice, scared that if I say it too loud that it may just set me off again.

The football crowds' voices stop abruptly and the determined clicking is no more.

"You at home?" Ty's voice has lost its usual playful edge and is now that odd blend of serious, yet soothing.

"Yes."

"I'm coming over. Have you eaten?"

"No. My Mum's at work and I couldn't be bothered to cook."

"Pizza?"

"I'm not hungry."

"…Ice cream?"

"…Haagen Daaz?"

"Sainsbury's does one that tastes just like it for half the price," he says wistfully.

I laugh, "I'm upset and you have Sainsbury's staff discount; Haagen Daaz please!"

"Fine, I'll get you the expensive stuff, just this once."

Present Day
September 2013

That night we ate 'expensive' ice cream in a blanket fort at the foot of my bed and reeled off all of the reasons why Nathaniel never deserved me.

It was one of those times that made me really appreciate my best friend. I don't know what I'd do without Ty.

3

Clique.

"Did you see the look on his face? Oh my God, I totally get that whole 'looking good is the best revenge' thing now," I squeal at Ty from my white compact student bathroom as I apply my soft pink M.A.C lip-gloss.

I admire myself in the mirror that hangs over the sink, rub my lips together, pucker and pout, fluff my curls, give myself the once over, and step outside preparing to measure Ty's reaction. If he likes it then I am all good to go for the Brompton Fresher's Rave tonight.

Tyson hasn't spoken much since we'd left the Fresher's Fair and I can't say that I blame him; Nathaniel being here didn't only bring back painful memories for me.

I knew I have should shut up about it, but I was so elated to see the surprise and regret that shone from my ex-boyfriend's face when he realised that it was me and how absolutely fabulous I looked.

I glance at Tyson before switching off the bathroom light and feel my happiness switch off with the bulb as I look at him. He is sitting on my bed staring at something that isn't there, on the opposite side of my room. His eyes hold this distant look that tells me that he hasn't been listening to me for a while; that I have merely become background noise.

I walk over to the bed slowly in my strappy Jimmy Choo's and slide up next to him.

"Ty?" I call softly, resting a generously bangled arm on his shoulder. He jolts from my unexpected contact and gives me a weak smile that doesn't reach his eyes.

"You look beautiful Ri," he says with a sadness which makes the compliment lose its charm. I hate when he gets like this; it's bloody awkward. Word to the wise; never get into a relationship with your close friend because you can never go back to the way you once were if it doesn't work out.

Sighing, I lace my arm around him and pull him to me. His head settles on my shoulder causing his braids to tickle my skin through my top.

"Thank you. Are you all right?" I ask resting my head on top of his. He looks down and nods, pulling away from me slightly.

"Yeah I'm cool. I'm gonna go get dressed now," he replies getting to his feet.

I stand up and face him but he keeps his eyes on the ground.

"Ty?" I reach out for him. He catches my hand before I can try and coax him into a hug again and throws me another pained smile.

"I'll meet you outside the Fresher's rave around 10. A few of the guys from my flat asked if I was gonna roll with them; I said yes. Sorry."

His confession doesn't sound as if he is as sorry about it as he should be.

Tyson knows that I don't have anyone else to go to the Fresher's Rave with, hence -as my only friend in Brompton…and life in general -he is meant to go with me, not desert me on the first night!

My expression sours and I tug my hand out of his loose grip.

"How could you say 'yes'? Who am I meant to go with?" I ask haughtily, folding my arms across my chest.

"Well...I figured you could holler at some of the chicks in your flat. If you're gonna be the Queen of the Brompton first years, you need some ladies in waiting, right?" He smiles, trying to charm me into coming around by using my plan against me. I would have gone for it, except his tone is tainted with sarcasm. As much as Ty is my right hand man, when he gets like this he can easily become public enemy number one. Well that's fine by me! If he wants to be off with me then I have no problem returning the favour. I shall assemble my clique of female cronies tonight and begin my reign over Brompton without him!

I arch one eyebrow, giving him my 'game on' smile as I take a step towards him so that I my face is merely centimetres from his. Tyson towers over me, staring down at me with an amused expression.

"Well I guess I'll see you there," I reply nonchalantly.

He shrugs, "I guess you will."

I bounce up on my tippy toes and plant a light glossy 'goodbye' kiss on his cheek. To my joy -and slight displeasure -the sadness etches its way back onto his face.

Without another word Tyson wipes the sparkly pink lip print off of his cheek and walks out.

With my makeup finished, I stand at the head of my flat taking deep measured breaths as I prepare to force myself to socialise -could I be any more of a loser? Rio, get a grip, they're just people. No one's going to attack you for saying hello!

Six dorm rooms line the off white corridor. The whole flat is occupied with female residents, which I am grateful for as it eliminates the chance of me awkwardly knocking on a door of a Brompton boy.

With false confidence I strut down the cheap scratchy carpeted hallway and stand outside room number one. Composing my face into a friendly (slightly needy) smile, I knock and a petite Japanese girl with doll-like eyes pops her head out of the door.

"Hi…"

"Hey, I'm Rio. I live at number 5," I say pointing to my door. The girl smiles back at me, and opens her door a little wider, extending a tiny neon pink polished hand towards me,
"Hi Rio, I'm Hideyoshi -Yoshi for short," she says. I shake her hand gently, scared that as small as she is I might break her by accident.

Yoshi looks like a little porcelain Lolita doll, with fair cream coloured skin and a few coffee coloured freckles scattered across her nose. Her eyes are as black as mine, but they have this adorable child-like quality to them which make her seem almost innocent. She has a small rosebud mouth, painted pale pink, and long raven and purple dip dyed hair under the new Obviously pom-pom hat I have been lusting after for weeks, which reaches the small of her back. If Yoshi knows about Obviously clothing too, then she is definitely meant to be in my clique.

"Nice to meet you, Yoshi! I was wondering if you're planning on going to the Fresher's Rave at Purple tonight?"

Purple is Brompton's personal student nightclub which holds pretty decent raves for a campus club. It is located a few yards away from the main campus entrance just off the main road.

Yoshi chews the inside of her lip and shrugs, "Hadn't really thought about it seeing as I never had anyone to go with."

"I don't have anyone to go with either. I figured that I could round up a few of the girls from the flat seeing as we'll be living together for the rest of the year. It seems like a good way to break the ice."

"Oh cool! Well I've met Carmen, Fontaine and Sky so far; they seem really nice, you should ask them," she suggests, pointing at each of their doors. I smile feeling this task become a little easier from her suggestion.

"I'm on it! Okay, well get dressed and hopefully we'll be able to leave by 10, so you've got 1 hour."

By the time 10 o'clock rolls around I am fully glammed up to the nines, looking like a ten and equipped with four equally glamorous girls; Yoshi, Carmen, Fontaine and Sky. They are all dressed so effortlessly, like the kind of girl I am aspiring to be; perfect hair, manicures, Asos dresses, designer heels and bags and flawless M.A.C makeup. It is as if this look is some kind of 'It Girl' uniform and each of us had put our own unique spin on it.

Yoshi is wearing a neon yellow midi dress, with equally bright neon jewellery in lime green, hot pink and electric blue. Her shoes and purse are excessive, quirky Betty Johnson creations, with make-up and hair to match. There is something gaudy about her style, but her Asian heritage makes it work in her favour.

The girl who had introduced herself as Fontaine, is a model. She'd informed me that Fontaine is her alias and that even if we do find out her real name, we are never to use it. That threw me off a little and I'd immediately labelled her as arrogant up until she started making goofy jokes moments after. Fontaine is an exotic beauty -a rare mix of Italian and Dominican. She is a hilarious loud-mouth girl from the heart of East London, with a head full of wild coppery-blonde corkscrew curls. She hails from Shoreditch, which is evident from her twangy East End accent, to her edgy fashion choices. Fontaine is the personification of the typical Tumblr girl; piercings, tattoos and a rebellious fashion sense. I can't help but admire her brave (extremely short) mesh panelled number teamed with thigh high leather boots that end a centimetre before her dress begins.

Sky, a self-proclaimed Irish fashionista with ruby red hair, is adorned in a simple yet thoroughly effective LBD and the baddest pair of spiked Christian Louboutin heels that only emphasize the surprisingly dangerous rear end she possesses. I don't know why it is still a shock to see a white girl with an ass when they had been popping up more and more frequently over the past decade, but Sky's just caught me off guard. If I didn't know any better I'd have thought she'd paid for it, but she caught me looking, wiggled it proudly in my direction and said, "100 squats a day!"

Finally there is Carmen; a Jamaican who was destined to be my wing-woman. She is average height with heavily lashed brown eyes and long black hair, which (thanks to the invention of weave) is almost as long as Yoshi's. She is fairly slender with a great pair of legs, ample bosom and a pierced tummy, which she flaunted with pride -I'm guessing the piercing is new. The thing that drew me to Carmen is that she is a bitch...but in a good way. She is brutally honest -which I find refreshing -and very....ballsy. Carmen describes herself as candid; I guess it sounds better than plain old facety. When I knocked on her door and asked her if she wanted to come to Purple with me, she replied with an uncomfortably loud,

"Thank fuck! I thought I was gonna have to go beg friend with that neek that lives in number three." After I told her to get ready, she cranked up her sound system and flooded the flat with Bashment and Soulful House (to which I practiced cutting shapes to in my wardrobe mirror…I don't want to embarrass myself on the dance floor now do I?).

The five of us clatter down the road giggling, yelling and screeching up a girly storm as if we've known each other for years. I am confident that I have chosen a good clique; simply being in their presence makes me feel more like I belong in this world with every click of my Jimmy Choos. I'm walking at the front of the group with Carmen at my side and Yoshi, Fontaine and Sky bringing up the rear, letting everyone know that this is the order of hierarchy. As we approach Purple, all of our chatter quiets a little -we don't want to be the irritating bunch of loudmouth girls that make the other ravers want to roll their eyes at. I'm sure that a set of girls like that will be present at this event sooner or later.

We slink over to where Tyson is standing with his new friends. Tyson notices us coming over and straightens up, his face showing that he is impressed with what I have managed to put together despite my social issues. He flashes his crooked smile.

Carmen grabs my arm, "You know him?" she asks in an excited tone. I giggle and shrug -guys like Tyson are a dime a dozen to me…well that's what I want the girls to think. In reality Tyson is my friend who just so happens to be hot; I got lucky!

"Yeah, that's my best friend, Tyson," I reply coolly.

"Girl, he is fione!" she sings releasing my arm so that she can smooth down her flyaway strands.

"Init! I clocked him at the Fresher's Fair today. You know bare chicks were doing some mad hating on you; I'm not gonna stunt, I was one of 'em," Fontaine confesses with a chuckle.

"I call dibs!" I looked over to my right to see if Carmen is being serious.

"Dibs?" Yoshi asks.

"Yes, dibs. As in he is a fine tuned automobile and I am calling shotgun to ride up front, ya get me!" Carmen laughs.

It is funny, but secretly I know she isn't joking. Carmen has her eyes locked on Ty and by the way she steps up the pace so that she will be the first of my crew to talk to him, she isn't trying to let any of the others get the upper hand.

I feel a twinge of possessiveness. Then and there I decide that none of them are allowed to date him; he's my Ty.

"Hey Ty," I smile sweetly encircling my arms around his neck for a longer-than-necessary hug, "How do you like my ladies in waiting?" I grin flourishing my arms towards the girls. Tyson runs his eyes over the group and gives them his signature lopsided smile again.

"You actually made some friends and the good kind too! Well your majesty, I must say I'm impressed –shocked, but impressed. So, how did I do?" he asks gesturing towards his group with a sly head movement.

My eyes scan the sea of masculine faces and my jaw falls open, "You have got to be kidding me! How did you_"

Tyson chuckles and cuts my astonishment short.

"Oi you lot, this is my bredrin, Rio," he calls to them over his shoulder.

A wave of Unfamous boys sweep coolly across the pavement to introduce themselves while I concentrate on trying to maintain a facial expression that doesn't give away how stupidly star struck I am.

Tyson's new band of buddies step up to his side, glance up from their phones and mumble nonchalant greetings at me 'You all right babes?', 'You cool?' and 'Nice to meet you darlin'.'

My reply is a squeaky, "Hi."

"Rio I believe you already know D-Man," Tyson smirks. D-Man licks his lips and smiles at me. I fight back my blush and smile back at him.

"This is Bless, Ace, Calvin, Shaquille and Manny."

Even though he speaks their names as if they are common everyday people, his eyes are bragging; Tyson has gotten himself in with the best of Brompton and he is rubbing it in my face for fun. Damn him!

Ace and Bless, who make up the event entertainment collective 'Moonlight Ents', are the hottest (in both the metaphorical and physical sense) new dynamic host and DJ duo of our generation. Ace is mixed race, average in height with honey coloured eyes and Bless is coolie (a mix of Jamaican and Indian), with a fade full of perfect glossy raven waves. They hold the most talked about events among the Unfamous, their most popular being the weekly showcase, Sunday Slam at Plan X in Brixton. Their line of work puts them amongst the most well connected guys in young urban London.

Calvin is one of the kings of Twitter; a very attractive white boy with a love of socializing, Instagram, designer clothing, Starbucks and (his main selling point) black girls. He has a huge following somewhere in the upper thousands, which means that even if you don't follow him (which I of course do), he will still appear on your timeline with his harmless witty banter, or because one of his many female admirers is talking about how handsome he looks in his new display picture.

Shaquille, an average looking brown skinned boy, is an international YouTube sensation, made famous by his unabashed humour on his weekly talk show 'The Shaq Attack'. Every week he passes hilarious comments on the lifestyle of the rich and famous, and occasionally the lifestyle habits of us Londoners.

Manny -one of the Unfamous personalities that I've been looking forward to meeting the most – is a well-dressed Korean with a buzz cut and an unchallenged exclusive trainer collection, who only dates 'models' and is the designer of the must have apparel that I stole from Tyson this morning -Obviously clothing. He nods at Fontaine. That small gesture of recognition from Manny make my girls look sparkly again. Fontaine knows him so that is a step in the right direction.

I give them a demure wave and proceed to introducing my girls (who compared to Tyson's new mates, don't seem as fabulous anymore, but there's potential there).

"Ladies this is my boy Tyson. Tyson this is_"

"Carmen." She jumps in front of me and extends her hand, holding Tyson's astonished gaze with that the undeterred confidence that I have only witnessed from Samantha in 'Sex and the City'.

Tyson take her hand and shakes it, "Nice grip," he comments, devoting his lopsided smile solely to her.

Most girls would've showed some sign of getting a little light headed from how extremely gorgeous that smile is, but Carmen stands her ground and replies unfazed, "I know." That conjures up a few impressed mumbles from his friends.

As much as I am all for her being the ballsy one of the group, I have to be careful that she doesn't steal my premature crown; I'm the one who is meant to leave an impression, not her.

I clear my throat and laugh off my minor annoyance, "Yeah so that's Carmen. This is Sky, Yoshi and Fontaine."

The others smile and wave as Carmen falls back in line, still holding Tyson's gaze. I have to admit, the girl is good…maybe I should stop blushing all the time and take notes.

"Why aren't you lot in the line yet?" I ask casting a glance at the too long queue for Purple that extends up the street and around the corner.

Ace looks up from his phone again, "Don't stress babes; you're with us, you won't have to line up."

"What, are you lot some campus superstars or something?" Yoshi chuckles -I raise my eyebrow at her; how does she NOT know who they are? Newsflash Rio; not everyone cares about the Unfamous as much as you!

"Course miss; I can make you famous if you like," Ace replies flashing a cocky, but sexy dimpled smirk in Yoshi's direction. Looks like I'm not the only one who it's easy to make blush; thank God it doesn't look as obvious on me. "Me and Bless are spinning tonight. We're just waiting on the ring leader to reach, then we'll bring you lot in with us," he assures her. I never imagined that any of this lot would class anyone as their ringleader with the high social statuses they each possess.

"Talk of the devil," Bless pipes up, pointing off into the distance.

Everyone peers into the shadows to see a tall well-built stranger approaching with a girl on his arm and 2 more following behind them. As they come into the light I feel my breath stop short.

"Ain't that the ACS president?" Sky asks, her attention now piqued.

"Yeah; Nathaniel Gibson aka sex on legs," Fontaine giggles.

I feel like the wind has been blown out of me and lord help me I am fighting back these tears with a vengeance.

Nathaniel is their 'King' and on his arm is the person who has absolutely no right to be there; the tramp that he had vehemently assured me 'didn't mean anything' is now silently claiming that she was the Queen to his King –Georgia.

I stand there rigidly, praying that I can uncoil myself before anyone notices that there is something wrong with me. I feel Tyson shift closer to me and discreetly stroke my hand; I clutch at his and he gives mine a small squeeze before letting go - he stays by my side.

I take a deep breath and collect myself, preparing to go to war if necessary. Georgia has already made me look foolish on this new turf once -she is not going to do it again.

Her green catlike eyes scour all of us before locking onto me and I hate the nervous jolt that flutters in the pit of my stomach when she does, but I meet her gaze with an uncanny blank stare, showing no sign of her presence bothering me, or that I even care that she is latched onto Nate like the leech she is. The crown is mine.

I turn my back on her and take my girls aside to address them privately.

"Just so you guys know; that is Georgia Daniels and I don't like her. In fact, she is the one person I can genuinely say that I hate. I know it's Fresher's Week and we all want to meet new people, but I won't fuck with anyone that fucks with her. "

The girls look uncomfortably from me to one another. I imagine it is something heavy to hear from a person they've just met, but if I'm to be their leader I have to set the ground rules from the jump. You're with me, or your with her -you can't do both.

Sky decides to break the awkward silence, "Not being funny, but your problem with her is *your* problem. Don't drag us into it, 'cause really, we don't know *either* of you."

I give her the same uncanny blank stare I gave my nemesis and she looks away.

"You're right, it is my problem, but that doesn't change anything. You're all free to make whichever choices you want, just like me, and I choose not to associate with anyone that associates with her. I'm not compromising on that."

"Why don't you like her?" Carmen asks. I sense that she is willing to side with me if I can validate my decision. Do I want to tell these strangers my business? No, not really, but if we are to be friends, they'll find out eventually right?

"She wasn't always the girl on his arm," I remark plainly, gesturing to the trophy couple. Fontaine's mouth falls open.

"You went out with Nathaniel Gibson?"

"Yes."

"What happened?"

I raise my eyebrow; isn't it obvious? "What do you think?"

The girls study at Georgia with new eyes. When they look back at me I see understanding, pity and resolve in all of their faces…except for Sky. She portrays the look of understanding convincingly enough, but I can still sense that she isn't completely with my 'No Georgia' rule, but still she says, "Okay."

I smile at her but it doesn't reach my eyes -if she isn't 100% on side then I have to be wary of her. All of my subjects are to be loyal to me and only me. I start turning away from her, silently deeming her as a potential traitor.

Just before I could turn away from her fully she adds, "She looks like a bit of a bitch anyway."

I glance over my shoulder and give her another plastic smile. Insulting Georgia won't get her out of the woods, especially when I know she is using the empty insult as a smoke screen to mask her true feelings on the matter, which she already made the mistake of making clear. Fakery doesn't sit well with me; I need every member of my entourage to be real. I'm not running a dictatorship, so anyone that goes along with rules they don't fully believe in is only doing so because they need to belong to something. Georgia might give her a better offer and she might drop me like a bad habit.

I hear the click of Georgia's heels come to a halt nearby and know that Nathaniel is now within touching distance. Slowly, I turn around to face them with my poker face in full effect. Nathaniel is staring at me.

Ace comes forward and flings his arm over Nathaniel's broad shoulders.

"Ladies, Ty, this is my boy, Nathaniel," he says proudly.

Nathaniel smiles cordially at the girls, ignores Tyson and set his brooding grey eyes back on me. I feel myself shudder involuntarily under the weight of his gaze and look away. It doesn't help much; I can feel his pull tugging at me, beckoning me back to him. Ignoring Nathaniel has always been an impossible task for me.

"We've met before," Tyson says stonily. I glance at him out of the corner of my eye to see him staring daggers into Nathaniel as if he would love nothing more than to rip his head off.

Carmen nudges me, "This is kinda intense," she comments quietly,
"Tell me about it," I laugh, trying not to let the intensity get to me.

"Oh, cool," Ace continues warily, conscious that the atmosphere has taken a turn for the tense. "Where do you lot know each other from?" he presses, trying to feel the situation out.

Tyson glances at me and brushes my hand lightly with the tips of his fingers. He understands that my business is my business and that when I'm ready to let **everyone** know then I will tell them myself...that is unless gossip does it for me first.

He settles with a vague, but honest answer, "We used to go to the same college."

Ace looks to Nate for confirmation; Nate responds with an abrupt nod, his stony eyes still studying me.

Georgia tightens her grip on his arm, clearly not enjoying the secretive trip down memory lane.

"So much has changed since then," she says tightly.

My poker face is replaced with a scowl –she is not going to make me look bad in front of everyone.

"Glad you noticed. Make sure you keep that in mind at all times."

"Only if you do," she sneers, resting her head on Nate's shoulder.

In his usual cool manner, he doesn't react –he isn't a fan of making a scene in public -but I notice the muscle in his jaw twitch in annoyance.

I summon the courage to return his gaze and smile casually. His lips part slightly as he takes in a swift breath. It's comforting to know that I still have that effect on him.

"I don't think it's me you have to worry about luv -it's nice to see you again Nathaniel." Georgia stops smiling and jerks his arm so he will stop staring at me.

Fontaine snickers.

"Well," she grins flinging her arm over my shoulder, marching me closer to the unhappy couple, "we're all here now, so Mr ACS President, we going inside or what?"

He is so painfully close to me now. It burns me to admit it, but time is definitely his friend; he is even more beautiful than I remember. His boyish prettiness has evolved into something deadlier, so much so that I experience the feeling I had the first time I saw him. My heart is racing at an unnatural pace, pausing in random places just so that it can catch up with itself. For the first time in over a year, Nathaniel smiles at me and the butterflies in my tummy that had lain quiescent for so long are suddenly shocked back to consciousness by the tangible electricity crackling between us.

"Let's go," he replies in his smooth-raspy voice.

4 Clubbin'.

We strut through the large black double doors of Purple in small groups of four, making our way down a dimly lit purple corridor with Nate and Georgia in the front, Tyson and I coming in second -the reigning King and his mistress followed by the intended Queen and her faithful advisor. Security is only letting us in a few people at a time and unluckily Ty and I have been lumped in with Beauty and the Bitch.

The bass pulsates around us as the muffled sounds of a popular Beyoncé track is playing on the other side of the second set of doors. The first DJ is busy getting the ravers into the mood with the warm-up session.

Before I can truly embark on my first Brompton Uni rave, we are stopped just by the entrance to give our jackets into the cloak room. This is the part of the night I have been looking forward to the most; showing off my fabulous outfit.

As Georgia is in front of me, she goes first. She is dressed in a simple black midi dress with simple chunky gold jewellery. Her pedicured feet are slotted into a pair of mile high black peep-toe heels with a shock of gold running horizontally through the front platform.

Her bitchy green eyes glare up at me from under a heavy fringe, not wanting to be outdone. I must admit that she looks good (as always), but this is my coming out party! I came to make a statement and I refuse to be outdone by anyone, especially the likes of her. I arch my eyebrow and step up to the little doorway where a girl around my age is taking the coats. I strip away my jacket.

Ta-dow! How ya like me now?

I stand proudly in a sheer chiffon leopard print blouse that hangs translucently over my black plunge bra that can barely contain my chest. The provocative blouse is tucked into a pair of tight high-waisted leather skinny fit trousers, which fit like a glove, emphasizing my curvaceous physique. I have a harlot red leather clutch to compliment my harlot red lips and acrylic stiletto nails. My fingers and wrists shine and clink with excessive amounts of gold jewellery and a long gold necklace drapes itself down my centre, stopping my navel with a heavy pendant. I hand the cloak room girl my jacket and a £1 with a smile. She gives me a bingo ticket in return which I slide into my purse.

My Jimmy Choos click across the floor as I subtly strike a pose. I had aimed for the overtly sexual vixen with a unique look that would stand out amongst the mass of Asos dresses, but with a touch of class. I have to set myself apart from the rest but still look relevant and I think this look has accomplished it perfectly.

Nathaniel clears his throat. Rio: 1, Georgia: nil.

"Looks like you won that round," Tyson smirks as we pass through the second set of doors. I fling my arms around him and laugh,

"This is why I love you! I beat her and it feels H'AMAZING! Who would have ever thought that I, Rio Greene, would ever be able to outshine the great Georgia Daniels? My plan is working; I'm on my way, I tells ya!" I wink.

"Happy much?" Ty laughs along with me, peeling my excited arms from around his neck.

"Yes, yes I am. It was like a cherry on top when Nate cleared his throat. Ooh that must have burned her," I cackle victoriously.

Tyson stops laughing and pulls me off to the side, "Yeah about him; what's with the staring and that?" he asks, his expression dead serious. Tyson doesn't play when it comes to me and Nathaniel.

I shift out of his protective grip and shrug, "I don't know and I don't bloody care! Nate can go suck a lemon 'cause tonight is my night, and I won't let him and his stupid torturously divine grey eyes ruin it!"

Tyson cocks his head the side. Swish goes his hair.

"Torturously divine?"

"Dude let it go," I fan him off, not in the mood to explain my teenage angst driven description.

After a few minutes, the rest of the group filters through the entrance. Tyson heads off with his boys, whilst I advance on to the next stage of my plan -becoming the 'It Girl Clique'.

"Now," I grin at the girls, rubbing my hands together making my bangles sing, "we need to find our spot on the dance floor." I run my eyes across the perimeter of the plush purple, black and chrome surroundings, stopping when I see a stage area with soft purple neon lights framing it near the DJ booth.

"Bingo."

"Mi will bruk yuh back when yuh come inna mi ramping shop," Fontaine screeches along drunkenly in my ear to Vybz Kartel as she gyrates her backside into Manny's crotch. I giggle (a little tipsy myself) and push her away. I am on such a high right now; my plan is going beyond well. My girls and I have captured the attention of the Bromptonians like moths to a flame. We've been doing our thing on the stage so well that DJ Bless had dubbed us the Fabulous 5. We got a name yo! Ooooh the other girls are so jealous and I LOVE it! They shoot us envious looks every time we start showing out with our vivacious dance moves, which let me know that we are a threat. I'm not sure if it is because our clique has been given a title or if it was because Bless is the one who gave it to us that makes their hate more potent, but either way, they (especially Georgia and her little gang of bum lickers) are throwing endless shade. Don't they know that throwing shade makes us cool!

Suddenly the whole rave goes into a pleasant uproar as Bless effortlessly mixes in Vybz Kartel's 'Virginity'. Tyson slides up behind me and plants one hand on my hips and laces the other around my leather wrapped waist. We rock, roll and grind to the heady beat, smiling, giggling and temporarily crushing on each other as our chemistry takes a firm hold of us. It is harmless of course, but all the while I feel a pair of eyes on us. Instinctively I look at the crushed velvet booth of the VIP area to see Nathaniel's glittering grey eyes staring at me disapprovingly over a glass of Moet as I sway. I look away and tried to re-immerse myself in the dance, but the weight of his stare will not let up. He is making me feel uncomfortable, as if I by dancing with Tyson like this I'm doing something wrong, which is ridiculous; after all, he is here with Georgia.

I stop dancing.

"Excuse me for a sec."

Tyson furrows his brow, "Are you all right?"

"Yeah, I just need to use the bathroom real quick." I lie.

I spot Carmen dancing nearby and drag her into his arms, "Carmen can take my place." They smile at each other and pick up where Tyson and I had left off.

I rush off in the direction of the ladies to collect myself.

A few minutes later I exit the bathroom with a bounce back in my step, deciding that things are going way too well for me to let my ex ruin my fun. So far everything has been going my way; my girls and I are dominating the dance floor, commanding the attention of the boys who are this year's superstars and making all of the girls wish that they were us. No one has ever wanted to be me before –the ego boost is intoxicating. If I keep it up then Georgia is definitely going to have to fall back and accept defeat. The fact that she showed up with Nathaniel means nothing. Tyson is right; we're not in college anymore.

Apparently -as some unspoken university rule –you're not supposed to get into any relationships in your first year. This is the year for exploring your options so that by the time second year rolls around, you will have a decent idea of who people really are and can make an informed decision on if it really is them that you want to be with.

Nathaniel is in his second year at Brompton and he has Georgia on his arm...maybe it means more that I think it should.

I turn the corner, preoccupied with caring about what Nathaniel is doing with Georgia and trying not to care so much that I am completely thrown off when I collide with a very tall, thick, impeccably dressed frame. I stumble backwards and would have most likely fallen flat on my bum had the person not caught me just in time.

"I'm so sorry," I apologise, now more flustered than before, "I wasn't looking where I was...oh!"

My words get lost on the way from my brain to my mouth as I am faced with the very person who has been plaguing my mind.

"Nathaniel?" I blink.

It's as if someone up there is playing a cruel trick on me. Every time I am near bubbling over with excitement they plant him there to take me down a couple notches. For the past year Nathaniel had only existed in my thoughts, but now he is physically here and it is nothing short of overwhelming.

Trying to catch my breath that seemingly whooshes out of me whenever I see him, I accidently inhaled his intoxicating scent. There are boys that smell nice because of whatever cologne they have on or detergent they use; and then there are boys that smell AMAZING because they smell like memories. It is a smell that even if they aren't around and you catch that particular scent in the air, it brings you back to all the times you used to lay in bed together, or bury your face into them when you hugged, or fell asleep in their t-shirt when they weren't there because you needed to be reminded that they were real. Nathaniel smells like Bold detergent and spiced apples. Nathaniel smells like home.

His large butterscotch hands cup my elbows gently so that I can regain my balance, then slowly, he releases me allowing me to try and stand on my own. I trembled in my six inch heels and stick my hand out so that the wall supports my weight. The impact of having practically every well sculpted inch of him imprinted against my frame again after so long is toying with me; I am too rattled by having him in such close proximity to keep myself from going weak at the knees.

"You okay?" He asks in his deep raspy tone that seems to command attention even when it is just above a whisper.

I exhale and give him a sharp nod.

"I'm fine," is my trembling reply as I step away from him. "What are you doing out here?"

Nathaniel waits patiently until I make eye contact and meets me with a gaze that has the power to disturb my anatomy in the best and worst way -depending on how you look at it. He looks breath-taking in his dark grey tailored trousers and black shirt with the top 3 buttons left open, showing teasers of his kissable collar bone and his tattoo.

I suck in a breath again and smell 'home' once more.

"I was waiting for you."

"Why?"

Nathaniel shrugs, "I wanted to speak to you."

"About?"

"Nothing; I just wanted to speak to you. You look…different," he comments simply as his eyes burn into me. I put more of my weight on the wall. Every time I interact with Nathaniel, even the smallest things seem epic because my mind will be all over the place. I'll focus on how close his glorious six foot something frame is to me, radiating his body heat onto my skin, how his deep raspy voice breaks into husky whispers in random places, the way his puckered lips seem to caress every word he speaks, but most of all, the way those alluring grey eyes are constantly seeing more than what is on the surface.

Nathaniel mimics me and leans against the wall in a similar fashion.

"This is weird right; us being here? I thought I'd never see you again."

I don't say anything. Instead I wrap my arms protectively around myself, not feeling like the 18 year old vivacious vixen I had been embodying all night, but more like my shy, awkward 16 year old self.

Nathaniel smiles gently and takes a cavalier step towards me, pinning me in place with his stare.

"I've missed you Ri."

In an instant I snap out of it and quickly side step him to return to the party. This is way too much to deal with right now - it was something I'd wanted to hear him say for what felt like forever. In my head, when I had fantasized about our reunion, my reaction wasn't the panicked one I am having now. This is real; Nathaniel is really here in front of me telling me that he misses me, and it terrifies me.

"I have to go," I squeak almost running towards the door. He catches my hand and pulls me back.

"Wait_"

"Nathaniel, just leave me alone…please," I plead. If I have to deal with this for a moment longer I will break down and I don't want to do that; not here, not tonight.

Nathaniel's mouth tightens and his eyes turn icy; he has never been able to deal with rejection well. He releases me.

"We're stuck here for at least the next two years Rio. You can't run from me forever."

"I know, so do us both a favour and don't chase me."

5
Facebook.

"Bruv, you need to drop her like a bad habit!" Tyson warns with a chuckle. My face is fixed in an expression of disgust at the information he has just offloaded on me.

"Are you being serious?"

"I'm a serious guy,"

"No, you're gassed."

Tyson laughs, "If I'm so gassed then how come I got piece?"

My jaw drops and I stare at Tyson in disbelief, "You're lying!"

"You wish I was. Sky is loose fam! The wickedest thing is, it's not even just me she's been with. I heard she fucked Calvin and Shaquille too."

I pulled another face, "No way! We've only been here for a week -how has Sky already had sex with three guys?"

Tyson shrugs.

"I'm not slippin' though; I gave her the dick first."

My hand flies up and connects with the back of his head - we are alone in my dorm room so it's ok to hit him now...sort of.

Tyson laughs mischievously and jumps off the bed to get out of my reach, meaning that he has more dirt to share.

"I'm not gonna stunt though, Sky has got ass for weeks! It was rippling like the ocean when I gave her the back-shot. I was like bang…bang…bang-bang-bang-bangbangbang," he says animatedly, screwing up his face like he smells something bad, while he happily demonstrates his doggy style sexpertise. I throw my pen at him and clamp my hands over my eyes.

"You're such a slag!"

"Thank you!" he grins proudly. I laugh at him and roll my eyes. Ty is so goofy sometimes, but people let him get away with it because he's cute.

He plops himself back down on the bed and rests his head in my lap. I run my hand gently through his braids till I reached the ends, twirling them around my fingers as I mull over what to do about this new information Tyson had bestowed on me. I can't have a hoe in my clique; it's not a good look. If word gets out that Sky is slack, people will associate that with the rest of us, which in turn would class all of us as loose in the eyes of our peers –birds of a feather flock together, as they say. I don't expect my girls to be celibate, they can sleep with who they want because -let's be honest -the way society is nowadays you have to be a certain calibre of loose to be considered a hoe as our generation standards aren't all that high. However, I do expect them to be selective. Exclusivity is the key to being seen as 'prestige' in our society of misinformed double standards. As the saying goes, "A key that opens many locks is a master key. A lock that can be opened by many keys is a shit lock." The lower a girl's 'body count', the higher the chance she has of earning the sought after title of some lucky guy's 'Wifey'.

Sky couldn't have chosen a worse university to be labelled a hoe. Seriously, she's trying to sleep around in BROMPTON and get away with it? Or maybe she doesn't want to get away with it –she's slept with Ty, Calvin and Shaquille in the first week of uni (lessons haven't even begun yet), a stupid move as they are all part of the Unfamous (well…Ty not so much, but he is definitely in there with them now) and part of the same Unfamous friend group. She doesn't know them from Adam, but she is quick to open up her legs to them. I'd never do something like that. What is wrong with her? Doesn't she care about her reputation?

I shrug to myself and sigh, unsure of what to do with her. Getting rid of Sky seems like the sensible option, but I like the nickname 'Fabulous 5'.

Perhaps I'm being too hasty; Sky isn't a bad person…she isn't my favourite person, but she isn't bad. I'll give her one last chance for the sake of the group and the atmosphere of our flat, but one more strike and she is out!

"What lessons you got tomorrow?" I ask Tyson, still absentmindedly playing with his hair. I glance down in my lap to find him staring up at me -God he is gorgeous!

I jerk my leg snapping him out of the moment, afraid that if I stared back the friendship lines would become blurry.

Tyson shakes his head and sits up. "Um, Introduction to Animation; you?"

"English Literature,"

"Fun!" he says sarcastically. There is a bite to his tone which I know I probably provoked by extinguishing the tiny spark of possibilities of our relationship before the fire had a chance to burn. I don't want to burn with Tyson; it isn't safe. Our friendship is safe and that's how I want it to stay.

Those few weeks after I'd broken up with him and we stopped talking were the worst. I had never felt so alone in my life. It was one thing to lose Nate, but to lose Tyson would kill me. If I lost him I would have no one, so I have to be the one to keep us in check. If we cross the friendship line again and something goes wrong, I'm not sure that we would be able to recover from it again. A relationship at the age of 14 is nowhere near the same intensity as it is at 18.

"I know right," I laugh overlooking his obvious attitude, "You excited?"

"Excited for what?" he asked in the same tone. He could be so stubborn.

I huffed, walked over to my desk and sat down. I'm not in the mood for this. I nudged the mouse pad bringing my Macbook back to life.

"'Cause it's gonna be our first uni lesson, init!"

"So! It's still a lesson. Just 'cause it's in uni doesn't suddenly make it fun."

Ugh, he's so miserable sometimes.

I fan him off, signalling that I am done trying to get him out of his funk and log onto Facebook -9 new friend requests, 12 event invitations, 5 inbox messages and 23 notifications. WOW! What am I doing with 23 notifications?

I click on the red bubble and a list springs up telling me that Amari 'DJ Bless' Richardson has tagged me in 23 photos. I smile and click the first photo.

"Oh my God!" I squeal bouncing in my seat, "I didn't know there was a photographer at the Fresher's Rave."

"That's because you spent most of the night dribbling over your dickhead ex," Ty mumbles loud enough for me to hear. Ooh we were going to fight in a minute if he doesn't fix his attitude. I force myself to keep my eyes on the screen and my mouth shut before I say something that will upset him.

I go through the rest of the pictures then deal with my surprisingly high number of friend requests. Disbelief sends a shudder through me when I see that the reason for Ty's bitterness and my so called 'dribbling' has requested me as a friend. I freeze. After our uncomfortable encounter at the club, Nathaniel still has the audacity to add me. We are not friends; far from it, so what the hell does he want from me?

I can feel myself getting wound up from over-thinking, I need air. I need to release this frustration, but I can't tell Ty, he's already in a mood and this will only make it worse…not that I'd tell him even if he wasn't in one.

The cursor hovers over the 'ignore' button but I can't click it. I should, but a part of me doesn't want to. If curiosity killed the cat, then what was it going to do to me? Break my slap-dash mended heart again?

I decide to leave it sitting there and go through the rest of my requests. I don't know why, but it's given me this satisfied feeling to know that he has bothered to seek me out on Facebook and request me even though I have blown him off. It also irritates me because this is exactly what I had asked him not to do. I wonder if he's following me on Twitter. I open a new tab, go to Twitter and check my interactions –'N. Gibson **@MrGrey** is following you.' For fuck's sake! Nathaniel is going to chase after me whether I liked it or not and I am scared to think of what might happen once he catches me.

I scroll through my interactions and squeal again. This time I am excited enough to clap my hands at the activity in my mentions. Ace has @'d me about the next Sunday Slam -the one event that I have heard about that oozed, dripped and glistened with the Unfamous. There is no way I am passing this up.

I spin in my chair to face Tyson with a stupid grin on my face. He is on his back on the bed playing with his iPhone. Since we came here and he got a couple new contacts all he does is Whatsapp people. When he chills with me I make him put it on silent because the amount of messages he will get in the space of 10 minutes is enough to make me want to 'accidently' drop it on the floor and hope that the screen breaks to the point where he can't read them.

"Ty," I squeak, trying to contain my excitement. He grunts in response keeping his eyes glued to the screen.

"I just got an invite to Sunday Slam; you know that one that runs every Sunday at Plan X in Brixton. Are you on it?"

Ty puts his phone down and smirks, his special smile playing around the edges as he looks at me.

"You are HAPPY!" he laughs slapping his hand on his thigh.

"Shut up!" I grin not caring that he is teasing me, because it is true, I am happy. I am ecstatic! Sunday Slam is the event to see and be seen at. Every Unfamous person goes there either to just jam with other un-celebrities (or real celebrities if you are lucky) or perform /host the show. If you want to be someone in their little world, you have to network with the people that matter. I want to be someone, so come rain or shine; I am going to be there.

"No I will not shut up. Rio, if you ever see the dirty grin on your face right now you would feel ashamed of yourself. STOP SMILING YOU NERD," he laughs harder. I try to reign in my smile but it is proving to be quite a task. I am being nerd right now but I'm being a nerd in the confines of my room with only Ty here to witness it, so I am going to continue.

"Whatever. Are you on it or not?"

"Yeah, I've been planning to go for a while. I got a *verbal* invite from Ace."

Ace's face flashes in my mind and I wonder if it would be worth my while to cosy up to him. I know it sounds **very** shallow, but do you know how Unfamous I would be if Ace was my man? I'd be Unfamous Royalty!

Unlike Sky, I plan to keep myself VERY exclusive and only go for the guys that I deem worthy of the Queen of Brompton first years. If I play hard to get enough, it will make me seem like the ultimate mountain to conquer to all the boys. The one that finally gets me will feel as if they have accomplished something because they would know that so many others would have tried and failed miserably. By the time second year rolls around I would have picked one of them and I'd be part of the steady power couple relationship that I desired.

"Don't even think about it." I'd completely forgotten that Tyson is here.

"Huh?"

"No not 'huh'. I can see the cogs turning in your head; you're trying to put Ace on your potential hubby list," he says knowingly.

"Yeah, so?"

"You're wasting your time. Ace wants Yoshi," he smirks, pleased that he has burst my bubble. Jerk. He is right though; Yoshi and Ace clearly have a thing for each other and Yoshi is cool so I'm about to step on her toes. If I am to rule, then I have to keep my subjects happy, and breaking the 'G' code is definitely the wrong direction to go in. I cross Ace off of my mental list.

I switch back to Facebook and look at Nate's friend request. I slam the laptop shut before I do anything stupid.

My camel Ugg boots shuffle up the stairs against the carpet of the almost full lecture hall. To come from a college classroom to this huge room that looks like it could be a miniature cinema (with desks) made the transition from further education to higher education all the more exciting. Just by being here I already feel more sophisticated and mature because I am now a university student.

I settle into a seat near the back of the room and pulled out my Macbook. How cool is this? I can actually do my work on my laptop instead of lugging around a stupid notebook.

I was enjoying the novelty of being a uni student so much that by the time I realise who I am sitting next to, the class had already started and it was too late to move.

"For someone who doesn't want to deal with me, you sure chose a funny place to sit."

I curse silently wishing that I had been paying more attention to my surroundings rather than ogling at how grown up I felt - something that is taken away from me as soon as Nate appears. No matter how far I come, I am always brought back to being that naive 16 year old girl who believed that it was me and the boy I loved against the world, when he's around.

I allow myself one small glance and end up staring. His hair is cut one millimetre away from bald, then from out of nowhere his thin, neat sideburns begin running down the length of his chiseled jaw then cupping his chin, before connecting to his just as thin goatee. His muscular frame is covered in a charcoal grey turtleneck jumper with the 'Zara' emblem stitched into the top right corner, black Armani straight leg jeans and charcoal grey, black and red Jordans'. Unconsciously, I bite the corner of my lip; he looks like a freakin' Calvin Klein model for God's sake! The way that the cotton hugs his arms and clings to the curves of his sculpted chest makes me weak. Why oh why did this beautiful boy have to do such an ugly thing?

"What are you doing here?" I hiss tearing my eyes away from him to try and focus on something else.

Nate snickers lightly and leans back in his seat, "Retake. Why are you sitting next to me?" he asks indifferently as if he doesn't really want an answer, but is enjoying watching me react to him.

"I wasn't paying attention. Trust me; this is the last place I want to sit."

"So you say," he shrugs.

I want to punch him in the throat. What's with all of the stupid little hints he is throwing about me wanting to be around him. I so do not want to be around him!

"Fuck off Nathaniel!" That makes him smile. He has a beautiful smile.

"Still as feisty as ever,"

"Don't talk like you know me because you don't; not anymore," I spit, my temper now getting the best of me. There was no need for me to be this mad at that minor comment, but he just provokes this anger in me that I thought I had laid to rest.

Nathaniel's misty eyes twinkle with amusement; he is enjoying witnessing my unfazed pretences wither away.

"What; are you different now or something?" A teasing smile plays around his lips. I draw mine in to form an unflattering scowl. Of course I have bloody changed, is he blind or something? I didn't look this good in college, nor was I this confident.

I peek at him and give myself a mental once over. I may look better than before, but no matter how much I alter my appearance I still don't measure up to his effortless good looks. I decide that I am going to take myself shopping as soon as the lecture is over for a much needed ego boost.

When we were in college I never understood why Nathaniel even looked my way let alone chose to make me his girlfriend. I was such a plain Jane and he was (and still is) the boy that practically every girl swoons over. In my mind, physically, we never made sense. Everyone thought that Nathaniel should be with someone like Georgia because she was on his level of beauty. It hurt to know that they didn't consider me attractive enough to be with him, but for whatever reason, Nate did.

When I used to try and explain to him how out of whack we looked together he would crouch down a little so that his eyes were level with mine and say in the most sincere voice, "You don't see yourself the way I see you and it's a shame, 'cause I think you're beautiful babe."

He would tell me I was beautiful –I never believed him but it still made my heart fly. If Nathaniel had referred to me as sexy or pretty then the compliment would be easier to digest. There is a big difference between someone telling you you're pretty/sexy/cute to someone telling you that you are beautiful. Beauty is more than skin deep; it means that someone not only sees what is on the outside, but what is on the inside too. I thought I was too plain, awkward and insecure to be beautiful. Funny, he thought that I was so bloody beautiful, yet he still managed to be unfaithful to me and to add salt to the wound, I come to Brompton and he has the wicked bitch of the North West latched to his arm every chance she gets, like some glamorous leech, in Louis Vuitton and Louboutins.

"Yes. In case you haven't noticed, I'm not 16 anymore," I sneer.

Nathaniel smiles and turns away from me.

"You don't fool me Rio," he says after a short silence. I huff loudly acting as if I am annoyed that he has decided to reignite the slightly unwanted conversation, but inside a lone butterfly tickles my tummy. I'm intrigued and dying to know what he means by me not fooling him.

"What are you on about Nate?" I ask not looking at him, afraid that the lone butterfly will multiply into the giddy swarm that had surprise attacked me at Club Purple.

Nathaniel gestures at me with a cynical expression. "All of this. What exactly do you think you're doing?"

"What are you talking about?"

The muscle in his jaw flickers -Nate is not a fan of bullshitting. Honestly, I don't know why I am trying to act like I don't know what he is talking about, or trying to fool myself into believing that one year apart would rid his memory of my mannerisms. It is safe to say that next to Ty, Nathaniel knows me through and through. Once upon a time, he even knew me better than Tyson, and that is saying something. I don't enjoy revisiting our past; it has a terrible habit of pulling at the stitches of the hole in my chest, but back then I believed that Nate and I were as close to perfect as a relationship could be. He was my other half; everything one of us lacked, the other made up for so it was silly of me to pretend otherwise.

"Cut the crap ok! I know you. This is not you. The clothes, make-up, the weave; you look like one of them. You, the person who used to burst into 'non-conformist' speeches to defend why you had absolutely no desire to resemble your peers in any way, and now here you are trying insert yourself into the world of the very type of people who you used to despise," he says tartly. He is getting mad. Good! I'm tired of being angry alone so he might as well join the party.

I jut out my chin in defiance; I refuse to explain myself to him. Unfortunately he takes my silence as an invitation to continue.

"Why does it still matter what 'they' think of you? Why are you trying so hard to get 'them' to accept you?"

"Ok Dr Phil, we're done here," I smile coldly, not enjoying his psychoanalysis. It is irritating me that he is trying to read me. Why can't he just mind his own business and let me live my life however I see fit? It's not like it's affecting him. Yes, I'm going in a different direction. Yes, I'm hanging around with the kind of people who use to irritate the life out of me with their shallow materialistic way of thinking. Yes I am trying to erase the old me; but this is his fault! The old me was so truly, madly, deeply in love with Nathaniel that I couldn't move on for months. It embarrasses me to know how badly I fell apart after him. I don't want to be that broken hearted wall flower anymore, hence I transformed into the new and improved Rio who is fabulous enough to be fancied by many and envied by more. I am popular...well, on my way to it, and important people care about what I think and it's not because of the reason they paid me any mind in college (because I was Nathaniel Gibson's girlfriend), it's because I am me; Rio Greene and for the first time in my life, that was enough. I wasn't about to sit here and listen to him criticize me when he's never known what it feels like to be treated as if you don't count.

Nate shakes his head and sighs, "I know what you're doing Rio and you are making a huge mistake," he warns.

"What I do is none of your concern anymore and it hasn't been for a while, so back off!" I snarl.

Nathaniel settled back into his chair, now seething, and looked at the lecturer who seemed oblivious to our heated conversation.

"You'll always be my concern Rio, whether you like it or not." His stony eyes burn as the muscle in his jaw flickers again.

I flip my hair over my shoulder and dip my head, making it drop forward to create a curtain between us. I breathe deeply, trying to force my emotions to shut down because his last reply has me open like a book and I hate it. Why does he still have to act like I matter to him? Why can't he just be an asshole and let me hate him without feeling like pushing him away may be a bad thing, because he really is only saying this to me because he cares.

I don't want to feel like this; I'm tired of it. I wish that feelings had an off switch because they have a tendency to become a little too overwhelming at the wrong times, and this is most definitely the wrong time.

I sneak a glimpse at him, and for one small moment, I wish that he was mine again; not because he is positively delectable, but because in my heart, no matter what happens, a part of me would always belong to him. I believe that it's damn near impossible to share such epic emotions and experiences with someone and at the end of the day have it boil down to nothing. If it does, then it wasn't real. Nathaniel and I was the realest thing I had ever encountered. I will always think of him as the boy I fell truly, madly, deeply in love with.

The lights are low and the room is hushed as we all sit and listen to our lecturer run us through the course outline on the overhead projector. I sit rigid in my seat trying my best to focus on what my lecturer, Rose Littman, is saying, as the sound of my heartbeat thumps loudly in my ear.

I'm annoyingly aware of everything and the darkness does nothing to aid my sensory displeasure. My breath seems too strained, my palms too damp and my heart is beating way too fast. I can feel his body heat against the left side of my body – he is so hot –and I can smell his mouth-watering scent, bringing me back to the times when love was, haunting me every time I inhale. I want to run out of the room; moving seats doesn't seem to be far enough because I'd know that he is nearby.

It is sheer torture sitting right next to him knowing that I would only have to move but a few inches to touch him once more. I knot my fingers together under the desk and lean away from him as subtly as I can, as to not draw his attention.

I had endured a whole year of crying, accepting and working on letting go of Nate, and now all that hard work is being thrown back in my face. Do you know how hard it is to let go of your first love? It's like a battle that you never truly win because as much as you may think you have let go and moved on to other people, you will always compare them to the first one. They don't kiss as good as, they're not as tall as, they don't understand me like, or they can't make me laugh like (insert name). It seems as if no one is ever enough because they will never be them. You may fall in love again, but love doesn't taste as sweet as it did the first time around. Love now has a bitter aftertaste of mistrust and cynicism. Love is now looking for signs that the new person may break your heart again.

I suck in a deep breath and shake my head furiously; I am not going to cry. Not here, not now. I can't. I have to stop thinking. I need to focus on something that has no relation to Nate, quickly. I scour the room and am met with various shadowed objects because of the lack of light. Fuck!

I raise my hand to my face, pretending there is something in my eye that I really have to get out. My head hurts and I can feel that stupid lump forming in my throat.

This is not fair! I'm supposed to be stronger now. I'm meant to be cured of my love sickness. I'm supposed to be out of his reach, so why do I want him to pull me to him and whisper that he is still as much in love with me as I am with him? It's times like this when you wish that life was like the movies and soppy shit like that really did happen.

As much as I don't want them to, my tears gradually fill my lower lash line to the brim and are due to fall any moment now. I grab the edge of my sleeve and tug it over my hand, pressing the material against my tear duct so that it can absorb the first tear. The other eye decides that it wants to join the pity party and before I can get to it, a hot tear slips from my eye and glides down my cheek. The routine cry baby sniff follows and I am officially crying and feeling like a total prat about it.

Would it look melodramatic if I swooped out of here in tears? Probably but I need to cry properly so I could get it out of my system and be done with it.

A pocket sized packet of Kleenex tissues land with a soft thud on the table in front of me. Nathaniel is still staring straight ahead refusing to look at me, but the corners of his mouth are turned down into an almost frown –I say almost because he looks frustrated too.

"Baby, stop crying," he whispers softly, taking my hand under the table. He brushes his thumb across the back of my hand lightly trying to soothe me, but it only made me cry harder.

I snatch my hand away and hide my face in the folds of my arms on top of the desk. After 10 minutes my tears subside and I now hide my face from the world because of shame. I can't believe I just broke down like that in the middle of my first lesson, in the presence of Nathaniel no less. All I can do now is wait until class is over, then I can escape to my dorm room and hide.

I contemplate what high calorie food I can tuck into to make myself feel better (which would inevitably end in me feeling like I would have to suffer a week at the student gym) when a small piece of paper slides underneath a small gap between my arms and the desk. I know it is from Nathaniel so I don't budge, making it clear that I don't want to be bothered.

By the time I stop being stubborn and raise my head, Nathaniel isn't even next to me anymore. I have a foolish moment where I try to convince myself that I had imagined him being there, and then I look down on the table to see that small piece of paper folded in half waiting to be read.

I glance around to see that half of the class has already left; the lesson is over and I have been too swept up in my teenage angst to notice.

I snatch up the note and my belongings, making a dash for the door. Once in the solitary confines of my room, I take out the note and read it:

When you're ready to talk
Nate x

His number is at the bottom.

6
iPhone.

"I'm gonna kick her in her neck! Is she dumb? No but Ri, is she really dumb though? Fuckin' dirty bitch! Watch when she comes in, it's gonna be ME and HER; watch!"

Carmen crosses her arms over her chest and settles back into her space on the bed next to a highly amused Tyson who is currently rolling around in hysterics. I pull in my bottom lip and bite down hard, trying to keep my laughter from exploding as well. Carmen is glaring at everything she sets her eyes on, so I don't think that me joining in with Tyson's raucous laughter is going to help lighten her mood.

Carmen growls and leans against the wall with her nails digging into her upper arms as if she is fighting to restrain herself from taking her fury out on Tyson. Her face is set in a calculating scowl with her eyebrows drawn inwards, creating angry creases in the space between them. She is seething. I have only known Carmen for a little over a month now, but we have established a somewhat close bond already, as I predicted we would. I'm familiar with some of her mannerisms, her volatile temper being one of them, and let me tell you something, you never (and I mean NEVER) get between Carmen and a boy she likes because she is likely to go off.

On this occasion, the opposing party is none other than fast ass Sky, who -since the promiscuous endeavours of her first week here -has made no attempt to slow down. Sky must have worked her way through half of Brompton by now, and unfortunately for her, she has made the mistake of sleeping with Carmen's conquest; DJ Bless.

Carmen's temperament is similar to that of Blair Waldorf's from Gossip Girl, in the sense that when someone messes with a guy that she likes, she sits and stews over the betrayal until she can think of a fitting way to retaliate. You can tell if she really wants to get even with the offending party if she threatens to kill them, though of course that's just gas. To Carmen, killing someone means insulting and threatening them in public. None of us think that Carmen can fight -she talks way too much -but that doesn't stop us from feeling for her victims (no matter how deserving) because Carmen has a volatile mouth on her and is nothing short of vindictive when pushed. Once she gets going, she doesn't quit until she is certain that she has won.

The last time I saw her in action was at our first coach rave up in Coventry, deftly named 'Rep Your Country'. Everyone was there – by everyone I mean all the Unfamous people that mattered from each Uni and then some. I acquired some promising new contacts that night. Anyway; the Fabulous Five was in full effect, each dressed stylishly in our country colours with our flags incorporated as an accessory in some way, resembling our cliques namesake exceptionally well if I must say so myself. I was repping Guyana, Carmen: Jamaica, Fontaine: Italy and Dominica, Yoshi: Japan, and Sky: Ireland. Word had gotten out about the Brompton Five, so we were kind of a hot commodity -which I was beaming about for days afterwards- all eyes were on us.

Since the Fresher's Rave at Club Purple, Carmen had been head-over-heels for Tyson's new friend, DJ Bless. Out of the 'Five' that night, Bless had set his sights on Carmen and had dedicated a song in the slow jam section especially for her, after which he -uncharacteristically for a DJ -left the booth to dance with her. From that moment on, Carmen was completely and utterly smitten with the attractive, high powered, young man. The girl was one Instagram like away from a restraining order. She and Amari hit it off pretty well and were now talking...like 'talking' talking, which of course in girl world now made him off limits to everything with a vagina.

On the night of 'Rep Your Country', Bless wasn't working so he was crushed up in the middle of the rave with the rest of us, whining to some sweet Soca music, when a pretty young thing from Langford University decided that she would like to sample his waistline on the dance floor. Carmen spotted the girl from a mile off, and later explained to me that her 'Hoe-dar' was going off because that 'tramp' was heading straight for Bless. She watched as this newcomer gyrated a few inches in front of Bless (trying to entice him with her fluid hip movements), waited until the girl was brave enough to raise her foot to take a step back so that she would be whining directly on him, and Carmen stuck out her foot. The Langford girl tripped and landed on the floor with her too short skirt exposing what it was meant to conceal; it was not a good look –she hadn't waxed! We all busted out laughing, and the girl ran away embarrassed.

You'd think that after witnessing Carmen react to a girl merely trying to dance with Bless would have informed Sky that perhaps **sleeping with him** wasn't the best idea, especially when the girl who is meant to be your friend has an impulsive mean streak. I guess she doesn't care.

"Shut up Ty!" Carmen sulks shoving him away from her as he rolls again. That fool better not dribble on my bed.

"Car, can you hear yourself? It's not that deep," he guffaws, "Sky sleeps with EVERYONE; that's what she does. As a matter of fact, any guy that hasn't fucked her yet is slippin' 'cause she is throwing her pussy out there like a free newspaper. It's nothing personal; this is just how some chicks operate. Let it go and let the hoe be a hoe."

"No! Why's she fucking Bless for? These times everyone knows he mine!"

"Well obviously not everyone cares! It's not like it even counted. Think of Sky as the Brompton boy's rite of passage; we all have to go through it at on stage," he grins.

Unmoved by his reasoning, Carmen kissed her teeth, "Shut up Ty!"

"Real talk," he continued, "I've mashed it, Calvin mashed it, Shaquille mashed it, Damon, Manny…shit, I heard that even Nate broke her off a piece." Tyson says the last part clearly and with more ill-humour than necessary. It delivers the effect that he wants because suddenly I don't want to laugh so much anymore.

Sky slept with Nathaniel.

My skin flushes with heat as anger consumes me. I had explained the situation between Nathaniel and I to the girls from day 1, and now she wants to turn around and do this? What the fuck? Nathaniel is not just some CRUSH to me; Nathaniel used to be my everything! He is the first boy I fell in love with, and I'm not convinced that I've fallen out of love with him even a little yet, so why couldn't she pass up the opportunity to wrap her legs around HIM of all people? GOD!

I'm with Carmen now; wait until she gets in!

Tyson and Carmen quickly strike up another conversation about lord knows what, as a subject change is needed after Tyson so willingly dropped the 'Sky and Nate' bomb. As engrossed in their tense trivial chit chat as they want to make out they are, they keep glancing at me, trying to gauge just how pissed off I am.

I really want to punch something, scream at the top of my lungs until my throat is sore and have one of those really dramatic moments where I shove every materialistic thing that I hold dear off of the table (iPhone not included). I am angry -the kind of angry where I am heavily inclined to be violent -but most of all, I'm hurt. 'Hell hath no fury like a woman scorned' had never felt truer for me than in this moment. The surge of adrenaline rushing around my body is making my blood boil with fury dangerous enough to make the Hulk himself tremble. Sky sleeping with Tyson is her merely trying my patience, but sleeping with Nathaniel is her asking to go to war against me. If she walked through the door right now I would beat her within an inch of her life. Better yet, if that bastard Nathaniel so much as walked past my building...

I'm mad at Sky, but I'm not so blinded by love that I can't factor Nathaniel in for the blame also. He should have known better. He's already trying to pry apart my wounds by continuing to deal with Georgia, and now he had added Sky to that list.

I didn't want to hate her; *technically* she had done nothing to me and I knew I was being silly by being **this** mad at her, but for whatever reason (love), it felt better to blame her because the less things I convinced myself that Nate had done wrong, the easier it is to try and forgive him.

Logically, I shouldn't even care if they had sex or not - he's not even my boyfriend -but like I said before...he's mine.

What I really want to know is when it happened, but I don't want to ask Tyson because he is likely to say something insensitive that will push my rage in his direction. This little escapade of Nate's has to have been recent; had it happened earlier, Tyson would have rubbed it in my face already.

As we have a class together, Nate and I are now on speaking terms...if you can call it that. We aren't friends; far from it. There is still the underlying animosity in every word I say to him, blended with my intangible looks of unchartered adoration, while Nate sits there brooding, unleashing those smouldering grey eyes on me every chance he can, his eyes speaking volumes louder than anything he dared to say. We are exes that communicate. To be honest, I find it emotionally exhausting, but there is this element of excitement because when things get too heavy, one of us is bound to slip up and say something that has been playing on our minds since we ended things. I thought we were making progress and were on our way to being more than just civil with each other, but like every other ex, Nate has done yet another thing to remind me why we aren't together anymore.

I pick up my iPhone and quickly fix my face before facing my friends. They know I am upset, but I don't want them to see how much because I'm supposed to be stronger now -Nate should not still have such a powerful effect over my emotions.

"You lot thirsty? I'm going to the kitchen quickly," I chirp in an overly-cheery voice that sounds strained even to me.

Carmen and Ty look up, both of them presenting me with different expressions; Carmen contemplating if she wants a drink or not, and Tyson fighting against feeling guilty because he knows that I am leaving the room so that I can be sad without an audience.

"Nah I'm good," he replies quietly, choosing to look at something else as opposed to my false smile and pained eyes.

Carmen shrugs lazily, "You got apple juice?" I nod in response and she flashes me a childish grin. A real smile glimmers on my lips briefly. I turn and leave before the tight smile returns, cradling my phone to my chest.

I clatter aimlessly around the bland communal student kitchen, trying to keep myself busy so that I don't have to focus on how betrayed I feel. I open my assigned cupboard for a glass then slam it shut. The sound of the cheap oak door smacking into the frame echoes though the kitchen and out into the hallway -so much for trying to keep my anger contained.

I need to yell at someone.

I go into my Whatsapp and scroll through my contacts until I reached Nate's stupid screen name 'Your girl is my groupie' and begin punching the touchscreen keyboard with my thumbs:

Sky?

I press send and go back to making Carmen's drink.

Why is it that when you send an important message that you want a reply to RIGHT NOW it seems as if the person that is on the receiving end of the message takes a billion years to reply. In the space of 30 seconds I check my phone four times and am to go for my fifth when the soft bell sound chimes out of it.

I click on it immediately, anxious to see how he is going to explain himself:

Correct.

Foolishly I try to scroll down even though there is clearly no more of the message left to display. Correct? That's all I'm going to get for finding out about his indiscretion; correct? What is he playing at?

Why?

This time I get a reply almost instantly; he's going to humour me while it still remotely tickles his fancy.

I didn't know that I was supposed 2 run who I slept with by u 1st

I'm not saying u do, but Sky? C'mon!

Rio, chill. It was just sex.

What is wrong with him? It's not JUST SEX when it affects my life as well. God he's so fucking obtuse sometimes!

U make me sick!

What's new lol

Nathaniel it's not funny! U slept with my friend!

What kind of friend would fuck ur ex behind ur back? I dunno y u even threw that in the argument when we both know that's not real reason y ur mad at me.

Oh really, then what is? Coz that seems like a pretty gd reason!

I glare at the screen expecting an instant response so I can retaliate some more, but there's nothing.

I growl and go back to angrily making Carmen's drink, now more riled up than before. Then came his reply, which stops me short:

Ur mad coz ur still in love with me Ri.

As much (or little) as we had spoken since I'd arrived at Brompton, neither of us have used the 'L' word…until now.

Instantaneously, I throw up my defences knowing that if I don't, this conversation will get real heavy, real fast.

U fuckin' wish!

Shit, why did I say that? I panicked and unfortunately it was the first thing that came to mind. It is a blatant lie and will probably hurt him a lot, but it's the only weapon I had.

I don't know what the prize is in this argument, but after putting in so much time and effort to become this new improved Rio, I'll be damned before I let him win. Pride can be a terrible thing.

Kl.

Oh hell no! I know this boy did not just give me the 'kl'; not even the full 'cool', but the abbreviated 'kl', which means he's pissed and as far as he's concerned, the conversation is officially over. I've got your 'kl' Nathaniel!

I jab the keypad once and pressed send:

K.

Ha! 'K' is much worse than 'Kl'. Suck on that Nate!

I fling my phone down on the counter now angrier than when I started out. I Whatsapped him to get answers and somehow he turned it around and made it about me. This isn't about me; it's about us, and it hurts that much more that I'm the only one who realises this.

My phone skids across the counter making a scratchy sound as it glides to the edge.

I don't want to be angry with Nathaniel anymore, but he seems dead set on making it as difficult as possible.

My phone teeters on the edge for half a second before it goes crashing down onto the blue speckled linoleum of the kitchen floor. For fuck's sake! I bend down and scoop it up to see a large angry crack running in a ragged vertical down the centre of the screen. As if I don't have enough to be pissed about already!

As I bend down to scoop my damaged phone up I detect the muffled sounds of a rapidly escalating argument coming from the hallway. Shoving the device into my pocket I make my way into the hallway to see its source being Carmen bellowing in Sky's face.

Sky's back is pressed against the wall, looking seemingly intimidated by Carmen, who is shorter than her with a slighter frame. Carmen doesn't even look threatening, but the tongue lashing she is delivering is. She's going for gold, stringing violent insults together with foreign curse words in a seasoned Jamaican accent. It's a pity that Sky has me to deal with as well. I quicken my pace, marching towards them like a solider charging gun first into no man's land.

"You know seh me and Bless ah do ah ting, so wha di bludclart yuh ah sex him fa?" Carmen screams, prodding Sky in her chest.

"I didn't think it was that serious. I mean, it's not like I'm the only other girl he's sleeping with!" Sky retorts.

"Tell me suttin," Carmen lowers her voice and put her face closer to Sky's, "Any ah dem fuckin' dutty gyal ah my bredrin?"

"Well no but_"

"But nothing; you know how much I like him and you still done it anyway! Me and you ain't friends no more," she yells, switching back to her British accent.

Sky gawks at her, "Car, are you seriously gonna stop talking to me over some guy?"

"No; I'm gonna stop talking to you coz I don't fuck with basic bitches."

Sky rolls her eyes, "Babe, you're over-reacting_"

"No she's not," I interject.

Sky turns her attention to me and her frame tenses up even more when she notices the eerie calm of my face. I know that my eyes have darkened even more than usual, making the onyx black bottomless. She stares at her shaken reflection in my pupils and shrinks back even more -she's right to be afraid because I am in the worst kind of mood right now.

"I think you've got some explaining to do," I prompt.

"What's there to explain?" her voice shakes. Coward! I almost feel sorry for her...almost.

"Nathaniel."

Deciding to find her courage (I guess I'm not as scary as Carmen) Sky sighs and pushes herself off of the wall.

“Are you two delusional or something? I’ve got one of you in my ear crying about me sleeping with some guy she’s not even with, who fucks practically every groupie he picks up in a rave, and now you’ve come along, pissed off coz I had sex with your ex who is meant to be seeing Georgia anyway. You’re both mad at the wrong person.”

"Funny, because in both scenarios the common denominator is you, Sky.” I point out.

Sky shifted uncomfortably as I hone in on her.

“You are a snake, and I swear to God if you go near Nathaniel_" Carmen nudges me, "Or Bless ever again, I will make you wish you never came to Brompton; I will ruin you. Understand?"

Sky blinks, "Excuse me? What makes you think that you have the power to ruin me? Just because you walk around here like you’re somebody, doesn’t mean that you are. Georgia’s in a few of my classes and she talks about you, you know. The way I hear it, you’re some wannabe trying to act like you belong so why don’t you do yourself a favour and get over yourself. You don’t belong with a guy like Nathaniel, Rio, you never did and you know it. That’s probably why he dropped you for Georgia in the first pl_ "

BAM!

I gawk at my palm in disbelief, slowly realising what I have just done. It had happened so fast that I couldn't stop myself. I was already mad and Sky's venomous words were the few extra drops of water that made the cup overflow. She spoke to me like she was one of Georgia’s bitchy college friends and it bothered me; people aren’t meant to regard me like that anymore. What else had Georgia said about me and to whom? How much did they know? Why was she set on keeping me down?

"What the fuck was that?"

Tyson is suddenly behind me tugging me away from a gob smacked (literally) Sky who is clutching her face on the floor. How hard did I hit her? My adrenaline hasn't worn off yet, but I’m sure that by the time I come down from my rush, my hand is going to let me know.

"That was a 5 star slap!" Carmen giggles through her shock.

"Rio what's the matter with you man?" Tyson growls, shoving me in my shoulder.

"I didn't mean to. Sky I'm so sorry…" I say pathetically. I honestly didn't mean to, it literally just happened. One minute I was getting ready to walk away, then the next my palm was delivering a powerful blow to Sky's face.

"Don't apologise! These times she was talking wicked - slap her, yes!" Carmen squawks.

"Talking wicked?" Ty asks, confused.

"Yes! If you ever heard the cheek of this common bitch talking about how Rio is some wannabe who never belonged with a guy like Nate, and that's why she got dropped for Georgia. If Rio didn't regulate her face, I would have," Carmen looks at me "and I wouldn't have apologised for shit!"

Tyson's expression softens and he searches my face. He knows how much I hate being reminded that I wasn't enough for the boy that was more than enough for me.

Hearing Carmen repeat Sky's scornful words revved up my anger back up to the point where I was sure that it would soon convert to bitter, salty tears. I spare Sky a poisonous parting glare and stalk off into my room with my broken iPhone in my pocket, and an ego to match.

I locked my door behind me and sit at my desk so I can assess the damage caused to my phone. There is a red bubble over the Whatsapp icon; Nathaniel had replied. I touch my finger to it but nothing happens; the touchscreen feature is screwed, which means that the phone is basically good for nothing until I send it off for repairs. How much of my student loan is this gonna cost me?

I sigh and throw it back down. Without my phone I feel like I'm disconnected from everything and everyone. Curiously, I wonder if the reason we cherish these extravagant pieces of communication so much is because in a way, they are like our hearts. We continue to get into situations that cause us to drop them and watch them break, then we pick up the pieces and put them back together knowing that it is not a good as it was pre-destruction, but it still works, except now it has a few nicks, bumps and scars. Eventually it breaks too many times and the pieces either don't fit together right any more, or it just refuses to switch back on because the power source has given up. When you really think about it, in this day and age our generation would fall apart without our phones; they keep us connected just like our hearts do. Maybe that's why people are willing to kill each other over one -the one they have is damaged goods so they need to steal someone else's only to ruin it all over again. Funny, isn't it?

By the end of the week, Sky has packed up her things and moved to another flat. Good riddance!

7

Mary Jane.

I pull my beige snood around my head and curse the icy November winds for penetrating my light blue jeggings. I knew I should've worn a pair of tights underneath, but foolishly I allowed the unusually bright winter sun to trick me. By the time I made it outside of my dorm building, it seemed long to go all the way back upstairs...plus, I needed to see him.

I stroll stiffly down the familiar cobbled walkway that runs alongside the green tinged babbling brook, overgrown with tall swishy weeds and berry bushes. I continue walking until I spot the break in the leafless hedges and carefully manoeuvre through it, feeling a few awkwardly positioned twigs nipping at my clothes. Once safely through to the other side I straighten up and force the feeling of cold out of my mind as I slink towards him.

Nathaniel is sat at our usual spot on the old creaky garden swing underneath the nature-made cove of Maple trees, with his oversized beanie hat sagging just right on his head, rocking the swing back and forth with a loosely laced Dr. Marten pushing against the soft earth. His eyes are cast downward, focused on lighting the blunt that dangles between his provocatively pink lips. As I get closer I noticed a strip of sliver glinting on the bottom left corner of his lower lip in the light as he draws his mouth in to take a long slow pull.

"You pierced your lip." I state, realising that the silver strip is a hoop that wasn't there the last time I saw him. His eyes flash up at me from under his heavy lashes, appearing as silver as his new piercing in the light. I suck in a breath and clear my throat; no matter how many times I look at him, I will never truly get over how beautiful he is.

Nathaniel raises an amused eyebrow at me, "You slapped Sky," he replies in a tone that has an implication of 'so what?' to it.

I straighten up and hold my head a little higher to indicate that I'm not sorry for what I did yesterday. It may have been a mistake that I'm not all that proud of, but that doesn't mean that I regret it. This isn't down to me trying to be *'Bad Gyal RiRi'*; it's because she hurt my feelings. Even as I stand in front of Nathaniel now with her words in my head, I feel as if I'm still not enough.

He puckers his lips into a small oval shape and blows the champagne laced marijuana smoke out into the air.

"You planning on leaving anytime soon?" He asks in his hushed husky tone. I shake my head; "Then take a seat. I won't bite," he smirks before sinking his gleaming white teeth into the soft pink flesh of his lower lip slowly.

Breathe Rio, breathe.

Nathaniel stops swinging long enough to let me sit next to him then continues stretching and relaxing his legs as we rock back and forth together under the Maple tree cove. My heart is fluttering, making me feel quite foolish because Nate looks so at ease as if my being here doesn't faze him in the least.

We've been coming to this spot for about 3 weeks now; just sitting, talking, remembering, feeling and rocking back and forth. The days are getting colder and the nights are coming faster, limiting our time our here and making me long for springtime.

During one of our talks, Nathaniel told me he had discovered this secret escape in his first year here; "No one else knows about this place but me."

"And me." I added.

Nathaniel had looked at me and smiled, "Yes; no one but you and me, Rio."

I remember the way my heart raced when he said it in his simplistically complex way. It was an innocent enough statement, but I could feel that he meant something more. I'm glad he had found this place; it allowed us to be alone together away from prying eyes and running mouths. It wasn't as if we were doing anything wrong -believe me our time spent out here was totally innocent -although there are times when he turns those pearlescent grey eyes on me and I am forced to stare temptation in the face and I just wanna...

Sometimes I think he does it on purpose just to watch me squirm; he hardly has to make much of an effort to do that. If Nate looks directly in my eyes and holds my gaze for longer than five seconds, that usually does the trick.

He takes another slow long drag from the blunt before offering it to me.

"You want a hit?"

I nod, take the champagne blunt from him and put it in my mouth, savoring the fact that it has just passed from between his lips. I take a small drag and came up short as the fire has gone out.

Nate produces a lighter and leans closer to me, cupping his hand around the trembling flame. He holds it at the end of the blunt waiting until it catches alight, and in a throaty tone he commands me, "Take it."

His eyes run the length of the blunt and land on my quivering lips -he is so close to me. A shiver runs up my spine and a quick flush of heat surges through me as he watches with intense fascination as I take a long deep pull to match his. I feel like choking because I've taken more than I can handle, but to avoid looking like a lightweight, I firm it, remove the blunt from my mouth, and suck the intoxicating smoke further into my lungs before taking another hit on top of that. I flick my tongue around the smoke, feeling it curl in my mouth before disappearing down my throat, then pass the blunt back to Nate. He hasn't moved an inch.

"Hold it," he coaxes me with a mischievous grin on his face. I'm wary as to why he wants me to hold onto the mind-altering smoke longer than I already am, but I obey.

Nathaniel's fingerless-gloved hand touches my face and his cold fingertips graze the taut skin along my jaw line, running slowly along it until he is cupping my chin, leaving behind the trail of his electric touch in its wake. Another flash of heat flares up inside me.

He turns my face towards his, "Hold it," he repeats just above a whisper. Well of course I'm going to hold it now; I've bloomin' forgotten how to breathe again!

His almond shaped eyes move from my mouth, up and up until they lock onto my ebony orbs. 1...2...3...4...5...oh God! I can feel the muscles in my stomach tightening and shuddering as the heat flares up once more. I squirm uncomfortably and notice the corner of his lips turn up in an amused smile.

He leans in closer, sliding his now slightly warmed hand down onto my neck.

"Blow it out, slowly."

As I exhale the smoke, Nathaniel leans closer still -our lips are almost touching -then inhales the dancing mist out of my mouth into his. My heart pummels against my rib cage and I crave to close the millimetre gap between our lips. I'm not high enough to do something so bold yet, but I wished that I was. I haven't kissed him in so long. As the last stream of smoke whirls into his mouth, he releases me and gives me back my personal space. I'm frozen where I sit, slightly disappointed. I think it shows because he smiles arrogantly to himself.

"It was about time you accepted my friend request," he refers to the Facebook request I had been avoiding since it had first graced my notifications, blowing my smoke out of his mouth.

I snap out of my daze and cross my legs, "My phone is broken."

"You couldn't wait until you saw me in class to find out what my reply was?" he smiles raising an eyebrow.

"We have things to discuss."

Nate rolls his eyes knowing that I'm referring to Sky, making me feel like I have just ruined the mood.

He takes another toke, "We have nothing to discuss Rio."

"You sleep with Sky and think we have nothing to discuss, but if the shoe was on the other foot I bet you'd have something to say," I snap.

Nate shrugs, "Probably, but I wouldn't. I find the idea of you and Sky together quite appealing."

"I'm not laughing." I scowl. I'm not in the mood for jokes.

He sighs, "Rio, I wouldn't say anything."

"Don't chat shit!"

"I'm not. As much as I care for you Rio, you are not my girlfriend and I am not your boyfriend. Who you choose to have sex with is none of my business," he states earnestly, looking at me from the corner of his eye. His underlying implication that I should have the same mind set as him is apparent, but I chose to ignore it.

"I don't care. I'm making it my business_"

"Why?"

"Because it's bad enough that you are with Georgia_"

"Ain't nobody **with** Georgia and you know that, so why are you bringing it up? We're talking about Sky."

"I was just saying_"

"Well don't! You wanna to be mad about Sky, so be mad about Sky."

I close my mouth and pout. I hate when he goes all alpha male on me because it makes me obey. At times it can be *very* endearing –what female doesn't like a man who can put them in their place? I kiss my teeth; what I want to say isn't appropriate when he's not prepared to hear it, so he finds a clever way to control the conversation.

I snatch the blunt from his lips –his eyes flash but he says nothing -and take a frustrated pull. If I get high enough I will say whatever is necessary and not allow him to talk me out of it.

"Do you know why I slapped her?"

"Because I fucked her."

"No, smart ass! I slapped her because she said, and I quote, 'You don't belong with a guy like Nathaniel, Rio, you never did and you know it. That's probably why he dropped you for Georgia'. Do you know how fucking embarrassing and hurtful that was to hear a girl who I don't even rate have something like that over me?" The volume of my voice escalates.

Nathaniel's eyes widen and understanding becomes apparent on his face; he knows what a sensitive subject that whole situation is to me.

"She said that?"

"Yes. Your stupid sidechick has been talking shit about me in lessons, according to Sky."

"I'm sorry. I'll talk to her."

"I'd rather you had nothing more to do with her. As long as she thinks she's won, she'll keep talking shit."

"Ignore her. People can only affect you if you let them, so don't let them."

"So you're not going to stop talking to her?" He doesn't respond.

I take another pull and sink forward feeling the drug take its desired effect and hand the blunt back to Nathaniel.

He frowns, "Don't let hateful bitches like Sky and Georgia bring you down. I've told you before, what other people think about me and you ain't important 'cause it ain't nothing to do with them. The only thing that matters is what we think."

"And what is that exactly? The way I see it, all this talk of a united front is a waste. You make it clear every time you pick her over me, Nathaniel." I stand up. I've had enough for today.

Nate sighs. His fingers catch my hand but I tug away before he can get a grip. Why do I keep doing this to myself? Why am I even here having these secret meetings with my ex, which always end badly, when I could be investing time in one of many potential second year boyfriends?

I pick up my foot unsteadily -the contents of the blunt compromising my co-ordination -about to walk away when Nate appears in front of me.

"I never picked her. I meant what I said when I told you that she was just there Rio; I chose you. I love you but you don't wanna forgive me_"

"THEN WHY THE FUCK AM I HERE NATHANIEL? All I've been trying to do is forgive you, but I can't."

"Then why are you here? Huh? What, you need someone to scream at, is that it?"

"No!"

"Then what is it Rio because honestly, all of this is getting old now. You either forgive me or you don't!" he snaps finally losing his temper.

I sigh, "I want to_"

"Then why don't you?"

"You broke my heart Nate," I confess weakly.

Nate throws up his hands, "For fucks sake Rio, you fucking broke mine too you know!" He roars. I jump at his outburst.

He takes a step back and breathes deeply to calm himself down. The muscle in his jaw twitches.

"Ri, you were it for me! Out of all the girls there was no one else I wanted but you. I know we were young, but it didn't matter to me because I loved you...so much..." his voice starts breaking in places.

I watch with astounded silence as Nathaniel takes on my usual role and falls apart -I don't know what to do. Suddenly my pain becomes irrelevant because underneath all of the brushed off comments and machismo, Nathaniel has been holding back his hurt but I had finally pushed him over the edge because it was all coming out now.

"I couldn't even see myself with another girl, and I felt so awful after I did that to you. I knew you would hate me but I told you anyway because I knew that it was better you hear it from me, but still, after all this time, you still won't forgive me even though I forgave you."

His pained expression tugs at my heart. I think he's going to cry and I really don't want him too; seeing a grown man shed tears is heart-breaking.

Nathaniel falls silent and I think that he's finished until he unleashes the full forces of his sky grey eyes and says, "Do you know how hard it was for me to deal with the fact that you...the girl I thought I was going to marry one day...killed my child?"

8

16 & Pregnant.

* April 2011*

I shift in the passenger seat of Nate's GTi, watching countless houses, trees and people whoosh past me, not taking any of it in. Choice FM plays quietly in the background providing a slight distraction from my guilty thoughts; did I do the right thing?

I couldn't handle the fact that I was pregnant in the first place; a baby was the last thing I wanted, I mean I'm still a child myself (no matter how much I try to convince my mother otherwise) and a baby was far too much responsibility. The moment the nurse confirmed that I was in fact pregnant with my 17 year old boyfriend's child, I made the decision that brought me to where I am today. I had an abortion.

I made the choice to kill my child and now I am being driven back to my home so that I can sit and mull over what I have done by myself, because from the look on Nate's face, he doesn't want to join me.

Just before they wheeled me off to the theatre, Nate had clutched my hand with this desperate look in his eyes.

"Baby, is this is what you really want? I mean, if you're having any second thoughts you can back out. Ri, you don't have to do this. We'll figure it out," he'd said with soft desperation. "I'll be here to support you, you won't be doing this alone Rio, I promise."

I couldn't even look at him because I knew that if I did, any resolve that I had left would crumble.

The whole process from finding out I was pregnant up until this moment is probably the most difficult thing I've ever been through. When I initially discovered I was going to be a mum (after a series of pregnancy tests to double, triple and quadruple check that the little positive sign on the stick was correct before I sought out a professional opinion) the first thing I did was curse. I glared at it trying to wish it away, foolishly hoping that perhaps if I stared at it long enough that the positive sign would turn into a negative, but of course it never did. I was quiet for over an hour, sitting alone on my cold tiled bathroom floor holding the latest result limply in my hand, trying to stay calm.

I knew the instant that I saw that I was pregnant that I didn't want it; how the hell was I meant to raise a baby when my mum was still raising me? I don't even have a job!

I'd decided that I wasn't going to tell my mum about this; she would kill me and then she would tell my family and family friends and they would kill me. That's a whole lot of killing! I didn't want to be the topic of the latest gossip and have to sit through lectures and then have people judging me and dictating what I should and shouldn't do.

I told Tyson first and it was him who made me tell Nathaniel. As scared as I was of telling my mum, at the time, the prospect of telling Nate was even more frightening because I was afraid that it would scare him off. Those are generally the stories that you hear when teenage girls reveal to their teenage boyfriend that they are pregnant -the boy gets freaked and walks out on her -but Nathaniel wasn't like that. When I first broke the news to him he smiled…up until I told him I didn't want it.

Nate was barely speaking to me, appalled that I'd even contemplate killing our baby. I'd assured him that we'd have our whole lives to make another one and that I was only 16 and wasn't in a stable position to raise a child. He didn't want to kill this one, but he supported my decision anyway because it was what I wanted and he loved me and he only wanted me to be happy. I wasn't willing to do the same for him because in 9 months it wasn't him that was going to be waddling down the road with people young and old judging him, writing him off as another statistic, and from what I had heard about the pain of child birth, I was really going to have to be up for it to push a fully formed human out of my you know what.

Before I could even undergo the procedure, it was a stream of endless battles with myself and with Nathaniel. As supportive as he was, he was always trying to get me to change my mind by talking about the things we could do with our kid, all the things we'd teach them, kissing my stomach and talking to the baby, thinking of baby names and all of that junk. At times, I loved what he was saying so much that I started to come around to the idea, but then I'd have morning sickness, or stand naked in the mirror and look at my once flat stomach start to protrude a little and all of those warm fuzzy hopes and dreams would be dashed and replaced by my negative logic.

The people at the abortion clinic weren't much help either. When I went to book my appointment they carried out the world's most frustrating questionnaire with me, filled with endless repetitive questions that all lead back to the same annoying question, 'Are you sure you want to do this?'

Even as I laid on the gurney in the hospital theatre before they put me under, the nurse said, "We're going to put you under now luv, but before we do I need to ask you one more time; are you sure you want to do this?"

I'd stared up at her helplessly as my lips quivered, wanting to translate the flurry of thoughts that were scrambled in my head 'Yes…no…I mean…I don't know…ye_NO! NO, NO, NO! I can't, I…yes. Oh just do it I just want it to be over, I want this to go away,' but I didn't say anything.

I felt a tear slip from my eye and I placed my hand on my stomach,

"I'm sorry," I whispered to my baby.

"What was that dear?" the nurse asked hopefully.

I pursed my lips and closed my eyes, "I said I'm…I'm sure."

She frowned, my answer clearly not being the one she wanted to hear. Weren't these people meant to be neutral? For fuck sake I already feel shitty enough without Nancy Nurse adding to it.

"Okay dear," she said in a resigned tone "I want you to keep your eyes closed and count backwards from 10."

I said the number 10, then 9 and then I felt the guilt rush over me; what was I doing? I'm killing my baby! I don't want to do this, I've changed my mind. I've changed my…

When I woke up I was in recovery feeling groggy and disorientated. The white washed walls and the smell of the hospital quickly cleared things up for me and I realised that it was done. I touched my stomach and felt a delayed pang of emptiness -my baby was gone.

I looked around and saw other women who had undergone the same procedure either sitting in silence staring at the walls, trying to behave as normal or crying their eyes out. Nathaniel was next to my bed looking everywhere but at me. His face was pale and pinched, with red rings around his puffy grey eyes. I'd made him cry and I hated myself for it.

Our baby is gone for good now and happy is far from what I'm feeling; I'm disgusted with myself. Sometimes we let logic get in the way of things that we should never apply it to and we end up making the worst decisions of our lives. Our baby is never coming back. I didn't know if it was a boy or a girl, it was never going to have a name, I was never going to see it smile, take its first steps, hear it laugh or cry or speak its first words.

I shake my head, blurring the thoughts of what was bound to be a beautiful bouncing brown baby out of my mind and try to focus on what the radio host is blabbing about. It's not loud enough to shove the thoughts away so I readjust the volume until I can focus on nothing but the irritatingly happy presenters.

"What's the matter with you?" Nate snaps, returning the radio to its previous background volume.

"It was too quiet."

"Well sometimes a bit of quiet is healthy. It allows you to think properly."

I roll my eyes and turn back to the window. More houses, more trees, more people -more nothing.

"That's the problem."

A few minutes later Nate swerves onto my street and pulls up in front of my house without bothering to park or turn off the engine. His hands are clenched around the steering wheel so tightly that his knuckles pale to a light pearl colour; the veins bulge against his skin making their bluish hue show through and the muscles in his jaw flicker wildly as he clenches and unclenches his teeth. He is mad and I know that he has no plan to accompany me. Looks as if I'm going to have to hold my pillow and cry alone.

"You not coming inside?" I ask already knowing the answer. Nate glares out of the windshield at a destination that will lead him away from me and my wrong doing.

He shakes his head stiffly, "Nah, you go ahead. I'll call you when I get home."

Just as I thought.

I want to be mad at him for not staying with me; this is definitely one of the times when I really need him and he is bailing on me to go and be angry, but what did I expect? If I had taken his feelings into consideration he wouldn't even be mad...but maybe I'd be unhappy. By now it's a tossup of which consequences would be harder to deal with, this or the shit storm of drama I'd have to deal with if I had decided to keep the baby. It's the same question I'd been asking myself for the past few weeks and even after making the decision and following through, it's still there. My mind doesn't care that there's nothing that I can do about it now, it still wants to chew over every detail. Fuck.

Sighing, I unclip my seatbelt, "Don't bother," I sulk, "I know you're upset so you go do that. I'll be fine."

"Cool," he replies in a clipped tone.

The sooner I get out of this car, the better. I can feel a lump forming in my throat but I need it to hold on for a few minutes longer, after all I still have to go into my house and face my mother so that I can pretend everything is hunky dory before I escape to my bedroom and break down. If she sees me crying she's bound to ask questions and the last thing I need right now was the Spanish Inquisition raining down on me, especially about being pregnant in the first place.

I look at Nathaniel and I just want to hold him and beg him to forgive me. If he forgives me maybe I can forgive myself too.

"I never wanted this you know. If we had been more careful we wouldn't even be in this situation. If things were different then_"

"THEN WHAT, RIO?"

I flinch at the volume of his voice that usually so velvety, has become an agonised roar.

He slams his palms against the steering wheel and growls, "I don't want to talk about this anymore ok. 'Shoulda, coulda, woulda' ain't gonna change shit, so drop it! I'll call you when I get home." He transfers his incapacitating glare to me –I cower against the car door. So many hostile emotions are thrashing around in his grey eyes like a terrible thunderstorm. At first glance his stormy anger is the overwhelming factor - if I push him too much I may end up regretting it -but as I look deeper I see his sadness and my heart quivers for him. Rio look what you've I done!

"Nate I'm so sorry_" I begin, reaching out to comfort him cautiously. He catches my hand before I can touch him and closes his eyes. His breathing deepens for a moment, his pronounced chest rising and falling slowly as he gathers himself, and then slowly he brings my hand to his face and rests his cheek in it. I tremble, afraid to move in case he changes his mind and pushes me away again.

His soft lips skim across the skin on my wrist before he kisses it gently, closing his eyes tighter.

"I know. I'll call you when I get home."

He releases my hand and reverts back to glaring out of the window. I don't want him to pull away but I realise that he had to summon a lot of tolerance to give me that small gesture. Even now as mad as he is, he's still putting my feelings first; I just wish he would stop punishing me for it.

I touch his tense shoulder lightly then get out of the car. Before I make it halfway to my front door, I hear his car engine roar and he presses down on the accelerator. I glance back in time to see him disappear into the distance. I bite back my tears and slip my key into the lock. All I have to do is get past my mum and then I can let it all out…alone.

I walk inside with what I hope is my normal day to day expression and call out to my mother to let her know I'm home. Instead of seeing her smiling face pop out from the kitchen I am greeted by Tyson's worried face.

"She's over at mine," he says, answering the question I didn't ask, "I told her that my mum's making dinner and that we'll be over soon. I figured you may need a minute to think."

"Thanks." I manage.

"So…did you do it?" he asks carefully. I manage a nod before my face crumples into my ugly crying face.

Tyson rushes over, sweeping me into his long, warm arms.

"It's okay, Ri," he soothes, rubbing my back and kissing the top of my head, cradling me to his chest so tightly that I no longer have to find the strength to stay on my feet.

I succumbed to the comfort and cry harder. Why couldn't Nate have been like this?

"Oh Tyson," I wail, "I'm a horrible person."

"Shhh; no you're not."

"Yes I am. He hates me Ty, Nathaniel hates me! What have I done?"

"He doesn't hate you Ri, he's just upset right now. Just give him time, he'll come around."

I shake my head, "I don't think so. You should've seen the way he looked at me. I killed…I killed our baby. I thought it was the right thing, I swear I did, but now I'm not so sure and it's too late to do anything about it."

For a moment he doesn't say anything, he just holds me.

"He loves you Rio; he'll forgive you."

"What if that's not enough?"

Tyson dips his head and tilts my face up to his.

"If it's real, it will be enough." There's a pregnant pause before he continues, "I can't imagine how you feel right now, but you need to remember the reasons why you did it and understand that it doesn't make you a bad person for wanting to be in a better position to raise a family, okay. The best thing you can do is to stop torturing yourself over it and take it as a lesson."

He pulls me against his chest and kisses the top of my head again then walks me to my room.

"Let's get you to bed. I'll be here when you wake up."

9

New Slaves.

Present Day
October 2013

"Shut up you any guy!" Carmen snaps comically at Tyson over a large pot of Tuna and Pasta.

I have just entered the dorm kitchen fresh from my encounter with Nate. Our parting conversation had stirred the recesses of my memory bringing the things I stuffed so deep down in my head to the surface; the walk home was not a pleasant one and I knew that if I was alone that it wouldn't be pretty so I opted to be around my friends to take my mind off of it all.

Carmen is preparing dinner while Fontaine, Yoshi and Tyson sit around the table playing black jack with a huge bag *Haribo Tangfastics.*

"What's good family?" I call out planting myself next to Tyson. He loops his arm over my shoulders and pecks me on the forehead casually.

"Where you been?" he asks, curving his cards slightly to stop Fontaine from peeking at his hand. She pouts then giggles settling back into her seat.

"I had to sort out something," quickly before he can ask what I put the spotlight back on them, "What have you lot been up to?"

Carmen flings down the pot spoon and skips over the fridge in her Ugg boots and blue silk pyjama pants. I swear to God this girl wears Uggs with everything!

"Listening to your boy chat shit," she snorts taking a block of cheese from the shelf. Tyson groans.

"What was he talking shit about this time?" I ask reaching for a sour cherry in Tyson's pile. He smacks my hand and throws me a warning look.

"Car shut up and stop hating 'cause you're poor!" he laughs putting an Ace of Spades down on the messy stack of cards arranged in the centre of the table. He glances at his hand and calls out, "Hearts."

"At least I accept my brokeness. These times you image hunters are rollin' up to the Gucci SALE with your STUDENT LOANS trying to PRETEND you are living the high life, then eating 20p noodles for dinner every night. Cool. Thanks. Shut up!" Tyson kisses his teeth and fans her off.

I snicker and get up to help Carmen prepare the food.

"Gucci sale?" I enquire.

"Yeah; Ty, Amari, Ace and Shaquille think that they are spice because they're goin' Eastpark on Saturday to buy out of season Gucci ACCESSORIES that rich people who can afford to buy Gucci suits don't want any more 'cause they know it's old and dead!"

"Ty, that's like what, a third of your loan?" I giggle joining Carmen on the mockery.

"Yeah but unlike you bums, I have a job."

"Um excuse me; I have a job thank you very much!" Fontaine interjects.

We all say nothing. It's not that her modelling isn't a real gig, it's just, well, aside from what we deem the REAL jobs for established companies (which are few and far between), most of the modelling Fontaine does is for up and coming labels -i.e. t-shirts with words printed on them -or music videos for rappers that we all know aren't really going to blow…ever. Her modelling career would be an utter success if it was based on Instagram likes.

Tyson breaks the silence before she has a chance to take offence.

"Fine Fonts, I'll let you off, but the rest of you need to shut up. Actin' like man's broke out 'ere; like man don't make p!"

"No one said you don't make p, you just don't make in season Gucci p," Carmen states. I am slowly sinking to the floor with laughter now.

Before my transformation, I never quite understood why people would move heaven and earth to purchase superfluous material items they couldn't really afford, so that they could flaunt it in front of their peers who were just as broke as them. It was like everyone needed to partake in this common fallacy to prove that even though they weren't rich, they were doing more than all right because they had the latest Celine bag or Ralph

Lauren polo shirt to back it up in order to avoid the veracity of their reality. It didn't make any logical sense to me back then, but it does now -we live in a society where we define each other by the things we own. We're slaves to materialism. It's natural that people first judge you by what you look like and in a world where we idolize the rich and famous, especially if your lifestyle is the complete opposite of that, we look down upon people who look broke. Brokeness is a disease that we feel we need to be cured of because the things associated with it will never be glamourized by the media in a way that will allow us to feel okay about it, hence we end up with kids partaking in illegal activities to try and get out of the hood for a better life like they see their favourite rappers enjoying. By purchasing certain luxury items you can pretend you are living the lifestyle and people will respond to you as if you are up there with the best of them. Having money equals status and status equals power and the more powerful you are the more money you can make to gain even more status, resulting in even more power. The delusions of grandeur we subject ourselves to plant the idea that these things make us worth of being a 'somebody'; for men it's the alpha male title and for women…it's Beyonce; it's always Beyonce.

As people were so desperate to appear affluent, a lot of them had knock offs, so ratings are awarded to the people that purchased the genuine article, even if they had to scrimp and save to get it. It's common to see the underprivileged in designer gear emblazoned with the logo just so people can see that it is in fact YSL, Chanel, Louis Vuitton, Armani, Gucci (etc), whereas the day to day people who are well off tend to dress more plainly in their designer gear. The poor want to look rich and the rich don't care how they look because they know they're rich; therefore they have nothing to prove.

It's easier for women to get away with not having to 'stunt' than it is for men because in our patriarchal society men are advocated as the bread winners and life has demonstrated many times over that the man with the money gets the girls, hence a lot of young men are jaded by the 'Money Over Bitches' mentality because they know that if they focus on getting money, women will come.

In order to move away from my old life I had to embrace new ideals, including ones I wasn't so hot on, because it would help me move forward. Before I came to Brompton the most expensive branded item I owned was an old Gap hoody that still managed to be a size too big that I'd held onto since secondary school. I didn't care about the latest trends and must have items, but 'they' do, so now, so do I.

Tyson pops a Haribo in his mouth, "Listen yeah, it's my money and I'll spend it on what I want. You lot can talk all you want but at the end of the day I don't care 'cause we all know how you females operate." The laughing came to a halt.

Fontaine is looking at Tyson over the top of her cards, "And how are we exactly?"

Tyson takes in our awaiting expressions and realizes that he's now put his foot in his mouth so he has to be very careful about what he says next.

He sighs, "Let's be real; if dudes don't look the part, no matter how attractive or thuggish they are, you lot won't rate them."

"That's not true," Yoshi pipes up looking genuinely offended.

"Don't gas. You're telling me that if Ace had stepped to you in Primark jeans, Hi-Tec trainers and a Gola hoody, you would give him the time of day?"

Yoshi trails her heavily embellished pink acrylic nails over her cards in a contemplative fashion.

"I dunno," she shrugs quietly "Maybe."

"That means no. I rest my case."

"That's not fair though. You said he was wearing Gola and Hi-Tec!" Carmen argues on Yoshi's behalf.

"So? Why does what he's wearing matter?"

"Because it's GOLA and HI-TEC!"

Tyson rolls his eyes, "Like I said; I rest my case."

I stay in the kitchen with them for another hour, long enough to eat and crack a few jokes before I decide that this distraction is no longer working. I force a yawn and an exaggerated stretch.

"I'm tired. I think I'm gonna have a nap."

"How are you tired already? It's not even 6 o'clock," Fontaine remarks.

I avoid their curious gazes and shrug, "It's been a long day."

They accept my answer and I scurry off into my room locking the door behind me, kick off my shoes, close the curtains and crawl into bed willing the sandman to make an express visit so that I can stop thinking about my baby shame.

Nathaniel's parting words ring in my ears, "D'you know what, maybe you shouldn't forgive me, 'cause standing here talking about what you did to our child, I'm not sure I really forgave you either."

I pull the duvet over my head and squeeze my eyelids together as tightly as I can, but still a determined tear slips out. I had hoped that all of the therapy sessions the doctor had sent me to would've helped me deal with the situation, but no matter how much I tried to deal with it (or ignore it), the guilt from me having that abortion never went away, and to hear him say those things to me only made the experience more painful to re-live.

It seems as if we'll never forgive one another for the pain we cause each other, or to ourselves.

What remained of our broken relationship was starting feel like a burden that hadn't finished crushing us yet.

10
Moet.

It's Sunday night and my girls and I are dressed to the semi-casual nines -which meant that every chance we got we would take snaps for Instagram, to show those who weren't attending Sunday Slam tonight how good we look, seated amidst the overflowing audience of the Sunday Slam crowd in Plan X, watching Shaquille work the stage with his charismatic hosting abilities.

The event was definitely living up to its over-hyped hype; Unfamous faces from all walks of popularity were dotted heavily around the place in their statement outfits -a mixture of designer clothing, heels for 'bad bitches', street wear, tattoos, eclectic hairstyles and piercings – it looked like Tumblr had regurgitated inside the building. Everyone was either paying attention to the show, networking, flirting, drinking, snapping shots for Instagram (cue the infamous 'duckface', contemporary poses and filters) and tweeting (as you do…#SundaySlam). I had selected the current understated urban girl closet staple; a black midi dress, Converses, my OBVLY beanie hat from which my weave fell out from underneath in waves of well sculpted curls, red lipstick, lashes and ratchet gold jewellery. There were several other girls dressed like this (as expected) but I convinced myself that I was rocking it the best.

Oddly for a Sunday night, Plan X had brought London to life; it felt like a Saturday night. Normally I'd be curled up on the sofa in my house clothes watching some film that I had seen more times than necessary on terrestrial television, too lazy to move because my mother's Sunday dinner had given me 'the itis' –a term black people used for that heavy exhausted feeling a generous plate of soul food would incur.

That was one of the many wonderful things about living in London, no matter what day or hour it was, there is always something to do. We are the British version of New York –the city that never sleeps.

Amari is lodged in the DJ booth chatting to Sky who (for whatever reason) is now one of the Sunday Slam girls (a set of wannabe models that Ace hires, whose job it was to walk around in too tight #TeamSundaySlam t-shirts and play hostess with the mostess with the crowd…which mainly involves them walking around like they own the place and hovering around the 'important' people), while Carmen downs multiple glasses of rosé and describes all the different ways she would kill her. Yoshi is cuddled up in the corner with Ace, giggling like she had no sense and Fontaine is trying to coax me into an unnecessary trip to the bathroom just so she can walk past a cute guy –whom she's giving her best 'come hither' eyes to -that is hovering by the stairs. The things girls do for attention. I don't really want to go because the way I see it, if 'Mr. Tall, Dark & Hench' (as she has so suitably dubbed him) was so interested, he would come and speak to her instead of having to witness her tactless tactics.

As you can see I'm not in the best of moods tonight. I had every intention of coming to here and continuing my charade of the up and coming 'It' girl, but once I got inside and saw Nate with Georgia in the VIP booth, my spark went out.

We haven't spoken to since our midweek fall-out at our spot when we made it clear that forgiveness for both of our wrongs wasn't on the card and possibly never would be. I am still upset about it, but our lack of communication is burning me. I really want to talk to him but I know that when he starts brooding, it is best that I leave him alone for fear that he might tell me a few more home truths that I don't want to hear. Can you believe that he sat right next to me in our English Lit lecture but never said a word; he never even glanced my way. It was as if he was acting like I didn't exist and I felt like he was either torturing me or maybe he had the same complex as me; he's mad at me but he can't stay away. I had spent a majority of my teenage years not existing to people and now when everyone is finally starting to pay attention to me, Nate isn't. It only highlighted my previous mind-set that being popular wasn't all it cracked up to be; so what if I had loads of friends? If the people that I really care about don't care about me anymore, what's the point?

I expected to see Nate here -this is his world after all -but I had hoped that with all of the progress that we'd made since we'd started talking again, that there was a possibility that I had made him push Georgia away. Guess I was wrong!

I noticed the two of them before they saw me and felt an already strained string pop in my chest, followed by a few more when she saw me and reached for his hand. At the time he was in the middle of a conversation with Manny -who is looking as swaggalicious as ever, decked out in his own clothing line looking like a walking advert for 'OBVLY' - but still his strong hands clasped hers gently, and he started rubbing his thumb across her skin. I used to love it when he did that to me; that small gesture used to indicate that a small part of him was focused on me, even if his mind was elsewhere because he cared. Now he cared about Georgia apparently. That was when I went and got my first drink.

I try not to look at them, but every so often my eyes wander over to the VIP to see them looking so picture perfect together. Georgia is sporting a pair of True Religion skinny jeans with a very expensive pair of River Island statement stilettos decorating her feet, and a lace shirt over a black bra. Her hair was arranged into a ballerina bun on top of her head, with a heavy fringe resting above her startling sea green eyes. Georgia is so pretty that even the fact that she is a total bitch can't taint her good looks.

She is stunning. He is stunning. I am drinking my way into a drunken stupor.

"Come on Ri, don't make me go by myself," Fontaine whines tugging the sleeves of my red leather jacket that I have decided not to remove because it is literally the only thing stopping me from looking like all of the other weave wearing, midi dress and Converse carbon copies in the building -outshone by Georgia's effortless fashion flair.

I take another swig of my wine.

"Take Carmen," I say monotonously.

"Carmen's busy!" Carmen snaps, finally taking a break from her plans of mass destruction to Sky's face.

"Doing what?"

"I can't leave, I might miss something important," she reasons with me.

I raise an eyebrow, "Like what?"

"Like Sky giving him a blow job behind the decks or something! You know can't trust that shifty hoe. Just go man; you need a break from drinking anyway." I roll my eyes and take another swig -she can bloody talk, she's drunk almost as much as I have.

A mass of copper and ash blonde curls hit my shoulder as Fontaine regresses into begging.

"Please Rio! Please, please, please, please, ple_"

"All right man, I'll come. Shut up already!" Fontaine grins and hops up.

I set down my glass for the first time all night, and grab my purse. Fontaine laces her arm through mine and practically drags me over to the stairway where she successfully catches the attention of her Prince Charming, a very tasty looking Ghanaian with arms as thick as tree trunks.

Once downstairs, I decide to check my jacket into the cloakroom before following a now ecstatic Fontaine into the dimly lit ladies toilets.

We stand in front of the large floor to ceiling mirror, Fontaine pouting and fluffing up her huge curly coif, me sulking and tugging down the hem of my dress. Why didn't I make more of an effort to stand out like I did at the Fresher's rave. Now thanks to my complacency, Georgia is in the lead.

Fontaine's biker glove brushes my elbow.

"What's the matter, Ri?" she asks in a concerned tone.

I shake my head and tug the dress down again with more vigour.

"It's nothing. I'm just being silly,"

"Probably, but tell me anyway." she smiles sweetly. I shake my head again not really wanting to get into it.

"It's Nate, isn't it?" she asks plainly, placing a gloved hand on her hip. I shrug feeling all the more foolish that it is obvious as to what's got my mood so messed up.

"Isn't it always?" I laugh weakly.

Fontaine sighs and shakes her head, sending her afro into a wild frenzy of gold and brown spirals, "Ri, you can sit here and sulk about him all you want, but he's not sulking over you, and that Georgia is lovin' it. The best thing you can do is at least pretend that you are okay."

"Pretending to be something is tiring; trust me," I say not only referring to tonight's problem.

Fontaine reapplies her tangerine Barry M lip gloss.

"Then make yourself okay. Everybody knows that the only way to get over an ex is to find someone new to fill their position. There are loads of hot single guys upstairs that have been checking you out all night, including Tyson_"

I throw her a warning look and she throws up her hands, "I know, I know, you two are JUST friends but I'm just stating a fact_"

"Well don't!"

"Okay! My point is, you've been too focused on finishing the Rose and sulking to notice, and that's not cute babe. Get it together, then we're gonna go and face our public and go and bag the hottest guys in the room and see how Nate likes it," she grins.

Sounds like a plan.

"How do you ladies feel about Champagne?" Prince Charming asks, flashing a superbly white smile at Fontaine. He had taken the liberty of introducing himself as Leon (@KingzOfLeon on Twitter. I'd seen his name frequently on the timeline so upon learning that information he instantly became more fascinating) when Fontaine and I re-entered the party from the bathroom, and after much batting of false eyelashes and bubble-gum smiles from Fontaine, he invites us to join him and his equally lush friend Carter Johnson, a highly respected Langford University legend, as notorious for his good looks and cool demeanour as Nate is at Brompton.

Carter Johnson is one of those modern day anomalies who keeps a very low profile (he isn't on ANY social networks), yet everyone knows him…or at least knows of him. He has an interesting face full of mismatched quirky features, that at first glance made him look almost awkward, but the more you look at him, the more attractive he becomes. His almost awkward features were comparable to abstract art; unconventionally beautiful. His skin is a pale white, decorated from the neck down with tattoos –he's covered in them. His eyes are a deep set hazel colour peppered with flecks of green under straight thick black eyebrows, Icelandic blonde hair, full on top combed into a VO5 quiff and shaved at the back and sides. The bridge of his nose is slightly crooked, possibly the result of a fight, and his mouth resembles the fullness of Mick Jagger's but are a deep shade of blushing red that contrasts with his skin. Further character is added in the form of a few scars here and there and a full face of dark stubble. In contrast to his physical appearance, his dress sense is fairly straight forward; a black t-shirt, black jeans and all black leather converses. His only adornment is a stylish Marc Jacobs watch with no numbers on it -understated yet highly effective.

We are standing at the VIP bar posing while Carter and Leon order several a bottles of Moet which they pay for with a thick wad of cash; I'm fascinated.

"You just spent £200 on champagne!" I exclaim as Leon collects the steel ice buckets and four champagne flutes. Carter shrugs and -to my delight –puts his arm around my waist as we walk towards the VIP section. Nathaniel finally looks at me.

"It's nothing," he says coolly, leading me across the threshold where the elite of the Unfamous reside. Calvin and D-Man are in the deluxe mix; they greet me and Fontaine and I I stand a little taller feeling like I belong in here because I actually know some people worth knowing. I smile coyly and take a seat next to Carter on the black studded leather booth of the VIP area. Leon and Fontaine bring up the rear, flirting in low tones.

I am biding my time to look up and let my eyes connect with the steely grey ones that I can feel glaring at me; I nestle against Carter. He takes my closeness as an incentive to put his arm around the back of the chair allowing his tattooed hand to rest suggestively on my shoulder.

Leon pops the first bottle and pours the tinted bubbly liquid into four flutes then hands them out. Cater takes mine from him then offers it to me pressing the cool glass against my lips.

"Drink," he orders with a devilish smile that although dazzling, is a little unnerving. I take the flute from him and have my first sip of Moet. It's delicious.

"Good?" he asks admiring the way my body relaxes, meaning that all the drinking I have done so far is finally kicking in. I nod taking another small sip.

"Good. Drink up, there's plenty more where that came from," his smile widens. It's even creepier.

I set the glass down and focus my attention on the show, making a point not to look at Nate. He wanted to act like I didn't exist; well I can return the favour just as well as he delivered it.

"Seems like just about anyone can get into VIP these days," Georgia leers looping her arm inside Nate's. My body goes rigid and I glare at her; is she really trying to pick a fight right now?

"You got a problem love?" Fontaine asks before I can make a spectacle of myself.

Georgia's gaze meets mine and she gave me a sardonic smile.

"No, just making an observation. I'm just curious as to how someone of a certain...calibre made it to the big league."

"Why? You threatened or something?" I challenge. Fontaine shoots me a look silently asking that I keep my cool. I can only try.

Georgia's smile tightens, her catlike eyes flashing dangerously at me.

"Now why would I need to be jealous? I'm no wannabe."

"Sure you're not darling. Just because you're latched desperately onto his arm," I nod my head in Nate's direction, "still doesn't make him yours sweetheart."

Georgia's arm twitches and I know that she wants to let go because of my factual remark, but the defiance in her eyes lets me know that she isn't going to back down so easily; instead she settles against him.

"Are YOU really going to talk about being desperate?"

"If the shoe fits," I shrugged taking another sip of liquid courage.

Georgia scoffs, "If the shoe fits indeed! Tell me, is your little plan to make a certain someone jealous working, 'cause from where I'm sitting it appears that they've stopped slummin' it and are occupied with someone a lot more worthy."

To rub salt into the wound she nuzzles her nose against the curve of his neck against the cursive tattoo that I love so much. I narrow my eyes at her.

Nathaniel shifts in his seat and looks down at Georgia sternly. She gazes up at him innocently at first like butter wouldn't melt in her mouth, before getting caught up with his sexy angry face and starts staring as if she's seeing him for the first time. I swear that I see her draw in breath and cease breathing – I thought I was the only one that reacted to him that way. His face edged closer to hers; swiftly shifting to the side of her face so that his lips graze her earlobe. She shudders. His lips twitch subtly as he whispers into her ear. Whatever he says puts a smile on her face and she finally exhales and nods. I frown.

Without another glance in my direction, Nathaniel takes her hand and walks out of VIP away from me. I pick up the glass, tipping it all the way up so that enough liquid will flow to flush the envy out of my system.

"Easy there, princess," Carter smirks taking my drained glass from me. I had forgotten that he was there -caught up in 'Nathaniel World' as per-usual.

What am I doing? I'm supposed to be making him feel like crap, not the other way around. It's pathetic; I'm putting so much effort into this façade while he quietly observes me make a total ass out of myself by arguing with his leech.

"You feeling all right?" Carter asks refilling my glass without asking. I nod and sway a little. Great! Not only do I look like an ass, I am also officially drunk, which is so not the best state for me to be in right now…

On the other hand, maybe it is. I'm feeling moody anymore, as a matter of fact, I feel wonderful...woozy, but wonderful.

"I'm great!" I settle against him once more.

Carter's arm drops to my waist and curls around my frame, hugging me closer to him.

"Sure you are!" he scoffs. "Tell me something; is he really worth going to war with Georgia Daniels over?"

I furrow my brow, "We're not warring, we just don't see eye to eye on certain things."

Leon chuckles, "I've heard Nathaniel called many different names, but never certain things."

"What makes you lot think it's about Nathaniel?" Fontaine asks, coming to my rescue.

"None of us are oblivious to the situation darlin'."

"What have you heard?" I ask hoping that the alcohol buzz masks my panic.

Carter gives a non-committal shrug.

"We all know that you lot did a ting back in the day."

"You don't even go to Brompton, how do you know that?"

"It's Nate Gibson," he takes a long drink from his flute before flashing me another disturbing smile, "People talk."

Right; I had forgotten that the Unfamous are like an elite cult and that they all know each other and each other's business. I wonder what else they know about us.

It's just gone 10pm, the show is over and the after party has begun but instead of raving it up with everyone else, I'm back in the bathroom again, in a stall this time, trying my hardest to keep my puke from going anywhere but in the toilet.

I curl over and heave once more, feeling sticky sweat beads form on my forehead. I need to breathe, but the flow of sour liquid spewing out of my mouth won't allow me to. My eyes are watering making stinging tears run from my eyes, smearing my makeup and blurring the unpleasant view of the contents of my stomach. I hadn't meant to drink so much; I wanted to get enough drunk so I would feel better, but unfortunately I've overdone it and am feeling absolutely, positively disgusting.

Once I am sure that I'm done, I grab some paper towels and sloppily wipe my mouth and dab my face; time to look in the mirror. I flush the toilet and stumble out of the stall right into the unimpressed stares of the numerous females that clutter up the bathroom. What's their problem; have they never seen a walking train wreck before?

"What the fuck are you looking at?" I slur angrily, glaring at the girl nearest to me. She tuts and looks away; the others follow suit. No one likes dealing with a mean drunk.

I splash my face with cold tap water, liberally chucking some in my mouth to try and rinse the bitter aftertaste of vomit out. The water feels so good on my clammy skin that I get carried away -still not totally sober -and end up wetting up the front of my dress.

"Fan-fucking-tastic!" I curse, now violently stuffing paper towels down the front of my dress, making myself look all the more ridiculous. A group of girls shoot me disapproving looks and mutter under their breath as they leave.

I finish cleaning my face; reapply my M.A.C concealer, kohl eye liner and lipstick, stuff four wads of Wrigley's Double Mint gum into my gob, then go and stand under the dryer for 10 minutes until I am sure that the huge wet path on my front is less visible.

I take a few moments to make sure that I won't fall flat on my ass once I rejoin the party by stumbling haphazardly up and down the bathroom aisle, bumping and shoving innocent bystanders as I do so. It isn't the steadiest walk, but I don't fall over so it's good enough for me.

I staggered out into the hallway to see Carter waiting right at the foot of the stairs. He has this strange look in his eyes but I can't completely decipher what it is -it's a cross between potent covetousness and a dark determination and it sends a chill down my spine. My mind is screaming for me to keep my distance because the way his stare is seeping into me is definitely not healthy...but then he smiles and after enough alcohol it doesn't look as creepy as it did before…just a little.

"There you are, Princess. I was getting worried, thought I'd have to go in there after you." He pulls me to him.

"I'mmm k," I slur, leaning into him to support myself.

Carter laughs lightly, "You don't look okay, plus I overheard a few girls talking about how Rio Greene is throwing up everywhere," he says gently, slowly rubbing my back.

I bury my face into his chest from shame. He was right, people did talk.

"Stupid girls," I mumble.

"So you were puking, eh? How you feeling now?"

"Like shit!"

"I can take you home if you want?"

I stiffen in his arms and take a wobbly step back.

"Nah, I'm fine. Thanks though."

Carter raises his eyebrow and looks me up and down in a way that makes me feel as if he has x-ray vision and can see through clothes. Instinctively I wrap my arms across my chest, swaying from the movement as I do so.

"You're fine, princess," he smiles, "But I really think you should let me drop you home; you look like you're about to collapse."

"But I don't even know you."

"Of course you do, princess; I'm Carter Johnson. I'm just trying to be a gentleman; my Mercedes is a lot more comfortable, cleaner and faster than public transport. I just wanna make sure you get home okay seeing as it's partly my fault that you're so hammered."

He drives a Mercedes? Well that changes things.

Against my better judgment, I pull in my lips and nod. Carter's smile grows.

"Fine; I'll go tell the girls you're giving me a lift." He stops me.

"No need, I already told Fontaine I'd drop you back. Give me your ticket; I'll go get your coat. Wait right here." I do as I'm told and Carter throws me a wink before heading to the cloakroom.

Foolishly I revel at how good leaving Sunday Slam with Carter Johnson in his Mercedes is for my Unfamous persona. I will definitely be a hot topic and as they like to gossip so much, Nate will hear about this. Good!

11
Fast & Furious.

Carter holds me steady as we weave through the backstreets of Brixton to locate his car. Every street we turn down is darker than the last, leading us further away from the bright city lights. Each time I ask Carter where he has parked his Mercedes he tells me that we are almost there -almost there seems a long way away from society. I'm beginning to get that uncomfortable flutter in my stomach that you get when your instincts suddenly kick in, but it's too little too late; we have turned so many corners that I'm no longer sure where we are or how I can get back. I'm too drunk to run away successfully.

"Why did you park all the way out here?" I ask to keep myself calm as the feeling of extreme discomfort continues to grow. If I keep talking I can delay my hysterics.

"It's more convenient?" he replies.

"Convenient for what?"

"Parking." He looks at me, "You seem a little shaky, princess; you okay?"

"Yeah, I think I'm just a bit woozy," I blame my nerves on my alcohol intake.

Carter stops walking and places his tattooed hand on my cheek. He strokes it softly.

"You wanna stop for a bit?" he asks in a concerned tone. I look around at the murky surrounding with all the locked up warehouse windows reflecting darkness back at me. This place probably looks less threatening during the day, but right now it looks like the last place I need to be.

"No. Maybe we should just go back to the girls." I suggest quietly. Carter furrows his thick eyebrows.

"My car is right around the next corner."

"That's what you said the last time." My tone sounds a little too panicked for my liking.

Carter frowns, "It is." He grabs my hand and drags me down another dark back road.

My throat is bone dry; my breathing has become loud and erratic. I want to scream but I know it would be futile because my voice will not project loud enough, and the fact that there isn't anyone else within a one mile radius doesn't facilitate much either. Carter's finger squeeze my hands so that I can't slip it out of his, something I've been trying to do as subtly as possible so he doesn't get suspicious. I'm forced to stumble after him. Making a run for it is probably inane, but at this point my gut is telling me that I would be sorry if I didn't even try.

"Let go of me," I squeak. Carter glances back at me as we round the corner, clearly fractious with my growing resistance.

"What is your problem Rio? You wanted to go home so I'm taking you home," he snarls.

"I want to go back!"

"Why? The car is right there!" he yells in an exasperated tone pointing at a black Mercedes jeep a few feet ahead. I blink testing to see if it was a chimera, but just like Carter had said, his car was parked right around the corner.

I stand dumbstruck, staring at the shiny midnight vehicle.

"You really were taking me to your car?"

Carter pulls a set of keys out of his jacket pocket and clicks a small button on the small device with the Mercedes emblem on his key ring. The cars headlights flash and the alarm system beeps once.

He shoots me a venomous look, "Where else would I be taking you?" he asks sceptically.

I drop my head ashamed of my assumption. I daren't tell him of all the awful things that were running through my mind, but my silence speaks volumes.

Offended, Carter lets go of my hand roughly.

"Are you being serious?" he yells running his hand over his face in disbelief.

"I told you to take me back but you wouldn't_"

"You're drunk for fuck sake, why would I take you back to the bar when I said I would drop you home safely? I mean, shit Rio - do you know who I am? I'm Carter fucking Johnson! It's not like there is a shortage of pussy being flung my way that I have to..." he doesn't even want to say it. The thought of it disgusts him.

"You are so lucky that you are drunk right now, 'cause if you weren't, I'd drive off and leave you here. Stop fucking about and get in." He presses another button on his device and the doors click to unlock. This is a fancy piece of machinery for a 20 year old university student, but it is apparent from our time in the Sunday Slam VIP that Carter is a man of means.

"I'm sorry," I mumble feeling like a naughty child being told off by their parent.

Carter sighs and gently takes my hand back in his, "It's ok; forget about it."

We walk the short distance to the car when a set of headlights light up the street. A tall dark figure exits the car and strolls over to us.

Carter chuckles darkly to himself then kisses his teeth as if someone has ruined his fun.

"I thought you went home Nathaniel?"

I can't believe my eyes. What the fuck is Nate doing here?

He fixes a tempestuous glare on Carter; he looks angry enough to take his head clean off with nothing but his bare hands. His chest is puffed out in an Alpha male stance making him appear dangerously intimidating. Carter doesn't flinch, but I do.

"Nathaniel?"

His eyes flicker to me with a softer pissed off look colouring them. Clearly, I'm in trouble, but unlike with Carter, he doesn't look like he wants to kill me.

I have seen Nate in action before and I had to admit that I was slightly afraid for Carter. Carter however doesn't seem apprehensive in the least; in contrast, he looks strangely amused.

"Rio get in the car," Nate growls in a tone that indicates that if I make him repeat himself, I am going to be in deeper shit than I already am. I had two minds to tell him to go and fuck himself and jump in Carter's truck anyway, but it is clear that there is more going on between these two than meets the eye.

I wriggle out of Carter's grip and walk as carefully as I can over to Nathaniel. His stormy eyes glare at me unmercifully as I stumble and clump towards him with all the grace of an injured ox.

"How much did you drink?" he hisses. I reply with a small shrug.

Carter pulls a Marlboro from behind his ear and lights it, "I kept her well supplied; she likes Moet, don't you princess? If you hadn't come along and ruined it I would've supplied her with something to get her sober real quickly." He chuckles and flashes that roguish grin at Nate.

Nate's jaw muscle tightens and he clenches his fists at his side.

"Listen; Rio ain't Georgia."

What the hell is that supposed to mean? Better yet, what does Georgia have to do with anything? Nate's words only make my already muddled brain more disorderly because they hold no significant meaning to me...but they meant something to Carter because his cocky grin vanishes.

"If you're so sure, then why the fuck are you even here, bruv? You scared something might've popped off?" he asks acrimoniously.

It's Nate's turn to look amused.

"Not even! If you thought you had a chance would you really need to get her this drunk?"

"That wasn't my doing; she was drinking of her own free will. If it happened to make my goal easier then so be it." He takes a drag of his cigarette, "Either way, drunk or not, by the time I had finished with her she would've been begging for more."

What?

"I had special plans for this one, but no worries, this is just a minor bump in the road mate -you won't always be there."

I wonder if he knows that I can hear him?

Suddenly Nathaniel is charging towards Carter at full speed and slams him into the door of his Mercedes. His fists seized the collars of Carter's jacket, and those few extra inches of height he possesses makes Carter seem a lot smaller than he was when I was next to him.

"There won't be another time pussy'ole," Nate growls, pulling Carter up to slam him against the truck again.

"Nathaniel what are you doing?" I scream. This situation has escalated far beyond my male testosterone tolerance levels.

"RIO, GET IN THE FUCKING CAR!"

"No, not until someone explains what is going on!"

"ARE YOU DEAF? I SAID GET IN THE CAR NOW!" he roars over his shoulder making me jump.

Defiantly, I stay put but I'm trembling at the volume of his voice. I don't want to get in the car, I want them to stop whatever this is and let me know what is going on because it obviously had something to do with me, but as usual, Nathaniel wants to control everything. He has a habit of shutting me out until he is ready to fill me in.

Why is everything always on his time? All of two hours ago he wasn't even speaking to me while he cuddled up with

Georgia right in front of my face, knowing just how much it would burn me, and now here he is gripping up Carter for trying it on with me, like it's any of his business –not that I would have done anything, but he doesn't need to know that. He owes me an explanation.

"STOP SHOUTING AT ME AND TELL ME WHAT IS GOING ON!" I scream back.

"GET IN THE_"

"FUCK YOU!" He grits his teeth and redirects his rage back to Carter.

Carter struggles under his grip trying to break free but Nathaniel stands strong, the curves of his bulging muscles sculpting his shirt.

Carter stops moving and exhales. Suddenly he is calm and it's scarier than Nathaniel's fury.

"Are you really this stupid Nathaniel?" he asks menacingly, "You of all people know what I'm about, so you'd better let go of me before I lose my temper."

"Do you think I give a fuck right now?"

Carter's expression darkens, "This is your last warning; get off of me or I'm gonna get you, and then," his eyes lock onto me and a chill runs up my spine, "I'll get her. Do you understanding what I'm saying, bruv?"Arrogantly, he takes another pull of his cigarette and blows it in Nathaniel's face.

Now I'm really worried; what does he mean by he'll 'get' us. What is Carter Johnson involved in? Whatever it is, it makes Nathaniel stiffen.

"You leave her out of this!" he warns.

Carter smacks his hand away, "You remember yourself and I will."

Nathaniel clearly wants to go for him, but whatever Carter's warning means and whatever Nate knows about him, makes him stop. He looks back at me, grits his teeth, and then steps away from Carter. One of the popped strings in my chest rethreads itself; he is putting his pride aside to protect me.

Just as I'm about to relax, Nathaniel lodges his boot into Carter's car door with a deafening boom that bounces off of the surrounding buildings and echoes back at us. It leaves a sizeable dent.

"Don't go near her again, I mean it. I don't give a fuck about Georgia, have her, but Rio…Rio is mine!"

Carter spits at his feet, narrowly missing Nathaniel's offending boot. He closes the gap between them and shoves Nathaniel back then gets into his car, scowling at the damage.

"I'll be sending you the bill for this. I know you're good for it so don't keep me waiting. Princess," he directs that unnerving smile at me "I'll be seeing you around."

I don't like the sound of that.

Cater drives off and Nathaniel visibly relaxes but the muscle in his jaw is pumping furiously. He swoops around and ushers me roughly into the car. I start to protest but decide against it when he glares down at me.

12
California King.

I open my eyes; I am sprawled out alone on a king-size bed that doesn't belong to me.

Groggily, I sit up -my head pulsates a little when I reached 90 degrees. I blink a few times and rub away the sleep that has gathered in the corners of my eye before focusing on my surroundings. Where the bloody hell am I?

The walls are painted light grey with only a large Samsung flat screen and Bose surround sound speakers adorning it. The bedding is unbelievably comfortable; I imagine it's the equivalent of lying on a cloud with black sheets made of the softest cotton I have ever felt, and plush silk pillows that are now the lucky hosts of my dribble stains. I frown at them and flip the pillow over hoping that the owner won't notice until it's too late, then I wipe my mouth on the back of my hand. The cherry wood shutters on the large window on the left side of the room are closed; were it not for the glow of the soft pearlescent light behind the head board I wouldn't be able to see anything –there isn't a lamp on the bedside table. There is however, a tall glass of water and a packet of paracetemol set out on it. Whoever brought me here knew I would need this like the desert needs the rain; God bless them. I pop two of the chalky white oblong pills into my mouth and wash them down with the slightly stale tasting water which I continue drinking until the glass is drained.

I swing my bare legs off the side of the huge dream bed only to feel my toes connect with the chill of the cherry wood floor. I shiver then stand up, coming face to face with my cataclysmic reflection in the full length mirror next to the closet. The mirror informs me that my weave is a mess of knots and limp curls -but fortunately not as messy as it could be thanks to the silk pillows –and that I'm in a man's white shirt and my underwear. Confused, I tug the hem of the shirt; where the bloody hell are my clothes?

A frenetic spin helps me spot them neatly folded on a chair in the corner of the room. Ok so my clothes are safe, now all I have to figure out is where exactly I've ended up. I run through last night's events and come up short, my memory going fuzzy after running down the stairs into the girl's toilets to puke.

I drag my hands through my knots in irritation, the shirt material brushing my nose as I do...and then I smell home; I smell him. He is all over me and the room is practically doused in his palatable scent. This is Nathaniel's shirt, which must mean that I am in Nathaniel's room...but where is Nathaniel?

Without further thought, I charge over to the bedroom door and fling it open, flinching as the crystal door-knob smacks into the wall behind it.

I'm now standing on a dark quiet landing in nothing but a shirt that luckily is long enough for me to maintain some sort of dignity in case someone sees me, not that the fact that it fits a little too well helps much.

With the choice of two other doors and a flight of stairs, I opt for the stairs, afraid that one of the doors could lead someone else's bedroom. I'm not sure if Nate lives alone or not –it's not a topic we discuss -but I wouldn't be surprised if he did; he possessed the means to do so. Being that this is London and property prices are ridiculous, for a 19 year old boy, this is nothing short of impressive.

I have never been to Nathaniel's place before; when we were together he still lived with his parents in Notting Hill. His family home is intimidatingly beautiful; white washed walls, high ceilings, breath-taking front and back gardens, a collection of contemporary art, and every room looked like it had been transported from a high end interior design catalogue due to his mum, Natasha Gibson, being one of London's most sought after interior designers. His dad, Daniel Gibson, is a successful architect –his parents are loaded. Unlike my upbringing, Nathaniel was raised in perfect family harmony. They were all beautiful, successful, charismatic, witty people to whom money was no object, and happiness was easy to come by. The first time he introduced me to his family, I envied him terribly.

I detect the same perfect interior design feel in Nathaniel's flat, but it's a simplified condensed version of his house without the more meticulous fineries that were more his mum's taste. I gawk at the impressive surroundings like Alice when she first found herself in Wonderland –funny, Alice followed the white rabbit while I drunkenly followed the white boy. I smile at my lame quip…what was his name?

I pad down the stairs only to be confronted by two more doors, one of which is cracked open a little emitting the unmistakable flickering of a television through the small gap. I push the door open wide enough for me to poke my head in and peer into the sketchy darkness. Isn't it strange how in certain lights objects can lose all colours and appear to be from a scene from a film noir?

Nate is lying on the sofa with his long legs dangling off of the edge, wrapped in a faux fur blanket, fast asleep. It's unfair that even in this limited palette he still looks like the most beautiful man I have ever known.

Longingly, I watch him sleep; he looks so peaceful and I wish that we were in a position where I could plant sweet kisses on his face like I used to when we were together, only to be taken aback by the intensity of his astounding eyes flickering open to stare up at me in that devastating way of his. I am tempted, but I stay where I am, pressing my hands into my legs as a form of self-restraint.

The time on the clock on top of the television reads 04:32. It would be rude of me to wake him up right now after all of the trouble he went through to come and rescue me from Carter...wait; CARTER, that was his name!

A few more scenes flash though my head jolting my memory and before I can stop myself I march over to sleeping beauty and smack him the centre of his chest, jolting him out of his sleep.

"What the fuck? Rio, why are you hitting me?" he groans.

"What the fuck was all that about earlier between you and Carter?"

Nathaniel groans again, "Forget about it, it's nothing. Go back to bed."

"Stop ordering me around like I'm a child. You're not my man; I don't have to do what you say!" I hiss.

Nathaniel sits up and the faux fur covers fall away from his body; he's shirtless. Shit! Rio, look away!

Suddenly my nails become very interesting.

"You're not my girl but I didn't have to come get you from him either. I also didn't have to bring you here and let you sleep in my bed while I slept on the couch, or make sure your hung-over ass had some paracetemol to numb the headache that I knew you would have when you woke up! You're welcome by the way!"

I open my mouth to say something back, but find that I have nothing to say that won't make me seem like an ungrateful bitch. Dammit!

"Thank you," I snap back –it's not a great retort but I feel the delivery of it will suffice. "Why did you bring me here?"

Nathaniel stands up making the covers fall away from him completely and towers over me in nothing but a pair of fitted Calvin Klein boxers. Oh for crying out loud!

Involuntarily, I bite down on my bottom lip. It's been a while since I've seen Nate in next to nothing –or any guy for that matter -and my memories definitely do not match up to what is standing in front of me right now…

.Sshhh Rio! Angry. Stay angry!

"You threw up in my car and passed out!" he informs me.

"Really?"

Staying mad at him is getting more difficult by the second.

"Yes. Do you know how hard it's gonna be to get the smell of vomit off of my suede seats?"

"I'm sorry...but if you had left me with Carter it would've been his car I was puking in," I say steering the conversation back in the direction I had originally intended it to go in.

Nate kisses his teeth, "Did you want to go with Carter?"

"Not particularly, but I want to know why you didn't want me to so much that you were waiting for us."

Nathaniel stares me dead in my face and says, "You would have fucked him."

My jaw falls open -talk about blunt!

"I would have done no such thing; I'm not a hoe! I have more sense than to sleep with someone I've just met."

"I never said you were a hoe, but look at how drunk you were; you couldn't even walk straight!"

"Fair enough, but I wouldn't have. Carter's creepy."

"If you say so," he says without an ounce of conviction.

I roll my eyes.

"Why does it matter to you who I sleep with? You're not even talking to me, remember?"

"It doesn't," he says unconvincingly, "You can sleep with who you like; just not Carter Johnson."

"Why not?"

"Cause all you are to him is a score that he feels needs to be settled."

I furrow my brow, "Is this the part where Georgia comes in?"

He nods and sighs.

"When you and I were together, Georgia was with Carter. She was the pretty little lighty from the block who all the guys wanted, and he was the bad boy who ran the block; the perfect hood match! They'd been together for about 2 years by that time, but he was starting to make her unhappy, so one day she plucked up the courage to leave him.

"After you and I split there was a bit of talk about me being the real reason she left him, so to this day Carter believes that it's my fault she walked out on him. She was the love of his life and now she's in love with me." Really? I never would have guessed that she loves you from the way she follows you around like some lost dog, but hey, thanks for confirming it, douche bag!

"You've seen a glimpse of the kind of person he is, so naturally we don't get along. Since you turned up at Brompton and made yourself so spectacularly known, Carter knows who you are to me, so to get even he wants to try and take you from me. I'm not gonna allow that."

"I'm not even with you so what's there to take?"

Nathaniel closes his eyes momentarily. When they reopen he is looking at me funny. I feel suffocated by the weight of his gaze and my heart is palpitating at an unusual rate. I can't breathe.

"Ri, I know it's selfish and that I have no place to say this, but I'm not ready for you to be with someone else…in any way…especially not him. I had to make sure things didn't go any further so I took Georgia home and came back for you. It was hell watching you with him in the VIP; cuddling up to him, smiling at him, letting him...touch you," he flinches at the memory "If I let it go any further I would have to endure seeing that on a regular basis, seeing as we run in the same circles now."

"You mean the way I have to endure you and Georgia?"

"Yes," he says guiltily, "And honestly, I don't know how you do it."

"I have no choice; you gave me no choice!"

Nathaniel shakes his head and takes my hand, wrapping his long fingers around it and rubbing his thumb along the back ever so tenderly.

"Of course you have a choice, you always have."

My stomach clenches nervously as he takes a step closer, almost sealing the small gap between us -almost.

"Don't say anything; listen to what I'm telling you," he says barely above a whisper. "Rio, I have never loved anyone else but you, and I hate the idea of you loving anyone else but me; not because I want you to stay hung up on me, but because I never got over you and I honestly don't think I ever will. I've been trying to. I thought that if I stopped talking to you that maybe that would be the answer, but it wasn't. You shut me out of your life for so long that I got used to not having you around, and then out of the blue you turn up on my doorstep and everything comes rushing back to me ten times over."

"Nate…stop," I croak feeling the dreaded lump rise in my throat.

"No. For once in your life will you just stop fighting me and listen. Don't you think this is hard for me to stand here and tell you all of this like I'm some fucking Romeo? I would never say shit like this to any other girl, but I'm here and I'm saying it to you. Doesn't that mean anything?"

"Well of course it does but_"

"But what? I know you have been just a miserable as I have, and for some reason someone up there brought us back together to give us a second chance, and all you want to do is find reasons not to."

"'Cause I'm scared Nate! I barely survived the last break up; you have no idea how much you hurt me or what that did to me. It took me a long time to be okay…I can't risk going through that again."

Nate's head falls forward and he lets go of me to cover his face. His large hands travel up his cheeks to smooth out the creases in his forehead then he throw his head back and sighs, his thick eyelashes clamping together as he exhales.

"You make me crazy you know that?" he mutters more to himself than to me.

He looks back at me but this time his eyes are sparkling like misty diamonds; he's not giving up. He's going to fight for me.

"I'm not going to put you through that again baby."

My heart flutters as he grabs me, pulling me close and entrapping me in a nostalgic embrace. I can't breathe and it is actually more than a little scary this time because I have genuinely forgotten how to as his hand slithers up the side of my body, rising and falling over my curves until they make it to my face.

"I love you and I miss you. I just want you to come back to me Ri."

Slowly he lifts my chin and lowers his mouth onto mine with a controlled hunger, kissing me delicately, allowing me only small doses. I go limp in his arms as I give myself over to the moment, encouraging his tender lips to kiss me stronger, deeper. He tightens his hold around my waist, pressing my anatomy into his own. I inhale rapidly as his warm, yielding tongue dances over my lips, parting them so that he can consume me. My arms encircle his neck as our kissing becomes more fervent -I hear him make the sweetest sound that causes my breath to quicken and the muscles in the lower half of my body clench so tightly that they begin to pulsate. I moan into his mouth, pressing into him even more attempting to meld us into one being.

He smiles against my lips.

"You still scared?" he pants sounding very pleased with himself.

"Yes," I whisper throatily, unable to contain my arousal. It's flaring up inside of me as if I've been doused in petrol and Nathaniel is my flame. My whole body is on fire and there was only one way to put it out.

He kisses me with more passion as he slowly loses control of his unsatisfied hunger for me, his large hands sliding up under the thin material of the shirt to grip my ass and press me into the firmest part of his statue.

"Good," he growls. I shudder in anticipation.

13

LaSenza.

My flesh is alight with the searing heat of seduction, yet covered from crevice to crevice in goose bumps. Every fibre in my body aches for the feel of wandering hands with curious fingers and hot puckered lips with tongues that dance untamed.

Nathaniel's lips rain burning butterfly kisses down my neck as he continues to squeeze my ass with his large hands, raking his nails over it every so often, delivering a multitude of sensations that have me jerking against him from over excitement.

I can't help myself; all logic has gone out the window and my inhibitions follow them as his lips travel down to the valley between my breasts, losing his face in the open collar of his shirt. I arch my back and moan as his teeth sink into my flesh. It hurts, but in a good way. I love the intoxicating adrenaline rush you get from sex that makes almost anything feel amazing. That alluring concoction of pleasure and pain coming together has a way of making you feel alive in the most aberrant ways. I run my hands down his back then up to his head to hold him in place so he can deliver another bittersweet bite. He does; harder this time. I cry out and fling my head back so that he can do it once more.

Nathaniel looks up at me -still nestled in my bosom -with his daunting eyes adorned with lashes so thick they resemble black lace, and smiles kissing the spot he's just attacked. Both of his hands travel up my body to the collar of the shirt and he kisses me harder, taking my bottom lip into his mouth. He moans against my lips and grinds his impressive erection into me. He curses and I sigh. Nathaniel is my favourite kind of lover; he's a talker. Once he gets going, the most panty dropping words fly out of his mouth like a Trey Songz slow jam. It's like having a cheerleader in the bedroom; the more he said, the more I did - which is great in the heat of the moment but often leaves me cringing when I think about some of the things we've done the morning after.

I take a step back so that I can make better use of my hands. I take my time slowly massaging his strong shoulders, stroking his arms and finally his perfect abs; it's like he's been carved out of marble. His muscles flex under my touch as I trace my fingertips between each crevice. I work my hands over him until I reach those sinful lines that disappear into his Calvin Klein boxers, tempting me to find where they lead to. I know exactly what awaits me at the end of that trail, and I'm trying my hardest to save the best until last, but I find myself becoming extremely impatient. I allow myself the slightest touch, skimming my hand over his hardness and kissing him with more passion in turn. He responds by securing his grip on the shirt even tighter and eventually tears away from my kiss.

Nathaniel stares at me with one eyebrow raised, panting like an Ulfric. A menacing tearing sound breaks through the almost silence, and suddenly the shirt is open; button-less from his haste, but open nonetheless. I whimper. I want to leap at him, pin him to the ground and take him right then and there, but his hungry stare keeps me in my place. I shiver as his eyes admire my scantily clad frame, wishing that I could hear all of the erotic thoughts that are running through his head. I squeeze my thighs together to ease the throbbing that had built into something so strong I felt I would come if he so much as touched my knickers.

Nathaniel smirks, enjoying my wriggling, "Take it off," he orders.

"I'd rather you did it," I breathe.

"I've already destroyed my shirt. If you like your lingerie, you will do it yourself," he warns. I gulp and squeeze my thighs together harder from the image of him ripping my frenchies off with the same savage strength. I'm tempted to let him do it...but La Senza underwear isn't cheap. Slowly I remove every last item of clothing until I'm stood before him wearing nothing but a seductive smile.

He bites his lip and groans, "Come here."

He restarts his tirade of burning butterfly kisses, his lips desperately try to connect with every inch of my bare skin while his hands waste no time in finding themselves between my legs, making me curse as he touches all the right places. I almost pass out from the ecstasy. He finds the spot that has me speaking in tongue, and stays there, until my words run together into something unintelligible.

"You feel so good baby," he groans as his expert touch stops my breath short.

His tongue sashays down my stomach and soon he is on his knees in front of me...

"Nathaniel!" I gasp as his mouth creates a new sensation between my thighs. He props my leg up on his shoulder, leaving me the difficult task of balancing on one leg as I try my hardest not to move too much in case I fall. I have the urge to pull away as the intense feeling builds in my centre, but his other arm is secured around my hips, holding me in place. I have a habit of running away when the feeling becomes too strong and it's clear from his grip that he remembers. I don't know why, but feeling like I'm going to violently combust frightens me; I'm scared for my life right now.

"Stop!" I pant; even though that's the last thing I want him to do. I grab his head trying to force him away from me, but instead he takes this opportunity to lock his endearing eyes onto me to watch me fall apart. I shudder.

I beg and beg but he keeps on until…

"Oh my God...oh my God...Nate, please! Nate...NATE...OH GOD NATHANIEL!"

I curl over him, shaking and screaming from the sweetest torture, clawing at his head crying for him to let me go so that the abyss that I'm lost in will disappear and I can return to earth, but he keeps going, taking me higher, moaning into me, and sending added vibrations through me. My legs go limp and finally he withdrew his mouth and his hands with a triumphant grin while I continue to convulse from the aftershock of my orgasm. In my book, if you don't experience the highly embarrassing jerky aftershock that comes with every good orgasm, well, you never really came sunshine!

"You all right?" he chuckles getting back on his feet and laying me on the sofa before sliding up alongside me. I nod and pant, unable to form words. He pecks me on the forehead and holds me, allowing my body to calm down. I kiss his face, refusing to give in to the rush of mass energy loss, and tug at his boxers clumsily, wanting him out of them this instant. It seems like forever since I felt him, and I need to feel him now more than ever to confirm that this actually real, that I am really with the man I love again.

Nathaniel smiles and pulls my hands away from him, kissing each of my fingertips softly.

I growl in frustration, "Fuck me!"

He laughs at my crudeness and kisses my throat, "Are you sure you're ready for that? You still seem a little shaken up," he says in his guttural baritone, making me even more impatient.

"Nathaniel, I swear to God_"

"Don't you think you've called on God enough today?" he teases. I blush.

Nathaniel strokes my face and kisses my flushed cheeks.

"Let's go upstairs, baby."

I lay trembling on the rumpled black sheets watching Nathaniel as he presses play on his iPod sitting in his lavish Bose docking station. The melodic sounds of Alicia Keys's 'Fire We Make' spills out of the expensive sound system and he turns to face me. I gaze at his glorious statuesque frame and bite down on my lip; I don't know why he's still affecting me so much, I mean, he's been half naked for a while now, but just admiring him makes me break out in goose bumps and causes my lower half to spasm uncontrollably.

Nathaniel fixes his luminous eyes on me and stands at the foot of his California King bed. He cocks his head to the side, and then ever so slowly, his hands find the band of his boxers. My eyes automatically snap to his lower region as I anticipate seeing him in all his glory. He tugs them down a little lower revealing more of his erotic lines. My breathing accelerates and my hand travel between my legs trying to ease the throbbing -his lips part.

"Nate..." I breathe, reaching out to him with my free hand. He pulls his boxers off completely and comes closer to me. I crawl onto my knees, grab onto his waist and kiss every exposed inch of him as torturously slowly as I can muster, biting into him, then soothing it with a gentler action before I perform my magic trick; now you see it, now you don't.

He groans and starts chanting my name like a sweet mantra.

"Rio. Oh Rio. Ohrioohrioohrioohrio... ohrio. Shit baby!"

Nathaniel grabs my hair pulling me off me completely and shoves me back on the bed in one swift motion. Before my body can stop bouncing against the bed springs, he is on top of me, spreading my legs with his own whilst flurries of impassioned kisses decorate my mouth. I tilt my hips, so eager to feel him, but he edges away, his lips still pressed to mine with a cheeky smile.

"Nah uh. I wanna hear you say it again," he coaxes kissing as his lips descend down my frame again.

"Say what?"

"What you said to me when we were lying on the sofa."

He wants me to beg more like. It was embarrassing when I summoned the courage to do it then, but I'm not brave enough to say it again.

I giggle and shake my head, "I don't think so."

He pauses mid-kiss and cocks his eyebrow.

"I want to hear you say it, baby." His tone is so persuasive but still I shake my head.

Nathaniel shrugs and smirks, "Okay." He stops kissing me and moves back up my body so that our centres are aligned, dips into me just enough to hear me gasp, and then pulls back out. That fucker!

"Say it baby." He does it again.

I moan a mixture of pleasure and frustration. I don't want to play stupid little power games with him anymore, we've wasted enough time doing that before we even got to this point so why are we still doing it? After all this time; all the tears, the arguments, the emptiness, I am in the bed of the only boy who had captured my heart and subsequently not given it back and I have no intention of wasting one more second.

Extending my hand, I stroke the side of his face lovingly, unconsciously getting lost in his pale eyes. Nathaniel stops smirking and is now staring down at me intensely. The longer I hold his unwavering gaze, the louder my heart beats over our heavy breathing, and just like that, the world melts away and it's just us. We're together and up until this moment I hadn't realised how happy I am. I smile and press my lips to his, pouring all of my love into that moment, pulling him as close to me as I can so that I can feel every inch of him. I'm not dreaming; this is real. I'm kissing Nathaniel and it feels wonderful.

At first my kiss takes him by surprise and he kisses me back with caution, trying to calm my feverish lips, but I'm in need of him so urgently that I clutch him tighter. Finally he catches on and now we're kissing like it's the first time. I have that same exhilarating feeling that I experienced the first time Nathaniel kissed me when I was 16; that epic first kiss rush when you feel like you have waited a lifetime to feel their lips crash against yours, that brings with it that nervous yet strong intensity that sings that from this moment on, nothing will ever be the same again. His tongue parts my lips and massaged my own as he began to move against me, sending illicit sensations through me. I arch my back to increase the pressure and sigh into his mouth.

"I love you Nathaniel."

He pulls away and stares down at me with a different look in his eyes. As cliché as it may sound, he is staring like this is the first time he's laid eyes on me and has decided in this moment that I am the most beautiful woman he has ever seen. I feel like he is staring into my soul and is finally seeing me for everything that I am now, and that he's okay with it. His misty eyes express a love that runs so deep that it scares me just to see how potent it is…because that's the way I stare at him.

"Will you say it again," he asks softly.

This I have no problem repeating.

"I love you."

He kisses my forehead.

"Again."

"I love you."

He kisses my cheek.

"Again," he breathes moving against me, finding his exquisite rhythm.

I tilt my hips to meet him.

"I love you Nathaniel," I gasp.

"I love you more."

He plunges into me and buries his face into the crook of my neck, cursing against my heated flesh as he tries to catch his breath. My breath has left the building -eyes wide, mouth open but no sound.

The world disappears again and all I'm aware of is him moving inside me with smooth inhibited motions, trying to allow my body time to loosen up and get used to him. If he stops for even a moment right now, my walls were likely to close in on him with an astounding tightness. As I pointed out earlier, I haven't slept with anyone else apart from Nathaniel, so the last time I saw any action was a little over a year ago, consequently leaving me very...snug.

"Shit," he curses throatily, pushing and pulling his length in and out of me. I push back making the contact a little harder, a little deeper, a little lovelier. My legs lift from the bed and lock around his waist, pressing him all the way into me until we become the beast with two backs. I scream feeling his pace speed up as he slams fantastically into the untouchable parts of me -it hurts so good.

I shriek and claw into his back like a woman possessed. He loops a caramel arm under my chocolate leg and lifts it onto his shoulder then raises his upper body and thrusts into me creating a new sensation. I feel like my insides are going to cave in, but I don't stop him, the pain is addictive, just when I think I can't take anymore a wave of uninhibited pleasure writhes and undulates through every fibre of my being. I hold on tighter and take it. Nathaniel pumps furiously, jerking my resilient frame against the bed so hard that the headboard begins to knock against the wall. I tug at my hair, drunk with desire. I don't understand the wild words that escape our throbbing lips; we're cursing and hollering like sinners, provoking each other on to say the things that you only say when the sex is so good that you become who you really are.

We perform our forbidden dance and he chants my name again, his sexy baritone making it sound like a tantric love song dedicated to me, his muse.

"Ohrioohrioohrioohrio."

I can feel our sexual energy forming into a ball of euphoria in the pit of my stomach, expanding and vibrating to the tips of my fingers and toes.

"I'm gonna come," I whimper digging my nails into his arms and flinging my head back; the fear of explosion resurfaces. Nathaniel groans, my erogenous declaration pushing him closer to the edge.

"Come for me baby," he pants as he starts to unravel.

The next few lines are a jumble of our names and colourful words as we arrive at our destination together with such ferocity that when we finally come down we are clutching each other and shuddering violently.

"I love you Rio."

For the first time in over a year, I fall asleep in Nathaniel's arms and I am truly happy. I have him and I want nothing else. He's all I need.

14
Stiletto Nails.

I don't know how long I've been awake; it's probably been a few hours because when my eyes first opened the windows didn't have this glorious glow of daylight framing the edges of the cherry wood shutters. Strangely, it feels as if time hasn't progressed from the moment I realised where I was and who I was with –Nathaniel; my beautiful Nathaniel. Time seems frozen because nothing else registers to me but him.

We have shifted positions from earlier on, and he is now sleeping peacefully on his back with one arm wrapped around me, cuddling me into his perfect chest, my head resting on his pecs and one of my legs draped across his hips. Images of last night replay over and over in my head and I'm fighting not to wake him from his slumber to re-enact them, deciding that I should appreciate the memory and savour this simple moment tangled in the sheets with him until I'm clear about what is going on between us. As amazing as last night was, where did it leave us? Are we together or is that a work in progress? I mean, he had said that he loved me, and I him, but here and now, what does that count for?

I never imagined that we would ever end up back here, but here we are and for the first time in a long time -I am happy. I am also scared. To be here with Nathaniel is like standing on top of the highest peak of Mount Everest, beyond the clouds where nothing but heaven can touch us, but it feels inevitable that eventually I won't step carefully enough and I'll slip off the edge, or he'll push me, then watch apologetically as my fragile body tumbles downwards, hitting every ledge as I fall, till I smash into the ground, shattering all over again. This kind of happiness is hazardous because recovery is not always guaranteed, but because it is so precious, we reason that just to be this happy, even if only for a few fleeting moments, it is worth the fall.

I kiss the smooth skin on his chest softly and smile as he shifts slightly; he is awake. As hopelessly pathetic as it sounds, I can't wait for him to open his eyes so that I can be dazzled by his loveliness again, but also so that I can see if he still has the same all-consuming love struck look for me.

I kiss a little higher up this time, my lips landing lightly on the curve of his throat, and he shifts again.

"Good morning," I whisper hoarsely from disuse (and overuse) of my vocal chords.

Nathaniel smiles with his eyes still shut, "I'm not awake yet." His morning voice is even more endearing than mine.

I smiled harder against his skin, "Yes you are, you plank!"

"Nuh uh! Sleeping Beauty can't wake up without true loves kiss," he chuckles.

I shove him playfully and roll off his body so that I am lying on my back with my arms crossed over my chest in an 'x'.

"Kiss me then."

I lay as still as a statue, trying to pull off being trapped in a deep enchanted slumber awaiting the moment when my Prince Charming comes to my rescue and breaks the spell with true loves kiss. I'll admit that this is so corny, but it's one of the perks of being with Nathaniel; we do silly romantic things like this and it's okay because it's us. When we're not fighting, this is who we are. This is part of the reason why I missed him so much.

The mattress moves as Nate sits up and I try my best to suppress my smile when I feel his face floating inches from mine; so close and yet so far. I wait patiently even though I'm tempted to take a small peek to see his now animated face. My heart flutters in my chest when his fingertips trace the outline of my trembling lips delicately as if he's afraid I will shatter if he's not careful enough with me. He presses his lips to mine and I am positive that he can hear the dramatic change of pace as my heart races from the feel of his faultless lips kissing me tenderly. I reach up and lace my arms around his neck to deepen it, relishing the way that once again, nothing else matters at this moment but the two of us.

After a lifetime, he pulls away and gazes down at me with that same all-consuming love drunk look in his eyes, that make their shade of grey light and sparkly like crystals.

"Good morning beautiful."

"Morning."

We're back downstairs in Nate's living room (as expected, he does live by himself) cuddling up on the sofa, eating buttery toast with strawberry jam and drinking sweet, steaming mugs of hot chocolate under the faux fur covers. We've already made love again twice -once after our 'good morning' kiss and again in the shower when we were supposed to be getting clean -now we we're both dressed in a pair of Nate's joggers and old t-shirts, rolling our eyes at the television screen where Jeremy Kyle is screaming at a grubby looking young Chav couple about sleeping around on each other. Neither of us are big fans of daytime TV, but as we've both switched off our phones, deciding to spend the day playing hooky from uni (and the outside world in general), this is what we have to put up with during our sexual intervals.

"I could never be on that show you know. He would make me ignorant," Nate comments, rubbing his fist like he wants to punch the arrogant, straight talking host through the TV.

"Oh, shut up!" I giggle.

"I'm serious; I would knock him out if he spoke to me like that."

"Sure you would!" I roll my eyes and sink my teeth into my toast.

"You think I wouldn't?"

"I know you wouldn't. He's got a bag of security guards waiting in the wings for your black ass to start feeling froggy. You won't even get the chance."

"Fuck his security guards! My boys will be in the audience," he laughs. I roll my eyes again.

"Yeah, 'cause they're gonna really let in a bunch of riff raff like you lot into the studio."

Nathaniel makes a face and pinches my hip under the sheets. I shriek and kick him.

"Ow!"

"Serves you right! Don't pinch me."

"What, you think you're bad yeah?" he challenges, rising up to tower over me.

"I know I'm bad," I grin and poke my tongue out at him. He smirks and I know we're about to engage in a play fight which will only lead to one thing. I put my breakfast down and bite the corner of my lip.

I giggle like a school girl when he pounces on top of me, pinning my arms above my head.

"Get off!" I squeal, struggling to break free before he straddles me.

"Nah, you're bad, remember? You should know how to handle yourself," he smirks.

"What are you gonna do to me?"

His eyes darken as he leans in close, "I'm gonna punish you."

My stomach clenches and my breathing hitches.

"How?"

Nathaniel expertly keeps a hold on my wrists with only one hand while the other slides down my arm, over my cleavage, to my waist and then… he starts tickling me. Well this isn't what I had in mind at all. I hate being tickled and he knows that which is why I guess he sees this as a suitable punishment.

I am choking on my heinously provoked laughter, trying to stop screaming long enough so that I can form words to tell him to stop, when the doorbell rings –saved by the bell indeed. Nathaniel automatically stops tickling me and checks the time on the digital clock on top of the television. His body goes rigid.

"Shit!"

"What's the matter?" I ask, worried by the abrupt change in his demeanour. Nate gets to his feet, pulling me up with him.

"Nothing baby; go upstairs for a minute, I need to sort something out quickly," he orders, pushing me in the direction of the stairs.

"What is it? Are you in trouble?" I panic, pushing against him.

"No, I'm trying to avoid it. Please Rio, just go upstairs," he pushes again.

The doorbell rings again, then the letterbox clatters open; "NATHANIEL YOU BETTER BE AWAKE!"

No. Not yet. We haven't enjoyed this long enough for it to all come crashing down already, especially not by the same girl who ruined us in the first place; Georgia.

I turn to face him slowly with a look of distress colouring my features.

"What is she doing here?" I ask.

Nathaniel grits his teeth and reaches for me. I step back.

"Nathaniel, what the fuck is she doing here?"

"Baby, it's not what you think," he pleads desperately, seeing the bond that we'd mended last night beginning to fray around the edges. The doorbell sounds again.

"WHAT. Is. SHE. Doing. HERE?"I growl.

"Nothing! We've both got lecture on Monday morning so we go to uni together, that's all, I swear."

"She lives on campus, why does she need to come here?"

He looks away and replies quietly, "She makes me breakfast."

"She does WHAT?" I scream the last part unintentionally; my emotions are getting the better of me. "Why the hell is she cooking you breakfast? I thought you two were just linking?"

"We are!"

"You don't come to your link's house and cook him breakfast Nathaniel so spare me the bullshit. That is something that a girlfriend does for her man!"

"What? Rio don't be silly. You cook for Ty," he fires back.

"I'M NOT FUCKING TY!"

My face is hot and my pulse is thundering in my ear drums as I felt my temper flare up. How dare he even bring Tyson into this! He knows the levels of our friendship, so what makes him think that he can use that to justify Georgia being outside on his doorstep waiting to be let in so that she can cook him breakfast? Am I a mug?

"You're right. I'm sorry ok, but you're over reacting. Do you really think that after all of this I'm still gonna mess with her?"

I look away –there's no need for me to say it; we both know what my answer is.

Nathaniel grabs my hand, "Rio, I love YOU, okay?" He stares into my eyes trying to get his words across mentally. I hold my angry face for as long as I can, trying to tell myself that the sincerity in his eyes is just a trick to cover up his lies, but I can't deny truth when I see it.

I sigh and grit my teeth, "Tell her to go away and never come back!"

Nathaniel relaxes and kisses me on the forehead, "Okay."

I wait with baited breath by the sitting room door, anxious to hear what he will say to her to make her disappear for good. The latch clinks then a small popping sound follows as he opens the front door.

"Hey babe," she says with a smile in her voice. I imagine her flinging her arms around him right now, hugging him like he's hers to hold. Nathaniel does not belong to her; she's not allowed to touch him.

"Hey G," he replies in a neutral tone. What's with all the niceties? Hurry up and tell her to fuck off, will you!

"Why ain't you dressed?"

"I'm not coming in today."

"Naughty!" she giggles, "Why not?"

Nathaniel pauses. He's probably contemplating how to tell her that she is really just a trashy rebound and that the girl he is madly in love with is waiting for him inside (ready to judo kick a bitch if she has to).

"Rio's here," he says plainly. I love the subtle 'go away' undertones of in his voice.

Georgia falls silent momentarily. Yeah bitch, that's right, I'm back!

"I thought she went home with Carter?" she sneers.

"Did you really think I was going to allow that?"

"Wait, you went and got her from him? I thought you said you were tired?"

"I lied." When he wasn't using it on me, I loved Nate's no nonsense approach. There was nothing you could say to him because you knew that he didn't care.

"I don't believe this...so you brought her back here?"

"It's my house." I. Love. Him.

"NO SHIT NATHANIEL!" Wait, is she crying? Oh this just keeps getting better!

"Georgia, calm down."

"FUCK YOU NATHANIEL!" She IS crying. Good! Now you know how it feels. I hope it burns you to know that you have lost him. He's mine and there is nothing you can do to stop it because he loves me and he has always loved me.

Suddenly I hear scuffling.

"Where are you going?" Nate asks in a firm voice that sounds a little strained due to the fact that he is trying to keep her outside.

"I want to speak to Rio," she sobs.

"What for? Georgia, let it go and go to your lecture. You're embarrassing yourself."

"Let it go? You have no fucking idea what I'm going through and you want me to let it go? RIO!" she screams.

What do I do; stay where I am so that the drama doesn't escalate, or go and see what she had to say?

"Did you hear what I said?" he growls.

Georgia ignores him and keeps screaming my name.

"RIO!"

I decide to go to the door, not just to hear what she said but so I can enjoy the view of her at her lowest; I may never get this chance again. When I get there, Nate's arms and legs are spread from corner to corner, blocking her entry while she tries to find a gap to ease through. Up against Nathaniel's 6 foot something frame, Georgia resembles a small, irritating Yorkshire Terrier, known for behaving as if they are bigger than they really are, when rubbed to wrong way. Well, she is a bitch.

"What?" I snap.

Georgia locks her catlike green eyes onto me. They look even more intimidating than usual because her black kohl liner is smudged underneath her lower lash line, with purple tinted mascara tears running from them, making her look slightly demonic.

Nathaniel looks behind to see me standing there with my short self, trying to look threatening with 'just fucked' weave and clothes that are way too big for me.

"Rio, go back upstairs!" he growls.

"Don't you dare! Not until I say what I have to say."

"Leave her alone!"

I walk closer and stand next to him placing my hand gently on his shoulder, "It's okay baby," I notice Georgia flinch. I don't hide my smile. Nathaniel sighs and steps aside, letting Georgia in then closing the door behind her.

She stares me down in her six inch heels and runs her blood red stiletto nails through her long, dark hair.

"I have something to tell you." The way she looks at me brings back feelings of insignificance. Even though I've won, it is clear that she still doesn't think I deserved to be with him.

I jut out my chin, "What makes you think that I want to hear what you have to say?"

"If you didn't want to hear it then you wouldn't have come down," she replies stonily.

"Maybe I just wanted to see how pathetic you looked," I smirk. She doesn't like that.

"You wanna hear what I have to say or not?"

I shrug, "Might as well if it'll get you on your way faster."

"I don't think I'll be the one that wants to leave after this."

Nathaniel puts his arm around me and kisses the top of my head as a sign of unity and I swear I couldn't possibly love him anymore if I tried. We're together and there is nothing that she can do to destroy us this time.

Georgia's buttery complexion flushes with red tinted rage.

"Just say what you have to say and get out, Georgia," he sneers. The anger in her eyes sobers as she frowns dejectedly at him, and I almost felt bad for her. Almost.

"That's no way to speak to the mother of your child now, is it Nathaniel?"

"What?"

"Congratulations," she smiles "You're gonna be a father!"

I've just been pushed off of the top of my imaginary Mount Everest. I let go of his hand and stare at him in disbelief, wanting him to tell me that there is no possibility that this is real.

"Nathaniel? Nathaniel, no. No!" I choke. He doesn't look at me; he's too busy glaring at Georgia.

"Georgia, this isn't funny."

"Who's laughing? I'm pregnant and it's yours," she turns to smile victoriously at me, "And you can leave now!"

The steadily crumbling bond snaps as my body finally reaches the bottom of the mountain.

15
Friendzone.

It's 4pm as I traipse towards my dorm building in last night's outfit, with my hair thrown into a sloppy bun revealing a few tell-tell weave tracks, and dried tears staining my cheeks. I am a far cry from the picture perfect potential 'Queen of Brompton' that I have been consistently trying to depict, but right now I don't care, I have bigger things to worry about. All I want to do is climb into my bed and sleep, and sleep, until enough time has passed for the pain to become irrelevant.

Nathaniel had dropped me back to campus against my will, leaving his newly acquired baby mother in his flat so that they could talk when he returned. Let them talk; I have nothing more to say to him. I mean, what is there for me to say? We had been happy together before and he'd ruined it with Georgia, then just as we get back to the good times, he ruins it all over again with the same bitch! He's gone an outdone himself this time; before I had to deal with infidelity, which was hard enough to move past, but now the twit's gotten her pregnant!

This feels like a huge karmic slap in the face; I was pregnant for him just over a year ago and I chose to get rid of our baby, so the universe, knowing how badly Nate wanted our child, gave him another with a girl who would keep it just so she could keep him. She's finally won her prize; that gorgeous, popular, powerful, wealthy young man is now hers.

What I don't get is why he'd have unprotected sex with his 'link'. I knew she was more than a bit on the side to him, the only person he was lying to was himself. Georgia cooks him breakfast and rides to uni in his car with him every Monday morning, they're always at events together, not to mention every time I see her with her claws clutching onto him when I see them around campus and now they're having a baby. How could he have been so stupid? He'd always claimed that he and Georgia we're never serious and that he had no plans to make it so, but what's not serious about a family?

If there is ever anything to mark the end of the Rio and Nate saga, this is definitely it. I can't compete with a baby. As he spoke I'd made a mental note to myself to go to the clinic and get the morning after pill; we didn't need any more baby mama drama than we had already.

The whole agonising ride back, he'd reeled off a string of apologies and promises that he would fix it and that we'd be happy. I didn't say a word, I just sat there crying and shrinking away from him whenever he tried to touch me –it was like we'd switched roles from that time he drove me home from the abortion clinic; now he's the sorry one and I can't stand to be near him. How can he possibly fix this? He can't force her to get an abortion, hence this can't be fixed. His pleas were falling on deaf ears.

How am I supposed to sit down and watch the man I love build a family right in front of me with a woman I despise?

I can't.

He kept on saying that nothing has to change, that we can still be together and that everything would be all right in time, but he is wrong. This changes everything, not only between us, but I can feel a change coming over me as well. I am sad. I know I moan a lot, but aside from my mini teen dramas I was actually quite content with my life. Education wise, I'm doing pretty well, I finally have friends outside of Tyson so my social life is booming, as is my social networking life (I almost had 1000 followers on Twitter and about 400 on my Instagram) –I was enjoying my independence. Unfamous wise, I'm excelling up the ladder faster than I'd expected, and I'd only been at Brompton for 2 months. Almost everything is perfect, but my pathetic love life just overshadows it all.

I enter my flat as quietly as possible praying that no one comes out of their room and start questioning me. The girls and Tyson have been hitting up my phone since yesterday upon discovering that I hadn't returned to campus, but I'd been too wrapped up in my fairy tale to let them know I was okay. The last thing I wanted to do right now is have everyone asking the dreaded question that will only worsen my mood; 'Are you okay?'

My hopes are squished when I spot Tyson sitting outside my door in one of my old beloved grey Nike hoodies and a pair of red flannel Simpson pyjamas, with his head resting against the door frame, his eyes are shut and his mouth ajar. Why was this idiot asleep in the corridor like a homeless person?

Despite my sadness, I smile at him fondly; of course he'd be here. I tip toe over to him and press my palm over his lips so that he won't make any noise when he wakes up. Tyson jolts upright at the feel of my cold hands, his pretty brown eyes slightly dazed from shock. I press my finger to my lips signalling to him to keep quiet then stifle a giggle at the way he nods warily up at me like a victim that is being rescued from his captors. I pull him to his feet and we enter my bedroom as quietly as we can, letting the door click softly behind us.

The state of my pokey dorm room makes me groan; it looks like Tyson's room -like a bomb of hit it. Whenever I get ready to go out I have a bad habit of turning my whole room upside down just to get dressed. My wardrobe doors hang open with a collection of shoes, tops, bottoms and dresses tumbling out of it. More clothes, some underwear and accessories have taken over my bed space, and pots and tubes of makeup with applicators scattered between them covered the rest of the available surfaces. I kick off my Converses in the direction of the wardrobe jumble so that they can join their sisters, and sweep all the crap off of my bed onto the floor. I'm not in the mood to tidy up right now.

"You gonna tell me where you were?" Tyson asks unearthing my matching pair of Simpson pyjama pants in blue from one of my wardrobe shelves -we bought them together in an ironic attempt of behaving like stereotypical besties. I pull my dress over my head and grab the pants from him, ignoring his distracted stare. He'll get over it in a minute.

"I don't wanna talk about it right now," I mutter climbing into bed in just my Pj pants and bra.

Tyson joins me and tucks the single bed duvet around us, making sure to tuck it a bit tighter on his side as I have a habit of rolling myself up in them and leaving him with nothing.

"Ri, I was going out of my head, I couldn't sleep. Fonts said that you had gone off with that Carter guy from Langford and that you were licked. I called you like a thousand times."

I sighed and rolled over putting my back to him.

"I wasn't with Carter."

"Then who were you with?"

I wasn't about to answer that at this moment. I really did just want to sleep and forget about this whole ordeal for a few hours, and if Ty knew that I had been with Nate, that wish would not be coming true for a good while.

"Ty, I just want to sleep, okay. Can we'll talk about it later?"

Tyson sighs and wraps his arm around me.

He kisses the top of my head, "Okay."

When I wake, it's dark and I'm alone in my bed, cocooned in the duvet, wondering where Tyson is. I reach up and pat my hand clumsily along the wall until I felt the cool plastic of the light switch. The florescent prison standard light flickers on, illuminating my now mysteriously tidy room. On my desk is a large pizza box, accompanied by a litre bottle of Pineapple KA and two plates. I shuffle out of the bed to peek at the pizza; chicken, pineapple and sweet corn stuffed crust on a barbecue base. This is why I love Ty; he knows exactly what I need to cheer me up when I'm feeling low, and comfort food is definitely one of them.

Just then Tyson came through the door with a few more eating utensils and two tubs of Haagen Daaz ice cream; Strawberry Cheesecake for me and Cookies and Cream for himself.

"I got the expensive stuff," he grins wiggling his eyebrows.

"Ty, you didn't have to do this," I gush taking a few items out of his hands so that I can give him a hug.

"I know, but you looked like you needed it."

"You have no idea."

After I finish spilling my guts it's more likely that he will need this than me. See the thing is Tyson has no idea that Nate and I had any contact with each other unless we were forced to be around each other because of our lecture or circle of friends. I'd kept it a secret from him because I didn't want to hear any of his bitching and jealousy provoked warnings about why it was a bad idea and how Nate would only hurt me again. Funny, now that I think about it maybe I should have told him; maybe I wouldn't be where I am now if Ty had the opportunity to talk me out of it.

After a quick trip to the bathroom to freshen up, Tyson and I arrange ourselves on the floor on top of a spare blanket that I kept under the bed, with the pizza box between us and two large glasses of KA balancing precariously on the uneven sheet. We pulled out my desk chair and put my small flat screen on it so that we could watch our all-time favorite film, Love and Basketball, while we stuffed our faces and waited for the ice cream to defrost.

"All right, spill," Ty said sinking his teeth into his first slice of pizza.

I take a long slow sip of my highlighter yellow pineapple flavoured soda and smack my lips.

"What do you wanna know?" I only intend answer exactly what he asks and nothing more. The less he knows the better. I'm not going to lie to him, but I'm not going to reveal things that I don't need to either.

Tyson cocks his eyebrow, "This must be bad if you're making me play 21 questions with you."

"Depends on how you choose to take it."

"Uh huh." He eyes me sceptically and I can tell that he is going to try and get as much out of me as he possible.

Taking another bite of pizza, he begins.

"Were you with Carter?"

"Yes." See, that wasn't a lie; it's not the whole truth, but it's not a lie.

"Why didn't you pick up your phone when I called? What were you doing with him?"

I shoot him a look; I know this boy is not trying to imply that I had sex with a guy that I hardly knew. Why does everyone think I'm a slut all of a sudden? Do I seem that desperate?

"It was on silent and we were walking half way around the world to get to his car so he could take me home," I reply in a frustrated tone.

Tyson nods, accepting my answers as something believable.

"Ok, ok. Did he do something to you?"

I shake my head, "No."

"Then who upset you?"

I take another long sip of my drink ate some pizza so that I have time to consider how to answer him without completely throwing myself to the wolves.

I swallow, "Georgia upset me."

That wasn't a lie either.

"Georgia? What did she do?"

"Ruined everything, as usual."

"Ruined everything in terms of your little plans for world domination…or is this matter a little closer to the heart?"

I scoff at his phrasing and take another bite of pizza to stall; this is about to get complicated. I can feel Tyson's eyes watching me, waiting for my answer with baited breath, silently hoping that it is the first option he mentioned. It doesn't take a genius to figure out that he doesn't want it to be the second option. Oh well.

"The second one."

Tyson makes an incoherent sound letting me know that he is not impressed in the slightest.

"What has he done this time?"

I pause not wanting to say it out loud as if that will make it more real, not that not speaking about it makes it less real, but still…

"He got her pregnant, Ty," I whisper.

It's Tyson's turn to pause.

"He what? Are you fucking joking?"

"I wish I was, but no. Georgia is pregnant with Nate's baby." My voice sounds like I have completely given up.

I'm exhausted from it all. I gave Nate everything I had and once again I'm left with nothing but these tiresome emotions that I'd rather tune out than feel. When you keep giving your love to someone that abuses it, it drains you, and eventually you will have nothing left to give. It had taken everything in me to move past my issues with Nathaniel and surrender to my true feelings, and I had thrown all of my heart into it thinking that this time it would be better, that we would be better. I knew I had said that to be that deliriously happy even if it was for a short while would be worth the fall, but now as I sit with my best friend, eating greasy junk food on the floor in our pyjamas, I'm beginning to reconsider. The hurt always seems stronger than the joy because every time you allow your mind to wander and some happy memory comes up, you feel even worse because it's a reminder of something that you don't have anymore.

My mum used to recite that generic 'Don't be sad because it's over, smile because it happened' quote to me whenever she'd catch me in one of my Nathaniel funks back then. The day that I suggested that she should take her optimism and be happy that she and my dad happened she finally shut up about it.

Why do we try and find all these useless things to make ourselves feel better after someone hurts us? It works for a little while, until you realise that it's only words, material things or another person who you're not really that into, and that they will never make you feel as happy as that person did, nor can they overshadow the pain that person left you with.

Tyson puts down his pizza and take my hand, "I'm sorry Ri."

"What are you sorry for? You didn't do it," I laugh bitterly.

"I'm sorry that he hurt you."

"It's my fault. I should never have gotten back with him."

"...What?"

I'd said too much.

Tyson slid his hand away from mine in disgust, "You got back with him?"

Guiltily I bury my face in my hands, preparing to reveal all.

"When Carter tried to take me home Nate was waiting to intercept me -he and Carter have some unresolved issues concerning Georgia. He took me to his house and looked after me because I was drunk..." I paused not wanting to tell him the rest.

"And?" he coaxes.

I huff and continue, deciding that I'm gonna have to get it all out eventually so I might as well just tell him now.

"He told me how much he loved me and then we...you know..." I hinted uncomfortably.

Tyson's mouth presses into a straight line "Yeah, I know," he replies tightly.

"So everything's going great, we were happy the way we used to be up until she shows up on his doorstep. He told her to leave because I was with him and she starts kicking off, crying and screaming, then she demanded to speak to me. I went to the door and he put his arm around me and everything....then she dropped the bomb. I told him to take me home."

Tyson is quiet, too quiet so I kept quiet too knowing that he needed a minute to process what I'd just revealed so he could try to deal with it accordingly. His normally cheerful face is solemn, his twinkly brown eyes now flat and void of anything pleasant. How mad is he?

This is ridiculous; I shouldn't have to be worry about how my best friend takes information like this because there is a chance that he may feel more for me than he is supposed to. It's infuriating. Right now I need him to be here for me and not make me feel like I have done something awful to him when I'm the injured party here.

I switch my eyes to the screen and watch as little Monica pushes over little Quincy and tells him that she doesn't want to be his 'stupid girlfriend anyway'.

Tyson closes his eyes and take in a slow, deep breath.

"I swear I don't get you girls sometimes. You know a man ain't shit, but you still go back. It's like you like getting fucked over?"

See what I mean! I brushed it off not wanting to get into an argument.

"Yeah well I've learned my lesson now! God is obviously trying to tell me something. It wasn't even a full 24 hours before it all went wrong. Maybe were not meant to be together after all," I said dejectedly. Suddenly I have a hankering for something a lot stronger than Pineapple KA. I think I've got some vodka under the bed. Mmm, vodka and Pineapple KA; it definitely has promising possibilities, me being too drunk to be upset being one of them. I roll onto my back and reach for the bottle.

"God has been trying to tell you other things but you just choose to ignore them," he mumbled. I act as if I'm too engrossed on my new quest for a drunken stupor, unscrew the bottle and take a swig. I feel bad brushing off his feelings like this, but now is not the time for him to jump on the whole 'I love you' wagon. I need him to be my best friend, not some lovesick guy trying to escape the 'friendzone'.

"So yeah, that's what happened." I go to pour some vodka into my cup but Tyson snatches it away, replaces the lid and moves it out of my reach.

"Don't do that," he snaps.

"Do what?"

"Ignore what I'm trying to tell you."

I narrow my eyes at him, "And what are you trying to tell me exactly, dear *friend*?"

"Forget it!" he sulks grabbing his half eaten pizza slice.

Oh I want to punch him! He's supposed to be making me feel better and what he's actually doing is making it worse by getting into one of his stupid moods and making this about him.

What does he expect me to do; throw myself at him and proclaim my hidden desire to love him until the end of time? I'm not gonna do that; not because I don't love Ty, of course I love him, just not the same way he loves me. I'm frustratingly in love with that bastard Nate, and no matter how much I try to push the feeling, the shit won't budge.

"I don't see why you won't just let me in, Ri."

Oh for crying out loud!

"Tyson, stop it," I scold him.

"No! Every time I try to tell you how I feel, you always want me to stop."

"BECAUSE YOU'RE GOING TO RUIN EVERYTHING!" I scream at the top of my lungs.

Tyson clamps his mouth shut and turns away from me. Now I feel bad. I hadn't meant to scream at him, but it's like he doesn't get what he would be ruining if we took it there. We're not little kids anymore; if we got together it would be the real deal and if it didn't work out this wouldn't be some little puppy love that we could recover from like we did (well, I did) last time, and lord knows where that would leave us.

I lay my hand on his shoulder, "I'm sorry. I didn't mean to shout."

He shrugs, "I get it okay. I'm not him."

"Ty, that's not even it."

"Sure it ain't."

"It's not. Ty, I'm glad you're not him, he's a prick! You're my best friend in the whole wide world and in a way I love you more than him, but it's not the same kind of love. Even though it hurts, I can deal with being without him, but it would kill me if you weren't there anymore."

He sighs and pulls me to him. Surrendering to his lovable nature, he kisses my forehead, "I'll always be here Ri."

"That's what you say now, but what if we did get together and something happened?"

"There is nothing that could happen that would make me leave you," he says so earnestly that I almost believe him. It's easy to make promises like that when things are good, but once someone hurts you, those promises become a lot harder to keep than you would have imagined.

"Ty, the last time when things got a bit heavy between the two of us you wouldn't speak to me for weeks. Do you know how much that hurt? I can't risk losing you again, you have to understand that," I plead.

"I hear you, Ri. It sucked not talking to you and I don't want to go through that again either, but I won't wait for you forever." Is it wrong that, that bothers me? I mean, I don't want Tyson spend lord knows how long waiting for me to (in his opinion) come to my senses –if I ever do –that's selfish, but I don't want him to not want me like that. I'm not the girl who drives men wild, the only real partner I've had is Nate, so when I didn't have him anymore, it was nice to still feel wanted by Tyson, especially as no one else was rushing to step up to the plate. I frown to myself.

Tyson gives me a playful nudge.

"I'm in high demand, you know," he grins trying to soften the bleak promise of his words. I go along with it and smile back, glad that he is easing up a little and reverting back to being my bestie.

We settle back into our positions and watch the rest of the film in silence. As I observe Monica and Quincy's relationship evolve I felt a flicker of curiosity; would Tyson and I ever have a 'double or nothing' moment? I peek at him from the corner of my eye and admire how his smooth chocolate skin hugs his immaculate frame, the way his lips are permanently puckered, the way his dimples pop in and out of view when he changes his facial expression, and how even though his hair (which is currently slicked back into a huge bushy ponytail) looks a hot mess, it doesn't disrupt his boyishly handsome looks.

He catches me staring and raises his eyebrow.

"Can I help you?"

I shove his head, "Shut up…idiot!"

Smooth Rio, real smooth.

16
Twitter.

It's been two days since the latest Nathaniel catastrophe and I still haven't left my room. I'm supposed to be in my English Lit lecture, learning the things that I took out this student loan for…but Nathaniel's in that class, so instead I'm lazing about in my grey Nike hoody (that I've temporarily nicked back from Tyson as I have no plans to leave my room), alternating scrolling through timelines on my iPhone of Twitter, Instagram and Tumblr to see what the rest of the world is up to - ignorant banter, ass shots and feelings as per usual.

I'm not in the mood to socialise with anyone besides Tyson –the girls don't like it much, they want to know what's wrong, but right now I'd rather keep my distance until I can think about the situation without crying.

Aside from avoiding my girls, I'm hiding from the rest of society because according to Twitter there is a lot of speculation about my sex life. The last 'they' saw or heard, I had gone off drunk with Carter Johnson after spending the night in VIP cuddled up with him, so my name is milling around the Twittersphere as they come up with misconstrued facts of what we did (or rather did not) do. I knew that leaving with Carter would spark off some discussion, but the fact that I didn't actually do anything but was still getting called out for it is getting to me. This so called 'gossip' was apparently juicy enough to warrant a few indirects on Twitter via @KissTheSky.

I thought that mine and Sky's little feud was dead now, I haven't wasted a thought on her in a while, but it would seem as though she was far from over our spat. The only reason I haven't blocked that tramp is to keep tabs on her, and it's a good thing too because she can't seem to keep my name out of her mouth:

@KissTheSky: So she wants to talk shit about me, but she's leaving Sunday Slam with a man she don't know. LOL okay.

@KissTheSky: She let him beat. It's bait.

@KissTheSky: I thought CJ had standards. How does he go from @GeorgiaPeach to this beg :/

I had been so tempted to @ her and say something foul when this got retweeted onto my timeline:

@GeorgiaPeach: @KissTheSky lol once you've had the best you can't do better ;) talk about downgrade!

That bitch was fanning the flames just for the fun of humiliating me. She of all people knew that I didn't sleep with Carter because she popped up and found me at her new baby father's home. You'd think that getting knocked up would give her a touch of humility, but no. I was tempted to tweet about her news, but I knew it wouldn't make me feel better. It would be another way of me confirming the truth to myself and then for everyone who knew our history to see that she had won once again.

This is the reality of being an Unfamous; the gossiping, the judgmental looks, the fake people that cluster around you -not because they actually like you, but because they think that they can benefit from being your friend -and constant trivial dramas that only escalate because people are too concerned with their image to let things go? Right now I'm craving my previous background status where I could go through this meltdown without everyone having an opinion on it and misconstruing the truth. It is my life and I don't appreciate it being broadcasted as entertainment for social networks.

It's common to hear people blow it off as 'It's just Twitter', but that saying doesn't count for much in a city like London. We're all crammed in to such a tight space (it only takes just over an hour to get from one end to the other…depending on traffic) and everyone knows everyone, so because of this, what starts online has a habit of carrying over into 'real life'. I wasn't about to let them talk me down over social networks so I opted for a simple, mature cop out.

@RioDuran: If they wanna talk, let them talk. The truth will remain the truth no matter what the haters say.

10 minutes later that urban wisdom earned me 14 retweets and three new followers.

Tyson emerges in a cloud of steam from my boxy student bathroom in the black basketball shorts that he had acquired from the Brompton basketball team and a vest top. He had practice today, which he hadn't planned to go to because he wanted to keep me company, but I convinced him that it was unhealthy for him to stay cooped up in the stuffy room with me as I was the miserable cow, not him. After much reassurance that I would be okay on my own for a few hours he went to his room to get more clothes and his kit. It was like he had moved in with me, and I was grateful for the company; lord knows how much more miserable I'd be without him here.

He looked over my shoulder at my Twitter and frowned.

"Don't entertain their shit Ri. You're better than that."

"Am I?"

"Well…no, but you should pretend that you are. Hashtag 'Image ting'!"

At 8pm, Tyson returns with his hair looking worse than before he left and is slick with man sweat. I had ordered a few dishes from the Chinese restaurant on campus 'Yum Chow', and was currently struggling to finish composing my 3000 word essay about John Steinbeck, over a plate of Special Fried Rice, Butterfly King Prawns and Kung Po Chicken. More comfort food was needed after Ty departed. My mature tweet hadn't deterred Sky and Georgia from posting more reputation damaging indirects and I didn't want to get into 'Twitter Beef' because that was tacky so I chucked my phone out of reach and dug out the menu from the top draw in my desk ordered then decided that I might as well tackle some work as I hadn't been to any of my lessons for two days.

Tyson dips his hand into my plate and picks up a prawn before I have the chance to stab him with my fork.

"Go away!" I growl, now protecting my plate.

Tyson pops the prawn into his mouth with a cheeky smile.

"You're so greedy man. I only took one, you've got five left in your plate."

"So! Your food is over there. Next time your hand comes in my plate I cut your fingers off," I threaten. I hate when people have their own food but yet they still want to eat yours. We have separate portions for a reason -Rio doesn't share food!

Tyson chuckles and goes to get his food while I sit eating one of my prawns and glaring at him for shortening my portion. His hand disappears into the white paper bag that holds 8 more prawns; one by one they go from the bag to his stomach in under a minute. Tyson is one of those guys that will eat for the world then say they are still hungry, but doesn't put on any weight. I wish I could do that, but my metabolism isn't as generous as his. I work out to stay in shape; Tyson doesn't need to, but he does it anyway because for some odd reason, he actually likes working out.

After he empties the bag of prawns he finally gets a plate and dumps the contents of his other two containers on it before taking a seat next to me with his sweaty self. I scrunch up my nose and shove him away. He smiles and sits closer to me.

"Has he hollered yet?" he asks, shovelling an overflowing spoonful of red sticky rice into his gob. I pause; for the first time today I' forgotten about Nathaniel and Tyson just had to go and drag it back up.

"Of course he has, but after reading 5 out of 11 'I'm sorry' messages I can't be bothered to read anymore," I say tightly.

"So...you gonna reply?"

"What for? Ty, he's having a baby. I'm done."

"Sure you are!" he snickers.

"I'm serious! I came to Brompton to start afresh, then I allowed Nate to enter my plans and all he did was complicate things. I shouldn't be going through this again. I'm finished for good." I said it with so much conviction that I almost believed myself. My performance must've been really good because even Tyson fell for it.

"Glad to hear it."

"I know you are," I tease.

Tyson rolls his eyes, "Not just because you're giving him the boot ...again, I just don't like to see you sad Ri -the frown lines are not doing you any favours!"

I scowl and jab him in the side with my fork.

"Fool!" I smile.

He laughs and draws me into a sweaty one armed hug.

"That's better."

He flashes his crooked smiled and pecks me on the forehead. I stroke his messy hair with my free hand and mouth 'thank you'.

At 11 o'clock I'm slumped melodramatically over my desk, 1,500 words in, deciding that I've had enough of writing this essay, while Tyson -after another steamy shower -is back in his pj's and knocked out in my bed. Listening to his quiet snoring is making me feel sleepy as well. I knew that if I had been talking rubbish on Twitter or taking cute bedtime selfies for Instagram instead of avoiding the world I would be wide awake, but uni work has a way of draining you, which in turn makes you sleepier a lot faster. Funny that. There is a plus side to this though; the sooner I fall asleep, the sooner I don't have to struggle not to think about Nathaniel. He had Whatsapped me two more times while I'd been trying to do my work and instead of sticking to my guns and ignoring him, I sat and read every single one in his thread from the start of the term until now. We are such a mess. We'd gone from distant to close, then happy, to sad. It was a familiar pattern.

I click the save button and shut down my laptop.

Switching off the rest of my electronic equipment (including the lights) I yank off my legging, pull on my pajama pants and clamber into my single bed, half on top of Tyson. I hate the way he sleeps! He has this habit of spreading his limbs all over the place like this is his double bed at home.

With cranky hostility, I nudge him awake.

"Make yourself small, this ain't the Hilton!" I snap, pushing him against the wall.
As soon as he groggily frees up some space I dive under the sheets and mould my frame against him so that we are spooning comfortably –this is literally the only decent way to share a single bed, unless you're gonna top and tail it.

After a while his arm entwines itself around my waist and he pulls me closer to him, tangling our fingers together.

His gravelly sleepy voice breaks the silence.

"Night grumpy," he kisses the top of my head.

"Shut up and go to sleep," I snap.

I feel his lips curl into a smile against my head.

"Love you too, grumpy."

"Yeah whatever," I smile.

As we begin to drift off to sleep, I lie in his arms and think about how nice this feels. There isn't that inexplicable rush of electricity that I get whenever Nate is near, but there is definitely something there. It's simple, effortless…safe. If I'm honest, there is always something there between Ty and I, but I always chose to ignore it because I don't think that what I feel for him is enough, and I know that Tyson deserves more, but as we lay here in the dark I can't help but wonder what it would be like to kiss him right now…

I know these feelings are being spurred on by the emptiness I inflicted on myself by reading Nathaniel's messages. The desperate cascades of I love yous and I'm sorrys are making me ache for him, but I know I need to keep my distance -it's not safe…but Tyson is.

I shuffle around to face my best friend and my conscience shakes her head at me 'Do you really want to do this to him?' No, of course I don't, but I need a distraction. It's just a kiss. How much damage can a little kiss do? 'You know exactly how much. He's in love with you. A little kiss to you is more than that to him!' my conscience scolds me.

Still I edge my face a little closer to his ignoring my better judgment. I don't mean any harm; I just want something to fill the void for a little while. The guilty sound of my movements ruffling the bed sheets seems so loud right now. I pucker my lips and I'm almost there when Tyson opens his eyes sleepily and frowns at me.

I jump and hit my head on the headboard.

"Fuck!" I hiss nursing my minor injury.

"Ri, you okay?" he asks in a soft voice, rubbing his eyes.

Cringing at my tactless stupidity, I sink lower into the bed and put the pillow over my face.

"No I'm not."

"What's the matter? Why are you hiding?"

"I…I was gonna kiss you," comes my muffled confession, "I'm sorry."

Tyson makes an amused sound, "Errr, why?"

"Because I'm an idiot!"

Tyson pulls the pillow away from my face and frowns again.

"You're not an idiot."

I look up at his gentle face and I can see the love and concern for me, and suddenly I burst into tears.

"Then why do I do these things Ty? Why do I keep making bad decisions?"

"Because you're socially awkward, you're not used to interacting with people so you get overexcited and freak out," he teases wiping my tears away.

"Shut up!"

"It's true. You just tried to sneak attack kiss me while I was asleep. Only socially awkward people do that."

"This isn't making me feel better," I sniff with a giggle. Knowing that his job is done, he settles back into the bed and pulls me back to him.

"So, how was kissing me going to help?" he asks still amused.

I shrug, "I dunno; you just make everything better so I thought it would work. I don't want to go through this again. I already know what it's like and I can't do it. It just…it just hurts…so much…" my voice cracks as a fresh stream of tears make their way down my face.

Tyson pecks my forehead gently and gives me a reassuring squeeze, and I feel safe. That was all the incentive I needed.

I lift my face and press my lips to his softly not wanting to come on too heavy in case he rejects me. He jolts from surprise then pulls away slowly. His eyes are wide, regarding me cautiously as if I've lost my mind.

His voice sounds like he's trying to talk me down from a ledge. "Rio, I don't think this is a good idea. You're ups_"

"I know, but please."

"Rio, no_"

I ignore him and kiss him again a little stronger than before. It's hot, desperate and brief because I pull away before he can push me off.

"Please, Tyson," I squeak as another tear falls, "Please, I need you."

I grab for the waistband of his pyjamas and he catches my wrists,

"Rio, stop!"

I kiss him and press my body to his.

"Stop. Rio…Rio…fuck…stop," he half orders, half groans as my lips caress his neck and I move against him.

His hold on my wrists ease up and I take the opportunity to tangle my fingers in his braids, tugging on them gently before panting into his skin a very heady, "…Please."

Tyson stops trying to unwrap me from around him and takes my face in his hands. He wipes my tears away again and sighs.

"Stop begging me. I'm not going to let you do this."

"But isn't this was what you wanted?" I sob pathetically feeling shame consume me.

"You begging for me to sleep with you? Yes!" he laughs despite the atmosphere, "But not like this."

Tyson spins me around so my back is to him and wraps his arms around me.

"Now go to sleep. Everything will be all right in the morning."

"No it won't." I sulk dejectedly. I can't even get the one boy who's been pining for me for years to sleep with me and now I feel like even more of a loser.

"Of course it will. We'll go to Starbucks and have a big overpriced breakfast, my treat."

"But you hate Starbucks."

"I know, but I love you, big head."

17

Sex and the City.

Early Saturday afternoon, after braving the cold for over an hour just to get here, the girls and I stroll fabulously through 'The City' in Eastpark shopping centre in Shepherd's Bush, one of London's hottest commercial shopping spots next to the Stratford branch and Oxford Circus. It's an elegant architectural cluster of luxury designer brands, high street shops, restaurants, a cinema and a few special attractions that change throughout the seasons. Right now there's an ice rink in the centre of the complex; it's late November, almost December, which only means one thing –Christmas is coming. With the holidays looming every commercial avenue is geared towards it; tinsel, jingle bells, snow, lights and SALES!

After being cooped up in my room for two more weeks after my horrific act of desperation with Tyson, the ladies had taken it upon themselves to be as irritating as possible and stood outside my door banging, screaming and singing One Direction songs off key (with everything but the catchy chorus either missing or improvised…badly) for almost half an hour before I cracked the door open to tell them to shut up and then...well, all fools rush in! Carmen claimed that I was being a dirty dorm hermit that needed an immediate intervention to save me before everyone forgot who I was and I died alone in my room. She could've been a bit less dramatic about it, but then she wouldn't really be Carmen then would she? So here we are, strutting through Eastpark trying to shop away my anti-socialness, looking like a page out of a Cosmogirl Fall 2013 fashion spread.

We sip prudently at our steaming Styrofoam cups of Starbucks's latest holiday venture, spiced hot chocolate. They didn't really taste all that great but we had already forked out damn near £5 to drink one so they were getting drunk even if it killed us.

"Did anyone pick up any sugar?" Yoshi asks, smacking her lips together from the odd aftertaste. We each shake our heads peering at the offending beverage, silently wishing that we had because lord knows this bitter drink needs it, but in the spirit of 'staying in shape' we had opted not to. We each take a sip and pull faces.

"Right, LiqFest is next week and we have to look fire," Carmen grins, the thought of yet another rave making her salivate as usual. I roll my eyes; I'm really not in the mood to be social; being in Eastpark is already more than I can tolerate.

Without consulting me the girls had bought me a ticket for one of the biggest, most talked about Uni raves of our generation; LiqFest. LiqFest (short for Liquor Festival) consisted of all of the universities being transported by coach to locations outside of London where we would spend the first half of the night bar hopping our way into drunkness and the second half topping up on more alcohol and dancing it off at one of the local super clubs. I had seen photos from previous LiqFest events and it looked like a wild night. Fontaine, our designated alcoholic, was the most excited to go.

We'd been planning to go to LiqFest for weeks now, but in light of recent events I really didn't want to. It was bound to be a night that I really wanted to enjoy but would end up wishing never happened because something (or someone a.k.a he who shall not be named) was bound to upset me. I was going to protest and demand that the girls sell my ticket to someone else, but I couldn't have my girls roll up to one of the hugest events of this term without their front woman, so grudgingly, I surrendered.

"Init! Everyone's gonna be there, and after the past few weeks of an un-united front," Fontaine gave me the side-eye "we need to show up guns blazing, so they know who runs dis!" She illustrates her statement by throwing up manicured gun fingers and pouting. I roll my eyes again.

I go into hiding for a hot minute and suddenly everything comes crashing down. As irritating it is to hear Fontaine refer to our slight decline in urban society, it was true. There were a multitude of rumours flying around about us (mainly me). We'd become important enough for people to start keeping tabs on us about where we had been, who we'd been with and what we were doing with them. My life has turned into a British version of Gossip Girl -some of the things they are saying aren't even true, namely me giving Carter a blowjob as a thank you for dropping me home. As if!

Thankfully none of my major bombs have exploded on the social grapevine…yet. I haven't told the girls about what got me into this state yet, but we were going to have a little catch-up session over lunch, which I am also not looking forward to. I would rather be holed up in the safety of my room, eating another tub of ice cream and watching soppy rom-coms to make myself feel worse.

Why do we do that? Girls I mean. Some asshole upsets us, and instead dealing with it in a healthy way, we shut ourselves away from the world, cry, eat copious amounts of comfort food that we will regret once it shows up on our thighs, listen to sad songs that relate to our situation so we can increase the shitty feeling, watch romantic films so that we can observe the kind of unobtainable, perfect Disney love that only exists in movieland then cry some more because we know that we will never have a love like that. Then comes the whole 'why' section; we ask why can't they love us as much as we love them, why they act like we're not good enough, why we can't find someone that will treat us the way we deserve to be treated (all the while none of us truly know our own self-worth otherwise we wouldn't have messed with this jerk in the first place). Then finally comes what I like to call the Beyoncé stage; the 'Tell me baby why don't you love me when I make me so damn easy to love?', 'You must not know 'bout me, I can have another you in a minute', 'Don't be mad when you see that he want it, coz if you like it then you shoulda put a ring on it', 'You turned out to be the best thing I never had' stage. You pick yourself up pumped full of female empowerment and declare 'from now I'm focusing on me!' and proceed to fill the gap with work, shopping, clubbing, sex, drugs, alcohol and other bounce back addictions. I take a sip of my hot chocolate –I'm not at this stage yet, I'm being forced into it by my friends.

Half an hour later in Top Shop, the girls had their pieces to go with their LiqFest T-shirts (which they would later cut up to make them look more flattering (and by flattering, I mean slutty). Fontaine had a picked out a tiny pair of cut off denim shorts -which the bottom of her ass fell out of -Carmen had a tight canary yellow pencil skirt, while Yoshi had settled on a pair of black slashed leggings.

I haven't found anything. Nothing looks amazing enough. I still don't want to go, but if I have to turn up I want to look as amazing as possible so that *he* could see me and realise what he ruined…again.

After the girls purchase their outfits, we head over to Nando's to get a bite to eat and get down to the nitty gritty. I'm silent the whole way knowing that not only is what I have to tell them going to test my emotional control, but that there was a chance that one of them could let it slip, giving the gossips more scandal to twitter about. Well, they're going to know eventually right? Georgia can't hide her pregnancy forever.

We end up on a table for four towards the back of the restaurant as requested so that we could have as much privacy as possible.

"So Car, any word from Amari?" Fontaine asks taking the seat opposite me. Carmen kisses her teeth and picks up her menu as if she's not even trying to complain about him today, even though we all know she wants to.

I raise an eyebrow, "What's going on between you and Bless?"

Carmen slams the menu down on the table, ready to launch into another '100 Reasons Why Bless Ain't Shit' rant.

"Options, is what's going on with Bless!"

"Options?" Yoshi asks.

"Yes; options. It's like every other girl on campus wants a slice of the pie. It's MY pie!"

"*Your* pie?" Fontaine teases, wiggling her eyebrows.

Carmen scowls at her, "Let's not get into technicalities right now,"

"No, let's. Car, Bless is not yours. He's not anyone's. He's a man-slut."

"A very good looking, powerful man-slut at that," Yoshi adds quietly attempting to have her say and not piss Carmen off.

"I know this!" Carmen snaps at them.

"Then what did you expect? He's a hot, powerful, *single DJ*; of course he's gonna have options. What you need to do is stop making him your priority while he's still treating you like an option," Fontaine advises. Yoshi and I nod and murmur in agreement.

Carmen pouts, “I know; I keep telling myself that but as soon as he comes around, all of my logic goes out of the door. He’s so sexy, and the sex_”

Fontaine cuts Carmen off by raising her palm.

“Please, spare us the details. We know what the sex is like, we live with you, remember.”

Carmen smiles proudly.

“Then you understand why it’s so hard to say no.”

“Well if you can’t say no to him, say yes to someone else too.”

“Yeah! If Bless has options, level up the playing field and get some options of your own.” Yoshi agrees.

“Easier said than done. It’s common knowledge that I’m with Bless_”

“For crying out loud Car, you’re not with him!” Fontaine groans.

“You know what I mean man! What is it with you and the fine print? Anyway, other dudes won’t holler because of our…arrangement.”

“What kind of dudes are you messing with?” Yoshi asks, confused that any man would turn down sex from Carmen.

“Well, I’ve been speaking to D-Man…”

“His friend? Oh c’mon Car; that’s rookie mistake, not even I’m that naïve. You never sleep in the same circle, some boys still believe in ‘bros before hoes’.”

“I thought all of those boys had already graduated university,” Carmen frowns, “They all had sex with Sky and the ‘bros before hoes’ rule never came into play once!”

“Because Sky is a prostitute,” I chip in before going back to browsing the menu.

“You need to throw your net out a bit further love. Go for someone more low key, not another bait face -fish in a different ocean, if you get my drift.” Fontaine winks.

“Okay love guru!” Carmen grabs her menu and the rest follow suit.

“Not even!” Fontaine laughs. “Haven’t you ladies noticed that I don’t moan about men half as much as you lot?”

“Maybe that’s because you haven’t met the right one yet,” Yoshi suggests.

Fontaine pushes her curls out of her face, “And what, you guys have?”

We all keep our eyes on our menus, avoiding Fontaine’s sarcastic smirk.

"Minus Yoshi, all you lot do is complain about what these boys are doing wrong, but yet you still hang about hoping that they'll wake up one day thinking the sun shines out of your ass and finally put you on top of a pedestal similar to the one you've perched them on. If these jerks don't realise how amazing you are by now, then it's likely that they never will, so let it go ok. There's plenty more fish in the sea."

Carmen and I share a look; 'but I wanted that one'.

I go up to the counter alone -needing a break from Fontaine's unwanted words of wisdom -and place our orders. As right as I know she is, a part of me still didn't want to hear it. I know all of this already; we all do, but somehow we females feel like we need to suffer to get what we want because it makes it more worth it in the end. We delude ourselves into believing that if we stick with him through all the bullshit, eventually he will get his head out of his ass and realise that we were 'the one' all along and then we can finally have our happy ever after.

How stupid are we?

Why must falling in love be so complicated? Correction; why do people make falling in love so complicated? You like me, I like you, so let's be together already! What's with all these stupid games we subject ourselves to?

I stab my fork into my Peri-Peri chicken with more force than necessary.

"So what exactly is wrong with you and Ace, Yosh?" I ask with a hint of sarcasm, not accepting that she could have any REAL problems like the rest of us. Ace and Yoshi have been sewn up from day dot, she got the one she wanted, he worships her…and I envy that. I wish I didn't because she's my friend and I should be happy for her, but I'm not, and I feel like a bitch for feeling like this, but I just want what she has so bad. Ace adores her, he takes her out all the time, he's always buying her gifts and showing her off, forever touching her…it's like she's magnetic. Whenever we're all out, unless he's preoccupied with work, he's at her side and if he's not, you always see him seeking her out in the crowd.

Yoshi shifts in her seat and pushes her spicy rice around her plate.

"I never said anything was wrong," she replies quietly not making eye contact with anyone. Maybe she feels guilty that we're all miserable while she gets to enjoy a doting boyfriend.

"Of course; I forgot, you lot are perfect."

Yoshi frowns, "There is no such thing as perfect, Rio."

"So there is something wrong?" I ask with a little too much enthusiasm. Fontaine raises her eyebrow at me.

"No. We're, fine. We have good days and we have bad days, just like any other couple. We're fine," she snaps softly putting down her fork and folding her arms almost as if she's hugging herself.

"I'm sorry; I didn't mean to upset you. It's just you don't talk about your relationship much."

"It's okay. Like I said, we're fine," her tone signalling that that is her final answer.

"Why are you being so secretive Yosh?" Carmen asks. Fontaine raises her eyebrow at her too.

"I'm not. I'm just a private person. What goes on in my relationship is my business and there's nothing wrong with that."

"But you know our shit."

"Because you tell me your shit; I don't ask!"

Fontaine reaches across the table and touches Yoshi's arm gently. I notice the way Yoshi flinches like she doesn't want to be touched, and I suspect Fontaine does too, but she doesn't pull her up on it.

"It's okay babe. You don't have to tell us anything unless you want to. We're your friends, and we respect that, don't we girls?" she asks shooting us warning looks. I nod so that I don't look like the bad guy while Carmen pops a chip into her mouth and chews with purpose.

I speak again before the tension can get any thicker.

"Well I suppose it's a good thing that you guys are fine. At least one of us should be happy. You represent hope, Yosh," I smile. She returns the smile but it doesn't reach her eyes.

"Well I for one would like to believe that all men are assholes so that my thing with Bless doesn't seem that shitty. If they're all rubbish then maybe I have the crème de la crème of rubbish. It's what keeps me sane," Carmen says stuffing three chips in her mouth at once. Yoshi's expression slips further, but she corrects it in record time -there is something wrong with her and Ace, that's why she won't say anything. She's embarrassed. That's it; none of us safe from disappointment! If Yoshi, hands down the sweetest of the bunch, can't find happiness, then what chance do the rest of us cows have?

Fontaine sips her bottomless drink, an unattractive mix of Coke and Fanta that was this murky brown colour.

"Sometimes it's good to go a little crazy, Car; healthy even. Sane is safe. You can't learn much from being safe," she says casually. I peer at my curly haired compadre with fascination - Fontaine is always so collected, what does she know about going crazy?

"What was his name?" I ask.

"Who's name?"

"The guy who broke your heart?"

Her head whips in my direction and she gives me an amused look as if she's pleased that I had figured out that her wisdom had been gained from an unpleasant experience.

Fontaine leans back in her seat, all eyes now on her.

"Nadia," she says simply. "Her name was Nadia."

It as if we're now stuck in our little teen bubble and everything outside of it has been put on mute. Lunch is suddenly a lot more interesting.

For a while no one says anything until good old reliable big mouth Carmen breaks the silence.

"You're a lezza?"

Fontaine giggles a little and shakes her head, "No Car, I'm not a *lezza.*"

"So you used to be a lezza?"

Fontaine shakes her head again, "I'm bi-sexual," she smiles taking another sip.

The stunned silence returns.

Now don't get me wrong, I have no problems with anyone's sexuality, I just assumed that Fontaine was straight. I have never even seen her so much as bat an eyelash at girl; she always seems to be all about the dudes, namely Leon as of late.

I hope that the silence won't last any longer; I don't want Fontaine to get offended, because this is genuine shock, not judgment, but I honestly don't know what to say. This has me thrown.

Astonishingly, Yoshi is the one who speaks up. "Like real-life bi-sexual, or 'this is just something I'm going to try because I'm bored, plus boys think it's kind of hot' bi-sexual?"

Fontaine laughs and I feel Carmen exhale next to me. The atmosphere is relaxed once again.

"If I'm being honest, I think it might have started out as boredom…and for more male attention –they love all that girl on girl stuff -but after I got into it, I realized that I actually do like women."

"Shut up, you like getting head on a regular basis," Carmen interjects.

"That was definitely a plus, but no, I genuinely like women. There's something amazing about being with one, that no man can replicate."

"Yeah; a vagina."

We all snicker nosily drawing a few disapproving looks from a few people around us.

"So, Nadia broke your heart..." I say after we've quieted down, ready to hear my first girl on girl love story gone wrong.

"Yup, she did. Fucking prick!" Fontaine curses, taking a swig of her discoloured drink in the same manner that you would knock back alcohol. It's intriguing to hear her insult her ex-girlfriend the way that we would insult our ex-boyfriends, but what did I expect? People are people.

"What did she do?" Yoshi asks finally unfolding her arms and picking up her fork to push her rice around her plate some more.

Fontaine tugs one of her curly copper/blonde locks and sighs, "She messed me about. Nadia was one of those girls that were insanely beautiful and knew it. Once a woman knows exactly how appealing they are it tends to go to their head and they use their looks to manipulate people so that they can get what they want. The thing about Nadia was that she didn't know what the fuck it was she really wanted. She was attracted to me but she didn't want to be," she frowned.

"She would tell me over and over that what we were doing was wrong but that she couldn't help herself because she loved me so much. I never got what was wrong about us. Yeah sure, we weren't traditional, but the way I look at it, love translates the same in any language.

"She was very on and off with me, but I stuck around hoping that because this was new territory for the both of us, that eventually she'd grow out of it and just accept us for what we were, but she didn't.

"After a year of the same tired arguments it dawned on me that maybe she didn't really love me; she was using me to fulfil a fantasy. But you know me; fuck the fake shit, I ain't no God damn fantasy, I'm real! I told her that she either did this with me properly or we were done. So she left."

She looked at Carmen, "It hurt like hell, but it was a lesson I needed to learn. If you give someone your all, and they still aren't willing to do right by you, then you need to let them go. Sometimes people just use you because you're convenient or you're good enough for 'right now' but they have no intention of truly reciprocating your feelings. Sometimes an ultimatum can be the key to your freedom. It may not feel like it at first, but it is," she smiles.

"I'm not as strong as you Fonts. I don't want to lose him."

"If you don't really have him then what is there to lose?"

Good question.

In situations similar to what she described, it would help to be as rational as Fontaine was, but yet we can't always bring ourselves to do it until we're all bruised and battered to the point that we just give up. Once it's over, THEN we rationalise everything, but by then it's too little too late anyway; the damage is done.

If Carmen gave Bless an ultimatum and he backed off, all she would lose is an illusion, but we all knew she wouldn't, at least not for now. Carmen still has hope.

Some people need illusions to make life a little more bearable, which raises the question; are they optimists or are they just scared of reality?

Carmen is awfully quiet and that is saying something as she always has something to say.

"You okay?" I ask, nudging her with my elbow.

Carmen shrugs, "I dunno. Oprah over there's got me feeling all shitty," she says glaring at Fontaine.

"What did I do?" Fontaine asks innocently. Technically she hasn't done anything wrong, but the advice she had given has lowered the mood a little...for Carmen anyway, I've been miserable for weeks.

"You spoke sense." Carmen snaps.

"That's a bad thing?"

"No, but sometimes we don't want to be reminded of how much life really sucks."

"Life doesn't suck, Bless does. If you want better, go get better, babe. You're gorgeous with great legs, a flat tummy and a killer set of knockers; it won't be hard." Fontaine smiles, swirling the ice around in her glass. The ice cubes clink noisily against the glass; the sound is calming, so for no reason other than that, I mimic her and shuffle in my seat to face at Carmen.

"Look, I protested and protested but you lot were adamant that we were going to have girl time, knowing exactly what it involves, and now we're having it. Don't complain."

"Init! I dunno about you lot, but I'm having a blast. This is so 'Sex and the City'," Fontaine chortles.

"How is this anything like Sex and the City? We're sulking in Nando's!" Carmen points out haughtily.

"Cause we're four fabulous girlfriends 'lunching' together and complaining about our love lives."

"Or lack thereof," I mumble. "More like Vex in the City if you ask me."

"I'm Charlotte," Yoshi yells shooting her hand into the air.

"Well we know that. You're the prissiest one out of all of us," Carmen snorts.

"If she's Charlotte then I'm Samantha," says Fontaine.

"What, cause you're a slut and you love it?"

"Exactly!" she laughs.

Carmen and I look at each other. There are only two characters left; Carrie and Miranda.

Before I can open my mouth Carmen says, "Trust and know that I ain't Miranda. She's ugly, and so is her baby."

"What, so I'm Miranda?"

"I never said you had to be, but I ain't that bitch."

"I'm Carrie!"

"There can only be one Carrie."

We look at each other and I get that same twinge of intuition I had about Carmen the night of the Fresher's rave. She won't say it outright, but it's obvious she still wants my spot.

"I like him soooo much and he just doesn't fuckin' get it! I'm better than all those other girls rolled up into one. Why doesn't he realize how lucky he is to have me?" Carmen growls. We have been discussing her issues with Bless again for a while now and I'm starting to feel like maybe these men aren't the problem; maybe it's us. After all, the heartbreakers (them) are happily living their lives while the broken hearted (us) are sitting in Nando's moaning about them but refusing to move on for our own good.

"Carmen, please," Fontaine begs in an exasperated tone, "Enough already. If you're not going to leave him then I don't want to hear another word."

"I want to," Carmen pouts "but he's so hot!"

Fontaine rolls her eyes which consequently land on me. From the glimmer of expectation in her eyes it is clear that all of the minor news is out of the way and now it is time for the grand finale. I finally get to reveal the shambles that is my love life. Lucky me!

"You ready to talk yet?" she asks.

"No."

"Tough. Spill!"

All eyes are on me and for the first time since starting Brompton university, I don't like it. I take a moment to gather my thoughts and then I begin.

"Okay, so you're all aware that I left Sunday Slam with Carter Johnson?"

"Uh yeah! Who isn't? Everyone's been talking about it for weeks. I thought it would have died down by now but you, Georgia and Sky indirecting each other on Twitter added fuel to the fire. Everyone wants to know what really happened, especially us!" says Carmen excitedly.

"Yeah, did you have sex with him or what?" Fontaine asks getting straight to the point.

"No," I register the disappointment on their faces when I deny the rumours. "When we got to his car, Nate was parked up waiting for us." The girls perk back up again.

Yoshi leans forward "No way! What was Nate doing there?"

"Apparently he knew that Carter going to try something because of some unsettled beef they had involving Georgia_"

"Oh yeah, I heard about that. She used to go out with Carter init?" Fontaine asks for confirmation. I nod.

"Okay, so what happened next?"

"They start getting into it_"

"They were fighting?" Carmen gasps

"No! Will you lot shut up and let me finish." They all bow their heads and press their lips together.

I continue, "They get a bit physical and Carter says something to Nathaniel…I can't remember what it was, I was too drunk to pay attention properly. Next thing I remember is waking up in Nathaniel's bed."

They all lean forward with excited looks on their faces. I narrow my eyes at them.

"Yes, we had sex."

My news is followed up by a chorus of gasps, cheers and oh my gods.

"How was it?"

"I lost count of my orgasms." I pause for another chorus of appreciative noises.

"We finally decided to give us another go…a few hours later Georgia turns up at his house."

Silence.

"He tells her to leave because he's with me and she decides to announce her fantastic news; the Nathaniel got her pregnant! Ta daaa. That's why I hate my life. Can we go home now?" I grimace. Hearing about the girls problems was easy. Hearing my own was as hard as it was the day everything fell apart.

"Oh my God, that's awful. Rio, I'm so sorry," Yoshi frowns running around the table to hug me.

Carmen is seething.

"How could he do that to you after_" I shoot her a silencing look. As she was the closest to me out of the girls, I'd told her about the abortion. I didn't want anyone else to know.

Fontaine clocked on, "After what?"

I shake my head, "It's nothing. Bottom line is Nate and I have a lot of history together, a history that Georgia participated in heavily, and the moment we finally work things out, she messes it up again. The thing is, as much as I hate her for this, I'm even madder at him. Why would he sex her raw? It's like he wanted to get her pregnant!"

"Now Rio that's not fair_"

"The fuck you mean it ain't fair?" Carmen snarls at her, more affected by the news than the others because she knew the deepness of it all.

"People make mistakes Carmen!"

"Are you really defending him right now? NATHANIEL got GEORGIA, the girl who broke him and Rio up before, PREGNANT! There's a mistake and then there's pro-creating with your side-bitch!"

Fontaine fans Carmen off and focuses on me.

"Have you spoken to Nate about it since?"

"No."

"Why not?"

"What's the point? It won't change anything. What's he gonna tell me? He's sorry? I know he's sorry. Nate's been sorry and to be honest I don't want or need to hear it anymore. Like you said before, some things ain't meant to be and Nate and I just happen to be one of those things."

"Has he tried to speak to you?" Yoshi asks.

I roll my eyes, "He's been calling, texting, Whatsapping, DMing, inboxing me on Facebook, emailing..."

"Woah! He must really wanna talk to you," she says returning to her seat.

"Init! I think you should hear him out?" Fontaine says. Carmen glares at her.

"Not gonna happen. I think I may just have to stay away from guys altogether..." I trail off dramatically hinting that there's more to my terrible tale. Instinctively, they lean in in perfect unison.

I scrunch up my face and confess, "I tried to have sex with Tyson."

"I'm sorry, what?" Yoshi asks as if she hadn't heard me.

"Please don't make me repeat it, I already feel like an idiot."

"Oh my God! When was this?"

"About two days after I came back from Nate's. I've never been so embarrassed in my life!" I wail burying my face in my hands.

"Why, what happened?"

"He said no," I mumble incoherently through my fingers.

"What?" they all chime.

I huff and tear my hands off of my face.

"He. Said. No."

"Didn't see that coming. The way Tyson carries on I thought he'd jump at the chance," Fontaine chuckles.

"So did I. He said he wanted too, but not with me in the state I was. I was crying and throwing myself at him. It was pathetic."

"Well I'm glad he turned you down," Carmen says approvingly, "When you two get together, it has to be because you both want each other, not because you can't have someone else."

Carmen has been trying to get me to give into Tyson for ages; she's convinced he's the one for me. I secretly wished that I felt the same; things would be so much easier.

18
50 Shades of Grey.

I decide that it is time for me to go back to lectures -no point in taking out this hefty student loan if I'm not gonna make the most of it. It's Monday morning and my first lesson is going to be the toughest to get through; English Literature -Nathaniel.

I strut into the lecture hall a little more overdressed than usual. I'm in black jeans with a pair of 4 inch patent yellow ankle-boots, teamed with a retro yellow 'Little Miss Sunshine' baby tee that I borrowed from Yoshi. As Yoshi's frame is a lot smaller than mine the top was VERY snug around my bust and left a bit of my midriff on show for all to see. Over the top is my black leather jacket, plus a huge pair plastic yellow half-moon hoops hanging from my ears.

Apparently there is talk of my social ascension being in decline but I'm determined to show the gossips that it's still early days and that I wasn't going anywhere yet. When my time is over it will be on my terms, not theirs.

I ignore the faces that turn to watch me as I make my way to my usual seat in the back. A few murmurs buzz around the room when they realise that I am going to sit next to Nathaniel; they knew something is up between us. Probably that bloody Carter rumour. Why am I going to sit next to him, you ask? Because I can. I'm still not a fan of his, but what strength can I show to my peers if I shy away from him? I need to seem like I'm still in control; sitting next to Nathaniel is merely a social statement. When we were in college and I decided to avoid

Nathaniel at every turn after we broke up, it only made me look like a victim. Worse than that, because I was no longer in his company, I no longer got to associate with his crowd –that is not happening this time. I can be somewhat civil if it will aid me in my quest.

I approach the back of the lecture hall, and there, smack-bang in the middle of the row of polyester-cushioned, burgundy, flip-down seats, commanding the attention of three admirers, is Nathaniel.

One of the girls, with a sprinkle of freckles across her nose, spots me coming and nudges her friend. "Oh my God; look who's back!" she gasps with a giggle.

Her friend with long Poetic Justice braids who I recognize as Tanya Woods, one of Georgia's girls, swings around to make a snotty face at me.

"Ew! Rio Greene. Finally ready to show her face again is she? And what is she wearing? We're in lecture, not Sunday Slam!" she says a little louder than necessary -it's obvious that she wants me to hear her.

At the sound of my name, Nathaniel stops talking to the leggy blonde girl on his left and glances at me. His expression gives nothing away but I notice him subtly lean away from blondie.

Freckle face leans closer to Tanya and says quietly, "Speaking of Sunday Slam, did you see her leave with Carter Johnson a few weeks back? I heard that was the same night she met him!"

"Ugh, she's so thirsty. I bet she fucked him too!" Tanya laughs.

Nathaniel's doesn't like that. The muscle in his jaw is clenching and unclenching.

"She never fucked him!" he growls at her. Tanya stops snickering and takes up a defensive posture,

"And how would you know? You weren't there."

"Because I know," he says plainly, unleashing his steeliest glare on her. She doesn't say another word.

I march down the aisle sneering at Tanya and freckle face who is sitting next to him. I don't recognize her as part of the 'in crowd' so I shall speak to her as tactlessly as I like.

"You're in my seat."

She looks up at me and returns an equally venomous look.

"What is this, primary school? The seats aren't allocated darlin', so no, I am in fact NOT in your seat." She cuts her eyes at me and turns back to Nate.

His amused eyes watch me curiously and as much as I don't want to, I meet his gaze. My stomach flips and my heart aches, while my brain screams for me to leave him alone; but I can't. If she isn't going to move then that is fine with me; after all, it's just a chair. I don't care about the chair.

I break eye contact with him and glare down at freckle face again.

"Fine. Stay here," I smile icily. I lock eyes with Nate again, purposely staring into them trying to show that I'm not shaken, even though I am. True to form, my body reacts to him and the edges of his lips quirk up.

"Can we talk?" I ask gesturing my head further down the aisle where no one is sitting. Nathaniel nods, picks up his things and follows me to a more private section of the lecture hall. Glancing over my shoulders I smile triumphantly at the girls.

Wordlessly we take our seats. My heart is hammering against my rib cage but I'm focusing on breathing deeply so as to maintain my cool.

Our lecturer, Rose Littman, walks briskly into the room with her Miu Miu frames perched on her astute nose and her arms clutching thick volumes while her kaftan billows out behind her. She dumps the books on the podium before pushing her glasses up and addressing us.

"Morning everyone, hope you all had a good weekend. This week we're going to be reviewing the works of some of my personal favourites; the Brontë sisters. You should each have your copy of Emily Brontë's 'Wurthering Heights'…"

Rose continues to twitter on and I take out my MacBook completely ignoring Nathaniel's impatient gaze. Eventually it becomes apparent to him that I have no intention to speak so takes the lead.

"So…how have you been?" He sounds nervous. I don't respond.

"I take it you're still mad at me."

I roll my eyes. He sighs.

"You said you wanted talk…"

I keep my eyes fixed straight ahead, "I lied. I don't want to talk to you, I just don't want you talking to them." I say flatly, switching my MacBook on.

Nathaniel pauses as if I've just slapped him in the face (the idea sounds tempting), then kisses his teeth.

"Are you being serious?"

"Yes. Now be quiet, I'm trying to listen."

He shifts in his seat to stand and return to where he is wanted but I put my hand on his leg to stop him.

"What is wrong with you? This is why we never resolve anything, 'cause you love to play these petty games."

"Where are you going?" I ask stonily.

"Back to my seat."

I scoff, "I don't think so. Sit down." If he thinks I'm about to let him cause me any further embarrassment by re-joining Tanya, freckle face and blondie after I'd made such a show of asserting my superiority, then he has another thing coming.

Nathaniel glares at me and yanks my hand from his leg.

Rose looks up at us and furrows her brow.

"Is there a problem Nathaniel?"

"No Rose," he says as calmly as he can muster through gritted teeth.

"Well can you stop distracting Rio please? She's missed enough lessons as it is." She says firmly.

"I told him to be quiet Rose, but you know Nathaniel; never listens." I smile only to wind him up further.

"Hence he's retaking this class." She resumes her twittering.

Nathaniel scowls at me, "You think that's funny?"

"Sshhh, you're distracting me." A cryptic smile plays across my lips. For once I am the one controlling the situation and it feels empowering seeing him get so riled up to the point that he's losing his cool in public. I relish his reactions to my passive aggressive behavior so much that my only desire is to make him madder.

Nathaniel's eyes light up and the grey storm clouds come rolling in. The muscle in his jaw is tense and embossed in his butterscotch skin.

"You're not the only one who can play games you know," he warns through clenched teeth.

The lecture begins. The house lights dim and the pearlescent glow from the OHP illuminates the room bathing it in a soft white light. My senses kicked into overdrive. Suddenly this doesn't seem like such a good idea anymore -I'm too close to him. His anger has warmed his skin so much that I could feel it through my jacket and now his face, his frame, his delectable scent is too much for me to handle.

He edges closer to me and slides his hand discreetly under the table and onto my thigh.

I stiffen as he leans in and skims the tip of his nose along my jaw line until his lips graze my ear lobe.

"Nathaniel, what are you doing?" I panic.

His hand moves higher.

"You may be mad at me, but you're still mine and you know it," he whispers.

I push his hand away, "Nathaniel, stop!" I hiss.

"Sshh, you're distracting me," he taunts putting his hand back, squeezing my thigh. "You need to watch your mouth Ri. Don't you ever for a second forget who you're talking to." He squeezes even higher and a hushed involuntary noise rushes out of me. It had been quiet enough, but I knew he heard it loud and clear. Nathaniel smirks and turns his head towards the wordy projection on the screen.

"Open your legs, Rio." He orders, sending bolts of eroticism through my anatomy. My cheeks flush with mortification.

"No. I shouldn't even be letting you_"

His quiet baritone cuts me off.

"Rio; open-your-legs." My stomach muscles tighten. What is going on here? We're supposed to be fighting and I'm supposed to be in control but my malicious taunting provoked him into turning this into a sadistically sensual power game. I don't like it, but at the same time I want him to do it again, because a little voice in the singing in the pit of my stomach tells me I should, and you know we should always adhere to what the little voices say...

I close my eyes wishing that my wayward thoughts would shut up but they don't. Instead they make my longing for his touch greater and cause me to part my legs a little, encouraging him to dominate me. No matter how angry I am with him, I don't think I could ever not WANT him like this. I can pretend not to want to be with him until the cows come home, but when it comes to sex, Nathaniel is undeniable. Even now as we sit here furious with each other, the sexual energy throbs around us like a pulse.

I lay my hand on his leg and my stomach flips. I'm scared of what we are doing; it's unpredictable and daring, which only makes its allure all the more inviting. Maybe this is why people like to have angry sex. The thrill of wanting to make someone pay for their wrong doing with perverse pleasure lures you deeper into the depths of its kaleidoscopic darkness. This is the equivalent of standing starving in a room of the sweetest, shiniest ruby red apples and not being allowed to eat them. I am Eve and Nathaniel is the serpent, beckoning me from the tree of forbidden fruit, daring me to take a bite. If I follow through with this, I'm afraid that I won't be able to turn my back on him ever again.

I'm about to be sensible and remove my hand when his fingers skim my centre. My stomach clenches again.

I don't know what getting an erection feels like for boys, but if it's the same tummy-shuddering-inner-wall-clenching feeling that we girls get when we get turned on, then they sure do hide it well. I'm finding it hard to sit completely still while this is happening. Every jolt runs from between my legs to the rest of my body and I have to tense up to keep from moving. That's why when we ladies climax we look like we're having an epileptic fit; it's all of the jolts merging together.

I stroke his inner-thigh with my fingertips. He reciprocates the motion. I exhale. My fingers travels higher, skimming the anatomic contours of his trousers.

"Tell me you're still mine," he growls increasing the pressure on my thigh a little, his fingers massaging small individual circles into my flesh.

Clench, clench, shudder, jolt, jolt, jolt. Shit!

"No."

His index finger pressing into the crevice between the end of my thigh and the beginning of my...

I inhale deeply and gasp.

Nathaniel leans over slightly and whispers an order in my ear, "If you won't tell me with your mouth, your body will speak for you. Open your legs; properly."

I shoot him a dubious look "What if I don't want to?" I challenge.

"You want to," he assures me with charismatic, masochistic determination. He presses against the crevice again.

Shudder. Clench. Release.

"Open your legs baby," his inner serpent hisses seductively. He manoeuvres his fingers to the right and caresses the sore spot, slowly working my legs open. I about to bite the apple; it's too delicious to pass up.

He turns back to the OHP and plasters a look of concentration on his devilishly handsome face. I surrender and followed suit, breathing in through my nose and out through my mouth.

"If you make a noise, I'll stop," he threatens adding another element to his game.

His large fingers stroke me up and down through my trousers, all the while his face remains casual as if he is unaware of what he is doing. I purse my lips, holding my war cries in as I fight to keep still while he tortures me sweetly in a room full of people. The pressure of his strokes increase and the movement under the fabric becomes more fluid. He focuses his attention on my epicentre, exchanging his strokes with rapid circular motions. My breathing is strained but I'm too scared to hold my breath incase I implode from adding light-headedness to the mixture. I squirm and whimper.

"Sshh baby," Nate hushes me pressing harder and circling faster. He is cruel. How am I supposed to stay silent when he is determined to make me come undone? I close my eyes and try and focus on getting my breathing back to normal.

When I almost have it under control he takes me by surprise and his fingers slithered up over the waistband of my jeans and into my knickers. His fingers are cool against my warmth and I gasp.

"I meant what I said, Rio. Don't make a noise or I'll stop," he threatens again, caressing me, skin to skin.

Shudder...shudder...shudder…gasp.

"Sshh."

Shudder...shudder…gasp…gasp.

"Hush baby. You're almost there. Be quiet." He plunges into me…oh dear God!

Shuddershuddershuddershudder.

JOLT!

I swear I tried my hardest to hold it in and the noise wasn't even that loud; it sounded like a mouse being gagged, but he tore his hand away and left me aching trying to discreetly gasp for air.

Two people in front turn to look at us suspicious, but we avoid their eyes, keeping ours fixed on the OHP as if nothing had happened. By this time Nate's hand is safely back in his lap and vice versa.

I wait for a moment for the heat to die down before trying to pull his hand back.

He shakes his head, "I told you, if you make a noise I'll stop. It's over."

"But_"

"No buts. You broke the rules."

He kept his word and didn't touch me for the rest of the lesson while I shook my leg in frustration trying to ease my arousal. I cursed myself for giving into him again after I'd sworn to myself that the last time was the last time. That's thing about addictions; even though you know they're bad for you, sooner or later, you always go back for more.

19
New Girl.

I'm sitting at a small study table behind a shelf of books in the economics section of the Brompton university library, buried deep in the back where hardly any students lurk, pretending to be deeply engrossed in a physics text book. I don't even take physics but it was the first book I could grab on my way in. My notebook lies open on the table; random scribbles are scrawled on the almost empty page. So far I've drawn three flowers, that stupid 'S' thing that we all did back in primary school and a few of those line houses that you draw without taking the pen from the paper. To an unaware passer-by it would look as if I was half-heartedly doing my work, but if they took the time to look a little closer they would notice the way I squirmed with delight in my seat with the hem of my midi skirt hiked up to the upper half of my thighs, legs parted, biting my lip and clutching my pen for dear life as Nathaniel French kissed me under the table.

These hidden erotic exhibitions have been going on for a few weeks now. Nathaniel and I pick fights with each other over our many unresolved issues and then the tantalizingly merciless game begins. On most occasions we would play our little game in our English Literature lecture while Rose and the rest of the class discussed the destructive relationship between Cathy and Heathcliff, but as of late Nathaniel had felt the need to branch out. So far we'd gotten hot and heavy in the girls bathrooms at LiqFest, behind the campus bike shed, on one of the more secluded walkways between two student accommodation buildings, in one of the computer rooms, an empty classroom that we'd happened to find unlocked one day, and now the library. All of those locations and I had had not been permitted to reach the point of climax in any of them! Why? Because I still struggle to keep quiet. Any legible noise I make, he stops.

I've often thought about finishing myself off, but I never do because I've been instructed not to. As infuriating as this little game of his is, I enjoy the feel of all that pent up arousal building up every time he leaves me hanging -it makes me want him even more. We hadn't gone all the way yet, but when we do, it is sure to be earth-shattering after all of this prolonged foreplay.

I arched my back, pressing my lips to his lips as I fight back the quivering moan in my throat, trying to handle this illicit heaven in silence. Slowly I gyrate against his mouth as subtly as I can muster, causing the chair to creak in time with me. He grips my hips, holding me still, and then he pulls me closer so I can feel his desire deeper within me.

I grip the table and whimper. He retreats.

"Fuck!" I curse under my breath smacking my palm against the table top in frustration.

Nathaniel emerges from under the table, his electric eyes burn roguishly. I scowl at him and yank my skirt down.

He smirks at me, then licking his lips he says throatily, "Mmm; you were almost there baby."

He walks off leaving me alone with my maddening ache and a clenched fist with his name on it. After a few minutes of allowing my body to calm down, I gather my belongings, shove the physics text book into a random shelf, too annoyed to put it back where I got it from, and exit the building to take a much needed cold shower before I meet up with Tyson.

It's early December and Tyson and I had decided that before I completely abolish the miserable remains of my student loan, that we'd go Christmas shopping in Southside. To tell you the truth I'm not in the mood to go shopping, at least not with Tyson anyway. Ever since the night I'd thrown myself at him like some desperate housewife, the energy between us had been a little weird. We haven't really spoken about it and although that's more than fine with me, I know that we have to in order to move forward otherwise we'd just be stuck in this weird place of friends forcing friendship on each other. Tyson carries on as if nothing had happened and tries to carry on as normal, which I appreciate of course, but I feel as if we're watching what we say to each other sometimes. It's constantly like having the first conversation you have with a good friend after falling out every time we speak and I hate it. I hate it even more because I know it's my fault. This isn't us.

I check my hair in my standardized student bathroom mirror once more before shaking my head in annoyance. Why am

I worrying so much about what my hair looks like? It's only Tyson; the boy who had seen me wet myself when I was 5 years old because I had been too focused on waiting until Power Rangers was over to go to the toilet even though I was bursting. I chuckle at the memory; me screaming as I run and wee on the way to the bathroom and Tyson's high pitched laugh while he points at me with one hand and clutches his tummy with the other. My nick-name was Pee-o for weeks after that. As I study my carefully crafted curls in the mirror I wish that those days of friendly innocence would return. Life was so much simpler when we were young. One day you wake up and you're not a child anymore and the world is suddenly complicated because you know too much, but you still don't know enough. I don't know why I'm double checking my appearance for my best friend. He can act like there is nothing wrong as much as he wants, but actions speak louder than words. If we were really okay then he would have come upstairs and chilled on my bed, yelling insults at me so I'd hurry up. I'm not completely satisfied with my appearance but I accept that it's too late for me to change it now. He Whatsapped me 5 minutes ago to say he is waiting for me outside by his car, and I had kept him out there long enough already.

I exit my boxy bathroom, slip my feet into my Ugg boots, tug on my Cossack hat, wrap my super long scarf around my neck three times, and fasten the belt around my fur gilet, stuff my fingers into my gloves, and pick up my River Island tote bag, ready to face the boy who used to be my best friend.

Tyson is leant against his car dressed in all black, with my Obviously bobble hat covering his braids. Pressed up against him very familiarly -to my complete surprise -is a tiny brown skin girl that I don't recognize, with huge brown Bambi eyes, a cute smile that makes Tyson smile back every time she grins adoringly up at him, and assets that make me wonder how she manages to stand up without toppling over. Her hair is cut close, sculpted into perfect ebony waves against her scalp, and every time she smiles (which is pretty often) these deep dimples appear in her cheeks. She looks like a sexy cherub; she's adorable. I hate her on sight.

"Hey," I say unevenly, studying the two of them.

The cherub eases off of Tyson and smiles at me.

"Hi," she waves sweetly. I force a polite smile back so as not to seem rude.

Tyson straightens up and pokes me in my side. I don't want him to touch me right now.

"About time Ri. We almost froze to death waiting for you," he jokes.

I roll my eyes and say, "Whatever," as lightly as I can, when what I really want to say is "I dunno why you're moanin' when all of two seconds ago you and this pixie looked like you were ready to sing each other love songs."

It's in that moment that I realize that I am jealous. I've been jealous of Tyson's female companions before, but never like this. THIS bothers me; I know it shouldn't, but it does. Ty hasn't mentioned a female of any significance to me in a while and he never brings the girls he's fooling around with around me, so who is she? Is she the real reason he turned me down?

I look at dimples then back at Tyson, waiting for him to introduce us. He purposely busies himself with getting his key out of his pocket so I decide to introduce myself.

I stick my hand out, "I'm Rio."

She shakes my hand and smiles some more, "I know, Sonny talks about you all the time. It's lovely to finally meet you. I'm Angelica," she replies cheerily.

Sonny? That's not even cute! If you're gonna shorten his name then it's Ty, T if you're pushing it, but not Sonny.

I release her hand and raise my eyebrow at Tyson who is still avoiding looking at me. Angelica had heard of me but I never even knew she existed -this is what I mean about us not being the same anymore.

"My girlfriend," he clarifies confirming my assumption.

I look at Angelica again in her cable knit leggings and tiny furry winter boots. I dislike her even more now.

"Girlfriend? Oh wow! Um, okay. How come I've never see you on campus before?" I ask fishing for information seeing as it is obvious that Ty is in no hurry to tell me. I see him look at me out of the corner of my eye.

"Oh, I don't go here," she cuddles up to him and slips her hand into his, her petite fingers are swallowed by his. Why is she so small?

"Oh! Where do you go?" More like how the hell do you two know each other!

"Herring," she says proudly. I mentally roll my eyes. It's not Brompton so it's nothing to be proud of. Herring is second in line for the trendy urban uni crown. They almost won the title this year but let's be serious, did they really think Brompton would give it up so easily? Herring is full of the people who didn't have the grades to get into Brompton, and the losers who wanted to start a new legacy. Angelica is one of these losers. Okay I need to stop; this girl is being perfectly nice to me and I'm being a bitch.

"Oh you're one of them," I say playfully trying to soften my snide undertone, "So how did you and Tyson meet?"

"What is this, 21 questions?" Tyson cuts in, tired of my digging. I narrow my eyes at him. First he tells me nothing about this girl then plops her in front of me and gets defensive when I ask questions. What is his problem?

"Sonny, don't be rude!" she gasps, swatting his arm.

There's that stupid nickname again. His name is TY, you irritating garden gnome!

"Yeah, *Sonny*!" I don't cover up my snide tone this time.

"We met about two months ago at Sunday Slam," she informs me dreamily, "We talked a little here and there, you know, through Twitter, Facebook and stuff and now, here we are!" she says with an animated flourish of her hands.

"Magical! I smile tightly.

Ignoring my bitchy sarcasm, Tyson laughs at her with a sickening fondness, and takes Angelica's other hand, pulling her into a full embrace. She gazes up at him and springs onto her tiptoes with her lips puckered. He unleashes the crooked smile and leans down to kiss her gently. They look like the personification of Jack and the Beanstalk; ridiculous! Ty is damn near 6ft and this girl looks as if she is barely scraping 5ft. I divert my eyes and clear my throat.

"Sorry," she giggles her apology, "he's just so cute."

"Oh, he's something!" I reply brandishing another tight smile whilst simultaneously glaring at him. He shrugs.

"You lot can discuss my many upstanding qualities in the car. We're already running late."

What?

"You're coming?" I ask her incredulously? She finally stops smiling and Tyson furrows his brow at me.

"Yeah; is that a problem?"

I open my mouth to reply, but Tyson beats me to it.

"Course not babe; Rio just ain't used to having to share me."

"Mmm," I agree through pursed lips. I sound constipated.

Angelica starts beaming again and touches my arm reassuringly, "Oh, I see. Well these things take time. You'll get used to it."

"Mmm," I repeat.

With arms full of festive themed shopping bags filled with gifts for our nearest and dearest, Christmas cards, rolls of sparkly wrapping paper, sellotape and tags, Tyson and I walk down the lamp lit street to our mother's houses. The air is so cold that we can see our breath, made even chillier by the icy wind that whips around us and whistles through the bare trees that line the street, all their leaves a muddy brown, strewn across the pavement and smushed into slushy muck, decorated with random assortments of the days litter and cigarette butts. The sky is an inky black with no stars visible because of the heavy clouds which shield the moon like a smoky curtain. I can hear the cars and buses rushing past on the main road, the faint click clack of the trains, and the sounds of chatter and televisions coming from the homes, some emitting mouth-watering smells of their evening meals, mixed with the smell of damp London. It had been a while since we'd visited our mothers so we figured that as we were in the area we might as well stay at home for the weekend.

Angelica had been dropped off at her Dad's house and I could finally wear my irritation on my sleeve; I'd been struggling with it all day and had decided that it was okay not to like her because I did genuinely find her extremely annoying. If I had to hear her giggle or squeal '*Sonny*' one more time I would have lost it. She was just too cutesy and it was all getting to be too much.

"Angelica seems nice," I comment casually, looking up at the hidden moon. Tyson grips his shopping a little tighter; we haven't said a word to each other since Angelica skipped out of his car and we'll be going our separate ways soon, so I dove straight in. This boy has some explaining to do. It's one thing that this girl is a significant part of his life now, but that fact that he kept his relationship from me hurt. I know I'm being a hypocrite as I hadn't exactly told him about my endeavours with Nathaniel, but that is with good reason; he'd go into one if he knew. Anyway this isn't about me; it's about him and his Oompa Loompa!

"Yeah, she is," he replies plainly, giving nothing more away.

I try another angle.

"You two seem serious."

"I guess you could say that."

"Hmm. I still find it a bit odd that you never mentioned her."

Tyson huffs, "Yeah well, you know now, init," he snaps.

What is his problem? I stop walking and shove him.

"I don't like the way you sprung her on me Ty; that wasn't cool. You and this girl have been talking for months and you never mentioned her once! What the hell?"

Tyson rolls his eyes, "Rio, don't start! I didn't feel like sharing her yet, that's all."

"What, and you felt like sharing her today? Surprise Rio, here's my secret girlfriend!" I yell waving my arms about.

"Yes. Can we talk about something else now?" he snarls. I shove him again.

"No we cannot talk about something else!" I scream. "We're supposed to be best friends, how could you not tell me you had a girlfriend?"

"How could you not tell me you're back with Nate?"

I'm silenced. How did he know? Who saw us? Who told him?

"No, no, don't go quiet just because the spotlight is on you now. Talk!" he half yells.

I look down and shrug.

"What do you want me to say Ty?"

"I want you to tell me why the FUCK you're still messing with him when not too long ago you were locked away in your room crying because of him."

"It's nothing…honestly."

"It's never 'nothing' when it comes to him, so spare me the bullshit, okay."

I sigh, "I dunno what it is. It's just sex...sort of… It's complicated."

"You're damn right it's complicated! It's like you'd rather be fucked over than have someone treat you right. Sometimes I think you deserve everything he does to you," he sneers.

My mouth falls open.

"How can you say that?"

"'Cause it's true! You two we're together, he cheated on you, and you broke up. A year later you get back together, and then find out that he got the girl he cheated on you with pregnant, so you broke up again -bearing in mind that this was in the space of a day! Then you come running to me like I'm some side man, knowing exactly how I feel about you. After all that, you're back there again, but this time you're playing the side bitch to his baby mum -who he's still sleeping with by the way. What the fuck is wrong with you? Are you *that* fucking damaged?"

I clench my fists by my sides fighting the urge to punch him in the face because I knew I shouldn't. Everything he said is true and I had been telling myself the same thing since I'd stupidly succumbed to Nathaniel's seduction, but when all the drama was bundled into one and thrown at me like that by my best friend, it felt like a heavy slap in the face.

A tear fell.

"I didn't know he was still sleeping with her?" I sniff quietly, "And I never meant to drag you into this Ty; you know I'd never want to hurt you. I'm so sorry."

Tyson shakes his head, "You're not sorry, 'cause if you were you would have stopped messing with him! Rio, I've had your back from day! Every time you needed someone, I was there and look at how you're doing me! You only wanted to sleep with me because you felt lonely. You expected me to do it because you know how much I…" he closes his eyes and take a deep breathe to calm himself down. When he looks at me again his anger is clear as day "How could you go back to him and then get jealous because I got tired of waiting for you?"

"I'm sorry," I repeat, "I can't help it. You know how I feel about him_"

"YOU KNOW HOW I FEEL ABOUT YOU, RIO! But I guess as long as you get what you want, nothing else matters. You're so fucking selfish!"

I purse my lips together and look away.

"D'you know what? I'm over it! Do you! But when he fucks up again, don't come running to me, 'cause I won't care."

Tyson looks me up and down then storms off to his house, barging me out of the way with his shoulder when he passes.

It takes a moment to register, but once I realise what I've done, something in my chest quivers and snaps. I've finally done it; I've finally pushed Tyson's heart so far that he no longer has the reserved sign tapered across it. After years of gathering dust on the shelf, he has taken it down and offered it to someone else. I should be glad that he's finally moved on, but I'm not. I've lost him again, along with a large chunk of my dignity and control of my life.

Tyson is right; I'm Nate's bit on the side. Of course he's still sleeping with Georgia; they're having a baby and he hasn't had sex with me since he found out. This whole sordid thing really is just one of his power trips; he just wanted to prove that I still (willingly) belonged to him.

Somehow, after all that had happened, Georgia still came out on top and I'm left to fade into the background as usual, not only with the love of my life, but with my best friend too. I'm becoming insignificant once more and it's all because I wasn't strong enough to stay away from the boy who I had established a long time ago, wasn't good for me. I'd put in all this effort to free myself of him and turn my life around, only to run right back into his shackles decorated with our pernicious love, and I had only ended up making my life even worse.

I am damaged.

20
Radio.

As soon as I open the front door to my mum's house I can hear her favourite radio station, Vibez FM, playing in the background (with her singing merrily along), and the smell of something tasty hits my nose. My mum is cooking -I have come home at exactly the right time. With all the love that goes into soul food, even the most miserable individual can cheer up a little.

Living on campus away from my mother's catering meant that I only really ate proper food every now and then; it seemed like such a hassle to prepare a good meal every day when I was living on my own. Most of the time it was easy to prepare meals, take away, or the student staple once funds began to run low – instant noodles. Towards the end of term you had to get creative with your meals and make the best of what you had left in the kitchen. The girls and I have recently begun to gather together our remaining random edible food and tried to turn concoctions like rice, eggs, tuna, all-purpose seasoning, instant noodles and half a bottle of ketchup into something that Gordon Ramsey wouldn't hurl insults at us for-it was a hit and miss affair. Every student, when necessary, finds a way to become a budget Master Chef. Boys were lucky around this time of year, especially if they had befriended (generally) African girls on campus, because if they ran out of food (or couldn't cook) they could still get fed a decent meal. I had seen traditional bread-winner and housewife group setups on campus within the African community (even if any of the members of the group weren't in relationships) where the boys would purchase the food, and bring it back for the girls to prepare. The boys would then spend the rest of the evening in someone's dorm room playing video games, watching football -or any other way they could think of entertaining themselves -while all the girls would be in the kitchen preparing these huge meals.

It was as if these boys had found replacements for their mothers on campus. I knew it was partially a traditional thing, but sometimes it made me think that these girls were auditioning to play the role of the 'wifey' in the hope that one of the boys would realize what a good woman she was and snap her up. No judgement; we all do it to some extent, some of us reel them in with our other …talents –there are two types of women. For example, Yoshi hardly has to cook for Ace and they're official. They spend a lot of time in the bedroom with the music turned up really loud, and then afterward Ace takes her out to dinner or orders in.

I hang up my coat and push aside the strings of red, black, green and yellow wooden beads that hang from the top of the kitchen doorframe down to the floor creating an earthy clicking, clattering sound -I think my mother is the only person below 70 who still has this particular design aesthetic in their house.

"Hi mum!"

My mum spins around embarrassed that I have caught her dancing and singing along to some Beres Hammond track with her makeshift microphone – the pot spoon. She smiles widely at me, making the coppery skin at the edges of her eyes crinkle up.

"Rio, I didn't know you were coming today! What you doing down here?" she sings advancing on me -half walking, half dancing – with her arms outstretched awkwardly, trying to avoid putting her dough covered fingers on me. I meet her halfway and hug her, snuggling against her chest like a child. That is the good thing about living away from home; whenever you came back to visit it makes you appreciate what you thought you wanted to get away from, so much more. It's safe and warm here and I know that no matter what I do, there is always someone here that won't love me any less because of it.

I love my mum; she's a bit weird (she says vibrant), opinionated (she says honest), loud (passionate), loves a good gossip (*shrug*), stubborn (when I need to be), disorganized (free), and at times overbearing ("Rio, I'm your mother, it's my job!"), but she's wonderful. Everyone who meets my mum loves her straight away. She's one of those warm, whacky people who just wants the world to be a happy place –because of this trait, she's not always good when it comes to dealing with the bad things…my dad was one of them.

"Me and Ty went Christmas shopping," I hold my bags up "and we figured that as were down here we might as well visit you old maids," I grin.

She kisses her teeth and swipes a dough covered finger across my forehead.

"The cheek!" She dances her way back over to the huge silver pot bubbling on the stove.

"Something smells good."

"I know. I'm making Oxtail soup," she brags, dipping her 'mic' into the pot to stir the contents. Her long dreadlocks hang down her back, swishing back and forth over her bottom with each move she makes, the small gold adornments that she's decorated them with glinting in the light. I walked over to her and tug one gently. She fans me off. I grin; I've missed my Mum.

"You mind making the rest of the dumplings for me?" she gestures towards a soft mound of white dough in the mixing bowl on the counter beside her. I nod and go to wash my hands. When I was a little girl I always used to make the dumplings whenever my Mum required them. There was something fun about the squishy dough. It was like playing with plastercine that you could cook after you finished molding them. My Mum often ended up getting irritated with me because I spent ages shaping each lump of dough into hearts, flowers, stars, letters and whatever else I could come up with at the time. I felt like making a broken heart but I couldn't bear the thought of it popping up in my soup bowl and having to add more pieces to the debris.

"So, how's uni?" she asks.

Here we go. Why do parents do that? You don't see them for a bit and you miss them, then they start being all 'parenty', reminding you of why you were so eager to get away from them in the first place.

"Fine."

"What does fine mean?"

I roll my eyes, "Mum I just got here and you're nagging me already!" I moan.

"It's my job to nag you. You know how you get when left to your own devices," she gives me a knowing look. I throw my head back and sigh, grabbing a clump out dough out of the mound.

"Mum, please," I groan.

"Rio, I'm only you asking how university is going. Are you studying hard?"

"Yes Mum."

"Are you handing in your assignments on time?"

"Yes Mum."

"Are you punctual to your lectures?"

"Yeeeessss muuuum," I whine, already tired of her questions.

What is it with adults? As soon as you begin education it's like they forget that you have a life and ask you the same robotic questions over and over. It starts with 'How is nursery? Are you being a good girl?', then 'How's school?' When you start your GCSE's 'What GCSE's are you taking? You got any idea what you want to be? What college do you want to go to? What are you thinking of study in college?' You finally reach college and the questions pile up even more 'What college are you going to? Was that your first choice? How are you finding it? What are you studying? Do you like it? You working yet? Are you going to university or are you going to work fulltime? What uni are you going to? Are you staying on campus? You thought about what you want to be?' And the questions only get more irritating by the time you finally make it to university with a few more long ass lectures added on for effect. It's jarring enough to have your parents bugging you about it, but then it's like the world and its mother wants to ask the same tired ass questions as well. I wish they'd all just give it a rest!

"Are you going to all of your classes?"

Shoot me now!

I pause, "Define all?"

My mother put her hand on her hip and makes a face, "Excuse me?"

"Oh mum, c'mon. You knew I wasn't going to go to EVERY lesson so I don't know why you're trying to look all surprised," I chuckle rolling the lump between my palms before flattening it and pressing my thumb in the middle. I hand her the first fully formed dumpling. My mum snatches the dumpling from me and dropped it in the pot. It lands in the soup with a cheery 'plop'.

"I was hoping that you'd buckle down and acknowledge that this part of your education ain't free. If you mess this up you still have to pay them back and that would be a complete waste."

"I know mum. I'm not going to mess up just because I'm not in EVERY class. If I miss a lesson there's always the lecture notes posted on the student portal. It's fine."

"Mmm hmm," she murmurs in the way that parents do when they didn't believe you but they were going to leave it alone for now.

"How's Ty doing?" she asked changing the subject onto something that I didn't want to talk about even more than uni.

I shrug in response, "He's okay I guess."

"I haven't seen him for ages now. What's he been doing with himself?"

"Living." I hand her another dumpling. Plop!

She raises her eyebrow, "What's the matter with you two this time?" she asks, pushing the dumpling under a piece of yam to keep it from bobbing to the top so that it can cook properly.

"Who said anything's the matter?"

"Rio…"

I roll my eyes again. I came home to get a break from my stupid problems and now my mother wants to talk about them. Whenever Ty and I have an argument, my mother can always tell by the way I react to the questions she asks about him. According to our mothers, Tyson and I aren't allowed to fall out. Whatever problems we have with each other we are forced to talk it out and work it out before the sun goes down because if we go to bed angry with each other it will only make things worse. How much worse can this possibly get? I knew that if I opened my mouth about the argument she would only fast up herself and drag Michelle into it, and the last thing I need right now was them doubling teaming me and Tyson; so I lied.

"Nothing, mum."

"Mmm hmm." There's that noise again.

I shoot her a look. Uni she would drop because she could always bring that up again; me and Tyson arguing, she wouldn't leave alone until it was resolved.

I could hear the cogs in her head turning as she tries to figure out a way to make me tell her what had happened. I love my mother to bits, but sometimes she drives me up the wall.

"So," she says casually, "What do you think of Ty's new girlfriend?" My hand slows as I reached for another piece of dough. How the hell did my mother know about this chick before I did?

I clench my jaw.

"Angelica?" I say as nonchalantly as I can muster.

"Yeah, that's the one. Michelle's in love with her…d'you like her?"

HE TOOK HER TO MEET HIS MOTHER! Calm down Rio, calm down...

I shrug "She's okay,"...for a tiny, irritating, sugar plum princess.

"You hate her don't you?" my mother grins mischievously.

I smile back, nudging her with my hip.

"No! I don't HATE her_"

"Liar!"

"Mum, I hardly know the girl."

"Fine, you don't *hate* her. You don't like her though," she giggles.

"I only met her a few hours ago. I had no idea she even existed up until then." I confess.

My mum furrows her brow, "Oh! Well that's strange. So is that why you're fighting?"

I fling my head back again and growl, "Oh my God! Mum, just this once can you please stay out of it!"

"You want me to call Michelle?"

See what I mean?

"No Mum; I want you to get a life so you can stay out of mine!"

Uh oh, she's giving me the 'authoritive parent' eyes.

"Excuse me? I don't care if you're in uni; me and you ain't size, so watch your mouth, you hear me?"

I sulk.

"Do you hear me, Rio?"

"Yes Mum."

"Good. Now hurry up and finish making them dumplings 'cause you're gonna need to make some more dough for Michelle and Ty."

OH, FOR FUCK'S SAKE!

21
Cartier.

It's finally the end of term! After three surprisingly eventful months we'll all be deserting Brompton for Christmas and my flat is buzzing with festive holiday excitement. The girls and I decided that before we all head home that we'd throw a little Christmas dinner party in the communal kitchen and invite our nearest and dearest that we'd gotten to know over the duration of the term. As the girls are my nearest and dearest, I invited Tyson, who thought that Angelica should join us as well. Great! I don't particularly want her here, but over the last few of weeks -after Ty and I were forced by our mothers to wave our white flags -I had gotten to know her a little more and much to my displeasure, she is as sweet as she looks. It was easy to see why Ty was so smitten with her. Yoshi invited Ace, Fontaine invited Leon –Mr Tall Dark and Hench from Sunday Slam that she had been getting quite friendly with as of late – and Carmen invited Bless. We'd advised her against it of course, but she started getting defensive about it, so to avoid dampening her festive spirit (and having her dampen ours with one of her trademark moods), we dropped it. Bless isn't going to change no matter how much effort she puts in; if he wanted to make her his girlfriend he would have, but she thinks that he just needs a bit more time, after all, it has only been three months of her cooking for him, cleaning up after him, following him from event to event, helping him out with his coursework, having multiple lengthy conversations and multiple orgasms. Sometimes you just have to leave people to their own devices so they can figure it out for themselves. As the saying goes, those who don't hear must feel.

I'd decided to go cold turkey on Nate –no contact whatsoever –so I didn't have a date for our little shindig. I had Tyson; my friend. With all of the drama that I've gone through this term, boys are the last thing on my mind.

The girls and I have been up since 9am doing a bit of last minute shopping, decorating the kitchen and cooking a variety of dishes for this evening. It's set to be a perfect evening and although I'm dateless, I'm content. Carmen strung pearlescent fairy lights around door frame and the windows, Yoshi covered the available surfaces that weren't in use with vanilla tealights, white glitter to represent the snow -Carmen told her it represented the mess she would be cleaning up all by herself -and 4 decorative angel figurines that she'd handcrafted out of polyester, paperclips, feathers and more glitter. Fontaine and I were in charge of trying to make the dinner table look presentable for the occasion. We had pushed the two medium sized wooden tables together to create one large one, and covered it with a white bed sheet and my gold brocade H&M pashmina draped down the middle for a table runner. To make it appear a little more festive and we had nicked a couple of Yoshi's tealights, which we arranged on a white plate in the middle of the table around a wine glass filled with 'Celebrations'. As we were students with limited resources, we had opted for paper plates and plastic cups with white and gold Christmas designs on them as opposed to our mismatched tableware. We teamed the plates and cups with some white plastic Smartprice cutlery from ASDA and a couple of cheap Christmas crackers from Poundland -our funds had begun to run disastrously low by the time Fontaine decided that we had enough alcohol. All in all, everything looked wonderful.

The fridge is filled with fruit juice, wine, a 6 pack of Stella Artois for the boys, and the ever necessary bottle of Bailey's Irish Cream –my favourite! There are also a few store bought desserts (chocolate profiteroles, lemon meringue and strawberry cheesecake), which (hopefully) will still be left over tomorrow so that the girls and I can pig out before we head home. I'm busying myself making sure that my large honey roast chicken and Aunt Bessie's crispy roast potatoes and Yorkshire pudding's (I don't care if it's cheating, the Aunt Bessie brand is delicious!) are cooked to golden perfection, Carmen is making a huge tray of macaroni and cheese, and a big pot of rice and peas...well more like the rice cooker is making rice and peas, but she had done her part by putting the ingredients in! Yoshi had put herself in charge of the starters as she can't cook that well. She is currently warming up readymade savoury treats from Iceland in the other oven, and spooning readymade coleslaw and potato salad into serving bowls. Fontaine, who is even more incompetent in the kitchen than Yoshi, had cracked out her electronic drink fountain and is making the only thing she claims to know how to - death juice. If you don't know what death juice is then you clearly have never attended a student party. It is a mix of almost every alcoholic beverage, mixed with a bit of fruit juice so that it doesn't taste completely God awful. Fontaine chucks some tinned fruit in it for good measure so that it looks less intimidating, kind of like a fruit punch. It smells like a hangover waiting to happen. Anyone foolish enough to drink enough of the stuff will wake up the next day feeling like they got a 'fruit punch' in their head!

"What time is it?" Fontaine asks, dancing around the kitchen to Destiny's Child's Christmas album. I swear to God, if I hear '8 Days of Christmas' one more time I will kill someone. It's the best song on the album hands down, but after hearing Beyonce brag, "On the 2nd day of Christmas my baby gave to me the keys to a CLK Mercedes" at least 10 times already, it is making me a little bitter that I am without a 'baby' this year. Even if I did have one, the only transport I'd acquire from him would probably be a ride around Hyde Park on a Boris Bike for the day. I haven't yet figured out how to find a man that would buy me a flashy car. That reminds me - if I am alone on Valentine's Day, I am going into hiding for the whole day.

Yoshi glances at her Marc Jacobs watch that Ace bought her last week, "6:45."

"Already? I need to go get dressed!" Fontaine panics, throwing her spoon down making the sunset coloured liquid splatter onto the counter top.

"Me too. I can let Bless see me like this!" Carmen shrieks gesturing disapprovingly at her tank top, Hollister track pants and Ugg boot combination. She checks the macaroni again before slamming the oven door shut and high-tailing it out of the kitchen after Fontaine. Yoshi giggles and finishes adding the final touches to her decorations. I smile fondly at her calmness, glad that she is not following their flustered leads.

"Aren't you gonna change?" I ask, stirring a pot of gravy.

"What for?" she asks pulling a plastic mistletoe from her shopping bag and pinning it over the door.

"For your boyfriend…?"

Yoshi pulls a face, "No. I don't need to impress Ace, I already have him. Plus, I like what I'm wearing. It's comfortable."

At the sound of that word I take the rest of her decorations from her and push her out of the door.

"Never get too comfortable, it's a relationship killer; keeping up appearances is key. Now go to your room, and slip into something that will give him a Merry Christmas." I wink.

"But I haven't finished decorating and my starters are still in the oven!"

"Don't worry about all that; I'll finish up in here. You go get sexy."

Yoshi hesitates, "Are you going to change too?"

"Yes, but I don't have a date coming so it's more important that you all look fabulous, so go."

It's 7:30 and none of our guests have arrived yet, but that's to be expected as black people do not know time – an age-old theory that many of us have proven repeatedly -which left me with some time to get out of my house clothes. The girls are dressed, swanning around the kitchen, picking at Yoshi's starters and testing Fontaine's Death juice. As soon as I return Fontaine shoves a cup of the questionable concoction into my hand. I sniff the fiery liquid and recoil warily as the spicy scent burns my nasal passage. This will definitely be the first and last time Fontaine's creation will be in my cup.

I take a quick swig to be polite.

"Oh dear God!" I splutter, involuntarily coughing up the liquid. How much rum did she put in this? It tastes like sugary paint stripper! I set the cup down on the counter and grab some kitchen towel to catch the offensive liquid before it drips onto my red jumpsuit.

The doorbell rings, alerting us that the first of our guests has finally arrived. I was going to answer it as I was the closest to the entrance but Carmen zooms past me in her silver dress and heels with the excitement of a child who'd just heard the ice-cream van pull up.

"Heeey babe," she sings, launching herself at Bless.

He smiles and kisses her on the lips.

"Nice dress."

"Thank you!" Her back is to me but I know she is grinning up a storm at the compliment because I can feel her giddy elation radiating from her. It's funny how another person can do that to you. When we're alone we convince ourselves that we're just dandy by ourselves...and then that person comes along who makes us question how happy we really were pre-them, because the way we feel when they're around is intoxicatingly euphoric. When the relationship is in its early stages, you experience that never-get-enough honeymoon period where hand holding, hugging, constant kissing and frequent spontaneous sexual urges are the thing. I like that part; it's the part of the relationship that compensates for when everything turns to shit. The down side is; those are the memories that make you miss that person even more once it's over. Why does the passion have to fade? Why can't love stay like that? Is it down to the individuals involved, or is that how love is –a slow decline into a comfortable routine?

Carmen and Bless enter the kitchen with Ace following behind. Yoshi smiles and makes her way over to his familiar embrace quietly. Her greeting is totally the opposite of Carmen's and so is her outfit. I told her to get sexy for her man and she interpreted that into a black turtle neck and black skinny jeans. If it weren't for her thigh high leather boots, her now bubble-gum pink hair tied up in a messy bun, and the excessive amount of silver rings on each finger, I wouldn't have thought she'd made any effort at all. Ace curls his arm around her tiny waist, she makes an awkward movement before settling into his hold.

He frowns at her expression.

"You okay babe?" he asks softly. Yoshi looks down and nods.

"You sure? You look a little off."

"I'm just tired. We've been busy all day."

"Yeah, you look tired. Maybe you should go put on some more makeup. A bit more concealer and blusher should do it," he suggests taking her face in his hands and studying it. Yoshi purses her lips trying to disguise her offence but nods and whispers, "Yes Ace."

I frown and open my mouth to tell him off when suddenly he grins at her.

"I got you something." He reaches into his varsity jacket and pulls out an oblong shaped package, wrapped in black wrapping paper and tied with a white ribbon.

Yoshi looks at it and shakes her head with a small smile.

"Ace, you didn't have to_"

"I know, but I wanted to." He strokes her face, "I wanna keep my baby happy. Open it."

For some reason, maybe because she knows I'm looking, Yoshi glances at me. Her smile becomes more convincing and she opens the gift.

"OH MY GAWD!" comes Fontaine's strong East End accent from across the room. She rushes over and snatches the opened box out of Yoshi's hand with eyes as wide as saucers.

"This is not what I think it is. A white gold Cartier Love Slave bracelet! Yosh, you officially have the world's greatest boyfriend!" she gushes handing it back to her. Yoshi stares at the expensive piece of jewelry.

"Ace, um, wow. I, I don't know what to say."

Ace takes her by the hand and pushes her sleeve up a little, then closes the bracelet around it. In the box is a tiny Cartier screwdriver to lock the bracelet on. He screws each bolt tightly. It looks like a chic handcuff.

"Just say thank you," he smiles.

"Thank you," she replies quickly. He deposits the screwdriver in his jacket pocket. Fontaine grabs Yoshi by the wrist, twisting and turning it in the light, mesmerized by its glimmer. Yoshi starts chewing her lip and Ace steps closer, rubbing small circles on her lower back.

"It's official Yosh; you're all his," Fontaine giggles.

Yoshi looks at the bracelet.

Ace smiles.

"Merry Christmas, babe."

I look at the Death Juice that I'd set down on the counter only moments earlier and remind myself that men just complicate things and have brought me nothing but trouble thus far. I don't need one. I pick up the cup and down it.

22
Guest List.

By 8pm everyone else was in attendance except for Fontaine's fancy man who by the looks of it was going to be a no show which had put her in a bit of a funk. She sat next to me around the table and we swirled and sipped our Bailey's.

"If he wasn't gonna come he could've just said so. I messaged him half an hour ago and he hasn't even bothered to reply," she pouts.

"Never mind Fonts; I'll be your date," I smile patting her shoulder.

Fontaine takes a generous sip of her drink and rests her head on my shoulder, "Fine, but I don't put out on the first date."

"Oh please," I scoff.

"Okay fine, maybe I do -but only when I'm *really* drunk."

I refill her cup, "Well drink up, sunshine."

"Desperate much?" Tyson chuckles, peeping at me from behind the black Polly Pocket who had decided that she preferred Ty's lap to her own chair.

I shrug, "Beggars can't be choosers."

"You're talking like there is a shortage of dick," Carmen interjects in her usual graceful manner.

"Maybe I'm tired of dick."

"You need to be tired of that drink 'cause it's got you talking rubbish! 'Tired of dick' my arse!"

"Carmen!" Yoshi hisses trying to remind her that we have company.

"What?"

Yoshi shakes her head and sighs deciding that it's better to let Carmen be Carmen.

"Anyway, are you lot ready to eat?"

"Do you even have to ask?" Bless replies patting his stomach.

"I'm starvin' like Marvin over here," Tyson adds. Angelica giggles. That wasn't even funny! Why is she being such a chick? Idiot.

I roll my eyes at Tyson, "Oh please Ty, I know for a fact that you ate something before you got here!"

"That was just a snack," he confesses, flashing his crooked smile at Angelica before planting a sweet kiss on her lips. From the way she blushes I sense that he isn't talking about eating food. I throw up in my mouth a little. I keep my smart comments to myself and the girls and I busy start getting the starters on the table. Angelica offers to help. I smile and tell her no.

Once all of the dishes are on the table everyone helps themselves, aside from Tyson, whose dutiful girlfriend takes it upon herself to serve him.

"Angelica you don't have to serve Ty; you're a guest. If anything he should be serving you," I smile, trying to hide my irritation. Why is she so on it?

Angelica smiles back as she continues piling up Tyson's plate.

"I don't mind."

"I know but_"

"Rio it's fine, really. I like catering to MY man." Maybe it's just me wanting to pick a fight, but I could've sworn she said 'my man' in that way that females do when they want to remind you that he isn't YOUR man. I looked at Carmen who shoots me a look back that only confirms my suspicions. Let it go Rio.

"Ok, but Angelica_"

"Rio, I've got it," she snaps. The girls pause what they're doing, looking back and forth between us, while the boys stay well out of it.

I arch my eyebrow, "I just wanted to tell you that YOUR man doesn't eat pork, sweetheart."

Angelica looks down at the four pigs in blankets she has put in his plate.

"Oh."

Yeah bitch. Oh!

I hear Yoshi and Carmen snickering quietly while Fontaine hums '8 Days of Christmas' to herself. The tension building between Angelica and I had always been more apparent on my side of the fence, but I had tried my best to be civil as she had never given me any trouble before. Today her charade of the sweet little munchkin finally dropped, and I knew things would only get worse between us from here on in. Oh well, if she starts getting catty it gives me leeway to open up my mouth and let her know how much I don't like her.

"So how come you ain't serving my food?" Bless asks Carmen as she puts a couple of Iceland mini spring rolls on her plate.

She raises her eyebrow at him.

"Are your hands broken?"

"No, neither are Tyson's but his chick's getting his food."

Carmen straightens up.

"Am I your chick?"

"No_"

"Right then, get your own food."

We all pause; astonished that Carmen is publicly calling Bless out on their lack of relationship. I wanted to snap my fingers sassily, roll my neck and say 'Mmmhmm' for added effect, but I restrained myself. No one was as surprised by Carmen's attitude as Bless; he was watching her with new found amusement.

"Babes don't be like that," he says smoothly, reaching over and placing his hand on top of hers, "I came to spend the last day of term here with you," his hand drops into his lap and subtly onto hers "Can you fix me a plate please darlin'?"

One look at him and Carmen falls right back into step.

"Give me your plate then, idiot," she snaps softly, taking his plate from him. Fontaine makes a face at me and I shrug. At least she tried -it was some kind of progress.

Fontaine put on '8 Days of Christmas' again, but lucky for her I'm now too 'merry' to care, so merry that I am singing along with her as we put the main dishes on the table. As we start howling that we're 'so in la-la-la-la-love', the doorbell rings.

Fontaine's eyes widen, "It's Leon!" she shrieks excitedly, almost dropping the rice.

I take it from her.

"Well go open the door then!"

"I can't. I'm drunk."

"Looks like Leon will be getting lucky tonight. Now go open the door," I chuckle, ushering her out of the kitchen. I move my stuff a seat away from her so that she can sit with Leon putting myself next to Angelica who I suspect had seated herself between me and Tyson on purpose. Aside from our little spat earlier on, everything has been going okay.

I was hoping that the little spat would be the only thing that would go wrong tonight when a surprise walked through the door that knocked that issue right out of the park.

"Carter, what are you doing here?" I scowl. I knew I'd eventually run into him again, that was unavoidable as he was one of the Unfamous's top players, but never in a million years did I think our next meeting would take place in my home.

He watches me thoughtfully from the doorway with that unsettling enigmatic smile of his that gave nothing away.

"Hello princess."

I straighten up and walk over to him ready to evict him from my premises. I stop about a foot away from him and repress a shudder. I still can't get past the unsettling aura he emits; there's something off about him -aside from the fact that he had attempted to bed me to get even with Nathaniel -something more, something I'm not sure I want to discover.

"Why are you here?" I hiss, trying to keep my voice down because everyone is watching us with interest. Carter's eyes crawl over me slowly, from top to bottom then back up again. I shift my weight onto my other leg and fold my arms over my chest.

His smile widens.

"Nice to see you too *Duran*," he teases.

I narrow my eyes at him.

"So you're stalking me on Twitter now?" I enquire, curious as to how he knew my profile name.

Carter smirks, "Get over yourself princess, you're not *that* important." After a whole term worth of schmoozing the big cats, I clearly still don't rank high enough on the food chain to be considered one of them.

I frown.

"Then why did you call me that?"

"Your name....the song...Rio by Duran, Duran...." he states as if it's the most obvious thing in the world –*Duran, Duran* isn't really popular amongst the general urban crowd. The only other person I know that knows that song (aside from my Mum – it's her favourite) is Nathaniel. When we were in college, sometimes he would greet me singing the chorus -*"Her name is Rio and she dances on the sand..."* -before humming the rest against my lips as he kissed me.

"So...you gonna invite me in or what, princess?"

"Why should I when I didn't even invite you here in the first place?"

Carter shrugs, "It's Christmas."

Before I can deliver a witty retort, Cater is ushered in by a very giggly Fontaine who is snuggled under the stocky arms of her latest conquest; Leon.

"Why are you lot standing in the doorway? Take a seat, we're about to start the main course," she smiles nudging him in the direction of my empty chair.

I glare at Fontaine; is she that far gone that she's forgotten that I don't like him, or has Leon's presence turned her brain to mush?

"Sorry, no can do; there's no chairs left. Guess you'll have to go home." I smirk.

"Don't be silly, it's Christmas. He can have my seat!" Angelica smiles as she hops onto Tyson's lap.

This. Basic. Bitch.

Carter smirks at me, "Aww ain't she sweet?"

I narrow my eyes at her, "Oh, she's something all right."

"There we go, problem solved!" Fontaine grins.

Judas!

Everyone is chatting animatedly amongst themselves while tucking into the indulgent deserts that are now on the table. Tyson is enjoying his third slice of Lemon Meringue with a side of vanilla ice cream. Angelica frowns and pokes his tummy that has protruded over his jeans a little from all of the food he had put away. I roll my eyes at her.

"What's the matter, princess? Short stuff not your cup of tea?" Carter asks lifting a piece of cheesecake to his mouth. His eyes are locked on mine, looking into them a little deeper than I'm comfortable with. Have you ever felt as if someone can look in eyes and see straight into your soul, but not in that romantic way, in the way that makes you want to grab a crucifix and yell
"MY GOD IS STRONG!"?

I shift in my chair.

"Why are you watching me?"

"Can't I watch you?" he asks, resting his elbow on the table and turning his frame in my direction so all he can do *is* watch me.

"No!" I snap, shifting away a little more.

Carter makes an amused sound clearly enjoying my discomfort.

"Why not?"

"Because I don't like you!"

"Noted." He makes that amused sound again and turns back to his cheesecake.

Carter ignores me for the rest of the night and although I knew it was what I wanted, it irritates me. Carter is an asshole; definitely someone I want nothing to do with, but in the back of my mind a nagging feeling tells me that maybe Carter Johnson isn't the right person to have rooting against me. He's one of them. If one of the Unfamous's elites won't vouch for me, that will leave my popularity in a bad place because the other elites will follow suit and I'll remain a wannabe. After all this work (not to mention, *stress*) I don't want to drop to the bottom of the pile again.

At around 2am our guests began to disperse to attend another end of term soiree that I had no idea was even happening till now -even Tyson knew about it before me. Carmen sulks as she watches Amari put on his jacket, wishing that he didn't have to leave, but Amari is part of the inner circle of the Unfamous and whatever this secret shindig is, he is determined to go. I have never witnessed any of these lot so up for a house party in my life so naturally, I want to know why. What's so special about this one and why is it so under wraps?

Angelica went to get her jacket so for the first time that whole night I finally had an opportunity to talk to Tyson without her listening in.

I corner him by the fridge with my hand on my hip.

"How could you not tell me about this super-secret Unfamous house party?" I hiss.

Tyson raises his eyebrow at me, "I didn't *not* tell you; I thought you'd been invited. Everyone else was…"

I frown, "Who's everyone else?"

"Me, Ace, Amari and the rest of them lot. Shit, even Sky's going."

My mouth falls open -the slut got an invite and I didn't. How dare they not invite me but invite *her*!

"Whose party is it?"

"Some guy from Herring Uni. Jade something…" he shrugs.

My heart stops, splutters and restarts. It couldn't be...

"…Jade Washington?" I ask barely above a whisper.

Tyson snaps his fingers and points at me, "That's it! Jade Washington."

I gawk at him in disbelief.

"You mean to tell me that YOU got invited to a party by Jade frikken Washington?"

Tyson shoots me an insulted look.

"Yeah, I did. What's the big deal?"

I want to throw a rock at him. What does he mean 'what's the big deal?' It's *Jade Washington*; the guy practically put the University of Herring on the Unfamous map! Before Jade touched that place, Herring was like any other university and now it's one of *the* uni's to be at. Jade could've easily come to Brompton and been 'that guy' here, but instead he went to Herring and blew it and himself up. Jade Washington is a God among men. I have never even seen the guy, but the stories of his 'live fast, die young' lifestyle and kinky sexcapades are endless –he is both myth and legend. Jade is now in his final year in Herring and word is that when he graduates he's going to LA to sign a modelling contract with Elite Model Management. I've heard that he is better-looking than Nathaniel -that is definitely something to see.

Invite or not, I am going to that party!

"How on earth do you even know him?"

"Ace introduced us at a house party."

"What bloody house party? Was I there?"

"Nah, it was Tanya Wood's one," he looks away guiltily. He knows not to maintain eye contact with me; traitor!

"Georgia's friend, Tanya? What were you doing there? We hate Georgia, remember?"

"I didn't know until I got there. It's not like it was Georgia's party anyway."

"Might as well have been!" I scoff, "If they're with *her*, then they're against me!"

Tyson chuckles and pats my shoulder.

"You take this rivalry way too seriously sometimes. Her friends don't care about you; you're not that important, Ri."

I stare daggers into his back as he walks away from me and back to his Oompa Loompa. For the second time tonight I've been told that I'm not *that* important, but this time it's coming from Ty, who social status has clearly accelerated past mine if he's attending Tanya's party and got an invite to Jade's. This isn't how this is meant to go!

Sulkily I watch out of the corner of my eye -pretending to be immersed in cleaning up -as everyone slowly files out of the flat to embark on having the time of their lives at Jade

Washington's super exclusive party, while I pretend that the reason I'm not going is because I'm too tired -not because I didn't get invited.

With his all-knowing smirk, Carter swaggers over to me spinning his car keys around his index finger. He leans against the counter while I busy myself washing the pots and pans. I don't acknowledge his presence.

"You not coming, princess?"

"I'm tired." I drawl, not in the mood to entertain him anymore than I already have.

"Anyone ever tell you you're a bad liar?"

I roll my eyes, "Carter, what do you want?"

He takes a step closer to me and leans in.

"I have a strong feeling you'd love nothing more than to attend a Jade Washington party. Tell you what, as an apology for how I behaved last time, I'll take you. Jade's my boy, you'll be cool with me."

I drop the washrag in the sink.

"Seriously?" I'm elated and I'm trying my best to hide it; I actually get to attend a Jade Washington party and it takes everything in me not to jump for joy.

Carter makes that amused sound.

"All right, don't wet yourself! I'll take that as a yes then?" he asks with a mischievous glint in his eye that makes me want to say no because a look like that will only bring nothing but trouble. Something's up.

I narrow my eyes at him.

"Wait; what are you up to Carter?"

He smiles at me and alarm bells sound in my head.

"What makes you think I'm up to something?"

I cross my arms and raise my eyebrow.

"Call it a hunch. You know that I don't like you, so why take me Jade's?"

"I just wanna make things right," he replies innocently.

"Now who's lying?" I scoff.

"One thing that you'll learn about me is that I do not lie. Withhold the truth? Yes. Lie? Never! Lying complicates things. Why am I even telling you, you should already know how complicated things can get, ain't that right princess?" he smiles knowingly.

I frown, "What's that supposed to mean?"

"I think you know what it means."

"No. I can't say I do. Now are you going to keep talking in riddles or are you going to enlighten me?"

Carter makes that irritating amused sound again. I clench my fists against my ribs; I know exactly what he's going to say. For a while he says nothing, he just stands there studying my reactions and smirking -I pull my arms a little tighter around my frame. Carter smiles and reaches out to touch my arm. I recoil and glare at him. As the silence extends, the tension between us intensifies; one of us has to speak soon, but it won't be me. I'm too chicken to open Pandora's Box because I knew that once I did, it would shatter any illusions I had left. As curious as I am to hear his explanation, the fear of what may come out of that box seals my lips even tighter; once I hear it, he can't take it back.

He breaks the silence with a malicious stony tone that makes his cryptic smile even more unsettling, "You're a liar Rio," he states confidently. My palms are starting to feel clammy. I shift my footing and look away.

"This whole 'Queen Bee' image you're trying to pull off is pathetic, not only because none of us are buying it, but because you don't even believe it yourself. That's why you accepted my invite to Jade's party, because you knew the reason you didn't get an invitation was because we don't think enough of you to invite you." As sternly as he says it, that smile never leaves his face; neither does that mischievous glint in his eyes. I hated the way he said 'us' and 'we' as if to remind me that they did classify themselves as a separate collective from the rest of us mere mortals. They knew they were superior and from what he had just said it was clear that they didn't deem me worthy enough to carry on the way I have been.

We both know he's right, so I don't bother to counter his allegations, but it confirms my suspicions -Carter can see right through me. According to what he said, they all can. It wasn't all in my head like I'd hoped. I'd thought I'd been doing quite well at making them think I could pass as one of them, but apparently I'm the only one who thinks so.

I glare at him.

"If you think so little of me then tell me what it is you want from me Carter. I'm not buying that whole 'make things right' rubbish."

"Look, if you don't wanna go with me, then don't. I was just trying to help."

"I don't need your help," I sneer.

"Fine, if you want to keep being seen as a nobody it's no skin off my nose," he shrugs. "I'm Carter Johnson -who are you?" He stars to walk away and with him goes a valuable chance of acceptance amongst the Unfamous. I glared after Carter contemplating his offer. I don't want his help after the stunt he tried to pull on or last encounter –it doesn't sit well with my pride -but also because accepting it would feel as if I am making a deal with the Devil. There has to be a catch, after all, you don't get something for nothing, especially not with this lot. What I really have to ask myself is not if I should accept his help, but if I'm ready to deal with the consequences.

Do I really want to be the only person NOT at Jade Washington's party?

I grit my teeth.

"Say I accept your help...what do you expect in return?" I call after him. Carter turns and flashes a smile at me indicating that I have asked the perfect question to his imperfect answer. Pandora's Box creaks open.

"Princess, for the last time I really am just trying to make things right. You accepting my offer is enough. I'm not going to make you do anything you don't want to. I said I will help you and I will; as long as you stick around. Do we have a deal?"

He walks back over and sticks out his hand. I hesitate; I know something bad will happen if I make this deal with him, I can feel it in my get, but I close my eyes and shake on it anyway.

"Deal -don't make me regret this!"

"I'll do my best."

His reply teamed with that satanic smirk does nothing to ease my nerves. What have I gotten myself into?

23
Victoria Secrets.

Carter's Mercedes races down the motorway with his sound system blaring James Blake to fill the silence between us. In front of us in Ace's Audi, Ace, Bless, Yoshi and Carmen are chatting animatedly looking as if they're having the time of their lives and behind us in a matching Mercedes truck is Leon and Fontaine (who's head keeps disappearing from view) and bringing up the rear in the Volkswagen GTi is Tyson and Angelica laughing and exchanging secret smiles. Everyone is enjoying a short road trip, while I feel like I'm in a temporary holding cell with a huge elephant inside of it. Truly, there is nothing for Carter and I to say to each other, but at the same time, there is too much to say. I want to ask him why he really let me come with him again because I'm unable to rid myself of the nagging feeling that it isn't for my benefit at all.

I huff inwardly and decide to keep quiet and keep my eyes forward; watching the little white lines on the road disappear under the car is therapeutically distracting and seems to be all I can do to avoid fully acknowledging the weight of Carter's fleeting glances every few minutes. Knowing how much Carter irks me, I put myself in this position anyway. I keep reminding myself that it's for the greater good; I don't like Carter, but as he is oddly in my corner -albeit for his own twisted reasons -being around him is necessary.

Eventually we turn a corner and my discomfort grows because we have reached that part of the motorway where there are no street lamps for the next few miles. My calming white lines are now only visible as far as Carter's headlights shine, and our only guide are the cat eyes in the road that reflect ice blue light back at us. Darkness engulfed the car as the translucent white of the moonlight casts shadows all around us, making the dashboard lights more vibrant. We have entered No-Man's Land.

I clear my throat and shifted in my seat, pulling my arms a little tighter around my frame. I can see Carter's brilliantly discomforting smile from the corner of my eye. He reaches a manicured hand between us and turns the music down so low that it sounds like white noise. Way to make it even more uncomfortable, asshole!

"We'll be there soon so I think it's about time I lay down the rules," he says.

I furrow my eyebrows, "You're giving me rules?"

"Yes. You're my guest so when we get inside, try and stay at my side or at least where I can see you -you're new to the scene so you can't just walk around like you own the place. Also, stay away from Nathaniel." As soon as the words leave his mouth, his eyes begin to analyse my reaction.

My eyes widen and my heart rate picks up. I have avoided seeing and speaking to Nate for so long now that it is becoming slightly easier to ignore the aching emptiness in my chest. Carter is throwing me into a situation where it will be damn near impossible to avoid him and any drama he has in tow, especially as I'm showing up with the one person he tried to keep me from in the first place. As if this whole situation wasn't awkward enough already!

I look at Carter.

"Nate's gonna be there? Are you sure?"

"Yes," he replies keeping his eyes to the front, his smile playing around his lips, "You sound surprised. I had assumed he was part of the reason you wanted to go so bad. You're a bit obsessed with him."

"Excuse me? I am not obsessed! And how dare you say anyone is obsessed when you tried to sleep with me all because you're still hung up on that slut Georgia!" I fire back defensively.

All amusement leaves Carter's face. His hazel eyes burn into mine painted with an uncompromising severity that I have never seen witnessed from him as he always donned the creepy smile. This is much more unnerving.

Carter pulls over, and then in one swift motion he closes in on me, his face hovering over mine with a look daring me to test him. I want to stand my ground and get up in his face too, but my instincts advise me against it, so instead I shrink back against the door, holding my breath.

Carter hangs there for a few moments, then exhales heavily out of his nose and closes his eyes. Slowly he eases away from me and slumps back into his chair. I stay plastered against the door unsure of what to do. Running seems like the best option, except we're on the side of the motorway and Tyson and Leon's cars have already zoomed past us –I have nowhere to run to.

I stare at Carter; he massages his temples and mutters something to himself.

"What the hell was that about?" I speak softly so as not to accidently provoke him. I don't really want to speak to him after this, but I figure that as getting the hell away from him is not an option right now, talking is all I can do to regain control of the situation.

He looks at me.

"Don't talk about her like that. You don't know her," he replies, dodging my question. He isn't going to let me control things that easily. This is his game and we are playing on his terms and his terms only.

I suck in a breath and ease away from the door a little.

"She stole from me the only thing that mattered. How else am I supposed to speak of her?"

Carter flips a switch on his steering wheel and his window slides down. He lights a cigarette.

"You say that as if Nathaniel had nothing to do with it," he snaps, irritated by my evident devotion.

I frown.

"I know this is as much his fault as it is hers, but she made it worse. Now because of her, Nate and I can never fix 'us', ever!" I blink back tears. I haven't thought about the damage that Georgia has caused in a while now; I can feel a fire building inside me, burning my heart and heating my tears until they sting my eyes.

"I hate her!" I croak, clenching my fists in my lap.

Carter blows smoke into the air.

"Hate is a strong word Princess."

"So is love. If you know what she's really like, you'd hate her too! I honestly don't know how you could ever love someone like her."

"And I don't know how you could ever love someone like Nathaniel, but you do."

"Because he loves me back! Georgia doesn't give a shit about you, and you know it!"

Carter closes his eyes, takes another shot of nicotine and rubs his temples.

"That's not true."

"THEN WHY IS SHE HAVING HIS BABY, CARTER?" I scream coming away from the door completely as the hot tears spill over and burn my skin. "You're right, she loves you so much!"

So much for staying calm.

Carter stops rubbing his temples mid-motion and his eyes snap open. For a while he doesn't say anything, he just sits there staring out into the darkness of the seemingly endless motorway, and breathing. Well, at least I didn't have to be torn up about it on my own anymore –misery loves company.

After about 3 minutes of strained silence I start to worry. I stretched my hand out tentatively and tap him lightly on the shoulder. He shrugs me off violently, flinging my hand away from him.

"She's pregnant?" He asks so quietly that I'm not sure if the question is directed at me or not.

"Oh she didn't tell you?" I ask snidely, already guessing the answer from his reaction, "I'm shocked!"

Carter says nothing. He just sits there and stares some more, the ash on his cigarette lengthening as the wind smokes it for him.

My sarcastic arrogance doesn't last long. The longer I watched him just sitting, staring and breathing; I begin to feel sorry for him. As much of a creep as Carter is, I see that this news was ripping his heart to shreds as it did to mine, even if his reaction is no reaction at all. His eyes are sad.

Georgia is his Nathaniel.

As life has demonstrated many a time, (generally) when a boy falls in love, he falls hard, so it will burn him even more if the girl he has chosen to love breaks his heart, because it took him that much longer to trust and open up to her. Any female that has successfully gotten a boy to lay themselves bare to them and truly love them, has had the rare pleasure of seeing sides of them that you never knew they could possess; parts of them that the rest of the world will never see. That isn't something to be taken for granted because once you break a man's heart he (generally) says 'Fuck love!' and winds up leaving a trail of broken hearts behind him, trying to forget about you, too afraid to fall in love that deeply again because the remnants of this love hurt too much. Broken hearts are the products of broken hearts.

I feel for Carter right now.

"Carter?" I try again, keeping my hands to myself this time.

"Rio?" he replies a little above a whisper.

"Are you okay?"

He laughs bitterly, "Are *you* okay?"

"...No."

"Then how do you expect me to feel? You've been dealing with this for a while; I just found out." He throws his burned out cigarette out of the window and lights another one. "She didn't even tell me…why didn't she tell me?" he asks in a pained voice.

He lights the cigarette and takes a heavy drag.

"I swear to God, I love that girl, but she's a conniving little bitch!"

I have the urge to hug him, but I don't. If it was someone else I probably would have, but it isn't someone else; it's Carter.

"Maybe she didn't want you to get hurt," I offer feebly.

"Bullshit! She's at Jade's with Nathaniel right now; she doesn't give a fuck if I'm hurt."

My heart rate picks up again.

"Wait, you knew they were there together?" I hiss, trying to contain my frustration.

In spite of his current mood he makes that amused sound again.

"Why do you think I agreed to bring you, Princess?" he smirks giving me a look that lets me know that this was the part of the truth that he was hiding from me. The smirk doesn't last long as he remembers that he is upset; he goes back to staring aimlessly out of the window and smoking. Bastard! I'm glad he's hurting.

"You agreed to take me just so you could continue with your stupid plan to humiliate Nathaniel?" I snarl accusingly.

Carter rolls his eyes.

"Yes," he replies plainly -he doesn't even care that I'm offended.

Once again I had allowed myself to be led into one of Carter's stupid revenge plots against Nathaniel and this time I refused to hold my tongue. I shove him as hard as I can and watched as his body slams against the inside of his car door,

"YOU FUCKING PRICK!" I howl.

Carter glares at me as if I had lost my damn mind. I return the look.

"This is the second time you have dragged me into one of your fucking pathetic pissing contests because you feel the need to get back at Nathaniel over a girl that doesn't even want you! She loves HIM. She's having HIS baby. Nathaniel still wants to be with me but I accepted that I had to let go. Georgia doesn't want anything to do with you and yet_"

"IT'S NOT HIS BABY!"

"...what?"

I'm having one of those moments where you hear something so shocking that you think you imagined it and it's necessary to hear it again just to make sure that your mind isn't playing tricks on you.

Carter's face is void of any kind of smile.

"The kid ain't his."

"How do you know that?"

"As if rich boy Nathaniel, would ever bareback gold digging, hoodrat Georgia; but I would, and I did. She's probably convinced him he did too; probably has him thinking that her feelings for him run deep enough that she wouldn't *dream* of running around on him."

He chuckles and takes another drag of his cigarette, "Poor sod."

Right about now I should be feeling elated that the spawn of that she-devil doesn't belong to Nathaniel, but it only make me angrier. I have the right mind to march up into the party and lay that bitch out once and for all, regardless of what anyone has to say on the matter, but there were two things wrong with that scenario; I will be on her turf, and she is pregnant -not for Nate (thank God), but pregnant all the same.

"When?" is all I manage to utter.

Carter runs his hand through his Icelandic blonde and sighs, "About 2 months back. We hooked up about 2 weeks before I met you, 'for old time's sake'" his tone drips with sarcasm as if the whole idea of 'for old time's sake' disgusts him.

What I can't seem to wrap my head around is why she lied; obviously she wanted to trap him, but this is just stupid. Why would she tell Nathaniel it's his baby when she knows it is Carter's? Carter is white; is she hoping that because both she and Nathaniel are mixed that the child would be passable? Is she seriously that thick? This is a very desperate move, even for Georgia.

"Drive," I order him with a scowl so he knows I'm not playing. He takes one last pull and gets us back on the road. A sign appears from the darkness: Hertfordshire (17 miles). We're getting closer to Herring University, closer to ending Georgia's charade…closer to getting Nathaniel back where he belongs; with me. I have to be smart about this; one wrong move can send me

plummeting head first to the bottom of the social pyramid. Georgia is one of their own -I'm not. An attack on her is like a game of Russian Roulette; I could pull the trigger and live to fight another day, or any
chance of becoming 'someone' could be shot to hell.

Carter pulls into the Herring student parking lot, his flashy truck outshining every other car effortlessly. In a way Carter's truck is a lot like him; it has that effortless cocky swagger that just made you stop and stare, but if you got too close, it could destroy you. By making this stupid deal with him I have given Carter the power to destroy me. In the back of my mind I know that sooner or later I will regret this decision, but hopefully it will be worth it, especially if I get Nathaniel back. Carter turns off the ignition and the low rumble of the engine stops.

I open the door and hop out of my seat immediately.

"Come on Daddy. I don't know how to get to this party so you need to take me there right NOW!" I demand.

Carter makes the amused sound and leads me to my salvation.

Georgia is going down!

24 House Party.

The air is sweet and sticky, laced with the nose crinkling scents of body odour, various alcoholic beverages, and smoke from cigarettes and shisha. The deeper we delve into the party, the stronger the inquisitive scent of cannabis is, diluted every now and then by a person drenched in cologne or perfume to salvage your lungs for a moment. Every dorm room on Jade's floor is part of the adulterated atmosphere. Everywhere I look I am surrounded by beautiful girls and some equally beautiful men. I am mesmerised by the way they slink and glide around each other with an air of pre-eminence in their swagger, each one dressed immaculately in designer clothing (home-grown designers included in the mix) and accessories, equipped with the finest hairstyles money can buy. I feel like I'm trapped in one of those fabulous American teenage dramas where practically everyone is at least a 7 out of 10, and I'm trying my best not to look star struck. So many Unfamous 'legends' are milling around me, making me want imitate them to try and capture a piece of their cool so that they will assume that I am meant to be here. These are the exact bunch that I need to make fall in love with me and claim to be my friends -yes, I realise how that sounds. Sadly, all of this perfection belongs to Jade. I'm envious at how one boy can possess such a magnetic aura that people gravitate towards him and clamour to befriend him. He commands so much attention from so many important people, just for being him and nothing else; amazing! Why can't I do that? I frown to myself; I have the capacity to be just as remarkable as Jade, if not better, but for some reason people aren't taking to me as well as they should. I bet that if I had opted to use my voluptuous frame and taken a few Candy Mag pictures -becoming a self-proclaimed model -then I would've been where I wanted to be a while ago...probably without a boyfriend (not that I have one now), but 'one of them' none-the-less.

Carter strolls along at my side, flashing his notorious grin at the females (who swoon when they see him), and bumping fists, slapping hands and giving nods of acknowledgement to the guys. Nobody says anything to me and I don't say anything to them. Some people spared me an ephemeral glance to see who I was, and then I guess they figured I wasn't anyone worth greeting because they just carried on about their business. I recognise a few of the faces, but when I make eye contact with them in the hopes that they will make me feel that there is a place for me here, their expressions register blank as if they do not have the slightest recollection of me. Am I still so forgettable? I hope that the girls and Ty are in here somewhere or will be here soon so I won't feel so alone anymore –Carter doesn't count as company.

"CAAAARTER!" an unfamiliar baritone sings from across the way. I spin 90 degrees to see who is so excited to see Carter, and then the most amazing thing happens. It's as if everything is happening in slow motion; everyone's attention diverts to where the voice had come from -the boys watching with contained jealousy that this person hadn't called to them with such enthusiasm and the girls smiling their best 'hey baby' smiles like glammed up robots, as if they were all programmed to desire this one person. The crowd parts like the Red Sea, making way for the owner of the voice. When I peek through the crowd I see that he has two stunning (and giggly) females attached to him.

Could it be? I know I'm being an uber loser, but if this is who I think it is, an introduction is absolutely necessary. As discreetly as I can, I loop my arm through Carter's and stand smiling pleasantly at his side. Carter's body jiggles from his silent laughter, he knows what I'm up to, but he snakes his arm around my waist anyway, right before the last of the crowd parts to make way for the living legacy that is Jade 'Holy Moses he's hot' Washington.

The moment he comes into view I know that it's him. The rumours are true; he reeks of perfection; a being more flawlessly designed than Nathaniel himself. This guy looks like what wet dreams are made of, so much so that my stomach clenches and shudders simply from admiring (vigorously gawking at) him . His skin is smooth, supple, and golden as if he'd been moulded out of a tub of Palmer's Cocoa Butter, with a shock of inky blue/black hair that flows like dark water past his shoulders. He smells brand new, like a pair of white on white Air Force Ones fresh out the box, with a hint of wild indulgence, tickling my senses in the worst way. Oh how I long to be one of the throwaway groupies on his arm just so I can experience the twisted pleasure of being used and abused by him, just to say that I did. Gosh, he's heart-stopping!

His eyes flicker over to me briefly and the light in the hallway catches them, lighting them up like emeralds. In that moment, I understand why his name is Jade.

Signed, sealed, delivered, (take me) I'm yours!

I have never seen someone so magnificent in my life! No wonder Elite Model Management wants him; this boy belongs on a 10-foot billboard hanging over Times Square in New York posing for Absolut Vodka just like Smith Jared in Sex and the City, because he has definitely won the title of The Absolut Hunk in my eyes.

Wow!

"Carter fucking Johnson; where you been at man?" Jade grins coolly, releasing a very reluctant girl to give a fist bump to his friend.

Oh his smile! You'd think that he's just what the doctor ordered; he smiles and then BOOM, it's like the word perfection is derived from his existence alone.

"I been about, handling business, the usual. What about you?"

"Same old shit bruv; smokin', drinkin' and pimpin'!" he laughs. His groupies laugh too. I just stare at him, unable to function and on the brink of drooling on myself. "I'm not gonna stunt though, this dissertation business had me on lock for a hot minute so I had to get my head down."

Carter raises his eyebrow.

"You mean to tell me that you actually did your own coursework?"

"I never said that. I said I got my head down," Jade winks, flashing his pearly whites again. Oooh the things I would let him do to me...

Carter chuckles breaking my train of decadent thoughts and shakes his head, "You're a dog, d'you know that?"

Jade nuzzles his face into the girl on his lefts neck, growls up to her ear and says, "Woof!" before taking her earlobe between his teeth. Her breath hitches. I sigh inwardly wishing that I was her.

"Anyway, Calvin told me about that trip you lot took to Amsterdam last week," Carter grins wiggling his eyebrows, making it apparent that he knew the gritty details.

Jade laughs and wags his finger at his friend, "That's a next story for another time; there's too many ears right now. Where's your drink?" Jade asks pulling the sulky girl back to his side. He nuzzles his face into her neck like he had done with the girl on his left, dragging his lips over the exposed flesh before sinking his teeth into her softly with a smirk.

I. Am. Jealous.

The girl giggles, and just like that, she is out of her little mood. Jade rolls his eyes and returns his gem-like orbs to his friend, awaiting his answer.

"You got any Remy?" Carter asks. Jade nods, then without a word he pats the giggly chick on the backside (to which she giggles at again), and she slinks off to get Carter's drink. If I wasn't making sure to control my reactions so carefully, my mouth would have been hanging open. Do you think any guy could pat me on my ass and send me to make his guest a drink like my name is maid? Nah mate, it will never be that time, Jade Washington or no Jade Washington. Stupid girl!

Carter readjusts his hold on me, drawing my body into him a little more, and that was all it took for Jade's jade green irises to lock onto me with some interest.

"Hello miss," he smiles politely.

I smile in response and feel myself blush. His smile widens and the glimmer of interest in his eyes flickers into something that I can only translate as 'she wants me'. Ya damn right I want you; look at you!

"Jade, this is Rio," Carter introduces me, sliding his hand a little lower onto my hips. Jade takes note of Carter's hand movement and backs away from me ever so slightly, but kept on smiling.

"Nice to meet you, Rio."

"Ditto," is all I can manage without tripping over my words like some love-struck teenager. Jade makes that irritating amused sound that Carter loves making so much. My smile falters.

The giggly girl arrives back at Jade's side in 30seconds flat with a red plastic cup of Remy for Carter and Rose for me. I thank her and she looks at me for the first time, then smiles.

Jade puts his arm back around her waist.

"You're welcome," he responds to me and I'm not sure if it's on her behalf or if he's taking credit for her getting me a drink, but either way I find it a bit too arrogant for my liking. I frown at him and he grins as if pleased with my reaction.

Casually, he slides both his hands onto the girl's asses. I watch him in bewilderment.

"So what, you two an item?" he asks.

I'm about to jump in and deny it to the tenth power but Carter gets there before me.

"Somethin' like that," he smirks. He squeezes my hip gently which I take as a sign to go along with it. I bite my tongue so that I won't ruin whatever image of me he's building of me to the king of the Unfamous.

Jade studies me briefly and makes the amused sound. I grit my teeth.

"So there is some truth to the rumours after all. Carter Johnson and Nathaniel Gibson's ex; interesting. Georgia won't be happy, and you know how she gets when someone pisses her off." He says speaking to both of us but looking at me. I lift my head and jut out my chin; I'm not afraid of her, especially now that I finally have the information to take her down – after all, knowledge is power.

"I can handle Georgia," I reply stonily.

Jade's groupies look me up and down but Jade simply raises his eyebrow.

"If you say so," he replies in a disinterested voice. His groupies snicker. They don't think I can –I'll show them.

Carter clears his throat pulling the attention away from me.

"Where's she at anyway?" Carter asks stiffly, his previous irritation rearing its ugly head.

Jade shrugs and glances over his shoulder, "Dunno. Last time I saw her she was following Nathaniel somewhere." Both Carter and I tense up at the information –he's better at disguising it than I am. His thumb brushes against my hip softly, trying to comfort me.

Jade looks at me with interest; his mouth is not smiling, but his eyes are.

"You okay miss?"

"She's fine," Carter answers for me firmly. Jade's eyes flick to Carter's. He shrugs and his face becomes disinterested again. For the first time, I find myself being grateful for Carter's presence. He still unsettles me but (oddly) I feel a little safer because I know he's in my corner.

"I'm gonna go find Georgia. See you in a bit man." Carter fist bumps Jade again before pulling me away into the crowd with him. I glance over my shoulder to get one last look at Jade for memory's sake and feel my cheeks flush when I see him staring back at me. He smiles. Trouble never looked so good.

After half an hour of searching practically the whole party for Ms 'Baby Mama Drama', I was ready to throw in the towel and just try to enjoy myself, after all, it's not like she can stay hidden forever. I managed to catch up with Fontaine (briefly before Carter came to fetch me) who was drinking with purpose. Apparently Nadia was here and Fontaine was refusing to let her night be ruined because of it. She looked as if she was doing the exact opposite.

"Where's Leon?" I asked, prying a bottle of tequila from her hands. Fontaine frowned,

"In here somewhere waiting for me to 'check myself'," she rolled her eyes and tightened her grip on the tequila.

"Check yourself? What happened?" I yanked the bottle away and gave it to Manny as he passed by.

"I may have yelled at him…" she stuffed her empty hands into her pocket and pulled out a blunt.

"Why?"

Fontaine made an exasperated sound, "I dunno, I just…ugh, where the fuck is my lighter?"

I handed her mine. She sparked up and took a long drag to calm herself down.

"I haven't seen Nadia since she left me, and now she's swanning around as one of Jade Washington's tarts. She's been on his arm all night! I dunno what to do Ri."

"Wait, Nadia is one of Jade's girls?" I choked.

"Yeah, the one with the dark hair and the pouty mouth."

"Oh. You were right, she's very pretty."

"I know! That's what makes it worse; couldn't she have gotten fat or something so this wouldn't feel so shit." I nod; it's bad, but it's always rewarding to see your ex-lover doing worse without you. It's karma; you fucked me over and you got fat, all is right with the world once more.

It bothered me seeing Fontaine like that; a few weeks ago she was delivering a few home truths trying to whip me and

Carmen into shape, and now she was the one who needed the whipping.

I grabbed her by the shoulders.

"Fonts don't you go soft on me now, you're the only one of us lot with any real logic when it comes to relationships. If you can't keep it together then we're all doomed, so suck it up, go find Leon, apologise and then continue the night as you would have if she wasn't here." I said firmly.

Fontaine cracked a smile.

"D'you know what, you're right! Fuck Nadia!"

"Exactly, fuck that bitch! Go fuck Leon instead, you'll feel much better!" I joked.

"Sounds like a plan!" she laughed.

I paused.

"Fontaine I was joking."

Fontaine shrugged, "Doesn't make it any less of a good plan. Sounds like something I'd come up with. Thanks Ri!" She gave me a hug and walked off to find Leon. I just shook my head and laughed.

While flitting about with Carter, I had been introduced to a few more V.I.P's, each time with Carter's arm laced protectively around my waist (or alternatively on my hip if the person reacted a little too friendly for his liking). Surprisingly enough, a few people admitted to hearing about me, but to my dismay, each made a face as if what they had heard was not doing me any favours. Great!

Carter and I are posted up in the hallway talking to some so-called models that are irritating the hell out of me. All they do is giggle like school girls and pout between what would seem like accidental poses. It's exasperating, even Fontaine isn't this vapid! Carter told me that I needed these girls to like me if I really wanted to get myself out there. Apparently getting boys to like me wasn't a problem because of my figure and the fact that, well...they were guys init, but with girls I needed to try a little harder. Coy smiles would get me nowhere. We have been standing with these two Amazonian looking women for almost 10 minutes having one of those regurgitated uni conversations that I had honestly tired of by now. I don't care what uni you go to, I'm not interested in what you're studying, I know coursework is long and you've been 'banging out them essays' –SO THE FUCK WHAT? So has everybody else! I don't care! By the time Roxy and Kia (I think) have finished their cliché drivel about how 'bait'

Brompton is and how they know "bare man from B-City" (cue eye roll) I had devised the perfect escape plan.

"Which way is the toilet?" Yup, that's right, I played the bathroom card. Pure genius! I don't know why I didn't think of it when Carter had me generically smiling and nodding at Coco (real name Chanel -give me a break!), while I ignored every piece of shallow twaddle that left her collagen boosted lips.

"Oh, there's one in 7B that's available. If that one's occupied you can probably use the one in Jade's room," Roxy smiles, seeming a little too cheerful to be directing me away from their 'riveting' encounter with the one and only Carter Johnson *swoon*.

I force a smile, "And Jade's room would be where exactly? The line for 7B looks a bit too long for my liking."

Roxy's face falls as if I had asked the world's dumbest question.

"You don't know where Jade's room is?" How the hell would I know where a complete stranger's room is?

I return the unimpressed look to her.

"No."

"Wow, that's a first," she laughs, "Practically every girl in here knows where Jade's room is," she says in a snide voice as if I should be embarrassed to have not been one of his many conquests.

"Well I'm not every girl, am I?" I retort, making no effort to hide the attitude in my tone.

Roxy stops laughing and looks me up and down.

"Well I can see that. Guess you're not his type," she sneers sweetly.

"If his type is girls who are proud of being fucked and thrown away like common whores, then no, I guess I'm not his type," I fire back with a smile. Carter makes his amused sound, and for the first time, it doesn't irritate me because it isn't directed at me.

Roxy and Kia glare at me and then gave me that scowl that every girl on earth had learned to perfect when they wanted to make it clear that they don't like you. Like I give a shit! So these girls don't like me, so what? They are just girls. In this little society of the unknown elite, the males hold most of the power. Females are a dime a dozen and as all of us want to be the 'It' girl, most of the females are in competition with each other and don't like each other much anyway. Roxy and Kia were no skin off my nose; there are plenty more where they came from.

I decide that I don't need to know where Jade's bedroom is and I set off toward 7B (by myself for the first time that night). As I strut, I make sure to flash a few flirty smiles at the guys I have been introduced to so far, for good measure. When I reach 7B, the queue is long enough to make me groan in frustration, but seeing as I don't actually need to go all that bad I stand and waited my turn patiently –it's better than talking to Roxy and Kia, that's for sure.

I busy myself by staring at the heavy layer of smoke that settles above our heads when the door to 7B bursts open and a sour stomach curdling smell wafts into the hall.

"Arr, 'llow it!" the boy nearest the front of the queue groans covering his face with one of Manny's classic Obviously t-shirts, moving out of the way for a girl in a sexy pair of thigh high heeled Timberland boots.

"Does anyone know where Nathaniel is?" she asks with her back turned to me as she edges out of the door. I straighten up at the mention of his name and narrow my eyes at her, willing her to turn and face me. Who is this girl and what does she want with Nathaniel? The boy in the Obviously T-shirt turns in my direction and points to the fire escape on the other side of the kitchen parallel to me.

"He's on the fire escape with Calvin and Damon."

I fight the urge to slip away to the fire escape; part of my deal with Carter was to stay away from Nate, and as he has so graciously held up his end of the bargain by giving me a little social boost, the least I can do is stay put. If I happen to be in the kitchen near the fire escape a little later, and Nathaniel happens to see me and come over, well, nothing I can do about that now is there?

"What's the matter; she okay?" the boy asks gesturing into 7B.

The girl shakes her head, "Nah, she just threw up. You lot might want to use Jade's bathroom," she advises. Everyone in the line groans and starts to make their way a little further down the hall to join the end of the queue to Jade's bathroom, which is even longer than this one was originally. Seems as if Jade's bathroom is the place to be!

"You want me to stay with her till Nathaniel gets here?" the boy asks. The girl nods gratefully and turns on her heel, making a dash for the kitchen. Wait, is that…OH MY GOD IT'S SKY! If Sky is running out of the bathroom to get Nate for the girl inside who has just thrown up then it can only mean one thing...SHE is in there.

I look down, hiding my profile from Sky as she weaves through the crowd down the hallway. I wait until she is lost in the sea of people before walking up to the boy who is preparing himself to enter the tangy smelling room.

I catch him by the arm gently before he opens the door.

"Excuse me," I call softly, putting on my best empathetic face.

He looks down at me as if he's trying to place my face.

"Yeah?"

"I was wondering...is it Georgia that just threw up in there?"

"Yeah; why?"

I make my eyes wide with worry and put my hands to my lips in a flustered fashion.

"Oh dear! I told her it was a bad idea for her to come here in her condition. Poor thing; this pregnancy is really taking its toll on her," I say innocently enough.

The boy's eyes widen with shock.

"She's pregnant?"

"Well yeah," I say as if it's so obvious. Inside I am grinning because as of this moment the gossip ball has been officially put in motion. Soon her secret will be the hottest piece of news on the rumour mill, which will most definitely take her stats down a few notches.

"You go ahead, I'll look after her. If Nathaniel asks you can tell him that Duran is with her," I smile softly, simultaneously patting him on the shoulder and ushering him out of the way. I didn't want to give him my real name in case he had heard about me (and if he had, it would be because of the love triangle drama – that's how the rest of them knew my name); Nathaniel would know who Duran really was. The boy sighs thankfully, happy that he no longer has to subject himself to a stronger version of the putrid stench. I'm not too chipper about having to face the smell either, but the thought of a very vulnerable Georgia without her cronies to back her up is too perfect to pass up.

I flash the boy one last smile and enter the room. I lock the door behind me.

25
Power Trip.

The bathroom door is wide open. Georgia's silver pumps peep around the frame as she huddles over the toilet on her knees, panting and groaning like a drama queen.

"Nathaniel?" she sobs theatrically, adding a few more groans for added effect.

I say nothing as I walk over to the doorway, holding my breath to delay inhaling the acidic fragrance of the contents of her stomach, which she had unfortunately (lol, not!) managed to get down the front of her chiffon shirt and in the ends of her weave. I stand glaring down at her, enjoying how pathetic and disgusting she looks, feeling oh so powerful because not only am I the strongest person in the room, but no one else can get in here unless I am prepared to unlock the door.

Georgia groans again.

"Babe, I feel like shit," she cries assuming that the person looming in the doorway is her stolen lover. This is going to be fun.

"Look what we have here," I say in a voice so sharp that it slices right through her miserable moans, cutting them short.

Georgia rolls onto her bottom to see me smiling victoriously.

"Rio? What are you doing in here? Where's Nathaniel?" she sneers, glaring up at me from the floor.

"Nathaniel will have to wait. You and I have things to discuss."

Georgia's green eyes darkened to a murky swamp hue as she forces herself to stand. There is no way she is going to allow herself to be intimidated by me, after all, who am I to be intimidated by? According to her, I am no one. I am nothing. I watch the globs of vomit dribble down her top and wonder how, even in this dishevelled state, she still finds the audacity to carry herself as if she is a force to be reckoned with. Tonight, that is my role.

"You might want to clean yourself up superstar, you're gonna be in here for a while," I sneer shoving a wad of cheap economy tissue at her. She doesn't flinch; instead she snatches the scratchy off-white toilet paper from me and cleans the curdled gunk off of what used to be a very nice shirt.

"You gonna tell me what it is you want? I hope you're not going to embarrass yourself and try to get Nathaniel back again. It's getting pathetic now," she says, removing the discoloured droplets out of her hair. Can you believe the nerve of this bitch! She's locked in a room, cleaning vomit off of herself because of a pregnancy that she lied about, and she has the audacity to call ME pathetic! Am I missing something here?

"I'm pathetic?" I scoff in disbelief.

Georgia smirks, "Well, yeah! I mean, how long are you going to chase after a boy that clearly is preoccupied with someone else? Honestly, it's really sad."

"Well you should know, you spend enough time doing exactly that," I retort, refusing to let her get the upper hand.

She is right though; it is sad that after all this time I'm still trying to interfere with her and Nathaniel's 'relationship'. If I had any sense I'd leave well enough alone and let them continue to live in their world of lies; they deserve each other. As much as I know I should just walk away and let them get on with it, I refuse to let Georgia win. I made a vow to keep Nate out of my life, and I plan to stick to it, but she can't have him. If I miss this perfect opportunity to destroy any chance she has with him, after all that she put me through, then frankly, I'm a fool. This is clearly karma finally delivering the great revenge I've longed for, so why should I pass it up?

"In case you have forgotten, Nathaniel and I are having a baby. I'm not chasing anyone sweetie; he's mine," she sang, all too happy to remind me.

"Is that so? Well if he's 'yours', then why was he messing with me a good month after you broke the news to him?" I ask smugly.

I watch with sadistic pleasure as her cocky smirk dissolves into a infuriated grimace. Yes bitch; this is how it feels to find out that your man is cheating on you with the girl that you hate. Sucks don't it?

Georgia takes an uneasy step forward, clutching the small student sized sink for support.

"You're lying!" she spits.

I simply smile at her some more, revelling in the way her catlike eyes let her 'tough as nails' demeanour down. She wishes I was lying...and secretly, so do I. As good as it feels to rub this in her face, I'm not proud that I had allowed myself to become Nathaniel's side –chick as I had always believed that I was above such a demeaning role. That's the thing about loving someone you can't have; sometimes you take what you can get because you know it may be the closest you can get to actually being with them. At the time, a little something feels better than a whole lot of nothing. In hindsight, you feel like a fool because you know you knew better.

Georgia looks at the ground and presses her permanently manicured hand to her stomach.

"But...I'm pregnant," she mutters to herself in dismay. I can't help but laugh out loud just to add salt to the wound.

"I'm pregnant," she repeats as she slowly sinks back down to the floor and takes her head into her hands.

"You're pregnant with a child that he doesn't even want," I sneer.

Her head snaps up.

"He does want it," she retorts. I detect that her tone has lost some of its edge.

"Ha! As if; like Nathaniel would ever want to get YOU pregnant!"

"Well he did, and he does want it. He told me so."

That catches me off guard. Why would Nathaniel tell her that he wanted her child? Was it to replace the one he lost or was he so besotted with the idea of becoming a father that it didn't matter who gave birth to it? He was supposed to want my baby and my baby only.

I swallow a small lump in my throat and take a deep breath to calm the rush of adrenaline in my veins that is gathering speed and making my temples pulsate so hard that it feels like my anger is trying to break free. Keep your head Rio; don't do anything stupid. Kicking her in the stomach until she bleeds from between her legs may seem like a tempting idea right now, but you'll regret it later...well, maybe not, but you shouldn't do it anyway!

"That was probably to keep you off his back, I mean, how much could he really want this child with you if every chance he got he was with me, doing things that he wouldn't even consider doing with you?" I ask in a levelled tone.

Georgia shrugs, "Look, I don't live in fairy-tale land like you Rio; I've accepted that all men cheat, they're greedy, it's what they do. The answer to your question is simple; why buy the additional cow when you can get the extra milk for free?" she snarls, trying to save face. I want to do something to her face that will leave it beyond any form of salvage.

"If that's what helps you sleep at night, then fine. It must feel so sickening to be you sometimes," I sigh.

"Me?"

"Yeah you; I mean, you must hate that no matter how hard you try, that no matter what you do, he will NEVER love you because you'll never be enough. You'll never be me. That's why you lied isn't it?" I ask innocently, drawing for the big guns.

Georgia furrows her perfectly arched brows.

"What are you on about?"

"The baby, of course!"

Georgia rolls her eyes.

"I didn't lie, you idiot! As much as you'd like our baby not to exist, it does."

"Oh, I have no problem with that THING existing now that I know the truth."

Georgia shakes her head and chuckles darkly, "Call my baby a THING again and I'll make it so you can never have a THING of your own," she threatens.
As much as Georgia is definitely an intimidating character, if she decides she's feeling froggy it won't be me that gets jumped, you feel me?

"And what 'truth' are you getting at, because honestly, I just feel like you're wasting both of our times. Say what you have to say then piss off," she snaps.

My temples thump louder, and just as I'm about to reveal what I know, the thumping is so loud that I am almost certain that it isn't in my head anymore. It takes another set of deafening thumps and my name being hollered through the keyhole before I realise that the thumping is coming from the other side of the locked door.

"RIO, OPEN THE DOOR!"

Nathaniel had gotten word that I was in here alone with Georgia.

Showtime!

26 Destiny's Child.

"OPEN THE DOOR, RIO!" Nathaniel booms again, hammering at the door like a police officer. My heart quivers at the sound of his voice, his presence reawakening the dormant part of it –the part that loves him too much for me to be sensible. He's yelling at me but at this moment, I don't care. I know it makes no sense but I am so happy that he is here. Deny it as I may, I miss him like the desert misses the rain, and it pains me to have to conceal my elation for the sake of keeping up appearances. Every time I see him, no matter how briefly, I always feel like this –like I belong to him.

Sigh.

If I allow myself to indulge in my emotions, I will end up right back where I started –entangled in his arms, allowing him to perform his every sexual whim on my anatomy, his soulful moans encouraging me to confess my affections over and over till my throat burns with my eternal love letter. After all of that, somehow my hedonistic love story will end with the same tragic fashion it always does; alone.

Will I ever learn?

Nathaniel is standing on the other side of the door, screaming at me so he can defend Georgia; I hate him.

And I love him.

And I hate that I love him.

"I WANT CARTER," I yell back.

The hammering stops.

"Carter?" he asks with disgusted disbelief. I can picture his face; jaw clenched with that tiny muscle flickering like a candle in the wind, eyebrows knotted together, and his bright eyes turning dark and daunting as the tornado of anger swirls inside his irises.

I'm afraid to open the door; not because I'm scared of what will happen when I do, but because of the overwhelming feeling of adoration I get whenever I see him that puts my memories of his beauty to shame. I need Carter with me to keep me focused.

"Yes. Where is he?"

There is a scuffle and a gush of loud murmurs. The music is turned off as the Unfamous now catch wind of the situation. I have made us the main attraction of Jade Washington's party. I am dreading looking at my iPhone, which is jingling sporadically, alerting me that Twitter is on fire. Shit! All of the people with tons of followers are crammed into this dorm, everyone's going to know my business and judge me publically. Once these kinds of stories make it onto Twitter, they spread far and wide. If no one was sure of who I was before, they will know tonight.

"Why do you want Carter?" Georgia asks warily, finding the strength to get to her feet again. This time she stands without holding the sink. Funny how as soon as she hears that her ex is being brought into the situation she isn't all 'woe is me, I'm pregnant' anymore. The risk of being caught in a lie has miraculous effects.

"You'll see," I reply icily.

I'm not sure if it is anxiety or fear, but something is in Georgia's eyes that I have never seen before and it only makes me want to see my campaign through till the end all the more. So my name will be blasted across Twitter *shrug* at least I will finally get my own back.

"Princess?" Carter's voice seeps through softly with concern, "You okay?" he asks.

Georgia tenses up and I feel myself relax a little.

"Yeah, I'm okay."

"Rio, what the fuck is going on? Open the door!" Nathaniel cuts in, sounding even more wound up than before. He does not like me associating with Carter one little bit. Yeah well, I don't like you associating with whores' either but you don't listen to me, so go ahead and be upset. Maybe you'll finally realise what you put me through every time I see you with her.

I straighten the hem of my top and smooth any flyaway weave strands with my palms, before striding over to the door like the diva I wished I was. Georgia watches me suspiciously as she slowly staggers out of the bathroom to sit on the bed. I roll my eyes at her -you only threw up, stop being so bloody melodramatic!

I grab the cool metal of the lock and twist it until I the bolt clicks back into place, sending a blunt thud through the wood of the door. Breathing slowly I press down on the handle and pull the door open.

Nathaniel's eyes glow like polished steel, framed by the thick black lace of his eyelashes that only intensifies his stare even more. His lip piercing glints in the light as the muscle in his jaw flickers rapidly as he clenches and unclenches his jaw. His glower softens a touch when he looks down at me; he is definitely still mad, but not as mad as he was before I revealed myself. That's what love will do to you. Whenever we used to argue way back when, I used to make sure I looked at everything but him. Looking at him weakened my resolve and resulted in me waving my white flag so that we could get past whatever issue we were fighting over, and get back to being happy. Nathaniel was the opposite; he would keep his raincloud coloured eyes on me, knowing that if he stared me out long enough I would get lost in his beauty and surrender. Cheap trick, but it worked every time...but not this time.

We're not the same anymore; we're not the 'us' that we used to be. We're a 'mangled, torn and re-stitched, only to be ripped apart once more' version that is beyond repair. I hate what we have become, but most of all, I hate why we became this way. Georgia. I swear to you, seeing him standing here in all his heated glory, knowing that he is here to defend the one person he should be fighting against (from the very beginning), makes me consider unforgivable acts that would put Georgia out of our lives for good! I hate her so much it scares me.

I used to believe that Nate and I would have survived OUR baby issues; it would always be a major bump in our road, but there would always be the chance to have a child later on down the line when the time was right, but then he went and cheated on me with her, the girl who bullied me all because she wanted him. As much as I hated him for what he did, love made me forgive him, but once again Georgia popped back up and ruined us all over again. You can't imagine how much it hurt to find out that she was pregnant when she had us believing the child was his. If I knew then, what I know now, we would still be together and we'd be happy. Georgia is toxic and the sooner I remove her from our lives, the better. Whether this will fix Nathaniel and I, is a mystery -our issues are deeper than this one girl -but as I stare up at him, trying to calm the beating of my heart, a part of me hopes that it is at least a step in the right direction.

Nathaniel and Carter enter the room and close the door on our audience. Carter stands opposite Georgia and leans against the desk, watching her with contained fury. She makes a panicked sound. Nathaniel eyes Carter from the doorway, silently warning him to keep his distance. Carter doesn't even acknowledge him; he just continues to glower at Georgia.

"What the hell are you playing at Rio?" Nathaniel growls. Hearing his gravelly tone rumble so clearly for the first time in a while makes a flash of heat shoot up inside of me. I want to touch him, hold him, kiss him until my jaw aches and my lips swell...but I can't. Instead, I step aside and let him tend to his damsel in distress, in pained silence. It takes everything I have not to reach for him as he brushes past me, and not to cry out as he kneels down in front of Georgia, stroking her face with concern.

Stop touching her like that. Stop looking at her in that way...please.

So much for wanting nothing more to do with him; the allure of Georgia being out of the picture forever has gone to my head and I am drunk on one last chance to make things right.

"Are you okay?" Nathaniel whispers, brushing Georgia's slowly crusting hair out of her face. She pokes out her bottom lip a little and nods.

"I'll be alright. I don't know why they call it morning sickness when it happens throughout the bloody day," she moans.

Nathaniel smiles and touches his hand to her relatively flat stomach.

"It'll all be worth it in the end," he says optimistically. I wonder how he is with her when it's just the two of them.

Georgia smiles at him with such love and adoration that it make me nauseous. You don't love him; the fact that you are carrying on this baby charade just to keep him around proves it. That's not love, that's twisted possession. You need to find your ass on Maury, in therapy or something.

Carter pushes away from the desk and stands next to me with an unreadable expression on his face, watching the two of them interact with each other like we don't exist. He takes my hand and squeezes it gently. I squeeze back and the corner of his mouth twitches slightly, hinting at a smile that isn't going to come. He looks at me, then at them, and nods.

Carter's releases my hand and I step forward. They look up and scowl at us, suddenly remembering that we're in here too.

"You should be ashamed of yourself," I sneer venomously.

Georgia rolls her eyes and sighs wearily, "Oh Rio, shut up! You're giving me a headache."

I cock my eyebrow.

"Keep talking and I'll give you more than a_"

"HEY!" Nathaniel booms, stopping me short. Carter makes that amused sound.

Nathaniel gets up from the floor and stands halfway between me and Georgia, making the figurative situation literal.

"You two can't keep doing this. All this bitching is getting on my last nerve."

Oh it's getting on YOUR nerves is it? How upsetting for YOU! Never mind that I'm the one who is getting the shittiest end of the stick most of the time while you two play happy fake families.

"Now I know the situation isn't ideal, but we need to be mature about this or we'll just be stuck in this rut and I don't want my child to have to deal with this, so drop it, BOTH of you." He is talking down to us like we are children and while it only adds fuel to my fire, Georgia looks down sulkily, playing the role of the obedient baby mother to the T.

I put my hand on my hip.

"First of all, don't speak to me like I'm a minor_"

"Then stop acting like one!" he fires back, "What the hell were you even thinking locking yourself in here with her, Rio? Who does that?"

"I was just talking to her_"

"She's PREGNANT!"

"I KNOW THAT," I scream, tired of being reminded of it, as if it wasn't something that had tortured me in my head each and every day.

"THEN ACT LIKE YOU KNOW!" he shouts, getting up in my face, the thick veins in his neck pressing through his skin. I flinch and experience that flush of embarrassment you get when someone mistreats you in front of people that you don't like.

Nate sighs and softens his tone, "I need you to let go of this stupid vendetta you have against her Ri. It's over."

I peer at him questioningly; the way he said 'it's over' sounded a little too absolute for my liking.

"What?"

"I said it's over, Rio. I've already hurt you enough, and I know that this situation is not something you can handle, so whatever it is that we've been doing...or not doing has to stop...for good."

The already ravaged edges of the hole in my chest deteriorate further, like they have been soaked in gasoline and lit, burning and crumbling to ashes with every heavy heartbeat. He can't do this to me. He can't leave me; not for her, not for anyone, not EVER.

I shake my head and back away.

"You don't mean that," I choke, speaking more to myself than to him. I know he means it. He has been chasing me for so long and now because of some child that isn't even his, he is prepared to give up -he was prepared for me to let go…for good.

This is not happening, I won't let it.

"Yes, I do. We can't keep doing this to each other Rio. I can't keep doing this to you."

I shake my head.

"Nathaniel, listen to me_"

He looks at the ground.

"Rio stop_"

I grab him by the shoulders, forcing him to look at me.

"Will you shut up and listen for a minute?"

Georgia snickers in the background, "Pathetic." I will bitch-slap her so hard that my hand will leave an imprint on the baby's face!

"I'm sorry, did you say something?"

We all stop what we're doing and look at Carter. He walks over to the bed and stoops down in front of Georgia. He strokes her face, mimicking the way Nathaniel had done moments ago. Georgia doesn't move a muscle and for the first time ever, her fear is out in the open; Georgia is afraid of Carter.

"You always have so much to say, don't you, G?" Carter coos running his thumb across her bottom lip, "Well now's your time to shine, so c'mon darlin'; speak up."

Nathaniel makes a move to go to her, but I block his path, communicating with my eyes that he needs to leave them to it.

Her voice trembles, "Get away from me!"

Carter smiles creepily and tuts, "Baby, don't be like that."

"I'm not your baby, Carter!" she hisses.

Carter makes the amused sound, and he stands up and begins pacing in his cool manner.

"Funny you should say that."

"What's so funny about it? She's not your baby!" Nathaniel growls territorially. I frown and step away from him.

"Well, the irony of course. She *thinks* she's not my baby, but she *knows* that the one in her stomach is; isn't that right," -he smiles at Georgia –"baby?"

The room falls into silence, which is instantly replaced with the gasping, laughing and commentary from the other side of the door.

I look up at Nathaniel; his face crumples as he struggles to accept what he has just heard. His lips are moving but they aren't forming any words and there is no sound. His breathing deepens and he clenches his fists; his lips are still going until finally he closes his eyes and mumbles, "It's over."

He looks at all three of us; first Carter, then Georgia and finally, me. We stare at each other, and I want to touch him, but he doesn't look right, in fact, he looks all wrong.

"It's gonna be okay," I whisper to him, edging closer slowly so as not to trigger any unwanted reactions.

He frowns at me and shakes his head, "No."

"Yes, it will."

"Will it?" he laughs dryly.

I edge closer to him and touch the tips of my fingers to his. He doesn't move -he just keeps frowning at me.

I run my hand up his arm and onto his shoulder.

"Yes, everything's going to be okay now," I curl my arm around his neck and
the other one follows, pulling him into a gentle embrace, "She can't hurt us anymore. It's over."

"Nathaniel?" Georgia croaks from the bed. The sound of her voice makes him stiffen in my hold.

He shakes his head and pushes me away.

"It's over."

He walks out.

27 Heartbreaks & 808s.

"Nathaniel!" Georgia shrieks going after him. Carter doesn't stop her.

All around the doorway, people are laughing, gasping and staring at the scene before them; I even hear the word crazy pop up a few times. I don't relish this attention 1 bit, but I don't have time to let my ego take the stage. I don't care what they think –I may care in the morning, but as of right now all I can think about are those two little words echoing in my head; it's over. It can't be over. I know that we're in a dark place right now but I refuse to let this be where the story ends. I need to salvage what's left of us before it's too late.

"You okay?" Carter asks gently as people continue to watch us, greedy for more drama.

"Why didn't you stop her?" I ask irritated that after finally driving a wedge between the two of them Carter had just allowed her to go after Nathaniel.

He shrugs and looks down, "She's in love with him, what's the point of stopping her when it won't stop the way she feels?" he asks quietly, his cryptic mask dissolving a little, allowing me a glimpse into the kind of pain that I knew I never wanted to experience. If my heart is broken, then his heart is lost. I need to find Nathaniel.

Without another word, I dart through the crowd, out of the bedroom, and into the hallway, pushing past Jade 'Do Me' Washington in the process -another thing to add to my list of things I will regret in the morning.

I spot them at the exit surrounded by Georgia's clique, and more busy bodies. I push through the crowd trying to make myself heard over the commotion like it's my last chance to speak to him –scarily, that's what it feels like.

"NATHANIEL WAIT! NATHANIEL. NATHANIEL WAIT...PLEASE, DON'T GO!"

He looks in my direction and he runs his hand over his head.

"Rio, not now!" He turns back to Georgia "Is it true?" he asks in a deathly calm voice that sends chills down my spine.

Georgia steps forward with tears in her eyes.

"Nathaniel I_"

"IS IT TRUE?" he booms in an awful rumbling tone, making a few people jump.

She bows her head.

"Yes," she squeaks. She reaches out to him, "Nathaniel I'm so sorry_"

He throws his hands up and backs away from her.

"Don't touch me."

"Nathaniel, please," she begs, her eyes glittering with tears of desperation. It should be giving me great pleasure to watch Georgia crash and burn in front of everyone, but it doesn't. It's sad. She keeps crying and begging but he keeps backing away from her as if she has the plague.

"Someone get her before I do something I WON'T regret," he threatens, looking towards her friends for assistance. Sky and two more of her friends pull Georgia away from him.

Georgia cries harder, "Nathaniel please, I never meant to_"

"You never meant to what? Trap me with another man's baby? Bullshit G, you knew what you were doing! I'm so fucking done, man."

Without so much as a backwards glance, Nathaniel walks out.

I go after him.

"Nathaniel, wait up," I pant, running out into the parking lot to catch up with him as he storms angrily over to his car.

"Go back inside, Rio," he says over his shoulder, refusing to slow up. I jog a little faster.

"No! I want you to talk to me."

"I'm not in the mood to talk."

I catch up to him and grab his arm.

"Fine, we won't talk." I step closer to him and rest my hand on his chest.

Nathaniel frowns at me.

"Rio, this doesn't change anything."

I frown back.

"What? Nathaniel, the baby isn't yours; this changes everything! We can be together now."

"No, we can't. I'm tired of all this fucking drama and I'm tired of being the bad guy."

"Then don't be the bad guy!" I say weakly.

"How can I when you make me this way? I've been bending over backwards for you for too long, trying to prove to you that I'm riding for you, and every time the road gets rocky you point all the fingers at me, you run away, you shut me out, and now, you've shown up at Jade Washington's party with Carter fucking Johnson, the person I specifically told you to stay away from, and you let him make me look like some dickhead in front of all my friends! Why couldn't you have waited and spoken to me about it in private like a normal person?"

"I needed you to know how much of a malicious, vindictive bitch she really is. I needed all of you to know."

Nathaniel sighs, "Ahh, I see. So this wasn't really about me? No of course not, I mean, why would it be when your social status is more important to you than anything else."

"It's not, you are!"

"I used to be," he mutters, and then he turns his back on me and walks away. I don't follow him this time.

Nathaniel gets in his car and drives away without a goodbye, leaving me standing in the middle of the car park alone, and just like that, it's the end of an era.

I wait for the aching in my chest to start so that I can cry him a river, but there is nothing. I feel nothing.

Tonight, I lost my heart.

Book Two.

Untainted love isn't real after the first, this she knows
So a brooding darkness follows wherever she goes
Coiling itself around her heart, holding the pieces together
Reminding her that there's no such thing as forever
So when she sees a glimpse of light she runs to it
Catching it before it fades, convinced it's worth the risk
If temporary happiness exists in an almost-stranger's lips
Then it should make for a bitter-sweet kiss
Let unchained hands wonder
Let his touch tear your defences asunder
Then revel in his body heat
And writhe to escalating heart beats
Just for tonight, believe in his poetry
Lie to yourself and say it's not as hopeless as it seems
Undressed before him, no inhibitions, exposed
For these rebellious highs overshadow the lows
You know that this won't do
You know he can't fix you
But right now you belong to each other
Right now for the both of you, there is no other
Explosions collide, the light glitters then fades
Back to the darkness, 50 shades of Grey
With looks of acknowledgement you'll go your separate ways
Tattoo his name in your memory as yet another mistake.

-The Broken Romantic
Scotty Unfamous
From the 'Smoking in Cursive' poetry collection

1
Nothing Was the Same.

March 2011

I sit huddled on the lid of the toilet seat in the cramped cubicle, hoping that my nose will soon become desensitised to the sickly sweet and sour smell of the girl's bathroom. I can't stand the smell of numerous bodily functions masked over with economy air freshener that only makes the smell even more disgusting than it was to begin with, and yet here I am. I have been hiding in here for the past half an hour with my eyes clenched shut, wishing that a secret passage door will magically appear in this cubicle so that I can leave college unnoticed, that way, I won't have to face THEM. No matter how hard I squeeze my lids together and mouth my ridiculous wishes, no door manifests. I know I will have to go out and face THEM eventually -I can't hide in here forever, although it feels like a good idea right about now. A part of me wants things to go back to the way they were before, when I was no more than an extra that moved about in the background of THEIR wonderful world…but he changed that. He changed everything.

The 'he' I am referring to is my new boyfriend of 4 weeks; Nathaniel Dante Gibson -who is most possibly the most beautiful person I have ever had the pleasure of meeting in my life. Nate is one of those rare treasures; jaw-droppingly gorgeous on the outside and just as amazing on the inside. He's kind, thoughtful, romantic, funny, and absolutely out of his mind to have even spared a second glance at me, let alone make me his one and only when there are tons of girls that are in the same league as him. He is WAY out of my league; that's what THEY said.

THEY are Georgia Daniels and her gang of followers; the most popular girls in my college who all pine for the attention of my boyfriend. My being with Nate has planted me on their radar and instantly classes me as the enemy. I haven't done anything to them, I haven't even so much as looked at them, but they took it upon themselves to follow me to the bathroom and bitch about me like I wasn't there while I tried to use the toilet.

Every word they spat while reapplying their lip-gloss, dripped with poison, made to burn me for my crime against the social order. They made fun of the way I dress, my hair, the fact that I am pretty much a loner, and made it very clear that I am in no way, shape or form, good enough for Nathaniel.

As I have never made it my business to draw attention to myself, people never really bothered to pass any sort of judgement on me because I was kind of insignificant, so to hear these girls lash out on me like that made it that much harder to stomach -hence I am still sitting here like a coward.

I didn't say anything back; one, because how 'cool' would I really look hurling insults at someone whilst hovering over a public toilet seat and two...because although I hate to admit it. I believe that what they said about me and Nathaniel being together is true, and that makes it hurt even more. I don't deserve to be with someone so stunning. We don't look right together. He is as flawless as a model, while I'm simply 'the girl next door'.

I don't think I'm ugly (definitely not as ugly as they claim I am), but I am nowhere near as perfect as Nate. No one was as surprised as I was when his interest in me extended beyond friendship.

As my only real friend at college (and in life in general) is Tyson, when he wasn't around during my free periods, I found myself in the library to pass the time until he was released from class. Sometimes I did college work, but most of the time I sat down at a small table that faced the window reading Mills and Boon romance novellas. Nathaniel was often in there as well, sweet-talking some poor girl he had brought along into helping him with his coursework.

One day he showed up by himself and planted himself right next to me. I looked up and the first thing I said to him (bear in mind I had never spoken to this boy in my LIFE) was, "I'm not helping you with your coursework."

Nathaniel smiled, opened his text book and said, "I wasn't going to ask for your help. All you do is read sex books."

I remember feeling my face flush with heat as embarrassment took over. I had the strong urge to fling 'The Billionaire's Mistress' under the table, but figured that as he had obviously clocked what I had been reading for a while now, it was pointless.

Haughtily, I had straightened up my posture to show that I wasn't fazed and asked him, "Well why are you sitting here then?"

He replied, "You looked like you needed company. You're always alone, and as we ALWAYS see each other, I figured that we may as well speak to each other. You're like my unofficial library buddy." He smiled and just like that, he had won me over.

College had always been something that I saw as a way to fill up my empty days and even more time to goof about with Tyson, but now it had the added bonus of Nathaniel.

At first we only really hung out together in the library every now and then because he was still sweet-talking naïve girls into doing his coursework, but after a while the girls stopped tagging along and he sat with me all the time. We would completely abandon what we were doing (me: my 'sex books', him: his coursework) and sit talking in hushed voices for hours. We spoke about everything there was to talk about from college, to politics, to musing over the difference between 'juice' and 'juice drink' (don't ask me why). Whether what we talked about had any point to it or not, I treasured every moment; every word, every dazzling smile, every innocent touch that flooded my insides with intangible warmth. Before long I was convinced that I was in love with him, but I kept my feelings to myself afraid that he didn't even look at me as more than a friend.

One day he turned to me and said in the simplest, sweetest manner, "Rio, I like you...a lot." He smiled and went back to his coursework, leaving me staring at him, speechless. Eventually I confessed that I liked him too and that, ladies and gentlemen, is how I ended up with the most mesmeric boyfriend in the world -the mesmeric boyfriend that 'could do a hell of a lot better'.

Their spiteful words play over and over in my head like one of those really crap catchy songs that you hate but can't seem to rid your mind of. I don't want what they think to matter, but it does because if they think it, does that mean everyone else does too?

My phone vibrates, and then the sound of Rihanna's 'We Found Love' erupts from the speaker, momentarily erasing any negative thoughts from my head. It's him.

I dig urgently into my pocket and press the receiver to my ear.

"Nathaniel," I breathe. I cringe hearing my love-struck tone bounce off the tiled walls and back to me. Could I sound anymore consumed?

"You've been gone for ages; where are you?" he asks, worry heavy in his voice.

"I'm in the bathroom."

He pauses for a moment, and then I hear him smile, "Errrgh, you're taking a shit aren't you?"

"NO!" I squeal immediately, my face flushing with embarrassment. Oh my gosh, how can he ask me that? I don't want him to think of me as a…human. I'm a girl and everyone knows that girls don't 'shit', fart or any other revolting bodily function that takes away from our allure.

"Don't lie," he teases.

"I'm not; I'm...I just wanted to be alone for a while," I say quietly, the humour fading from my tone as the bitchy words begin to play all over again.

Nathaniel pauses and I am sure that he is trying to think of something that would put me in a better mood.

"Which bathroom you in, baby?"

"The one by the common room," I sulk.

There is some rustling in the background and then I detect the faint sound of his Nike Air Max 110s hitting the ground.

"I'm coming."

Before I have the chance to argue, the main door creaks open, and the foul air swirls about, now laced delicately with the warm spiced apple undertone of the boy I love.

I slip the cracked plastic lock back into place and slowly pull the door open. Despite my mood, I can't contain my smile when I see him. He is leant up against the sink counter, with his hands stuffed in the pockets of his jeans, and his head dipped low enough that the peak on his Supreme snapback conceals the top half of his face, leaving only his soft pink lips on show.

"You know boys aren't allowed in here," I scold him softly, preparing myself for the moment when those startling eyes finally lock onto mine and leave me breathless. I walk over to him, bracing myself for all that he is, only I guess I'm not walking fast enough because his hand reaches out and grabs me by the waist, pulling me to him and pressing my miniature frame into his sizeable one. I gasp.

He lifts his head and looks down at me. I stop breathing.

"I don't care. What's wrong?" he asks lowly.

I exhale and tear my eyes away from his.

"It doesn't matter."

"Whatever it is, it's upset you -it matters." He presses his lips against my forehead and lets them linger there for a moment before

pulling away so he can tilt my face up with the tips of his fingers and turn me into putty in his hands. I sigh; mould me.

"I overheard some girls talking about me," I confess, leaving out the fact that those girls are his stupid 'friends'.

His eyes tighten, "What did they say?"

I look down again, "That you could do better."

Nathaniel's whole body tenses up, "They're wrong." As quickly as his body had tensed, it loosens and melts around me as he relaxes and embraces me tighter. I breathe him in and feel myself get a little lightheaded.

"You are the best thing that could have ever happened to me. For me, there is nothing better than you," he says softly.

I roll my eyes.

"Nathaniel, have you seen yourself? You could date Lauren London if you wanted," I chuckle bitterly, looking up him again.

He frowns and takes my face between his hands,

"Rio, I don't want Lauren London; I want YOU. I love YOU."

Come again?

I suck in a sharp breath and forget to exhale as I stand staring into the face of the boy I love more than life itself, trying to get my heart around what he had just said. He stands tall and unwavering, his feelings projected as clear as the breaking of day on his face. I couldn't love him anymore if I tried, but the fact that he loves me back makes me want to.

"You love me?" I ask, dazed and confused that this exquisite creature could possibly love me.

Nathaniel draws my face closer and lowers his head until our lips touch; warm, moist and yielding. His kiss is strong yet tender, leaving me breathless and yearning for more.

He ends it all too soon, panting heavily, his heart thudding against my chest with urgency.

Smiling, he gazes into my eyes and nods, "I love you."

Present Day
January 2014

I hate my life.

2
Nobody's Business.

The cruel, icy wind smashes unrelentingly against the windows of Tyson's black GTi, making me grateful that I didn't have to travel back to campus on public transport and risk getting doused by the swollen rain clouds that loom overhead, decorating the sky with assorted shades of grey. I can't wait for spring time. The miserable winter weather reminds me of him –grey and cold. To be completely honest, everything reminds me of him, even the most insignificant object is able to trigger a memory from a time when love was. I detest that I miss him the way I do; it puts me in a bad place, a place I had vowed I would never revisit. I have broken many vows lately, and each one makes me wish that I possessed the capacity to be stronger.

I am a mess. I spent my entire Christmas holiday shut away in my bedroom, playing melancholy love songs to torture myself further.

They say that time heals all wounds, but if you have a piece ripped out of you, it will never really heal. You'll just be scarred and every time you see that scar it will remind you of what you lost. I've lost my heart; I'm un-healable.

That night when he left me standing in the parking lot after telling me that he wanted nothing more to do with me, he shot my worn and torn heart into a black abyss, obliterating the familiar ache in my chest; I miss that ache. Now all I feel is emptiness because without him, I have nothing -he was my everything.

"Rio, this doesn't change anything."

I wince at the memory and readjust my defeated position in the passenger seat.

Tyson glances at me and frowns, "You okay Ri?"

Oh how I am tired of that fucking question... NO, I'M NOT OKAY, NOW STOP ASKING ME!

I nod stiffly and try to force a small smile, but it comes out looking like I have a bad taste in my mouth. Tyson makes a face that lets me know that he doesn't believe that I am okay, but he is going to leave it alone for now.

We've been driving back to Westchurch in silence, but unlike the drive up to Herring University with Carter, it isn't tense, it is just silent. I don't want to talk and Tyson is content with just having me by his side so he didn't try and make awkward small talk. Before the whole incident (even though we had made up) things between Tyson and I weren't exactly back on track, but having to throw himself into best-friend-mode after tracking me down in the parking lot at Jade's party, he is my Ty again. If anything good has come out of this whole ordeal, it is that we are back to being besties again -something I didn't realise I had missed so much because...

"Ahh, I see. So this wasn't really about me? No of course not, I mean, why would it be when your social status is more important to you than anything else."

"It's not, you are!"

"I used to be."

Over the holidays, Ty had made the effort to come and see me every few days, and he also made sure that he called me every day so that I wouldn't have the chance to let my sorrow consume me completely –too late. Angelica hadn't liked that much; the distant period between Tyson and I was all she knew, she was used to having him all to herself, but now that I am officially back on the scene again, she has to share 'Sonny' with me -by the way, I STILL think that is a flipping stupid-ass nickname. I want to smack her in the throat every time she says it).

We hit the roundabout and zoom past Westchurch High Street -the butterflies begin to flutter around in the pit of my stomach. We are almost at back at Brompton; I will have to face everyone soon. For the second time in my life, I clench my eyelids together and wish for a secret trap door to magically appear when we hit campus so that I won't have to endure their judgemental stares and hushed gossiping as I walk by. I had made a complete and utter fool of myself at what was the biggest dorm party of the year and naturally, everyone was on their phone in minutes informing the entire cyber world of my endeavours. If they only half rated me before, they didn't rate me at all now.

"I wanna go home," I sulk.

Tyson kisses his teeth at me.

"Shut up. We're almost there and I ain't turning back now. You're gonna bop up to your room like you own the place with your head held high and no one will say anything, got it?" he orders me, choosing to follow his tough love approach. I nod obediently knowing that he is right; if I make it look like I am bothered by their opinions, it will give them more ammunition to work with because they will know how much it really affects me.

This year's façade is going to be even harder to pull off than last year's because not only do I have to win the respect and adoration of my peers all over again, but I have to develop an indestructible mentality if I am to survive the nasty comments that will be thrown my way. I sigh; in the past few months I have tried to recreate myself so much that you'd think I was Madonna.

"You ready?" Tyson asked observing me warily from the driver's seat.

We have successfully made it to campus and are now sitting in the car park outside of my block. My eyes are closed and my fists are clenched so tightly that my knuckles have paled from the strain. Brompton students swarm all around, hauling their suitcases back to their temporary student accommodation, a majority of them in a far better mood than I am. They are happy to be back. I can't wait for this term to end so I can hide away again.

I take a deep breath to calm my nerves, and compose my face.

"Yeah, I'm ready."

I open the door and swing my legs out swiftly, wanting to get this over with as quickly as possible, and strut to the boot of the car to fetch my suitcase. Tyson meets me around the back of the car with a stony look on his face, daring someone to say something. I mimic his expression.

"Shoot me now," I mumble.

"Suck it up." he opens the trunk, hauls my suitcase out and sets it at my feet.

"I can feel them looking at me," I hiss.

Tyson looks around and sees that I'm not being paranoid; they are all staring at me.

He shrugs and pulls out his suitcase.

"If they're gonna look then give them something to look at," he nudges his head towards my bust and flashes his crooked smile.

I make a face and punch him in the arm, smiling softly.

"Pervert!"

Tyson grins. He takes my hand.

"It was just a friendly suggestion."

We marched up to my block hand in hand, bypassing all the sceptical and curious sets of eyes that are trying to watch me on the sly. Needless to say, I am relieved once we hit my dorm, which is already in full swing with the girls running around and screeching childishly at each other. Carmen is already shuffling around in her favourite pair of Uggs, making a huge pot of tuna and pasta, and telling crude jokes about her sexual escapades with Bless over the holidays, while Fontaine unloads the never-ending selection of alcoholic beverages from her backpack (already tipsy) and Yoshi is sitting quietly at the table, drinking anything Fontaine shoves at her and giggling at Carmen, her usual vibrant attire replaced by a dark, shapeless jumper and yoga pants. I've missed them.

Over the holidays we hadn't spoken much because I had screened everyone's (except for Tyson's) calls, but every now and then I forced myself to pick up out of guilt...that and if I didn't answer I was never going to hear the end of it when I got back.

"Bitches!" Tyson squeals in a camp voice opening his arms wide for a group hug.

Fontaine bounds over to him first and throws her arms around him, and then me.

"Ohmygaaawd, you're baaaack," she slurs happily in her drunken cockney twang, planting a big wet one on my cheek and her boisterous golden curls tickle my skin.

"I knaaaaw," I reply in the same ditsy tone.

"I fackin' missed yooooou," she sings into my ear, still squeezing me.

I pat her on the back and push her away gently, "Okaaay, I missed you tooooo, now get off," I laugh. Fontaine pokes out her lip and releases me, only to be replaced by Carmen and Yoshi, who aren't as enthusiastic, but are happy to see me nonetheless.

Carmen shuffles over to the stove.

"You lot reached here just in time; drunkard over there," she gestures at Fontaine "has a sack full of the loudest Thai I've smelt in my life, and the pasta is almost ready. Can you say MUNCHIES?" she hollers, hopping up and down on the spot animatedly.

I grin; weed is just the thing I need to get my mind off of...

I shake the thought from my head.

"Good stuff! You lot got cheese to go with the pasta, right?" I ask, taking off my jacket.

"Of course! It's in the fridge," Yoshi says returning to her seat.

"You lot are going in, init! Pasta, weed and liquor; 2nd term is starting off correct!" Tyson grins, rubbing his hands together and taking a seat next to Yoshi. Fontaine thrusts a drink into his hand.

Carmen raises her brow, "I'm sorry; last time I checked, you didn't live here. You need to go see what Calvin and the rest of them are doing in your dorm, 'cause this is for flat mates only."

Tyson's face falls.

"No food for youuuu," I tease in a goofy voice.

"Shut up. If she ain't feeding me, best believe I will shorten your portion nicely."

I put my hand on my hip.

"You're gonna really try and take MY food when I'VE got the MUNCHIES. You must want to die tonight," I joke.

"It's true; you're craven! Car, 'llow me man, you know I'm good for it," he says, flashing Carmen his signature sexy crooked smile and wiggling his eyebrows suggestively.

Carmen looks him up and down.

"No thanks!"

Laughter erupts in the kitchen and just like that, I'm less pessimistic about being back on campus. That's the best thing about friends; no matter how down you are feeling they are always able to lighten your mood. You can be as popular as the Jade Washington's of the world, but unless you have that small circle that you know are 'for real', none of that matters. All the friends in the world can't compare to being around people who really love you, flaws and all.

Two hours later we're all slumped in different positions around the kitchen table with an empty pot of pasta in the middle and five equally empty plates stacked up next to it. The rest of the table is strewn with empty bottles and discarded plastic cups (left over from our little dinner party last term). Along with that mess, there are Rizla papers, severed cigarettes, and random mounds of ash from where each one of us had missed the makeshift ashtray (another plastic cup).

For the last thirty minutes Carmen has been babbling about how hot Bless is –one of her favourite subjects. I'm zoning; her voice is now background noise, which I respond to by sloppily nodding, umm-ing and ahh-ing in the wrong places, making all of us break out into fits of raucous stoner laughter.

We calm down again for the umpteenth time and Fontaine raises her hand.

"Alright Car, you've been talking for the world. My turn," she says taking advantage of an opening to speak before Carmen can take the floor again. Silently, I thank God.

"I have got really, really, really big news," Fontaine grins, spreading her arms wide to emphasize just how big her news is.

"What?" I ask, half-heartedly not caring. Fontaine is the most intoxicated out of all of us, so her news is probably just more mindless babble.

She claps her hands together and purses her lips as if she's going to reveal a juicy secret.

"I'm in a relationship!" she grins.

"What, with Hench McGym-bo?" Carmen asks, referring to Carter's muscle-bound friend, Leon, who Fontaine had been seeing casually last year.

Fontaine makes a face, "Oh God no! I finally got him into bed and let me tell you, the only thing that is hench about him is his muscles."

"That's probably down to those steroids he's been taking. I heard it makes men's dicks shrink," Carmen snickers.

"He doesn't take steroids, that body of his is 100% dedication. His dick is already the size of a clitoris; if he took steroids it would bloody disappear altogether! I had to fake my orgasm just so he would think that size doesn't matter; poor thing. To make matters worse, he doesn't even give head –I couldn't believe it! It's 2014; I thought boys that don't give head were extinct now! Quite frankly, the whole experience was fucking depressing."

Tyson's eyes widen with amused horror.

"Is this really how chicks are going on these days? Talking about guys like…guys."

Yoshi puts her hand on his shoulder in a reassuring fashion, "Ty, this is nothing. Believe it or not, they're toning it down because you're here."

"Anyway, Nadia and I are back together!" Fontaine squeals. We all fall into silence.

Fontaine's smile falters.

"Well? Aren't you happy for me?"

Carmen, Yoshi and I look at each other, but say nothing.

"A chick? That's hot!" Tyson grins smiling to himself. It is obvious from the way his smile widens he is picturing Fontaine with another girl and that he likes what he sees -pervert.

"Was Leon's dick that bad?" I ask.

Fontaine laughs, "Yes, but my relationship has nothing to do with his shortcomings. A few days after Jade's party, she called me and asked to meet up. We went out for drinks, one thing led to another and then_"

"You had a *real* orgasm!" Carmen finishes for her with a smirk.

"Did I ever!"

"So, is she for real this time?" I ask seriously.

"Yup! She asked me to be her girlfriend, and I said yes. We're official guys!"

"So she's out of the closet now?"

Fontaine shrugs, "Pretty much."

I furrow my brow, "Pretty much?"

"She hasn't come out to her family yet, but we're a couple in public now and that's good enough for me_"

"For now," Carmen interjects again.

Fontaine nods, "For now. I know how difficult it is to come out of the closet; it's scary, especially when it's those closest to you. Not everyone will be okay with it. Luckily for me my parents are quite liberal so it doesn't bother them, but there are some family members who won't speak to me anymore, and on the off chance when they do, what they say isn't nice. Nadia's family are devout Catholics; I can understand why she's not ready to tell them just yet."

"As long as she tells them eventually; exes have a funny way of making history repeat itself, reminding you of why you broke up in the first place." I mumble.

Fontaine leans back in her chair and chews her lip; she's scared that I could be right.

Yoshi, being the sweetheart that she is, reaches over and gives Fontaine's hand an optimistic squeeze.

"Well I'm happy for you and I'm sure that things will be much better this time. If she didn't love you she would've stayed away, but she came back. Don't worry about the bad stuff before it's even happened, just be happy. So, When do we get to meet her?" she asks.

Fontaine's face lights up again, but just before she can give Yoshi an answer, Carmen's horrified voice cuts through the air.

"WHAT THE FUCK IS THAT?" she screams grabbing Yoshi's arm.

Yoshi's eyes widen with panic as she tries desperately to yank her hand back before the rest of us can see the large bluish-purple mark that is peeking out from under her jumper sleeve. Carmen holds strong and pulls Yoshi's sleeve up as far as it can go, revealing an array of angry bruises and scratches marring her skin.

"Yosh, what the hell happened to your arm?" Fontaine gasps taking a closer look.

Yoshi tugs her arm out of Carmen's iron grip and hastily yanks her sleeve back down.

"I had an accident over Christmas. It's nothing!" she snaps defensively, folding her arms protectively across her chest.

In that moment, everything falls into place; the unexpected alteration of her personal style, the way she flinches sometimes when people touch her, the way she gets edgy when Ace is around, why she's so private about their relationship, the random expensive gifts (which he said were to keep her happy, but are no more than material apologies), the way how when we're out, if he's not with her, he's watching her. I thought it was because Ace was an attentive boyfriend, but now I can see him for what he really is; abusive.

I look at her and frown.

"What kind if accident does that to your arm Yosh?" I ask calmly.

Yoshi rolls her eyes trying to make out that she's getting annoyed, but I know better; she's avoiding making eye contact.

"I fell down the stairs at my parents' house when I was playing with my niece."

"Is that what he told you to say?"

Tyson, Carmen and Fontaine's eyes widen when they see where I'm going with this.

Yoshi looks at me and scowls, "I don't think I like what you're insinuating."

"So you came up with that excuse yourself?"

"Ri, Ace is our friend," Tyson steps in, "He loves Yoshi; he wouldn't do that to her."

"What's love got to do with it? My dad loved my mum and look what he did to her!" I yell. Tyson doesn't say anything else; he knows how touchy the subject of my father's treatment of my mother is.

I look back at Yoshi.

"Ace did this to you, didn't he?"

"No! I just told you, I_"

"Fell? Well, let me tell you something, if you don't get out of this soon, one day you'll 'fall', and you may not get back up!" I growl.

Yoshi glares at me stubbornly.

"Rio, ease up." Fontaine says gently, giving me a warning look asking me not to push the subject anymore, "If Yoshi says she fell, then she fell; leave it alone."

I huff and lean back in my chair deciding that it's probably best to back off. Yoshi's not going to talk, and if she's not going to talk then that means she has no intention of leaving him yet. Having a go at her won't do anything until she's ready to be helped; I saw that first hand every time my mum lied to Michelle whenever my dad did what he did to her.

Yoshi looks at the ground and bites down on her trembling lip.

"I'm tired. I'm going to bed," she says quietly. We watch her leave.

They say that love is a form of insanity; maybe that's why it has the power to make us behave so irrationally at times. Love has proven time and time again that it can be one of the most dangerous things that exist in this world; it can take us to exhilarating highs one moment, and then send us to crushing new lows the next. I will admit that I am one of its victims, but as far as I would go for it, I have my limits -my lover putting his hands on me being one of them.

Yoshi's multihued arms ends our night of fun on a very tense note and I'm afraid to see the rest of the marks she is hiding away underneath her clothes because I am betting that we haven't seen the worst of it. Carmen and I were ready to go over to Ace's flat and go off but Fontaine told us that we should stay out of it because the fact of the matter is, it isn't any of our business (SO!), and that we won't know for sure that Ace is the cause of the bruises until we have solid evidence -so we left it alone...for the moment.

You can take a horse to water but you cannot force it to drink; until she is ready to fess up there isn't much we can do to help and it pains me that she is defending him when in fact she needs defending from him.

3

Nude.

A slither of pale winter sun peeks through the small gap in my curtains; it's daytime -time to get up and face reality again. I throw back the covers of my single bed and sit up, relieved that my dream has ended. Nowadays my dreams are just as bad as being awake because in each of them I am still without him. Every night before I go to sleep he is always the last thing on my mind, so naturally he is in every dream I have. Every night, in every dream -no matter where we are or what we are doing -he leaves me, and every morning I wake up. Alone. Sometimes my dreams are so vivid that I relish waking up because for a few seconds, everything is all right…then reality sets in and the emptiness comes rushing back to me. I don't know which is better: feeling the pain of my loss, or feeling nothing at all. Either way I am miserable; stuck in my own personal purgatory, unable to feel anything, the hole in my chest collecting dust. When he walked away he took my heart with him and as far as I'm concerned, he can keep it. It's his. It will always be his.

I pick up my iPhone from the windowsill and look at the time –its 5 o'clock *already?* Well looks like my 'alone time' is going to have to be cut short because I have to start getting ready for tonight's event. Before the new term officially begins, everyone is heading to Moonlight Ents's official re-fresher's rave, Bad & Beautiful at the *The Suite* in Leicester Square, to celebrate being back at university. Why they think being back is something to celebrate I will never know, but this rave is the first big event of the year, so I have to go. Naturally, I have that anxious feeling in the pit of my stomach that people are going to stop, stare and gossip when they see me, but like Tyson said; I can't hide forever. He thinks that if I just throw myself into the lion's den, then it's more likely that the buzz about my name will die down faster because I'll be old news after that. I hope he's right.

After a long leisurely shower, I smother my skin in Palmer's Cocoa Butter and pull my outfit out of the cupboard -I purchased this from a small fashion boutique in *The Denes* shopping centre in Bromley, so it's near enough exclusive. I have been saving this dress for a special occasion, but as I need to return to the scene with a bang, I figure that tonight is special enough. It isn't something that I would usually wear when I'm raving because it's too impractical for the way I dance, but I look *beyond* amazing in it. I finger the chocolate jersey fabric and smile to myself. Even though I won't admit it out loud, I'm also choosing to rock this dress just in case Nathaniel shows up. I know, it's a little pathetic making an extra effort to look good just in case the boy you like (in my case, the boy I love) sees it, but we've all done it, so don't you judge me.

I step into the dress carefully, admiring the way the soft cocoa material caresses my skin as I pull it up my legs, over my hips, torso, and bust, then I tie the thin spaghetti straps around my neck. The dress hugs my voluptuous frame and stops just below my knees, the plunging halter neckline dips down to my cleavage; high enough to be tasteful, but low enough to make eyes and minds wonder. As it is the same cocoa complexion of my skin, it has that coquettish quality that makes me appear nude at first glance. The back of the dress is almost non-existent as the material doesn't begin until it hits the dimples at the small of my back. I am walking sex.

I keep my makeup and hairstyle understated, keeping the colours neutral, and slicking my hair up into an empress bun. Even my shoes are simple –nude suede pumps. I glamourize my ensemble with a pair of large gold disc earrings from H & M, a statement gold cocktail ring from Accessorize, and a hand beaded gold clutch from Top Shop. You know those random occasions when you look so good that you just stand and stare at yourself in the mirror for ages, then you realise that you're being really vain but you don't care because you're a goddamn *vixen*, so you start posing, pouting and practicing your 'come hither' looks and possible modelling positions for Instagram, until your *flawlessness* drives you to feel narcissistic enough to actually *take* pictures for Instagram and post it up, then wait for the 'likes' to roll in (oh this is so going to be my new avi…maybe I should post it on Twitter too -@RioDuran: New avi!☺) ...or is that just me? Whatever! There is no way Nathaniel can think badly of me when I look this good. I'm sure of it.

Friday night and Leicester Square is ablaze with lights, laughter and lots of people. Black cabs and those shifty looking bike carriages strung up with fairy lights (some with sound systems) line the road. The sound of plates and cutlery and glasses clinking, flows out of the restaurants. An artist sits by the railings drawing impressive (but cheesy) caricatures for the tourists. A busker blows his saxophone to the tune of George Michael's 'Careless Whisper', with the case for it open at his feet filled with small change, surrounded by a few merry drunkards who dance about to their own rhythm in front of him, whooping and cheering. The police are posted around waiting for some trouble, which will inevitably start as the night wears on. The pretty pavements the government lines this London tourist spot with, are littered with flyers from the numerous club promoters, who walk around, dressed to impress, trying to offer deals mostly to female club goers. The city is alive and it's hard not to love it.

We've been inside of The Suite for just over an hour and I have already been approached seven times by six different guys (one of them couldn't take the hint). My dress is working its magic effortlessly, it's only drawback being that my dance moves are a little limited. I'd spent most of my time seated on the white leather couches, bubbling and swaying to the music, while my girls dance in the VIP section without a care in the world, drunk off too many complimentary bottles of wine and champagne, courtesy of Ace and Bless's drink tab.

When we'd first entered I got a few expected dirty looks from random girls that I didn't even know, but the way the men were watching me pushed the negative sneers to the back of mind and I revelled in the attention. Now all I need is for Nathaniel to see me, where *is* he? I have been scanning the crowd since we got in here, and all now there is still no sign of him. I really hope that he does show, otherwise all of this is for nothing. Once you put someone up on a pedestal you find that the attention of others is nice, but meaningless, because you only care about what that one person thinks. I want him to see me and freeze for a moment to take me in, then watch his steely eyes turn into liquid silver as the burning desire he would surely have for me, melts his defences like butter in my mouth. I needed to see that exquisite look in his eyes that lets me know that a part of him wants me in his life. I'm jolted out of my wistful reverie by my iPhone vibrating inside of my clutch purse -Tyson.

Where u @ fish face?

I roll my eyes and smile to myself, happy that at least he is here; there will be one element of normality to the overhyped atmosphere. As much fun as I am having turning heads with my illusionist dress, my problems are still there waiting for me to become unoccupied so they can torment me again. This makes me more than grateful for Tyson, because even though they never completely go away, when he's around they seem somewhat bearable. He is my medicine; when it all becomes too much to handle, he comes and take the hurt away for a while. What I really need is my cure, my love -Nathaniel -to make me all better. Seriously, where is he?

Shaking my head, I turn my attention back to the rave, not wanting to crawl back into my little black hole of nothing while I am in public. I continue to sway to whatever deep house song is playing. I don't know what it is and I don't care, I just need to focus on something else. Everywhere I look there are young, glamorous girls, flaunting their best assets, dressed in provocative outfits, twirling, dipping, cutting shapes, and shaking their hips to the beat as if they are performing a pre-mating ritual dance. The boys that aren't already lost to the music hover nearby, biding their time before they pounce on an unsuspecting female, watching and waiting with thirsty eyes, like predators stalking their prey. Everybody else is bubbling around the edges of the dance floor, making friends with the walls as if they are in a school disco, or at the bar. The bar crowd are either drinking to get tipsy enough so that they can come out of their shell, or trying to get stone cold drunk so that they can act a fool –enter the boy in sunglasses and gaudy designer clothing, holding up a bottle of Moet that he bought with his student loan, trying to play the role of the big spender.

I Whatsapp Tyson back, telling him my location, secretly feeling a little smug that I am able to tell him that I'm in VIP; I have my foot in the door –even if it's being held open because my friends are sleeping with the event planners. Bored of standing in one place too long and a little thirsty, I decide to treat myself to a cocktail. Usually I'd buy a glass of wine and call it a night, but as my dress has me feeling like I can play the role of the whole 'grown 'n' sexy' diva, I think a pretty, overpriced, fruity alcoholic concoction is right up my alley -plus, student loan has just dropped, so I can spare to splash more cash than usual (please note this does not put me in the same category as those Moet spraying, sunglasses in the dark wearing, student loan stunters…it's just a little treat that I feel I deserve). I Whatsapp Tyson again, letting him know that I'm going to the bar, then I signal to Carmen -who is gyrating on top of the table as if she bought it. I don't think she sees me because she's reached the point of whining where you close your eyes and make ratchet faces because you know you are going IN. All right SPICE!

I chuckle quietly to myself and sashay through the crowd, mumbling, "Excuse me," repeatedly. Why won't these idiots move? I'm walking here! You can go back to grinding on that ugly boy once I've passed. Finally I have shoved and squeezed my way through the crowd and am now at the slick bar area, lit by florescent blue neon lights. I spot an opening around the perimeter of the bar and fling myself in it before anyone else can beat me to the punch, accidently shoving the extremely well dressed guy next to me in my haste. I turn towards him to deliver the obligatory apology so that we can both get over it and move on with our lives, but when my eyes connect with his magnificent green ones that glow with an ethereal intensity due to the blue lighting -making them all the more hypnotic -I freeze.

Shit!

Jade 'in–your-dreams' Washington peers down at me irritably and furrows his brow. Of all the people I had to fall into, why did it have to be him? It wasn't enough that I had caused a major disruption at his party (he probably thinks I am a total loser now), but now I am falling on him; 'why?' I cringe!

As quickly as I can muster, in a desperate and slightly awkward attempt to redeem myself, I look down coyly, then, back up at him from under my lashes, "Sorry."

Jade's expression softens and he gives me an amused but forgiving smile. "Don't worry about it...Rio, isn't it?" he asks, flashing his perfectly straight white teeth, rendering me speechless -as if his model-esque looks aren't enough to send the butterflies in my stomach into a frantic flurry. I am slightly astonished that he even recognises me, let alone remembers my name. I, Rio Greene, have been retained in Jade 'kiss-me-now' Washington's memory -that has to count for something, right?

I blush furiously and smile back at him, trying to control the size of my grin, as I don't want to look too overjoyed. I've witnessed first-hand how Jade regards females that fawn over him, and I will be damned if I give him cause to roll his eyes at me. He turns to me fully, his long glossy locks swishing over his shoulder in a way that makes me pine for a new weave. I wonder what he is mixed with, because I would breed for him in a heartbeat! It's funny how we can meet a guy we barely know, take one look at their hair and decide then and there if we would have their baby. Of course, 9 times out of 10 we wouldn't *actually* go through with it because, well, that's just crazy (and a tad scary), but it is entertaining to imagine what pretty babies you'd have together.

I toy with my cocktail ring, still smiling, "Yeah. Jade, right?" I reply sweetly, admiring the way the club lights make his emerald orbs glitter like jewels –what can I say? I'm a sucker for pretty eyes.

Jade lifts his drink to his full lips and chuckles. "Don't be cute; I know you know who I am," he says arrogantly before taking a sip of the strong smelling dark liquid in his glass.

My sweet smile falters as I sense myself skirting the possibility of receiving the dreaded eye roll. I have two options; I can either laugh it off and hope for the best, or find a witty reply to shoot me out of the deep end. I do neither. Giggling like an idiot will do me no favours, and I'm on the ball enough tonight to say something cleverly humorous within a decent time frame. Instead I fire back at him with the same level of arrogance, "Well then I guess I'm not the only one being cute, 'cause you obviously remember me too."

Real smooth, Rio! You should've just smiled.

Jade's lips twitch as he processes my reply, then they fall, erasing all traces of his brilliant smile. I guess he isn't used to being spoken to like that. He sets his glass down on the counter and narrows his wicked green eyes at me. Slowly, he leans in close enough that the heat from his buttery toffee skin radiated onto mine and sneers, "Well how could I forget the desperate little girl who made a spectacle of herself when she ran out of MY party after the guy that still didn't want her, even after she exposed Georgia Daniels?"

I tense up and try to give him my best 'who do you think you're talking to' eyebrow raise.

Jade pulls back, smirking triumphantly knowing that he has hit a nerve.

"Something like that is bound to leave an impression, don't you think?" he taunts. Yup, definitely should've just giggled and braved the eye roll. It would have been a hell of a lot more bearable, than having Jade 'douche-bag' Washington mock me for my indiscretion. Suddenly I'm not thirsty anymore. Shooting him a furious partying glare, I snatch my clutch purse off the bar and turn on my heel to storm off.

He catches my wrist, his mocking smirk now replaced with an amused smile.

"Are you always this dramatic?" he chuckles.

I strengthen my glare and yank my hand away.

"Yes, now fuck off," I growl, feeling my little crush on Jade 'total-asswipe' Washington withering away as my anger builds. How dare he say those things to me! He doesn't even know me. Right now I don't give a toss about who he is, he has no right to speak to me like that. Why do some of these people think that it's okay for them to belittle the people beneath them just because of their social status? Yes, I get it, I'm not one of you, so in your eyes I'm not entitled to receive the same respect as one of your peers, but I'm still a person goddammit! Urgh, they are so infuriating! Makes you wonder why I want to be one of them so bad right? I don't want it to be okay for them to speak to me like that anymore.

The people surrounding us have become distracted from their conversations at the sound of me cursing at their 'King', and are now waiting to see what happens next. This ain't television bitch, don't watch me!

"Yes?" I ask them haughtily, talking out of my neck like a hoodrat. A few of them grumble and give me dirty looks, before muttering things along the lines of "That girl's too rude, about 'yes?'", while the rest of them find my attitude amusing.

Jade laughs again, "You like causing a scene, init?" I roll my eyes; why is he still talking to me?

"Not even, I just can't stand self-entitled assholes," I retort.

His thick shapely eyebrows knot together. "You calling me an asshole?"

"What, are you deaf now too?"

Jade throw his head back and laughs again, sending his lustrous tresses flying, creating a rich fan of glossy black silk. I don't get what's so funny?

"Wow! You're rude y'know. I was just messing with you miss," he smiles reaching for my arm again.

I step back. "Don't touch me," I hiss.

Jade cocks his eyebrow in mock surprise. "Well, that's a first! All the girls want me to touch them; init babes?" he smirks, demonstrating his point on a girl nearby -his slender fingers slowly tracing the contours from the nape of her neck, to the tips of her now trembling fingers. He throws in a cheeky wink for good measure. She giggles. I roll my eyes for him.

"You're a prick," I spit, unimpressed by his frivolous sexual antics.

Jade dismissively turns away from his new admirer and shrugs. "You're too sensitive. Let me buy you a drink; what's your poison?" he asks casually, hailing one of the all too eager female bar staff.

I furrow my eyebrows in confusion.

"I've told you to fuck off, called you an asshole AND a prick, and now you're offering to buy me a drink?"

"I know; you're very rude. Maybe someone should discipline you…" his suggestive smile is slow and undeniably sexy and if I hadn't already decided that I dislike him, I would be blushing and trying to reign in my eager smile.

I roll my eyes, "No thanks, I'll pass." I try to make an exit, only for him to grab my wrist again.

I smack his hand off. "I said, don't touch me!" Suddenly a lot more people have tuned into our little mini drama. I wait with baited breath, as the realisation of my actions sink in. I can't believe I did that, it's practically social suicide! I have just hit Jade Washington; surely he is going to end me now.

Jade's light-hearted smile is no longer present - I have well and truly crossed the line.

He sighs and takes another sip of his drink.

"Okay, we're even now. I pissed you off, you've now pissed me off...A LOT, so here's what's gonna happen; I'm gonna take you and that lovely little number you're almost wearing to the dance floor, and we're gonna make it up to each other," he says seriously. I swallow.

"I don't want to dance with you," I say, quiet but firm, trying not to push my luck any more than I already have.

Jade shifts closer to me, his proximity distinguishing just how much taller he is. He stares down at me with his eyebrow raised, not saying a word, and I can feel his body heat again. Defiantly, I stare back up at him, my jaw tense and my chin jutting out. The longer we stand like this, the more attention we attract, and the more I want to step away and disappear into the crowd. It's as if he's getting a kick out of me fighting with him - perhaps he has one of those 'I like a challenge' complexes that most gorgeous womanisers have.

I feel his insistent fingertips sear his touch along the bare skin at the base of my back as he pulls me closer, keeping his sparkling eyes locked on mine.

"Yes you do," he murmurs in a compelling manner. He is right, I do, but I will be damned if I admit it.

I open my mouth to deny his assumption when I spot Tyson breaking through the crowd behind Jade. Thank God! I rip Jade's lingering arm from around me and walk stiffly (I'm a little dazed from my close encounter with Jade, and trying to hone in on any composure I have left) over to a territorial looking Tyson.

He reaches out and pulls me to safety, keeping his eyes on Jade.

"What's going on Ri?" he asks tautly, still looking at Jade.

I tuck myself under the nook of his arm and gave shake my head, "Nothing," I lie.

Tyson looks down at me and frowns, "Didn't look like nothing."

Jade turns and leans brazenly against the bar to watch us, his expression is unreadable.

"It doesn't matter, you're here now," I say, forcing a smile so that he will let go of what is already a (in)tense situation.

Tyson sighs and tightens his grip on me. Jade notices; the corner of his mouth quirks up in amusement, as if to say that not even Tyson can save me from him.

"Whatever. Let's head back; Carmen is trying to do the splits and we both know that it will not end well," he laughs, pulling me along with him into the crowd. I giggle imagining what a mess Carmen must look like; she has been trying to do the splits for ages because she claims that she's done with 'all these basic bitches being able to do it while I can barely hold one leg horizontally!'

Just before we are swallowed by the sea of people completely, curiosity causes me to glance over my shoulder; Jade is watching me with an enigmatic look in his eyes that I can't decipher, but I am pretty sure that whatever we started at the bar is far from over. He bites the corner of his lip and winks before turning his back on me.

God, give me strength.

4
Madonna.

The disappointment of not seeing Nathaniel at *The Suite* the other night looms over my head like my own personal rain cloud. Why wasn't he there? Why isn't he *anywhere?* As one of Brompton University's 'Kings' he is sort of obliged to at least show his face at major events, something he normally relished doing. Maybe he didn't hear about it...okay, that's ridiculous; of course he knew about Bad & Beautiful, there wasn't a soul in the realm of the Unfamous that didn't. Nathaniel is Brompton royalty, he probably received several invites; not that I'd know seeing as he has taken the liberty of deleting (and possibly blocking) me from his Facebook, Twitter and Instagram so that I have no idea of his whereabouts, what he is doing...or if he even thinks about me at all. Along with cutting off our cyber connections, Nathaniel has blocked me from his Whatsapp and has avoided picking up the phone or replying to any of my desperate text messages. I don't bother trying to get through to him anymore because every unanswered call and text makes it clearer that he meant what he said; it's over. I wonder if the reason he didn't show up to the rave was because he knew I'd be there...surely not; he can't want to keep away from me so badly that he'd avoid being where I am altogether...can he?

My question is answered when I turn up to my English Literature lecture on Monday morning and his seat is empty. I scan the entire room, desperately hoping to see him occupying one of the other chairs; any other chair. I don't intend to bother him; I just need to see him, to know that he is here and that he is okay –to see if our separation is eating away at him as much as it is me.

Nathaniel is nowhere to be found.

Stoically, I take my usual seat at the back of the lecture hall and close my eyes -it is all I can do to keep my tears from falling. I had been counting on him being here to break the torturously elongated thread of distance and time between us - and to feel my heart beat. It's been a while since I felt the inexplicable tremor of love's anxiety. What I would not give for that ache in my chest.

The entire lecture ends up being a waste of my time because I didn't pay an ounce of attention to what Rose was talking about. Instead, I bounced between restraining my tears beneath my eyelids and staring at the door, waiting for the boy that I know would never come. It got to the stage where I wanted to see him so badly that I sat and stared at his chair and imagined that he was there. At one point, I actually reached out to touch my hallucination so that I could hold his waiting hand under the table and revel in the gentle way he would brush his thumb back and forth over my skin. When you lose someone you love, you miss the smallest things that you took for granted when they were there, like the way they held you in their arms so securely, that it felt as if you were pieces of the same puzzle that were meant to fit together. Or, the way that even after kissing for ages, they still had to sneak a few extra pecks on the lips before they were satisfied enough to pull away completely.

God, I miss him.

I had intended to return to my room after the lecture so that I could be alone with my memories, but somehow I find myself strolling absentmindedly along the familiar cobbled pathway that runs alongside the glittering stream. I am heading towards Nathaniel's field that lay just beyond the prickly hedges adjacent to the stream. He is bound to be here; it's where he comes to be alone. My dark eyes scour the spiky leafless hedges for the small inconspicuous gap that will take me to the other side. The moment I spot it, I break into a chaotic sprint and charge through the gap, ignoring the sting of the jagged twigs scraping into my hands and face, breaking the skin in some places. Please Lord, let him be here. I need him to be here. I emerge on the other side of the hedge, scathed and panting, into the vast field surrounded by towering masses of Maple trees with their autumnal sunset leaves blowing arbitrarily in the chilly wind. The breeze whips the weaker leaves from the branches and scatters them haphazardly across the muddy grass. The bleached pale-yellow sun hangs directly above the surrendering scenery, casting opaque shadows under the trees. I peer cautiously into the almost darkness of the canopy of trees that hold up the old rusty swing for some sign of him -there is none.

Of course he's not here you idiot! Why would he be here? He has a frigging house. What use is sitting out here in the freezing cold when he can pretend that you don't exist from the comfort of his own home? Get a grip! After mentally scolding myself for being so naive, I sigh and close my eyes, fighting back a fresh set of tears. When am I going to accept that the fairytale is over and let this harsh reality finally set in? In the real world, there are no such things as happy endings - just endings. If a rift between lovers doesn't separate them, then something else will. We are all doomed to lose each other one way or another, but it saddens me that this was the way our ending has panned out. Even something as tragic as death seems more romantic; very Romeo and Juliet, who loved each other until they each took their last breaths. My Romeo doesn't even want me anymore. All I have left of him now are bittersweet memories that only encourage me to stupidly keep holding onto something that is far beyond redemption. If only we could erase all our wrong-doings and make it like it was, when the only thing that mattered to us, was loving one another. What I wouldn't give to have my heart back…

April 2011

Nathaniel tears his swollen lips from mine, panting raggedly as he fights to unclasp my arms from around his neck. I try to hold on, to no avail, as his strength overpowers my own and he breaks free. "Ugh!" I growl, flinging my head back in frustration. Why does he keep doing this to me, it's infuriating! Every time we're alone in the house and it is clear which direction our fervent kisses are heading, he pulls me off because he doesn't want us to go too far before he's sure that I'm ready. The only thing I seem to want to do these days is 'go too far' with him, but apparently my boyfriend values my virginity more than I do. From what I heard, boys are supposed to be a barrel of raging hormones that thinks about sex constantly -my predicament baffles me.

The first few times we reached this stage I thought it was sweet that he reigned us in before we crossed the point of no return, because it showed how much he valued and respected me, but now it is downright irritating!

I look up at him and scowl, "For FUCK sake Nathaniel! Again? Really?" His eyes sparkle like Swarovski crystals; he smiles down at me, amused by my displeasure, making it hard for me to stay mad at him. I cross my arms under my bosom and look away, determined to be a moody little cow this time.

Nathaniel snorts and presses his full lips to my forehead.

"You're so cute when you're mad," he teases encircling his arms around me.

I huff and push him away, "Shut up!"

He laughs, uncrosses my arms and drapes them around him. Stubbornly, I let them go limp and fall back to my sides. Mature, I know. Realising that I plan to make this as difficult as possible for him, Nathaniel grunts.

I get that he wants us to wait to make sure that I am positive that I would be making the right choice in sleeping with him, but what he doesn't seem to understand, no matter how much I reassure him, is that I am MORE than ready. I know, beyond a shadow of a doubt, that Nathaniel is the only boy I want from now until forever. That unwavering certainty lets me know that losing my virginity to him is the right thing to do. I won't have it any other way. So many girls before me have made the mistake of handing over their innocence on a whim because they got caught up in the moment, but I don't need to be swept away by the feel 9of his luscious lips caressing mine to know that I want him –I want him all the time! Every day I fantasise about how wonderful it would be to feel his warm flesh pressing against mine, to feel his hot mouth suckling on my breasts, to experience the foreign sensation of him entering me for the first time. I can feel the most rigid part of his anatomy pressing into me right now, and judging from the size of him, it will hurt, but it will be worth it. Thinking about all of the explicit things I would let him do to me is not helping me ignore the heated pulsations between my thighs.

Nathaniel brings his hand to my face and drags his index finger along the flushed skin of my cheek.

"Ri," he sighs, tilting my face up to look into his, "Why are you in such a hurry to do this? I'm not going anywhere. I just want everything to be perfect for you, so you don't regret it once it's over," he says softly, grazing his lips against my forehead.

I cup my hand over his and nuzzle my face into his palm. "Nathaniel, having you here, knowing that you are mine and I am yours is about as perfect as it's going to get. I don't need candles, rose petals and Maxwell to make this special. All I need is you."

Nathaniel sighs again and closes his eyes, "You say that now_"

I cut him off, "And I'll say it a thousand times more if it will make you believe me."

He pulls me to him and finally plants his kiss on my head.

"Rio, I'm not only holding out for your sake –I'm holding out for mine too," he confesses brushing his lips across my skin, clearing the canvas to plant another sweet kiss.

I look up at him, my frustration morphing into confusion, "Why? You're not a virgin."

Nathaniel smiles, "I know that genius! I'm just a little scared..." he says sheepishly.

I tilt my head, "Scared? Of me?"

"Yes," he admits, opening his eyes to reveal his brooding grey orbs.

"Why?" I ask, more confused than before.

"Because I love you Ri. I've never had sex with someone I loved before; the last thing I want is for us to do this, and then for you to regret it."

I sigh and take his face in my hands carefully, realising for the first time that Nathaniel is breakable and that him being in love with me gives me the power to break him.

I kiss him.

"Listen to me; my whole life I have never wanted anybody as much as I want you. Sex never plagued my mind as much as it does now. One day you may not be mine anymore, and one of my biggest regrets will be that I never made love to you as much as I possibly could have, so please..." I trail off and allow my body to do the talking. Standing on my tiptoes, I brush my lips against the hollow of his throat and lay one single kiss there. Nathaniel's lips part and he allows me to plant a trail of invisible love prints up his neck, along his chiselled jaw line and finally on his lips. His response takes me by surprise when he groans and clutches me tighter than ever before, crushing both our bodies together until we look as if we have merged into one. Layer by layer, our clothing is discarded and flung God knows where, as we kiss and touch with more urgency.

We are almost there.

As he lays me down on the bed and slip on a condom, I am unsure of how I am supposed to feel. I'm experiencing a multitude of emotions all at once and I can't focus on one; it's overwhelming. I just want to feel my love for him, and I know it is in there somewhere, but I am incapable of bringing it to the forefront of my mind because as each moment passes, his body gets closer. When the tip of his member brushes against my opening, I shudder and everything becomes even more surreal. Now instead of emotions, all I can think is –oh my God, we're really doing this!

"Rio?" he breathes, hovering over me.

"Yes?" I whisper.

"Are you sure about this?"

Despite the heightened atmosphere, I roll my eyes.

"Nathaniel I love you, but if you back out of this right now, I will find a knife, cut your dick off and take it home so I can do it myself," I threaten.

Nathaniel smiles and leans down to kiss me. "You really are cute when you're mad."

I have never ***not*** *regretted something so much in my life.*

Present Day
January 2014

"Rio! What are you doing here?"

I had been staring out at the leaf-strewn grass, so caught up in my daydream that I didn't even notice the tall dark figure watching me from the shadows, dressed head to toe in black.

"Nathaniel!"

5 Broken Strings.

Rain clouds loom overhead while the weak sunlight, lost in the infinity of the sky, fails to illuminate much beneath it. Everything is grey and dreary - a bad omen. Nathaniel emerges from the shadows with a belligerent scowl on his face, his handsome features contorted into something odious; but even in his fury he is still one of the most breath-taking people I have ever met. His normally well-kept 5 o'clock shadow of a beard is fuzzy and unkempt –I can only imagine what state his hair in under his black beanie hat. Dark-purple half-circles ring his glorious eyes, making it apparent that he has suffered a few too many sleepless nights. The once polished steely grey of his irises now look like tarnished silver -worn out and abused. His skin has lost its golden butterscotch glow, and the darkness of his hair only makes him appear more drawn -he is tragically beautiful. It's almost unbearable to see him in such a state; he had always looked so perfect. It gives me a glimmer of hope.

I fight the urge to run to him and cradle him against my chest. I inhale shakily and make my way over to him, walking as if I'm heading down the Green Mile. I have wanted to see him for so long, and now that he is here, I have no idea of how to approach him. It's clear that he still doesn't want me around from the way his eyes bore into me like knives as I get closer to him and the tumultuous storm clouds gathering around his pupils -he is not happy to see me.

I stop about a foot away from him and swallow the lump in my throat.

"Hello Nathaniel," I breathe.

He winces at the sound of my voice and looks away.

"What are you doing here?" he repeats icily, fighting to conceal any signs of my presence getting to him. He is doing a good job of it; I almost believe he doesn't care...until I see the muscle in his jaw twitch.

"I wanted to see you."

"Why?" he growls. I frown. The unmistakable burn of heartache ignites in my chest but I welcome it. I knew Nathaniel had unknowingly been keeping my heart captive all this time. It was beating loud and erratically, jolting the edges of the theoretical wound in my chest –a bittersweet pain. I cross my arms to keep from fidgeting, but my palms start to get clammy; needless to say, I am *super* nervous right now. It's so arduous talking to him when he gets like this, but as I have thought of nothing but speaking to him during our time apart, I'm prepared to brave his foul mood if it allows us another chance to make things right.

"I wanted to see if you were okay. You've pretty much cut off all contact with me and then I haven't seen you anywhere since we've been back; I was worried about you," I explain softly, clenching and unclenching my fist against my ribs.

His jaw muscle twitches again.

"Well I'm fine, so you can go now," he snaps.

"You don't look fine."

He glares at me.

"That's because you're here; now go away," he snarls taking a threatening step towards me. He's trying to scare me off with his temper but I'm not going to let him.

I take a shaky step towards him, "Please don't be like that, I say, "This is me, okay. I know you're mad at me, and with good reason, but I'm trying to fix it. Nathaniel, I know you're hurt, you don't have to hide it from me, so drop the tough guy act."

"It's not an act. Rio, I don't want anything to do with you; what part of that don't you get? I don't answer your calls, I don't reply to your texts, I delete any voicemails you leave before I even listen to them. I don't want you in my life, okay? I don't want to fix anything; now will you just leave me alone already!"

I shake my head and take another shaky step towards him.

"You don't mean that. You're just speaking out of anger," I reason.

"That's the thing; I'm not. I meant what I said then, and I still mean it now. We're not good for each other Rio. The sooner you realise this, the easier it will be for you to let me go."

I look up him incredulously; how can he even think such a notion is possible? Doesn't he understand how much I love him? I couldn't let him go if I wanted to…my heart won't let me.

"Don't be stupid; you know I can't do that."

"Yes you can, you just choose not to," he argues matter-of-factly.

I furrow my brow, "How can you ask me to do something that you haven't even grasped, no matter how much you obviously want to," I gesture at his dishevelled appearance. Nathaniel runs his hands over his overgrown beard, trying to smooth the prickly wayward hairs down.

"Who says I haven't?" he retorts stubbornly.

I place my hand on my hip.

"Those bags under your eyes do. How are those sleepless nights treating you?" I ask cockily. Of all the people that he would try and put up a front for, I am amazed that he would actually try to do it with me. There isn't another person in this whole wide world that knows Nathaniel like I know Nathaniel -not even Nathaniel himself. It's clear that he is trying to push me away, but I don't think we've reached the end of our road just yet. Call me desperate if you want, but when you find the person you know that you could spend the rest of your life with, from time to time you will have to fight for your love. There are so many things out there willing to get in the way and destroy what you both have built together, and it's always easier to walk away, but in the long run the latter option always hurts more. Nathaniel is worth fighting for; he loves me and I love him, and after all that we've done to each other, that one fact remains the same because it's unconditional, and unconditional love is hard to find. How can I let that go without a fight?

Nathaniel scowls harder, "You're not funny."

"I'm not trying to be. I just want you to see that the direction you're trying to push us in, is the wrong one. Nathaniel, I love you okay_"

"Well that's just too damn bad," he snarls, cutting me off, the storm in his eyes now flashing with hot white lightening, "'Cause I don't love you."

All of a sudden, all the pain I had been spared over the past few weeks comes crashing down on me like a ton of broken hearts. Never in my life would I have dreamed that he would utter those words to me, and now he is standing here saying them with so much vengeance that I have no choice but to believe that it really is over. You can't fight a battle when your opponent won't even show up to the battlefield.

"You don't love me anymore?" I ask, eyes wide, choking back salty tears. Nathaniel allows himself a small glance at me and nods sharply. My breath quickens as I struggle to breathe normally and I can feel my knees giving way, but I am too weak to stop myself from falling. I collapse right into his chest, grateful that he still cares enough to catch me. His strong arms hold me securely, but his body is rigid -he doesn't want me to touch him. What do you do when the one you love doesn't want you to touch them?

You cry.

The sobbing begins in short bursts of grief, but once my tears gather momentum, my breathing becomes even more uncontrollable than before, my body starts shaking and I can't even form a comprehensible sentence to beg him to take back his words.

Nathaniel drags my limp frame over to the creaky swing and makes me sit down until I am calm enough to speak without hyperventilating. He sits at the other end of the swing, sparing me a few pity glances to check that I haven't keeled over and died in my angst, but aside from that, he sits in silence, staring angrily at the sky as if he is having a heated conversation with God, demanding to know why I was here when he had already made his feelings clear at Jade's party. If I didn't get it then, I sure as hell get it now;

Nathaniel doesn't love me anymore.

"Why?" I croak, figuring that a one-syllable word could be uttered without the interruption of yet more tears. I swear, I have never cried this hard in my life.

Nathaniel sighs heavily and drags his hand over his beard.

"Rio just let it go okay. You're already in a state; nothing I say will make it any better. If anything, it will make it worse."

I take a deep breath, preparing to speak again.

"How do you think I will...feel...if I never know...why...you...fell out of love...with me?" I splutter pathetically.

Nathaniel grimaces at my words and grits his teeth.

"Fine; I don't love you anymore because aside from our obvious issues, you're not the same girl I fell in love with Rio. You've become so obsessed with becoming another status-chaser that you've lost yourself. You never used to care what those people thought; you were happy being you, the sweet, awkward girl who loved reading tacky Mills and Boon romance stories. Now, you're a hypocritical, manipulative, attention-seeker, who acts on what she thinks will make her more popular. How can I love someone I'm not sure I even know?" he asks.

I clutch my hand to my chest.

"I'm still the same girl Nate, I've just grown up," I argue.

"There's a difference between maturing and forgetting who you are Rio," he sighs, "I'm not mad at you for changing -I know it's partially my fault, and I'm sorry -but this is exactly what I mean when I say we're not good for each other. Every time one of us does something wrong it alters the other too much. We never used to be like this Ri," he explains softly, losing some of his hostility.

"We don't have to be like this," I say in spite of myself.

Nate furrows his brow in annoyance, "You say that like we have a choice."

"There's always a choice."

"Stop it!" he snaps, "Stop being so damn optimistic and get real. There is no choice when it comes to us because we will never forgive each other for all the shit we've done."

"I'm willing to try."

His jaw muscle flickers again.

"Look at how long you've been trying to forgive me...look at how long I've been trying to forgive you...I can't."

My breathing slows as I realise that he is referring to the baby again. I look away, embarrassed - this is my least favourite subject. On top of the emotions I'm experiencing right now, I don't need that guilt piled on top of it.

"I'm sorry," I whisper, hoping to avoid going down this road again.

"I know, but that doesn't change anything. It still happened; no apologies will ever erase that, especially since I had to go through all of that again with Georgia. I lost another kid, and this one wasn't even mine." His face crumples into a look of despair as he mentally relives that moment in his head again.

I don't know what to say, we seem to have said it all. The moment he told me that he didn't love me anymore, this whole conversation became irrelevant - I became irrelevant. I had always believed that I was extraneous to this world because I wasn't an Unfamous, but a part of me felt like I belonged somewhere because he loved me...and now he doesn't.

Shakily, I get to my feet. I don't want to here anymore, knowing the way that he feels about me –it's too much. Nathaniel stands with me, reaching out his arms to steady me as I prepare to walk away for the last time. I shy away from him; I don't want him to touch me because I know that the feel of his hands will linger on my skin like a handprint in a memory foam mattress.

Nathaniel takes a cautious step towards me.

"You want me to walk you back?" he asks sheepishly, all of the harshness of his tone gone. Without looking in his direction, I shake my head and concentrate on putting one foot in front of the other -the quicker I get away from him, the better. In spite of himself, he continues to walk alongside me, his hands stuffed in the pockets of his jeans to keep from offering his unwanted help to steady me. I keep my eyes locked on the small gap in the hedge; once I am through there I will run as fast as my legs can carry me, away from this nightmare and back to my room, where I can dream of better days. I stretch my hand out to push a few of the more volatile twigs out of the way –I am already leaving this place with enough scars.

Before I can ease my way through the tangled pathway, Nathaniel grabs my coat and yanks me to him, slamming my body into his lofty frame. I was going to protest, but his lips crush against mine before I even have the opportunity to form words. His kiss is harsh and desperate, like he had to sneak one more in before we part ways for good, whether I want to or not.

I don't kiss him back; it will only add salt to the wound. Raising my arms up between us, I push against him weakly. He stops as quickly as he'd started, and releases me, avoiding my eyes.

"Goodbye Rio."

I turn back to the hedge and continue walking as if nothing has happened, feeling the pressure build in my chest.

The moment I am back on campus, I run.

6
Louis Vuitton.

Another day, another session of 'self-pity shopping' in Eastpark with my nearest and dearest, which today consists of only Ty and Carmen. I had planned to come here by myself so that I could indulge in my retail therapy without people being there to control my spontaneous spending habits, but Carmen had insisted that she come along as well because Bless had pissed her off, so she needed this as much as I did...not likely, but whatever. I am secretly glad for the company; if all of the girls tagged along I would have refused, because then I'd have to put on a semi-brave face to avoid being asked if I am okay every time my face slips back into its perpetual sulk. Carmen doesn't do that; being that she's a bit of a moody cow herself, she understands that you only need to be asked once, and if you say you are fine even though you're clearly not, then that's it, you obviously don't want to talk about it.

As we were leaving, Tyson showed up at the entrance of our dorm block in a pair of faded sweats and an old t-shirt with the words 'I KNOW' etched on the front of it, causing Carmen to tell him, "You must know that you look like a fucking tramp!" Obviously, this t-shirt was meant to be worn when he was having one of his better days. Tyson had been coming over to keep me company and chat shit until I cracked a genuine smile and forgot about...

So anyway, after a sufficient cussing from Carmen, Tyson decided he wanted to tag along to Eastpark with us. Out of all of my friends, it is easiest to be around Carmen and Ty because they just seem to get me the best. Ty had run back to his flat to 'fix up' (as Carmen put it in her ever delicate manner), and now here I am, trudging through the too bright, impeccably clean, white-on-white Eastpark shopping centre with a bestie on each arm, listening to Carmen entertain herself by insulting every crime against fashion that she can see.

"Look at this confused bitch!" Carmen says, blatantly gesturing at a young dark-skinned girl sporting a honey-blonde lace-front wig. I cringe on her behalf then slap Carmen's hand down.

"Stop it!" I scold her.

"Me? Rio, she's as dark as 11:59, with a Beyoncé wig, looking like a fucking ghetto firefly; she's the one that needs to stop! Dark-skinned females get enough shit without these rogue bitches dragging us through the dirt with them." Carmen replies as the girl walks past. The girl looks us up and down like we're the ones rocking the waste of an £120 wig.

Stifling a laugh, I nudge Carmen. "She can hear you."

"Good! She can see me too; take note, this is how you do it!" she says even louder this time, stepping out of line and twirling in front of the girl to show her what she thinks 'dark and lovely' is meant to look like –fabulous clothes, heels, French manicured nails, threaded eyebrows, MAC makeup…and a 21 inch Brazilian weave in 1B. The girl carries on walking, shaking her head at us.

We head towards 'The City' to go and look at all of the expensive brands that we can't really afford. It's a complete waste of time, but sometimes being surrounded by Gucci, Miu Miu, and Kurt Geiger is the closest thing we have to sampling high society (once our student loans begin to dwindle). You can browse the shops and try on fabulous things that you know you can't buy just yet, but vow one day that you will make enough money to do so without a second thought. We hold our heads high as we pass the middle-class people showing off at the glitzy Champagne bar, secretly wishing that we could join them without having to consider how much a glass of bubbly would affect us later on down the line.

"That's it!" Carmen exclaims, looking longingly at a lush Salvatore Ferragamo winter coat. "I'm gonna find me a rich old white man in a loveless marriage and become his mistress, then make him buy me that coat!" she says pressing her palms against the pristine shop window.

Tyson laughs "What about Bless?"

"Fuck Bless! I want that coat!"

Tyson smiles places his hand on her shoulder.

"And to think, we've been telling Bless that he should actually consider being with you," he mocks her.

Carmen turns her attention away from the coat and narrows her eyes at him. "And so you should. If Bless doesn't end up with me he might get one of those irritating candy blossom pixies like you did. Lord knows we don't need any more of those little *pests* flittering around."

Tyson's expression turns serious; he tends to get very defensive if anyone says a bad word about his 'Little Angel' - another gag worthy nickname from their Disney-perfect relationship. As he fixes his mouth to retaliate on his midget's behalf, his iPhone starts to ring. The ringtone is one of my favourite tracks –Adorn by Miguel –which can only mean one thing...it's Angelica...again. I turn my head away from him so I can roll my eyes; I know she's his girlfriend and all, but she doesn't need to call as much as she does. Most of the time, she ain't even got shit to say and I'm starting to think she just wants to interrupt whatever it is Tyson and I are doing. The more time Tyson spends with me, the more she calls –she bugs the hell out of me. It's like, you know we're chillin', so why are you calling? When Tyson is ready to sit and listen to your irrelevant chatter, he will call you! Shit!

"Hey Angel, what's up?" he asks smoothly, his irresistible crooked smile being wasted on another pointless phone conversation. Carmen abandons the Ferragamo window and links arms with me.

"The same thing that was up when she called 10 minutes ago...NOTHIN!" she answers for Angelica, not troubling to keep her voice down. I press my face into her shoulder and snicker; this is why I love Carmen -she says all the things that I won't. Tyson shoves her in the back of her head and kisses his teeth.

"Nothin' babe. What were you sayin'?" he says into the phone, reassuring his dwarf before continuing his conversation. Carmen whips her body around to face him, dragging mine along in the process, and screws Tyson -who quickly lets go of my arm and moves a safe distance away from us so that any other comment that Carmen has to add will not be heard by Angelica. Does he not know who he is dealing with? Carmen doesn't have shame!

"SHE WASN'T SAYIN' SHIT! SHE NEVER SAYS SHIT. TELL HER TO STOP FUCKING CALLIN'! SHIT!" As funny as it is to hear her insult Angelica with no remorse, I am embarrassed because now everyone is watching us as if we were ghetto scum that obviously didn't belong at this end of Eastpark.

I can just imagine what they're thinking 'New Look is down there 'blud''.

Sometimes, shame is a good thing to have.

I yank Carmen towards the closest store, not actually intending to look at anything, but needing to get out of the public eye for a minute so that the Eastpark shoppers have a chance to get over her big mouth.

Carmen makes a face.

"Why are we in Louis Vuitton? I don't want nothing from...hello!" she breaks off mid-complaint, and a dazzling smile transforms her face.

I raise my eyebrow at her. "Why are you grinning like that, you twat?"

"Boy," she grins, quickly pointing at who I suppose is a hot guy, behind me. I roll my eyes; I'm not in the mood for any other male that isn't Tyson, and even he's pushing his luck right now.

"Thirsty much?"

Carmen scowls at me.

"Fam, turn around and look at...oh shit he's coming over," she says diverting her eyes, "Be cool," she murmurs to me. Is this idiot really telling me to be cool when I have no idea what all the fuss is about, and she is the one looking like she has a mental disorder. Why is she looking at cufflinks, she doesn't even have a man! I sigh as Carmen throws flirtatious glances at the *boy*, over my shoulder. Is he really that hot? Carmen's continuing stream of smiles and the ever popular looking up at someone from under your eyelashes thing (that she is milking) is making me curious. I don't intend to join in with her ogling –like I said, men aren't all that appealing to me right now -I just want to see what got her practically waving panties in the air.

I pretend to check out a LV tote bag to my left so that I could catch a subtle glimpse of this supposedly fine specimen, but as soon as I do, I wish that I hadn't.

His 6 foot something frame is clad in a black vest top that hugs his body so right and so tight! He wears this indecent yet delectable garment underneath a cream blazer with a brown Louis V scarf slung effortlessly around the smooth skin of his long neck. His straight cut jeans sag just enough to portray his wilder side without making him look like a road man, and on his feet, he sports a pair of trashed worker boots. His long raven tresses are pulled up into a messy bun, which on any other boy would look a bit gay, but on him, only adds to the mouth-watering effect. The only thing technically wrong with his outfit is the fact that he is wearing a pair of Ray Bans because they hide his smouldering emerald eyes.

"Hey beautiful," he says silkily, flashing his Hollywood smile at me, and trailing one slender finger lightly over the top of my hand. My skin burns along the trail his feather light touch leaves behind. Of all of the shops in all of the shopping centres in London, why does he have to be in the one I'm in? I scowl at him and snatch my hand away; trying to hide how much his touch makes my insides run hot.

"Jade." I utter tightly, forcing myself to look away from his devastatingly handsome face. I can feel Carmen's stunned eyes on me with a look that screams 'AHKYDSHJIGIG…YOU ACTUALLY KNOW HIM?!?' I glance at her briefly and roll my eyes - translation: yes, but he's a conceited asshole. Carmen huffs and rolls her eyes back at me: 'Of course he is.' Don't you love when you reach that stage in your friendship where you can communicate with each other with just a look? Carmen frowns slightly and looks at Jade again, taking in his heavily lashed almond eyes that hint at their loveliness behind his opaque shades. If he takes them off I think she will start hyperventilating and disregard my judgement...so would I, but at least I'd have the sense to act like I don't care. Jade's 1000-watt smile doesn't falter; he is amused by my adverse reaction to him.

"You don't look happy to see me," he chuckles lightly.

"Well aren't we observant! What gave me away?" I retort sarcastically, leaking a little more attitude into my tone than necessary to let him know that I haven't forgotten the way he had spoken to me the other night at *The Suite.*

"Your friend looks happy to see me," he states plainly, unruffled by my words, gesturing at Carmen. She unconsciously bites down on her lip, her eyes locked onto his mouth, clearly appreciating the way his full pink lips fashion every word he speaks with such enthralling movements that the only thing you can think about is what it would feel like to kiss him. I shoot her a look: 'stop it'. She frowns. I roll my eyes and turn back to Jade.

"She's not happy to see you. Get over yourself!" I snap. Jade laughs dismissively and steps around me to address Carmen –who is letting the side down in EPIC proportions right now -in his alluring manner. Stop smiling at him you fish! We don't like him and his tall, muscular body that is making me want to test my theory that he may just taste like a Hershey's Kiss...

Dammit Rio!

He stands in front of Carmen -as close as he could get to her without actually touching her, and I can bet on my life that she can feel the red-hot heat his body emits, seeping through her clothes onto her skin. He stands so close to her that she has no choice but to tilt her head up to look into his incomparable face. I'll give her props though, she doesn't look the least bit uncomfortable with his unreasonable proximity; instead she holds his unwavering gaze with a confidence that makes me feel like a loser, because I would have looked away by now to collect myself.

"Hello friend," he smiles.

"Hello hot guy," she smiles back –traitor! Jade laughs; it is an impressed sound. Sure she is dazzled by his good looks, but she is unashamedly upfront about it, and that confidence alone saves her from the eye roll. Ever the unabashed ladies' man; Jade looks down and lifts his Ray Bans so that they rest on top of his silken tresses and takes Carmen's hand. He brings it to his soft puckered lips and lays a gentle kiss on it before throwing the 'looking up from under the lashes' ploy back at her to the power of 10. Carmen gasps as the surprise of his astounding eyes makes her re-evaluate his magnificence. He had clearly done it on purpose (ass), but the way he executed it was effortless, making it evident that this isn't the first time he's pulled the 'Hey, guess what? Not only am I hot, but my eyes are green!' trick on an unsuspecting female. Carmen fell for it; hook, line and sinker. I roll my eyes again.

"What's your name, friend?" he asks, allowing his fingers to caress her hand as he releases it from his hold.

"My name?" she asks, slightly befuddled from losing herself in his glittering irises. She looks to me for help. Can you believe that with all the mouth this girl has on her, she's actually forgotten her own damn name! I sigh.

"Her name's Carmen," I mumble lazily, rolling my eyes yet again. Why am I introducing them? They don't need to be introduced because I'm not planning on having any more contact with this douche bag if I can help it. Jade's mystical eyes widened with realization, and he steps back a little, his smile now a little less 'you could get it' and more genuine.

"Oooh, so you're Carmen," he sings knowingly.

Carmen's' sculpted eyebrows knot together in confusion.

"Um...do I know you?" she asks, also stepping back, uncomfortable with the fact that this person she doesn't recall meeting knows who she is.

"I'm Jade Washington; everyone knows me," he shrugs. All right, *modest*!

"Oh you're Jade! Yeah, I was at your party last term. I didn't get a chance to meet you, it was so hectic in there," she smiles.

Jade looks at me and smirks "Yeah, it was hectic, wasn't it?" I scowl at him. Jade laughs to himself and looks back at Carmen.

"You know Bless?" It comes out as more of a statement than a question.

Carmen blushes and nods, "Yeah, I know him."

"I thought so. I knew your name sounded familiar." He gives her a casual smile to mask whether he's heard good or bad things. Carmen is fickle enough when it comes to good-looking boys not to pick up on questionable behaviour if it isn't immediately obvious.

"Well, now that we're all acquainted..." he says, suddenly sliding his rippling arms over mine and Carmen's shoulders in one fluid movement, "There's a silent rave coming up at Malaysia Blaq about five days from now, you lot wanna come? I'll get you in for free." His delicate fingertips barely graze the exposed skin of the nook where my shoulder ends and my neck begins; I suppress a shudder. As much as I want to fight it -because he is such a colossal asshole -I can't seem to rid myself of my borderline fanatical crush on him; he is just too gorgeous! I don't want to let him know that I think that though, so I manoeuvre myself out from under his arm. Jade cocks a thick plucked eyebrow at me and shrugs.

Carmen's mahogany eyes light up at the sound of Malaysia Blaq, one of London's most exclusive nightspots where it isn't out of the ordinary to see a famous face or two. One of Carmen's goals is to be a high society chick, and now (for at least one night) Jade is practically handing her, her dream on a silver platter. Not only is entry to Malaysia Blaq (possibly one of the hardest nightspots to get into, in the city) guaranteed, it is also going to be free! I don't want to go. I know this is some stupid ploy for him to get closer to me, and to be honest, it excites and frightens me at the same time, for the same reason –he is *Jade Washington.*

I open my mouth to decline his invite when Carmen shoots me a look. I close my mouth and fold my arms sulkily.

"Fine," I pout. Carmen's face lights up again. Jade studies my exchange with Carmen with intrigue. He knows Carmen is still under his spell, so he turns to me. His eyes pierce into mine.

"You don't want to go?" he asks, clearly perplexed that I would turn down such an elite invite.

I shift my weight onto my right leg, fidget with my fingernails and shrug, "Not particularly, no."

"Hmm…why not?"

"Cause I don't want to!" I say, -that and the fact that I don't like your egotistical ass! I am sure he can read what I am *not* saying all over my face because I'm not making the slightest effort to hide it.

He flashes me a smile of tainted innocence.

"Well...you kind of have to come," he says apologetically, finally releasing Carmen. I didn't realise until that moment that I had a problem with him holding her for so long. I clear my throat.

"Oh really, and why is that?" I ask, sounding disinterested. Jade grins and with the same fluidity, he grabs my hand and tugs my arm, curling his inwards as I lurch forward so that I spin into him. We are now standing with my back pressed unwillingly into his front, our hands still clasped, his strong arm holding me in place, my heart racing so fast that I am certain that he could feel it, as his plump lips skimmed my earlobe.

"You still owe me a dance, miss." He pecks me on the cheek and unfurls his arm so that I spin back out into my original position. The look on my face must be a sight to see because almost everyone in the store is smirking at me.

Leave it to Carmen to comment, making an awkward situation worse.

"I'll have what she's having!" she snickers.

Jade steps back, admiring my reaction to him with an indulgent look in his kiwi eyes, seeming very pleased with himself. I am too stunned by his tactics to deliver a salty one-liner to wipe the mesmerising smile off his face. Instead I grab Carmen's hand and high tail it out of the shop as fast as my feet will allow me, but not before hearing Jade holler, "So it's a date then?"

"No!" I yell over my shoulder.

Jade chuckles, "We both know that, that means yes really, don't we? Carmen luv, bring Bless along; we'll make it a double!"

"Okay," she replies between fits of laughter.

I glare at her and yell back at Jade, "We're not coming!"

"Yes you are. I'll text you the details."

I stop walking and turn in his direction. He is leant coolly against the frame of the Louis Vuitton entrance, looking as immaculate as one of the store mannequins.

"You don't even have my number," I spit.

Jade wiggles his eyebrows mischievously, "Wanna give it to me?"

"No!"

He shrugs. "Fine, I'll get it some other way. You ladies have a nice day and I'll see you on Friday."

"Okay," Carmen grins back. I yank her arm.

"No you won't!"

Jade snaps his Ray Bans back into place, tilts his head down so that I can see his eyes over the top of the frames, and winks.

"Sure I won't."

Asshole!

7

Text.

It's another bothersome Monday on the restless campus of Brompton University. My alarm shrieks at me mercilessly from across the room on my desk, emitting that nerve-grating sound that resembles one thousand people dragging sharpened fingernails over a blackboard over and over in an abrupt rhythm. I open my bloodshot eyes that ache from not nearly enough sleep -I couldn't tell you last time I had a decent night's sleep. Have you ever tried sleeping with a broken heart?

The green digital numbers on the stupid alarm clock flash, informing me that it's 7am -time to get up. Fuck that! I cover my head with my pillow in a frivolous attempt to drown out the irritating sound, but as expected, the shrieking seeps through the material with an even more annoying muffled wail. I yank the pillow off of my head and fling it with all my might, praying that it will knock the devil clock to the ground, breaking it forever so that I can go back to sleep to live in my dreams of *him*, that will never come true. The heavy foam stuffed pillow sails through the air then merely thuds the clock of Satan softly, then spitefully shoves my beloved iPhone, sending it skidding across the length of my desk to meet its doom. Ain't that a bitch! I flinch at the sound of my phone thudding onto the thin scratchy carpet; all the while the alarm clock continues to mock me with that awful sound. Guess I have to get up.

Wearily, I roll out of bed, turn off the alarm and retrieve my life-force with a frustrated scowl colouring my puffy features. Glad that it hasn't suffered any apparent damage, I put my phone back down on my desk and am about to hop in the shower when it buzzes and tinkles. Who the hell is bothering me this early in the morning?

I glance at the illuminated screen; it's a text message from a number that I don't have stored in my device; I hope it's not one of those annoying PPI things.

The preview of the first sentence shows on screen and thankfully, it's not PPI.

"Who the hell is this?" I grumble. I haven't given my number to anyo- oh-my-God, you have got to be kidding me! As the realisation of who this unknown number belongs to dawns on me, my palms become clammy and I almost cause another phone catastrophe in the space of a minute.

Jade Washington.

I delete the message without reading it.

True to his word, he had used his powers of persuasion and obtained my number from someone. If I ever find out who gave it to him, they are going to pay, dearly. If I hadn't already endured the displeasure of conversing with Jade to the point that his legendary allure had become tarnished with arrogance, then I would undoubtedly be salivating like an eager female fan at a Trey Songz concert about him adding me to his infinite list of contacts. Unfortunately, I know better.

I know girls that would sell their souls just to be pursued by Jade Washington and here I am shrugging him off as if he is some run-of-the-mill wasteman. I know what you're thinking; you wanna be Unfamous so why are you turning down one of their rulers? Unfamous by association is the easiest (but most unrated) road to take to the top, which is what most females and a few boys do, but after the rubbish I had put myself through last term trying that shit with Carter Johnson, I am determined to make it on my own.

I have been doing the 'socialite' thing with Carmen for a while now, but it isn't getting me anywhere fast enough. It was fun at first, but after a while raving, comedy shows, fashion shows, variety shows etc, all becomes very passé. We revolve in the same circles as the Unfamous, so it's always the same venues, the same DJ's, the same music and the same bloody people, causing the same bloody conflicts to be brought to light. It's tiring. I think being a socialite is more Carmen's scene; raving is like crack to her, which is one of the reasons why she and Bless would work as a couple -Bless goes to raves for a living (to DJ of course) and Carmen lives for raving. What could be more perfect?

I had given modelling some consideration, but as I've said before, my physique is not built for fashion. With thick hips and thighs, and a more than ample helping of breasts and booty, I'm more suitable to be a Candy Mag glamour girl -that's a straight no-go-area in my book –I'm not about to be some glorified Instagram model. Plus, Fontaine is already the model of our little collective, with her svelte 5"8 frame, flawless dulce-de-leche skin and her famous sun kissed mane of untameable curls that gave her that watered down 'ethnic' look that was perfect for the mainstream media; black, but not too black.

Yoshi's position in the group can't be challenged simply because we all lacked her artistic talent and love of Anime/Manga. Yoshi's talent is uncommon in the Unfamous world, making her more sought after due to lack of competition, and the fact that she is Ace's girlfriend doesn't hurt much either - Unfamous by association, with added talent to validate it. She has recently teamed up with Manny on his Obviously clothing line, to design some new age hippy illustrations for his next collection. Once Manny drops that line, Yoshi will blow up. Lucky break or what?

My girls are doing things that work for them, and then there is me, the leader of the gang, who is totally clueless. There's always the latter option of being bait for the sake of being bait, but the Unfamous don't really respect that...unless you're a guy (exhibit A: Calvin). If you have an occupation that ties into your un-fame, then you're Unfamous-ness is validated. Yoshi, Carmen and Fontaine are all validated. Shit, even Ty's validated -without him even trying, once again! Shaquille got a glimpse of one of Tyson's animation projects then paid him to create a slick motion graphic opening for his YouTube show, The Shaq Attack. On top of that, Tyson has passed the 1000 followers mark on Twitter; stupid boy. It bugs me when the others surpass me, but it's even worse when it's Tyson because I know he doesn't even care about being Unfamous. I just want to punch him in the face sometimes.

I NEED to be validated, not just so I have an excuse and a better chance of beating Mr Popularity, but so that I give the Unfamous a GOOD reason to remember me once we all grow up and realise how petty and superficial we were when we were younger. Even though my drama from last term is now old news, it's all people associate me with. Hello, my name is Rio Greene and I am Nathaniel Gibson's desperate ex-girlfriend! When I finally figure out what occupation I'm going to take up, I'll banish that memory from their minds. I'll be Rio the 'insert-Unfamous-job-here' chick, and they will love me!

I set the phone down again, and this time I make it as far as the bathroom door before it vibrates and tinkles again. I eye my phone suspiciously from across the room before giving into curiosity. Part of me fears the worst; what if it's Jade again? Then I consider the more likely possibility of it being Tyson, Whatsapping me to remind me about our scheduled 'I'm banging out this coursework' session, this afternoon in the most popular computer room on campus -Joe Crankford -where we will spend hours feebly trying to complete our coursework but will inevitably end up writing bugger all. It's almost the end of January, which means that EVERYONE has coursework that should've been completed over the Christmas holidays to hand in, therefore EVERYONE will be in the computer rooms. We can just as easily do our work in our dorm rooms, but where's the fun in that? People like Tyson and I (that are fans of quality banter) will be in Crankford, while the people that have actual intentions of buckling down and getting their work done will be in one of the quieter rooms, giving the fun a miss.

Almost everyone that enters the Crankford building goes in with the best intentions…then we cross the threshold, take a seat where most of our friends are, and it's all downhill from there. We'd make fun of the idiots that have to hand in 3000 word essays the next day and hadn't even written so much as their name on the top of the page, move onto more trivial topics like the latest episode of Love & Hip Hop, talk rubbish and tweet from our phones, even though there are perfectly good computers in front of us, because we are THAT cool. After all of that, we'd start gossiping and end up streaming a flurry of adulterated insults about the most scandalous topics. Eventually (after hours of doing fuck all) we'd each admit to ourselves that coming to Crankford to do coursework was a stupid idea, and leave. What a way to waste a day!

I grab my phone and sigh when I see the same unknown number scroll across my screen -it definitely isn't Tyson. My thumb hovers over the button that will reveal the message that I am sure will make me want to cut up my sim card into tiny indistinguishable pieces, but (though I shall never admit it out loud) will flatter me all the more because he has gone as far as to actually get my phone number. This is 2014; young people generally don't call/text each other anymore -what for? Why use regular forms of communication like everyone else when you can use apps that deliver texting equivalents! I tap the screen and the message appears:

I figured ur attitude problem may compel u 2 ignore my 1st msg (I'm right aren't I?) so I thought I'd send another, just in case. C u Friday, sexy!
Jade x

For crying out loud! Why me? I contemplate switching my phone off to avoid more unwanted contact from Jade 'guess what? Not only am I hot, I'm a stalker too' Washington, but decide against it, partially because as much as he irks me, I am secretly happy that he is on my case, but also because, well...why would I be without my iPhone ON PURPOSE? That doesn't make any sense! I like that Jade is persistent, but I plan to make him work for my attention 10 times harder than anyone, just to see how much rejection he can handle before he gives up…or what he can do to make me give in.

I had patiently endured two long-ass lectures, and one equally long-ass seminar and I'm now kicking back with my friends in the Joe Crankford computer room, NOT doing my coursework. My half-written essay glares at me from the sleek white Apple Mac computer screen, silently yelling at me to start writing, but my attention is elsewhere (as I had suspected it would be). I am posted along the side of Tyson's long torso with his slim, yet well-defined arm wrapped securely around me, forcing me to inhale his heady aroma of Versace Blue Jeans and Dark and Lovely hair oil. At the other computers in our little area are Fontaine, Ace, Calvin, Manny, D-man and Shaquille, who is subjecting us to watching a video on World Star Hip Hop of a mouthy young female getting knocked out by the seemingly timid guy she was laying into, whilst pointing and laughing like the jerk he is. As I mentioned earlier, Shaquille is Tyson's friend who has the wildly popular YouTube show 'The Shaq-Attack', so as far as everyone else is concerned Shaquille can do no wrong, even when he is wrong. I don't think the video is funny.

"Bruv, look how man has her on the floor!" he cackles. I roll my eyes.

"How can you laugh at that? It's not funny," I say sitting a little straighter against Tyson's side. I feel his braids brush my cheek as he glances down at me and his arm squeezes me gently.

Shaquille turns to address me.

"Yes it is. Rio, you can't tell me she didn't have it coming," he chuckles.

"I don't rate a man that puts his hands on a female, definitely not like that. It's wrong," I reply, sneaking a glance at Ace. Although Yoshi likes to pretend that we never saw the horrid marks on her arm, I still haven't forgotten.

Ace furrows his brow at me -I guess he caught my little look, therefore noticing my indirect. I make a mental note not to make eye contact with him for the rest of the day.

Shaquille shrugs his brawny shoulders -they have an excessive amount of muscle for a boy so small- I guess he compensates his lack of height with masses of time in the gym.

"Fine, whatever, that's your opinion. I'm not saying I agree with hitting females, but there comes a time when some chicks get a bit too wild and a slap is the only thing that will keep them in line."

"I hear that," D-man chimes –I frown at him. D-man is built like Shaquille, but he has the added bonus of the height, which made his stature the most menacing out of Tyson's clique. I shiver at the thought of him putting his hands on a chick. A slap from D-man looks like it will equate to INSTANT DEATH!

"Oh shut up, that's why you man ain't got no chicks," Fontaine scoffs trying to lighten the mood.

"Fonts, what are you talking about please? All man does is have chicks! The numbers are just beginning to dwindle 'cause you keep turning them," Shaquille fires back with a cheeky grin. Fontaine sighs with a look that says 'here we go again'.

"What can I say, it's a gift," she grins, flicking her bouncing mass of curls. It was no secret that Fontaine swung both ways now. Since she'd gotten back together with Nadia, she wanted to make sure that it was out in the open, more so to give her peace of mind in regards to her flighty lover than for her sexuality to be known.

"So how is naughty Nadia doing anyway?" Calvin asks licking his petite lips, his deep brown eyes shining with lust as they sweep over Fontaine's long slender legs that are currently wrapped in a pair of tight leather trousers. As irrelevant as Nadia's attractiveness is to the other girls and I, the fellas do nothing but fantasise about illicit ménage trios, including them, Fontaine and her sexy lady friend. Like that's ever going to happen...but then again, with free spirited Fontaine, you never truly know, which is probably why these lot kept electing themselves for the role of the lucky guy.

Fontaine smiles; amused by Calvin's transparency. "She's cool."

"That's good to know. Tell her I said hi, yeah."

"Will do!" she gives him a very cheesy, very sarcastic 'thumbs up'.

"What for? These times even if Nadia was interested in getting some dick, it wouldn't be Calvin's raw meat looking, white boy ding-a-ling," Shaquille interjects. The boys (all except for Calvin of course) burst out laughing.

"Man said your piece looks like uncooked Cumberland Sausage bruv; don't have it!" Manny howls, rubbing it in.

Calvin kisses his teeth. "My dick don't look like raw meat!"

"It's pink ain't it?" Tyson continues.

Calvin puts his hand behind his head and leans back in his chair. "Nah it ain't. Don't believe me? Ask your girl." he smirks.

"OOOOOH!" we chorus like school children. Tyson's body goes rigid beneath me. I told you he was sensitive about his midget; his boys know it too, so whenever they want him to lay off of them, they make a crack about Angelica and Tyson's pride keeps him quiet for a while. I look up at him and see his liquid brown eyes turn solid.

"I told you lot before_" he growls.

"Yeah, yeah, yeah we know. Chill Ty, it's just a joke," Shaquille interjects before Tyson can drone on anymore. I silently thank him. I love Ty, and I want to see him happy, but my God Angelica is not worth the energy he puts into her; she's not the right girl for him. The sooner he realises this, the happier we will all be...me especially.

We resume our senseless chatter and continue to avoid actually doing any work. The atmosphere is back to its fun loving normality when I hear the entrance door swing open. I peep around Tyson's arm to see who is coming to join the party -the moment my eyes lock onto him I wished I hadn't.

"Yo Nate, what time do you call this?" Ace hollers sliding his seat over to make space for the last person I want to see. Tyson's tightens his hold on me slightly, to remind me that he is here, and I am grateful.

Nathaniel's eyes land on me, and a tiny jolt in my chest sends my heart rate up a couple of notches. It's that uncomfortable jolt that you get when the person you have a conflict with suddenly pops up without warning. I don't know what to do with myself; am I supposed to smile and play civil, pretending that I it isn't killing me that he is so close within my reach, and yet so very far away at the same time, or should I play the role of the woman scorned and ignore him completely? If I smile at him, he may not smile back and then I'll look like a fool...but what if he does smile back? That would suck too, because the wonder of his face lit up like that would only highlight the fact that he is not mine even more. He is no longer the dishevelled shadow of himself that I had seen back in the field on that frosty winter day; he has returned to his former immaculately preened glory, standing before me looking like a God among men, with eyes like crystal lightening ready to strike me down. I touched the very tips of my fingers to my lips, remembering the unforgiving recklessness of his parting kiss, and wishing for a split second that we were back on the border of the field so I could relish in the shock of the cool silver of his lip piercing imprinting itself into my lips...

I squeeze Tyson back and discreetly nuzzle myself against him some more, the feeling of his sturdy frame anchoring me to what little sanity I have left. I take a deep whiff of him for good measure; it is going to take a whole lot of self-control to keep me from revealing how much I miss him. I watch with sombre eyes as Nathaniel strolls into the room so coolly, and greets everyone except for Tyson and me. I press my lips together and grit my teeth -well screw you then! Boy, am I glad I didn't smile at him because he has obviously gone with the immature option of acting like I don't exist. If anything, I should be acting like HE doesn't exist, not the other way round. HE broke MY heart.

Shit! Why do I keep doing this to myself?

Every time he upsets me I swear that I shall have nothing more to do with him and I convince myself that if I give myself some time, eventually I'll be okay, but how can I do that when he keeps popping back into my life. It's hard enough to deal with trying to get over him when he's not there, but putting him right in front of me is like the serpent waving the forbidden fruit in front of Eve. I'm not strong enough to resist loves temptation, even if it is unrequited.

Tyson dips his mouth to my ear, his long black velvet braids tickling my face again.

"Do you wanna go?" he whispers. I look around at the awkward faces of our friends, who wait with baited breath to see how this reunion of former lovers will pan out. You'd think that they'd be used to it by now. Any time that Nathaniel and I are together around them is never pleasant because there is always some stupid issue, but I guess that the danger this time around is that our issues have thinned the ice so much that a misplaced footstep can cause it to crack and splinter beneath our feet. Our baggage is too heavy this time; we're in danger of falling through, unable to stand on solid ground together anymore.

I chew the inside of my cheek, mulling over the intense relief I would feel if I withdrew myself from this situation, but also how cowardly I would look fleeing the scene after Nathaniel had bravely placed himself in it, especially since he had a lot more to be embarrassed about than me. Georgia had made a complete mug of him, (and to an extent so had I), but here he is with his head held high, undefeated and beguiling. I shake my head and reach up, taking hold of Tyson's hand that hangs casually over my shoulder, giving it a small squeeze. As long as Tyson is here I will be okay...or the best version of okay that I could pull off.

"I call it 3 o'clock. Get off my nuts," Nathaniel replies in his husky West London accent that only a true Londoner would be able to distinguish.

Shaquille kisses his teeth, "No one ain't on your dusty nuts rude boy. I don't get how everyone else turned up at practically the same time and it's only now that you're turning up, like say man like you is some rassclaart celebrity."

Nathaniel smirks "I had better things to do."

"Like what?"

"Like getting my dusty nuts polished, now don't ask me no more questions." he chuckles. The boys (except Tyson, who rolls his eyes and gives me another squeeze) laugh and lean in to hear the gory details of who, what, when and where. Nathaniel's eyes flicker over to me cradled in my best friend's arms; his smirk falters around the edges. The transition is so slight that only I notice it; one of the perquisites of knowing him so well.

"Bruv; who?" Calvin asks, too impatient to wait for Nathaniel to start dishing of his own accord. Nathaniel shakes his head, keeping the altered smirk on his face.

"Don't worry about it."

"Boo, you're shit!" Shaquille groans.

"No, I'm grown. Grown men don't kiss and tell, but you wouldn't know anything about that would you Shaq."

"Init, Screen Munch King!" Ace agrees referring to the countless times Shaquille had taken it upon himself to screen capture his saucy Snapchat conversations with a few... *expressive*, young girls. When they step out of line, Shaquille is notorious for posting the compromising conversations on Twitter, and being that he is a YouTube sensation, he has a tonne of followers, which means the girl will receive a tonne of insults in her mentions.

With the heat off of himself, Nathaniel glances at me again and I see his jaw tense. Although he has chosen to ignore me, he is still decent enough not to rub his sexual escapades in my face. How generous of you! I would appreciate it if you hadn't actually gone and slept with some other girl already, you prick! As cliché (and pitiful) as it sounds; I lay in my bed at night unable to sleep because all I can do is think of you, whereas you lay in bed next to some other girl, doing things to her that you used to do to me. It's a bit too late to worry about my feelings now; besides, you're only doing it because you will have to witness the expression on my face if I get upset. It's so easy to hurt someone when they're not there in front of you for you to see the effects - the guilty party can't stand noticing that the person who used to adore them can no longer look at them the way they used to, because it's a reminder of what they did to them.

I take another calming inhalation of Tyson to ease the Supernova of anger that explodes inside of me. I can't even imagine being with someone else, and Nathaniel is already whoring around. Figures; at least this time it's not behind my back. I release Tyson and turn to my computer hoping that actually doing my coursework will provide a sufficient distraction and help release some of my fury. I want to fling my head back and howl expletives until my throat is sore, but that's the downside of being in public, sometimes you have to fight your impulsive urges for the sake of your dignity.

I lift my hands to write something when my phone vibrates in the pocket of my jeans. I pull it out and peek at Tyson and Fontaine to see if one of them had sent the message so that we could talk on the sly. Neither of them is paying me any mind and when I finally looked at the screen I realise why. Instinctively I kiss my teeth.

"Piss off!" I cuss under my breath, not bothering to open yet another message from Jade, whose number I have aptly stored under the name 'The Mighty Douche'.

Fontaine catches my quiet cussing and looks over. Her eyes flit between my face and my phone before an excited smile breaks out over her face. "It's Jade, isn't it?" Way to keep a secret Fontaine! I had told her about Jade's recent contact on the way over here and I made it perfectly clear to her that this wasn't public information because any story involving Jade would spread like wild fire, and I'm not ready to be back in the limelight just yet. My eyes shoot up and examine my audience to see how they respond to the cat being let out of the bag, saving Nathaniel till last and completely avoiding Tyson -I don't need that kind of pressure just yet.

Nathaniel isn't looking at me. To the untrained eye he seems impervious, but I can see that jaw muscle of his flickering like a candle in the wind. He is livid. Good, that makes two of us!

"Jade who? Washington?" Tyson asks, spinning in his chair to look at me; make that three of us.

"Of course Jade Washington; how many other Jade's exist that are worth mentioning?" Fontaine swoons. She had done a photo shoot with Jade over the holidays for the new United Colours of Benetton ad campaign, where she had been subjected to Jade's notorious charm -she is now a dedicated member of his fan club.

I peep at Tyson who isn't trying nearly as hard as Nathaniel to conceal his temper.

"Someone gave him my number," I sigh, figuring that there is no point in withholding information anymore. There are two reasons I didn't mention Jade's new fascination with me to Tyson: one, Tyson could get too over-protective, which was a mixture of our deep friendship and his romantic feelings for me that haven't completely vanished as yet, and two, I have no real intention of getting mixed up with Jade, so there wasn't really anything to tell him.

"Who?" Ty asks, sitting a little straighter in the desk chair. I roll my eyes.

"Well I don't bloody know, but when I find out they are going to hear about it," I scowl, mentally cursing the person who had opened this new can of worms for me to deal with. Tyson nods in agreement, but the look on his face leads me to believe that he wants to do more than make them hear about it.

"Oh Rio, hush! Whoever gave Jade your number did you a favour, though I can't fathom why you didn't do it yourself. Do you know how many girls would give their soul to be pursued by Jade Washington?" Fontaine gushes.

"I don't care what those stupid girls would do. I'd rather it were them than me. Jade is an ass!"

Nathaniel smirks a little.

"Oh c'mon, he's not that bad. A little arrogant yes, but that's kind of part of his appeal,"

"Then you fuck him," I retort.

"Who said anything about sex? He can't seriously be going through all this trouble *just* to sleep with you."

"You do remember who we're talking about right?" Shaquille chuckles.

"Thank you! See Shaquille understands."

Fontaine pokes her bottom lip out.

"I think you lot are being unfair. Jade's all right," she says.

Shaquille kisses his teeth. "You would say that, you're a girl. You might as well book a room at Etap, cop a bottle of Alize, make a mix CD of slow jams, and sit waiting for him in your best lingerie ripe and ready to get dash 'way like a used condom the next day. Fuck it; you may as well start crying from now, since you are electing yourself as spokeswoman for the 'Gassed On Jade Washington Society'."

Fontaine makes a face. "Whatever, Shaquille! The way I see it, basing your entire opinion of someone based on what you hear is never a good idea because you're purposely letting what could be some of your best memories, pass you by. Yeah so Jade is kind of a womaniser_"

"Kind of? Bredrin, Jade is the biggest bludclaart gyalis in the history of gyalis-ing!" Shaquille roars.

"Shut up Shaquille! Rio, all I'm saying is_"

"Fonts, I don't want to hear it. Jade is bad news_"

"You don't know that!"

"What, and you do? I hear what you're saying, but I'm not taking any chances okay. Not with Jade."

Fontaine folds her arms and sighs, accepting defeat.

"Fine; what'd he say anyway?" she asks, trying to sound disinterested.

I huff and open the message:

I'm sitting in my lecture and all I can seem to think about is you in that God damn dress. Would it be too bold if I described in vivid detail what I would relish doing to you right now...or would you prefer to find out for yourself?

"Rio?" Fontaine's impatient voice snaps me out of my involuntary trance, in which I was considering all of the tempting possibilities of what Jade wanted to do to me, in spite of myself. I know that everyone is watching me, so I purse my lips to keep from smiling as my eyes retrace his suggestive words over again; Jade's borderline explicit prose concocting blue images in my mind. Him on top of me, me on top of him, front ways, back ways, sideways, horizontally, vertically, diagonally...let me stop. As insatiable as I am, I really shouldn't leave such long periods between sex. Unfortunately, the only person I really want to have sex with is no longer an option.

Mental note: must make a trip to Ann Summers.

"Rio!"

"Huh? What?"

"What does it say?" she asks again.

"What does what say?" I ask, playing dumb, hoping that she will just drop it. No such luck!

"The text message, dummy!" I read it again. The X-rated images ran through my head again. Fuck it, I'll hit up Ann Summers today if I have to.

Exhaling, I try to imitate Nate's reserved expression.

"It's nothing worth repeating," I say plainly, looking into Fontaine's face but purposely avoiding her eyes. Fontaine isn't the most observant person as her focus usually revolves around herself, but when she finally decides to venture out of her little bubble and take some interest in what the rest of the world is doing, she is very adamant in seeing that she makes the most of it.

She arches an eyebrow and smirks mischievously, "Lemme see!" Before my brain even has a chance to register her movement, Fontaine snatches my iPhone out of my hand and starts reading Jade's message, conveying a series of shocked and borderline aroused facial expressions that completely give away the nature of the text. Clearing her throat, she hands my phone back to me saying nothing. We exchange a glance.

"What did it say?" asks Shaquille, the only boy bold (and nosey) enough to say what is on his mind, as per usual.

Fontaine shoots him a look. "It said, mind your business!"

"Yeah right! It was probably him giving you the room number. £17.50 biz init Ri," Shaquille winks. I want to punch him in the mouth.

Nathaniel finally looks up and looks me directly in the eye. It is hard to decipher the look he is giving me, but I know it isn't a good one because his eyes are like the eye of the storm; a false uncanny calm hiding exactly how angry he really is. I arch my brow at him and shrug; you can be angry all you want, I'm not the one who just came back from fucking someone else. Nathaniel's eyes widen at my dismissal and the tumultuous storm flashes, lighting up the grey of his irises. Tyson lean a little closer to me, his solid chocolate eyes transmitting a warning to Nathaniel: you cool fam? Nathaniel juts out his jaw; he is not about to let Tyson punk him in front of anybody. Our little group falls into silence; the atmosphere is thick with tension that has been building up for a long time between Tyson and Nathaniel. When Nate and I first got together, they were on speaking terms, tolerating each other only because of me, but once that bond was severed, Tyson made it his business to inform Nathaniel of just how much he didn't like him in a very public argument in the college cafeteria. If I hadn't stepped in when I did, it would have come to blows on account of Nathaniel despising public humiliation and Tyson...being Tyson; overprotective and slightly in love with me.

I touch Tyson's hand.

"I'm hungry -Ty, you hungry?" I ask, hoping that he will say yes whether he is hungry or not so that we can avoid this situation, instead of hanging around to see if things will escalate. Tyson looks down at me, his eyes still hard, but not as hard as they were when they were glaring daggers at Nathaniel. I'm guessing this anger is directed at me; hence I had avoided eye contact with him. He isn't happy about Jade Washington pursuing me anymore than Nathaniel is. I ignore his hostility and plead with him with my eyes.

"I'm really feeling for some Yum Chow's right now; you on it?" Drop it and let's go, please, my eyes beg.

Tyson stubbornly looks back at Nathaniel to get his point across, and then sighs. "Yeah, let's go."

8

Canon.

"Rio, you're a plank! Seriously, this time you have successfully succeeded in making me lose all respect for you," Tyson says with a straight face.

My eyes tighten.

"Thanks for the support dude." I sulk, folding my arms. Tyson pushes me playfully, giving me his crooked smile in an attempt to get me to soften up after he had basically stomped on the dream that I have had for all of 5 minutes. I whack his hands away from me and continue to pout.

"Ri, you can't seriously be upset?" he laughs.

"Why not? I'm here trying to better myself and you're basically telling me that I'm a shit individual who can do nothing but dress up and go to events." Tyson rolls his eyes and picks up his food, twirling several threads of egg noodles around his plastic fork. We had come back from Yum Chow's not long ago and were now chilling in Ty's pigsty of a room. For someone who looks as well kept as Ty does (the majority of the time) and is so well-organised, you would never believe that his room could get to be in such a state. It isn't always like this of course; this is just one of Ty's bummy days. As I don't count as a guest in his eyes, he doesn't even bother to tidy up when I come over. Tramp! I had to kick a heap of discarded clothing, books, and XBox controllers off the bed and onto the floor, before I could sit down without fear of a stinky sock growing legs and attacking me.

In an attempt to avoid having to endure an unnecessary lecture about keeping away from Jade Washington, I had shared my 'validated Unfamous-ness' idea with him. After much thought, I had decided that my best option to rocket to 'unfame', is to become an events photographer - I mean, how hard can it really be? All I'd really have to do is buy a fancy camera, go to events, point and click, go home and adjust the brightness and contrast of the photos till they didn't look quite so amateur, and then slap a logo in the corner. Bada-bing, bada-boom; I'm a photographer! I'm surprised I didn't think of it earlier, it's actually quite genius when you think about it. None of the work and all of the benefits!

"Rio, you are not trying to better shit! What you're doing is GASSING yourself. You're not even willing to take a flippin' photography course you muppet, so why are you on becoming a photographer? These times you still haven't learnt how to master your dead digital camera; what are you gonna do with a big boy camera? You can't just leave it on the automatic setting all the time like you do with your regular camera."

"Why not? Who's gonna know the difference? As long as I edit them good, no one will be any the wiser," I say matter-of-factly.

"You say that now, but when your pictures come out looking crap like that photographer from the Sunday Slam, you will know."

I cross my arms.

"They will never look that bad!" I pout.

"Says you," he scoffs bringing a large clump of noodles to his mouth. He flashes his infectious smile again before cramming the lot into his gob. I kiss my teeth and fold my rice in with my sticky scarlet sweet 'n' sour chicken.

"Screw you dude. I'm gonna do it no matter what you say."

"I know this," he replies with a mouth full of noodles muffling his words so that they came out sounding like "Oi mow dish" instead. He swallows. "You never listen to me and that's how you always end up in some bullshit drama."

Oh boy, I can see where this is heading.

"I don't see what the big deal is! Being a photographer will help me kill two birds with one stone; I will be kept busy enough so that I don't end up in some *'bullshit drama'*, AND I'd become an Unfamous at the same time. What's wrong with that?" I ask, hoping that my diversion is working.

Tyson sighs, "If you say so Ri. Me personally, I think you need to leave that whole world alone and just get on with your life. If it's meant to happen for you then it will, if not, oh well, you'll always have me." He smiles that perfectly, imperfect crooked smile, throwing in a cheeky wink to give it more animation.

"You're forgetting -dearest friend -that you are a part of 'that world' now." I point out.

"No I'm not. I'm popular, not bait. People just like me because I don't reek of desperation like you do," he laughs. I contemplate throwing my fork at him...but then I'd have to get up to retrieve it then go and wash it off. That's way too much effort for a shot that's not even guaranteed with my bent aim. I settle for a simple insult instead.

"Dickhead!"

"Umm hmm, whatever. You know it's true; I'm just a likeable guy."

"No you're not bitch, 'cause I don't like you!" I poke my tongue out him.

"Oh you don't like me now huh? Is that because I'm so freakin' awesome, or is it because you like that slag Jade Washington?"

Here we go.

"First of all, that was a CRAP way to work Jade into the conversation, and secondly, I don't bloody like him! Why doesn't anyone understand this? I think Jade is a prat!" I scream.

"Well you make sure you remember that, Ri. I don't want you getting mixed up with this guy. I've heard enough shit about him to last me a lifetime, and while I may rate him for his escapades, I don't want you to become a part of that. I know you think that I'm overreacting, but it's only because I care okay."

Tyson stretches out his hand, his palm facing upwards for me to put mine in it. I know that to take his hand is me agreeing to some kind of unspoken deal, which is as good as me giving my word, but I can't guarantee that I can keep Jade away as he seems pretty adamant on pursuing me. I know it's foolish of me to be thinking like this, but I am enjoying the unwanted attention a little (why lie?), and the fact that it has the added bonus of pissing Nathaniel off is fantastic! I set my food down on the bed and get up to hug Tyson instead. He sighs knowing that I am avoiding sealing the deal and pulls me into his lap. I rest his head on my chest, and play with his long silken cornrows.

"Just be careful, okay Ri." I peck him on his forehead.

"Okay Ty."

9

Super Rich Kids.

THAT IS IT! I've had just about enough of this crap, I've put up with it long enough. It ends NOW! Since Jade 'can't take the hint' Washington got his greasy mitts on my phone number, he has been randomly texting me (or rather he has been 'SEXting' me) for the past four days. Though I had been mildly amused by his...*colourful* use of the English language in the beginning, my patience with him is now rapidly wearing thin. I had refrained from responding to any of his erotic text messages, assuming that my lack of participation in his frivolous, sexual mind-games would deter him from sending more, but I had been proven wrong every time he sent another - each message more forthright than its predecessor. He had started out slow with suggestive prose that allowed my over-active imagination to run wild, but as time wears on, he has been making his sexual intentions for me more defined.

What irritates me the most isn't that he refuses to throw in the towel, it's that I'm starting to want him to make good on his words. The more I try to repress my desires, the more my desires carry themselves over into my dreams, creating lusty scenarios that are all too vivid. I find myself waking up with skin so hot and damp with sweat that my pyjamas cling to my body, accompanied by a strong pulsation between my thighs. My only option to ease the undulating throbbing is to make use of my latest mechanical purchase from Ann Summers - I was dead serious when I said that I was going to take a trip there. Best thing I've spent my student loan on so far if you ask me!

It's 4am, Friday morning, and yet another heated session of dream lovemaking with Jade 'say my name' Washington, filled with black velvet visions of our bodies tangled in incomprehensible positions, has been cut short by the harsh vibrations of my iPhone. It's another tummy fluttering *sext,* which only adds to the frustration that the deep heady sex I was engaged in is only a figment of my imagination. In the sext he describes the illicit pleasure he would take in binding my wrists behind my back with a black silk scarf, and laying me face down on his bed, trailing ice cubes up and down the centre of my back with his mouth until my spine is numb. He says that he would then reignite the trail with splashes of hot candle wax, entering me as slowly as possible so that he could savour the way I feel as I shudder all along his length...

FUCK! I want him to do it so badly and I know that I shouldn't. Jade is trouble. I have to put a stop to this before I end up doing something I may (…or may not) regret. Gritting my teeth and trying my best to ignore the way my pulse is mercilessly hammering away at my centre, I press the call button. The phone rings three times before he picks up. I take a deep breath to steady myself, and I'm about to tell him to fuck off, when his husky 'after dark' voice leaks through the receiver and caresses my eardrums.

"Rio," he purrs. I can hear him smiling victoriously, "I was just thinking about you. What are you wearing?"

"You're not funny you know," I snarl pathetically, trying to keep my head in the game. Who answers the phones like that, and why does his voice have to sound so...*oooo* when he speaks? I'm trying to be mad here!

"I wasn't tryna be funny babes, I'm dead serious. I REALLY wanna know what you're wearin'"

"I'm not tellin' you what I'm wearin' Jade," I snap letting my temper get the best of me.

"That's cool babe. Wanna know what I'm wearin'?"

"NO!" I shout into the receiver, completely disregarding the fact that there are other people in this flat trying to sleep.

Jade chuckles, "It's a trick question; I'm not wearing ANYTHING. I sleep naked. Care to join me?"

"What? No!" I splutter feeling my face flush at his invitation.

"Suit yourself babes. I can wait."

"Well you'll be waiting a long bloody time, sunshine!"

"I don't mind, you'll be worth it," he replies, all traces of sexuality now void. I shift uncomfortably in my bed, the cheap prison standard mattress suddenly seeming less hospitable than usual. I don't like the way he says that I will be worth the wait; it unsettles me. He said it as if he knew beyond the shadow of a doubt that I would succumb to his advances.

I exhale and resume my mission.

"Whatever Jade, all I know is you need to stop sending me those stupid texts 'cause you're really starting to piss me off," I snap firmly.

"You want me to stop?" he breathes, his husky voice saturated in untamed lust as if we were in the midst of lurid love-making. How does he do that? One moment he sounds freakishly normal and the next I feel as if I'm having involuntary phone sex.

"Quit it!"

"What?" he asks innocently.

"You know what! Stop being...sexy!" I couldn't think of a less cringe-worthy way of describing his demeanour in the allotted response time. I whack myself in the head for having such a wonderful way with words.

Jade chuckles again and groans, "You want me to stop being sexy? You think I'm sexy, Rio?"

"I never said that!"

"You said that I should *stop* being sexy. In order for me to *stop* being sexy, I would have to be sexy in the first place, alie?"

"Well...yes but_"

"Exactly; so you DO think I'm sexy." I roll my eyes and sigh. No matter how much I protest that clearly isn't what I meant, Jade is going to find some way to twist my words in his favour. Arrogant prick!

"You're annoying me. I'm going to bed. Don't text me anymore." I hang up and roll over ready to return to the land of nod where I don't have to front like I don't think Jade is the inventor of the multiple orgasm, when my phone buzzes again. I growl into my pillow knowing it's him.

Don't b mad bbz, I think ur sxc 2 ;). I'll c u 2nite. Sweet dreams lol x

Sugar!

Honey!

Iced!

Tea!

I'd completely forgotten that Carmen had guilted me into going on a double date with her, Bless and Jade to Malaysia Blaq tonight. Fantastic! Now I have to endure a whole night of Jade 'I'm-too-sexy-for-my-shirt' Washington. This is exactly what I *don't* need right now! It's hard enough staying mad at him over the phone; how am I supposed to stay mad at him when he's right in front of me looking, and talking in the way he does? Who can fight that kind of temptation?

A succession of over-excited raps on my bedroom door, accompanied by a shrill chorus of incomprehensible squeals, wakes me up twelve hours later.

"RIO, OPEN UP. QUICK!" Yoshi's high voice sings over the racket the girls are making. I drag the covers over my head trying to muffle the noise - right now they're like having another alarm that I don't even have the option of turning off.

"GO 'WAAAY!" I growl, not appreciating my precious sleepy time being disrupted again. I had just reached the peak of my dream and they've successfully ruined it with their big stupid mouths'.

"BUT RI THERE'S A PACKAGE FOR YOU."

"NO DERE AIN'T, STOP LYIN'. I DIN'T ORDA NUFFINK," I shout back, lazily slurring my words because talking just feels like so much effort right now.

"I'M NOT LYING RI. THERE REALLY IS A PACKAGE FOR YOU. IT'S A GIFT...FROM JADE." They unleash another stream of fan worthy screams at the sound of his name.

I bolt upright and flip the covers off of me. A gift? From Jade? What the hell!?! Now I am awake. I toss my mechanical mate down the side of the bed (don't judge me, I couldn't help myself. Hearing his deep husky voice on the phone last night didn't exactly douse the flames that my dreams had started), then shoot into the bathroom to wash away any evidence of excessive drooling and crusty eye-bogey. Once I am sure that I don't look like road kill anymore, I run to the door, flinging it open impatiently so that I can satisfy my curiosity. It is exciting enough that I have received a gift, but the fact that it is from Jade 'it-feels-so-good-that-my-mouth-is-wide-open-but-no-sound-is-coming-out' Washington, adds an element of mystery.

I am greeted by a huge gold box tied with a black velvet ribbon, and the top of Yoshi's huge black and magenta streaked bouffant, adorned with Hello Kitty character clips, love hearts, and stars. She pops up on her tiptoes and smiles at me with candyfloss pink lips and ridiculously long false eyelashes that make her achieve that too-cute anime look she loves so much. My eyes widen at the size of the expensive looking package.

"What the hell?"

"I know right!" Fontaine grins, mindlessly tugging on her curls, while Carmen bounces up and down next to her, trying to avoid messing up her freshly manicured toes that still have her pink foam toe separators wedged between them.

Greedily, I yank the oversized box out of Yoshi's hands without so much as a 'Hello' or a 'Thank you' and bring it into my room -the girls hot on my heels. I place the box on my bed and tug gently at the ends of the ribbon, flinging the note attached to it that simply reads *'From Jade'* on it, to the side.

"What is it?" Fontaine asks, hovering right over my shoulder.

"Your guess is as good as mine dude," I reply, handling the packaging with as much care as I can muster in my excitement. I lift the lid off, revealing several layers of black crepe paper that conceal my gift. Anyhow this was some freaky sex kitten outfit – straight 'return to sender'...though when you think about it, I shouldn't be accepting *any* gifts from Jade 'Rio-is-on-my-To-Do-List' Washington. I tell myself that no matter what is inside this box, I am going to give it back, kinky outfit or not. Nothing in this life comes without a cost – extravagant gifts from uncompromising admirers included.

"Hurry up man! Unwrapping all slow and shit like this is some movie," Carmen yells impatiently.

I giggle and lift the rustling paper, unveiling two gorgeous dresses; one a deep shade of red and the other, the purest white. Each dress has a name card pinned to it; the red one is for Carmen, who is grinning like she has just been informed that she is getting free Brazilian weave for life, and the white one is for me. He thinks he's slick; I know a ploy to sweet up the friend when I see one. Why do boys assume that cosying up to a girl's friends is some sort of shoe-in with the girl. A girl's friend's opinion of the man pursuing her is important...but not so important that you should go and buy them an expensive ass dress! If a girl likes you then she likes you -point blank -and nothing that her friends say, good or bad, will change that...most of the time.

Carmen lifts her sultry ensemble out of the box and holds it lovingly against her slender frame.

"This dress is SEXY blud! Oh I can't wait to get dressed 'cause I am going to look so nice and it will make Amari want to do dirty things to me. I like it when he does dirty things to me..." she trails off into her filthy little fantasies. I simply stare down at my dress, dumbstruck. I don't even want to touch the milky fabric, afraid that I will fall in love with it. Fontaine senses my hesitation and takes the dress out of the box to see it properly.

"Oh my God, I'm so jealous right now," she squeals stroking the snowy georgette with her fingertips, "You lot are so friggin' lucky!"

"I'll say!" Yoshi agrees from across the room, fawning over the racy neckline of Carmen's dress, while Carmen occupies herself by admiring the way the deep rouge of dress looks against her chestnut skin.

"I wish some dude would have tried this hard to get into my pants," Fontaine pouts.

"D'you know what I mean! Jade is going for GOLD!" Carmen laughs, not removing her eyes from her reflection. Fontaine and Yoshi cackle along with her, but I don't join in. I can't get my mind around the beauty of our dresses. Why is he trying this hard? It can't just be because I am proving to be a challenge to win over, there has to be something more, something that I'm missing. Jade hardly knows me and yet so far he has gone out of his way to obtain my phone number behind my back, he keeps sending me erotic text messages, and is taking my friend, her…um, lover, and me to freaking MALAYSIA BLAQ for FREE. On top of taking my attitude, he has purchased two amazing dresses for me and Carmen to wear tonight. It just doesn't add up.

"Car, put the dress back in the box. We're giving them back, and you can forget Malaysia Blaq 'cause I'm not going," I say firmly, grabbing my dress from Fontaine and shoving it back in the box.

Carmen looks at me like I'm crazy. "Fuck a not going! Bruv, do you SEE this dress? I'm not giving back SHIT!"

"Car, I'm serious. I have a bad feeling about this."

Carmen rolls her eyes and huffs, "Rio, you have a bad feeling about EVERYTHING. Chances are that you are right and Jade is just trying to get into your pants, but so the fuck what? He's fuckin' HOT mate! No one said that you're obliged to give him the *pussoir* just 'cause he gave you a dress; FUCK a dress! Whether you do anything with this dude or not, will be because it's what you WANT, so stop stressing because technically there is nothing wrong with possibly the hottest man ever created - who, may I add just happens to be a God damn rich ass MALE MODEL -giving you GIFTS and taking you on a DATE to a fancy pants nightclub that most people can't even get on the list for. I'm not understanding how you can consider all of that, and sit there gassin' 'bout you wanna give back dress and not got to big boy club for FREE because JADE WASHINGTON wants to sleep with YOU. I should actually punch you in the face and smash your phone for saying such things!"

I laugh and sigh, "I hear that Car, but_"

"No buts; we're keeping the dresses, and we're gonna go to the club with two sexy ass boys, and we're gonna have the time of our fucking lives, and when it's all over at least one of us is going to get some DICK, and that's what's gonna happen. Cool. Thanks." Carmen swiftly folds her dress over her arm and marches right out of my room.

"I'M STILL NOT GOING!" I yell after her.

"YES YOU ARE BITCH!"

Watch how I'm not going.

Yeah so...I am SO going! I don't want to like the dress -I REALLY don't -but the moment I see myself in it, I get an empowering feeling of indestructible sexuality, and I fully understand why Carmen is so against giving them back. They are incredible, and the fact that I had never even heard of the designer only makes them even more desirable because it is unlikely that there will be several other girls swanning around in the same thing like it's a common Asos dress. Before I'd put it on I was adamant about not going anywhere with Jade 'I-already-mentally-fucked-you' Washington, but I let my curiosity get the better of me and told myself that I was just going to see what it looked like...and then I saw myself in it. Vanity is a sin!

The virgin white of the georgette contrasts against my dark skin; its threads are luminescent, giving it an ethereal glow whenever the light touches it. The layered strapless bodice of the dress clings to me adoringly, accentuating my voluptuous figure, before one layer of the sheer fabric billows out from my hips, with two thigh high slits in the front, allowing gluttonous views of my legs when I walk –it's devilishly angelic couture. From that moment on, all of my earlier qualms dissipate into nothingness, and I convince myself that Carmen is right; I mean, how bad can going on a flashy first date with the boy of my dreams (literally) be? Besides, this dress deserves to see the inside of a glamorous club like Malaysia Blaq, and after all of the crap I've been through lately, I deserve to be fawned over by a sexy, rich, male model.

Carefully I remove the dress and set it on my bed amongst various other items that I have selected to wear with it, and dash into the shower, anticipating putting it back on.

Two hours later, Fontaine and Yoshi are adding the finishing touches to mine and Carmen's hair and makeup, when the intercom buzzes.

"They're here," I gasp nervously, looking at Carmen. She smiles at me excitedly and springs to her feet, pulling down the hem of her little red dress.

Fontaine styled Carmen's hair with a simple centre parting, leaving all 21 inches of it to cascade straight down her back and over her shoulders. Whenever Carmen moves her head, large gold hoop earrings swing out from beneath the strands. Her wrists are cuffed with gold Cuban link bracelets, and a short thick Cuban link chain rests on her collarbone, which only draws more attention to the deep V neckline of the dress -and to her pert breasts that it just about covers. On her feet, her favourite pair of ridiculously-high black Louboutin pumps. Yoshi lined Carmen's eyes with an inky black Kajal stick and applied false lashes, making them look sultry and exotic, and she gave her deep red lip-gloss to match the dress -she looks *beyond* incredible.

Carmen teeters into the hallway and presses the 'talk' button on the intercom.

"Hello?" she purrs silkily –I think the dress has given her an ego boost.

"It's me babes," I hear Bless respond. "You lot ready?" he asks hopefully.

"Yeah, we'll be down in a minute."

"A'ight. Don't take long you know, 'cause if I have to come up there and get you, there's gonna be trouble."

"Whatever!" Carmen giggles, and it is clear what kind of trouble she is hoping she and Bless will get into.

We get the rest of our things together and slink into the lift, taking full advantage of the mirror that lines the back wall. As much as I will front like I don't care what Jade thinks of me once we get downstairs, I have to make sure that there isn't so much as a hair out of place. Thank God I had gotten my weave redone last week, because the previous one was on its last legs - I'm talking separating, clumping and stiffening with every move I made, so much so that there was no point in rescuing it anymore because two seconds later it would look like I had bought cheap synthetic weave.

Fontaine had curled my hair into voluminous waves and swept it over my right shoulder to show off my small silver studs, pinning it in place with a few bobby pins. I looked like I wouldn't look THAT out of place on the arm of a man as stunning as Jade 'you-were-created-I-was-sculpted' Washington.

"I can't wait for them to see us," Carmen babbles excitedly, "I swear, I have never been this hapz to look good in my life," she beams readjusting her breasts in the bra so that they look even more buoyant than they already are. I watch the floor numbers descend and run my fingers through the ends of my hair as my anxiety grows.

"I've never been so nervous," I reply shakily.

"Why?"

I look at her like she is stupid.

"It's JADE WASHINGTON!" I almost scream.

"Point taken."

The lift pings, signalling that we have finally reached the ground floor and my heart rate goes into overdrive.

The lift doors slide open...

10

Armani Exchange.

"Hey babe!" Carmen smiles with outstretched arms, eager to embrace her 'Blessed' bad habit. Under normal circumstances I would have remembered my manners and greeted Bless as well, but unfortunately I find myself dumbstruck on account of the model-esque young man that is standing next to him, mentally devouring me with those magnificent jade-green eyes.

His weave-worthy midnight tresses are casually flipped to one side, framing his glorious profile perfectly, giving him the harlequin romance aura of a young Fabio Lazoni. He is wearing a simple black Armani shirt with a black bow tie purposely left undone, dangling out of his collar, with the shirt tucked into the waistband of his black skinny jeans and the sleeves rolled up to his elbows, giving his simplistic look that young rebellious London edge. He looks like trouble. His choreographed look is finished off with a pair of black leather Brogues and a single earring with two raven feathers hanging from his exposed earlobe. It is Jade toned down, but even these subtle quirks in his outfit could not make him disappear in a crowd; Jade has an undeniable presence that you can't ignore even if you wanted to.

I am fighting not to stare at him, but as soon as my eyes leave him, a moment later they are back to gazing at him as if he is every woman's dream man, manifested. I walk over to him with a strained expression of indifference on my face. I want to scowl at him so that he knows that I refuse to be swayed by his impeccable taste in gifts or his distractingly good looks, but the way he is staring back at me won't allow me to; it only increases the butterflies in my stomach. If he is trying to conceal the fact that he thinks I look at least halfway as delectable as he does, then he is doing an awful job...but then again, when does Jade ever hide his thoughts from me or anyone else?

In the short time I have known him, I've learned that Jade is one of those rare individuals that says and does exactly what they feel, no matter the consequence. If you don't like how Jade is...well, it doesn't really matter because he is Jade 'close-the-door-on-your-way-out' Washington, the most arrogant, reckless, charismatic, sinfully sexy, unspoken ruler of the Unfamous, and he knows it. People can despise him as much as they want, but at the end of the day, we are disposable and replaceable - Jade Washington isn't. I am clearly anti-Jade, so why is he refusing to dispose of, and replace me?

I clear my throat and swallow in an attempt to compose my vocal chords so that I don't sound star-struck. I part my lips to greet him grudgingly...but then he smiles at me and no sound comes out of my mouth. Jade takes my hand in his, and then he slowly bows his head as he brings it to his lips. His long eyelashes tickle my skin as he places possibly the lightest prelude to a kiss on the back of my hand, sending a shock of tiny goose bumps shooting up my arm then down the centre of my back - the butterfly effect. I repress a jolt followed by a blue shudder, subject to his lids retracting to reveal his Caribbean sea-green eyes, staring right at me. He releases my hand and chuckles silently at my bewildered gaze before pulling me to him. I inhale sharply at the shock of feeling him this close to me.

Jade strokes my face with the back of his hand and says, "Nathaniel is a fool for letting you go."

We pull up outside of the entrance to Malaysia Blaq in Jade's Lexus, feeling every bit the V.I.P as Jade and Bless exit first then open the door for me and Carmen. We step onto the black carpet bordered off with black velvet ropes that stretch all the way down to the end of the pavement from the elaborate iron-clad doors. The boys lace their arms around our well-dressed waists and we instantly become the envy of every female partygoer waiting in the disgustingly long queue that snakes all the way down to the end of the street, and disappears around the corner. The black building is lit from below, with huge iron structures encompassing roaring flames that throw hundreds of amber sparks up into the night.

A short tanned oriental man walks over to us dressed in the traditional Malaysian male attire of a black *baju melayu,* with an intricately designed *kain samping* made of black and gold *songket* cloth wrapped around his waist, and a black *songkok* on his head. He bows slightly and takes Jade's car keys from him, he then give him a small black tag with the number '42' embossed on it in gold.

"Selamat malam; good evening Mr Washington," he says in a typical London accent, ruining the ethnic illusion a little.

"Good evening Sharin, how are you?" Jade smiles, shaking the valet's free hand.

"Very good sir; and yourself?"

Jade looks around, already disinterested by the conversation, and shrugs "I'm not too bad."

"Glad to hear it, sir." The valet greets the rest of us briefly then turns back to Jade, "I hope you and your friends have a good time tonight," he smiles, looking me over in a way that makes me switch my footing.

Jades' fingers expand slowly over the curve of my hip. "Don't worry," he grins, flashing his 2000-watt smile at me, "We will."

The valet smiles politely and slides into the driver's seat. Without another word, he zooms off down the road and we proceed along the black carpet.

The closer we get to the doors, the more I can feel the waves of excitement rolling off Carmen.

She leans over to me.

"Bruv, valet parking! We've made it!" she gushes in hushed tones. I roll my eyes.

"Shut up!"

"You shut up! This is the life I was meant to lead fam; walking up the black carpet with my trophy man on my arm_"

"What?" Bless asks incredulously. Carmen grins at him innocently.

"Huh? You say somethin'?" Bless cracks a satisfied smile.

"That's what I thought," he replies knowing that he has her under manners (and that funnily enough, she loves it). They giggle at their stupid private joke, seeming (oddly) more adorable every moment, whilst I try my best to glide along the carpet as smoothly as my date, in silence. I have nothing to say to him, and anything he has to say to me, I'm not particularly keen on hearing because all it will do is irritate me. It had been like this in the car as well, Carmen and Bless talking up a storm, whilst I sat quietly in the back pretending that I couldn't see Jade's eyes watching me in the rear-view mirror whenever he got the chance. I don't know why he thought that bringing up Nathaniel to pay me a compliment was a good idea. As flattering as it was supposed to be, the sound of his name only brought the sadness, that I am constantly battling, to the forefront of my mind, and now Nathaniel is all I can think about. I wonder what he'd say if he found out that I'm on a date with Jade 'Mr. Lover Man...SHABBA!' Washington?

Would he even care?

11

Fine China.

Amazing! This club is AMAZING!

Malaysia Blaq is, hands down, the most beautiful nightclub I have seen in my life, decorated in the most simplistically complex decor of black on black with gold detailing. It is a club worthy of hosting one of Diddy's infamous celebrity soirées and I can see why people make such a fuss about coming here. The walls are completely covered in black satin wallpaper, with angular wall lamps encased in convoluted gold leaf structures. The floor is made of black marble speckled with tiny gold flecks that glitter whenever the translucent gold strobe lights hanging from the black ceiling travel across them. There are three different floors, each decorated similarly, but each with a defining feature. The first floor has a selection of gold leaf lanterns clustered together in the centre of the ceiling to create the illusion of a grand chandelier that glows from within. The second floor has long black organza drapes that waft out from the centre of the ceiling like big black pergola, and a large gold leaf statue of statue of Happy Buddha at the far end of the room. The third floor is a grand, open-plan rooftop terrace, equipped with a black and gold shisha bar, an oxygen bar (how pretentious) and a manmade heated pond filled with cream and black koi carp. The most intriguing thing is that there is no music; not until you put on the complimentary headphones provided on entry. The headphones come with a digital tuner with 3 channels that allow you to tune into one of the three DJs who are posted on separate floors, playing different genres of music. The dance floor is a sight to see; masses of bodies dancing to different beats –it's rhythmic chaos, but it looks unbelievably fun. So this is a silent rave.

We are situated in the V.I.P section on the first floor, lounging against the large circular booth -wrapped in black leather with gold piping, sipping on a complimentary bottle of

Nicolas Feuillatte champagne from gold-rimmed champagne flutes. I am sitting next to Jade (because I have to) and Carmen is next to me, nuzzling under Bless's arm with her flute steadily streaming the bubbly liquid into her mouth. I am hyper aware that Jade's arm is stretched across the back of the booth, his slender fingers within touching distance of my bare shoulder, but he has made no move to touch me. He doesn't need to; the heat emitting from his skin and the sheer prospect of feeling his bare hands on my flesh is enough to keep me in a state of heightened anticipation. I had thought about leaning back a couple of times, but I can't help but feel that it will translate to me surrendering to him, which is not on my to-do-list...yet.

"I feel like I've died and gone to rich," Carmen says, smiling into her third glass of champagne.

"Well you sound like you've died and gone to *drunk*! Don't you think you should ease up on the champers?" I suggest.

"Why? It's free. I like free," she giggles

"But you're not really a drinker."

Carmen rolls her eyes, "What part of 'IT'S FREE' are you not getting?"

I sigh and shrug. She's in the VIP of Malaysia Blaq, she's not going to listen to me.

"Whatever Car."

"Are you always this much of a buzz kill?" Jade asks sitting forward, the warmth of his body heat suddenly intensifying with his proximity. I allow myself a small peek at him.

"Only when I'm taken on dates against my will just so my friend can get drunk on free champagne," I retort miserably.

Carmen rolls her eyes.

"Oh my God, you're so moany! Look where we are. Look at who you're with. Why are you in a mood?" she snaps. I fold my arms -choosing to ignore her stupid question because she knows damn well why I'm in a mood -and sit back in the chair, forgetting that Jade's arm is still there waiting for me. The burn of his flesh sends a peppered rush of adrenaline pumping through my system. He is so hot.

I go to move away from him when his arm shifts and curls over my shoulder, his fiery fingertips now scrawling small heated patterns along my exposed collarbone.

"Babes, loosen up."

"Yeah, I bet you'd love that," I scoff.

Jade smiles and bows his head so that I only I can hear him. "More than you know. I haven't told you half of the things that I would do to your_"

I jump up, putting a safe distance between us. If ever there was a time that I didn't need to hear his dream inspiring words of self-forbidden temptation, it is now, especially when he is right in front of me looking as good as a tall glass of ice-cold water to a parched mouth.

He grins up at me devilishly, enjoying my discomfort, and bites the corner of his lip. I wonder if he is aware that he is teasing me further, or if he is just THAT sexy.

"That dress really does look good on you babes," he purrs getting to his feet, reminding me of how much taller than me he is. He closes the distance between us, transforming my safe zone into a danger zone; my palms dampen, my mouth goes dry and inconveniently my voice goes missing because I don't hear it relay any of the objections that my head is screaming when he pulls me close and drags the tip of his nose along my jaw line, stopping just before his beautifully explicit mouth almost makes direct contact with mine. "I think you owe me a dance."

He almost had me.

His arms were around me, his rock hard abs were pressed up against me, his enthralling scent was making my head lighter every time I inhaled -and his eyes, his beautiful, BEAUTIFUL eyes -were gazing into mine like I was the only woman in existence. All I could think about was dancing with him…then Amber came over...and Chantal…and Alyssa, and India, and Pixie and about 20 other female admirers, and they just kept on coming. I am furious! To think that I had allowed myself to get caught up in his Jade Washington-ness like some naive little girl; I know better than that.

Bless and Carmen make a swift escape to the rooftop terrace to smoke shisha, and I can't say that I blame them. If the atmosphere wasn't awkward enough before, it's as tense as one of my date's smooth golden pecs -which he is ever so *charmingly* allowing one of his groupies to stroke through his shirt.

There are three tasteful yet scantily clad girls hovering around him like flies to shit, completely disregarding the fact that I am clearly here with him, even if it is against my will. I look at the willowy blonde closest to me - who feels compelled to flip her mile long hair every two seconds like she is in a Pantene advert - and scowl. I'm not sitting RIGHT NEXT TO HIM for the fun of it you know; get lost! She cocks her eyebrow at me and flips her hair again then continues to make whore eyes at, Jade along with the other females who are vying for his divided attention.

By now I gather that in the wonderful world of Jade, having a female by his side doesn't count for much. I should have known better really, he doesn't have the most monogamous reputation. The first time I met him he had a girl on each arm like it was nothing, and neither of them seemed to mind all that much. Well I'm not some thirsty groupie, and I don't reside in The Land of Simple Bitch, so if Jade refuses to respect the fact that I am supposed to be his sole focus of the night, then he can stay with his fan club without me sitting here having to witness it.

The Pantene girl giggles a little too hard at a joke that he cracks - that obviously isn't that funny because he rolls his eyes at her - and swats at his firm chest playfully.

"Jade, stop," she chirps at him in a voice that clearly means she want him to continue. Jade winks at her and flashes his 2000-watt smile very briefly, but it is enough to make her and the other two party-crashers pause momentarily to admire him.

I get a familiar pang of inadequacy - this reminds me of being in college with Nathaniel; me by his side, dejectedly fading into the background while Georgia and her cronies pout their lips and bat their eyelashes at him. The difference between then and now is that Nathaniel was enough of a gentleman to ask them to ease up because he was with me; Jade however, winks, smiles and suggestively touches these girls with his burning fingertips, encouraging their behaviour as if it isn't disrespectful to me in the least. Now, I know I have no hold over the desirable Mr Washington, but you'd think that after all the bother he'd gone through to get me here, that he'd have the decency to keep his hoes at bay. I have been contemplating different ways to get rid of these girls without causing a scene, but the way Blondie had looked at me when I mean mugged her, told me that removing them wouldn't be the easiest thing to do. Every possible scenario I come up with ends in a fight, and when I think about it properly, as much as I would love to slap a bitch, I am not about to make a fool of myself in Malaysia Blaq, especially not over Jade 'what's-your-name-again-babes?' Washington. I get to my feet and walk away as gracefully, and with as much dignity, as I can, to buy myself something a little stronger than champagne from the bar.

The black top bar is at the opposite end of the room dripping with wannabe wags, semi-pro footballers and broke, thirsty women, hoping that if they loiter at the bar long enough, some big shot would want to get into their pants enough to buy them a drink or two. My white designer dress seems even more lethal than my 'picture me nude' brown one, because every couple of steps I take, another hopeful guy tries it on with me. I find that due to the majority of the crowd being white men, it is more amusing than irritating because they like to use cheeky chat up lines that I really can't take seriously. The best one so far had to be, "I miss my teddy bear. Would you sleep with me?" -'cause that was *really* going to work!

I have successfully smiled at, shrugged off and pushed my way through the sea of grabby men (and less than friendly females) and I'm finally at the bar. I raise my arm to hail one of the 5 Malaysian bartenders made up of three strikingly beautiful females dressed in simple black dresses and an assortment of golden Hardy lilies in their hair, and two equally handsome men in black vest tops and harem pants cut from the gold embroidered songket cloth that the valet's wore. They all looked like models - despite their lack of height -and it only made the Malaysia Blaq experience more overwhelming. The longer I stand here waiting for someone to serve me, the more irritated and unimportant I feel. Every member of staff looks like they have just stepped off a Harpers Bazaar photo shoot, and are making the other beautiful people crowding the bar their main priority. This, on top of being ignored by my date, is not exactly helping my self-esteem. I thought that I looked like a million dollars, but these people make me feel like a tarnished penny - damn near worthless and unwanted.

I shouldn't have come here. Jade hasn't lived up to being the distraction I'd hoped he would be. Fight it as I may, I can't stop thinking about Nathaniel.

The feel of a male frame resting against me snaps me out of my one man pity party and brings me back to the present. I pause for a moment to give them a chance to back off, but it appears that they are comfortable where they are because they don't attempt to move.

I clear my throat to ask him if he has a death wish, but he interrupts me.

"I was wondering how long you were gonna allow me to press up against you, princess. Firstly, put your hand down, we ain't in primary school, and secondly, it wouldn't kill you to smile. No wonder they don't want to serve you!"

My stomach flips from the shock of hearing the familiar sound of the arrogant voice that still refuses to let on more than absolutely necessary, and I bet my life that he has that unnerving know-it-all grin that I despise on his face.

I must really be having a terrible time, because before I can stop myself I spin around and fling my arms around his neck as if it is him that I miss instead of Nate.

"Carter! Oh my God I can't believe it's you." I twitter excitedly, squeezing him tighter. Carter stiffens against me at first, caught off guard by my unusual reaction to him, and then gradually he relaxes into it and hugs me back...briefly. The feel of his embrace brings me back to my senses and I let him go, making sure to put some space between us. Carter and I aren't close enough to exchange hugs with each other, so now that my moment of madness is over, I am swiftly settling into how I usually feel around my 'friend' (if that's what you'd call him) – *awkward*, with a fresh splash of embarrassment to top it off.

His hazel eyes glint, highlighting their green flecks, and a menacing smile contorts his lips.

"Wow, a hug. Anyone would think that you actually missed me, princess," he smirks, zoning in on how uncomfortable he is making me.

I jut out my jaw.

"As if! It was an adverse reaction to having such a crappy night. I would have been happy to see the devil," I say sourly, knocking our love/hate, almost friendliness back into balance.

Carter's smile widens in approval at my jibe, and he slides into the small gap next to me at the bar.

"I'm the next best thing," he replies turning my devil insult into a twisted compliment. I roll my eyes.

"What are you doing here anyway?"

He looks at me like I'm stupid. "It's a club, princess. Just because places like this are a novelty to you, doesn't mean it is to me. Uni raves are my idea of slumming it."

With a flick of his Rolex-clad wrist, and a heavy dose of unwavering eye contact, he catches the attention of one of the female barmaids. She smiles at him and slinks over. Can you believe this shit? I have been standing here with my hand up for almost 10 minutes, trying to get someone's attention, with no luck, then along comes this creep and all it takes is a small hand gesture and a dose of bedroom eyes and Little Miss 'love you long time' can't wait to serve him.

"Hey handsome, what can I get you?" she asks leaning forward slightly, allowing Carter a small glimpse of her perky C cups. He looks at them shamelessly and smirks.

"I'll have a Gin and Tonic. What do you fancy, princess?" he asks transferring his focus from her bosom to me. He retrieves a wad of £50 notes from the hidden pocket inside of his tailored grey suit jacket, causing me to stare at him in disbelief -what is this 20 year old university student doing with all this money? I have never once heard Carter mention having a job, and student loan doesn't stretch that far, especially not for a tailored suit (that judging by the quality of the material and the cut, it's definitely designer), a Rolex, and most definitely not his magnificent Mercedes truck. I shrug and let it go. It's unlikely that he'd tell me if I asked anyway. Carter likes being enigmatic; the less people know about him, the better, especially amongst the Unfamous. With all the haters, fake friends and the people who want in, privacy is hard to come by because people are forever in your business trying to find a chink in your armour that will take you down so that they can replace you. It's a Unfamous-eat-Unfamous world and information is currency.

"I'll have what he's having...without the tonic...and make mine a double," I say to the barmaid, not bothering to keep the attitude out of my tone.

"No she won't," Carter snaps flashing me a stern look before she can make our orders. He placed his hand on my shoulder firmly, "Are you planning on embarrassing yourself tonight or something?"

"No, just trying to ease the suckiness a bit," I shrug dropping his gaze.

He sighs and gives my shoulder a squeeze. "No matter how bad it is, never let it show. Every bad decision you make provides your critics with ammunition to take you down when you surpass them, so I hardly think that leaving the club drunk with pretty boy," he gestures at Jade "will help your already tarnished image. They want to see you fall, never forget that." He turns back to the waiting barmaid and flashes his devilish grin, which she enjoys - I swear I'm missing something, to me his smile is creepy!

"Get her a Screaming Orgasm; she's in desperate need of one," he chuckles making the barmaid giggle along with him.

12
Floetry.

Carter and I are leant up against the DJ booth, sipping our drinks and stiffly catching up with each other. I had tried to talk to him about Georgia to see how he has been handling the whole baby situation, but he clammed up and brushed it off with an open ended "I'm dealing with it", and then changed the subject.

"So, why are you so mad at Jade?"

"Who said I'm mad at Jade?"

"Jade did." He smirks.

I purse my lips then take another sip.

"If he knows that I'm mad at him then why is he still encouraging those sluts?" I fume.

Carter cocks his eyebrow, "You think he's encouraging them?"

"I don't think, I know. I was sitting right there when he was doing it!" I snap.

Carter makes the amused sound.

"Jade doesn't have to do anything to encourage females, he's Jade! What did you expect?"

"Oh I don't know; for our date to actually feel like a date!" I reply, my voice heavy with sarcasm.

Carter rolls his eyes at me.

"Don't be so naïve, princess. No one has actual *dates* with Jade," he scoffs like I should have known better - which I should have. "Girls are content with being the main chick of Jade Washington's for the night, and here you are complaining like one of those girls rubbing up against him wouldn't gladly take your place."

"Oh what, so I supposed to be grateful?"

"Flattered, actually," he smiles.

"Well I'm not! I don't care who he is, I won't be treated this way. After all the trouble it took for him to get me to be here with him, you'd think he'd recognise that I'm not one of those stupid girls that feels 'flattered' to be here with him and respect the fact that we're on this stupid date."

"Why? No disrespect princess, but who are you for him to treat you any differently?" That is all it ever comes down to with these people; I have to be *someone* to be treated like what I think, say, do or feel matters. I swear, sometimes I feel like being a teenager is a job! If you can do it well you are rewarded with status boosts, but if you can't...well, SUCKS TO BE YOU!

I frown already tired of this insulting conversation and Carter's company, when out of the blue he smirks in a way that doesn't make me recoil.

"What?"

Carter chuckles to himself and continues as if I hadn't spoken.

"I don't believe my eyes," he mutters stifling another laugh. I cock my eyebrow.

"What?" I repeat, not appreciating being left out of the joke. Carter takes me by the shoulders and spins me around to see a slightly disgruntled Jade heading straight for us.

We watch Jade glide through the crowd -which parts for him at will -with the grace of a gazelle; tall and strong. His devastating eyes are focused on me, the darkness of the club dimming their brilliant hue into the rich earthy green of a rainforest.

"I think you could possibly be the first female to make Mr Washington jealous," he laughs.

I blush furiously, wanting to break the intensity of Jade's colourful stare, but I can't. It's as if he's hypnotising me with his splendour, sucking me deeper into his very being. My irritation begins to crack and break away. His full blushing lips are fixed into a small mysterious smile, which I am learning is his accustomed facial setting, but his eyes are blank. How did Carter come up with the ridiculous notion that I could ever make someone so...immense, jealous? I shake my head to disagree, simultaneously releasing myself from Jade's spell.

"Oh please! Did you see how many girls -models at that -were throwing themselves at him? He's not jealous, and even if he is -which he is not -he'd have some bloody front, don't you think?"

"Of course, princess, but surprisingly he is. I know Jade better than most -I have a gift at reading him. The plot thickens…"

"How so?"

"It seems I may have spoken too soon; I think he may actually like you," - my stomach flutters in spite of myself - "Either that or he's up to something," - then drops. I prefer the implausible idea that Jade may actually be into me, it seems a lot easier (yet even more daunting) to deal with than suspecting that his interest in me is all part of some convoluted plan. If he does like me –which I'm sure he doesn't -it wouldn't change anything, but it would be nice to know that someone of his elite stature has a genuine interest in me, that goes beyond the leather studded fantasies that intrude my dreams.

"That's what I thought," I reply coming across more disappointed than intended.

"But not what you'd hoped?" Carter asks, sounding as if he has already come to the correct conclusion.

I look up, Jade is almost near us. I tear my besotted gaze away from his quickly advancing figure and turn to meet Carter's stupid grin.

"Well obviously not! Who would want someone to mess with their head?"

Carter shrugs. "I dunno. You seem like the kind of girl that enjoys a good mind fuck," he smirks.

"Hardly!" I retort, picking up on his double entendre. I take my bottom lip into my mouth and huff. "Do you really think he's up to something?" I ask, now more concerned about Jade's motives than I was initially.

Carter makes a face and shrugs again. "It's hard to tell with Jade. When you think you've got him all figured out, he turns around and does something completely out of character that makes you re-evaluate who he really is time and time again."

"I thought you said you knew Jade," I tease.

"I said I know him better than most, doesn't mean I *really* know him...no one does. Well, whatever he's up to, just make sure you keep your guard up, okay princess. I worry about you enough as it is." Carter gives my hand a quick squeeze, making sure he doesn't linger long enough for it to become sentimental, and I see the flicker of a genuine smile peek out from underneath his usual sardonic grin. I smile back. As offbeat as our relationship is, Carter and I share a mutual level of respect and understanding with each other, especially since the sour night I stupidly played

Russian roulette with the man I love. We will never be BFF's, but we look out for each other as much as is necessary (and no more).

I feel his presence before I hear his voice.

"I've been looking for you," Jade croons in his melodious baritone that harmonises smooth with hoarse so perfectly, that I imagine myself sitting up till all hours of the night listening to him speak about nothing. I jump at the feel of his blushing lips grazing my ear - I'm so happy that I can't see him because I would have been incapable of delivering my response.

"Oh please! What happened, are you're groupies bored of you already, or is it the other way around?" I snipe.

His musical laughter wreaks havoc on my hormones and I fight to stay focused.

"Don't be like that babes," he manoeuvres around to the front of me, blocking Carter from my view, so that all I can focus on was the way his eyes smoulder with the intensity of a thousand suns. I forget to breathe. "I promise you, it was nothing." I frown.

"If that's nothing, then I sure as hell don't want to see something!" I spit, closing my eyes and creating a new safe zone so that I can't be distracted.

"Personally, I'm pretty sure you'd LOVE to see something," he jokes stepping closer to me, invading my self-imposed safe zone again. A scarlet light flashes in my head: DANGER, DANGER! The heat radiating from his body rolls off him in turbulent waves that crash and burn against my skin, igniting an internal fire of my own. He is so close –too close.

I look around for Carter in the hope that he will save me from myself and Jade 'I'm-so-sexy-all-I-have-to-do-is-blink-and-you'll-sex-me' Washington, but he is nowhere to be found. Thanks friend!

Jade touches my arm with his scorching fingertips, rendering me catatonic, and says, "Dance with me."

I say nothing as he takes what is left of my Screaming Orgasm out of my trembling hand and tips it down his throat, before setting down the glass on a nearby table. His halo of glossy midnight hair undulates around his face as he moves. It's like he has his own personal wind machine, and I'm blown away. He grasps my clammy hand (cringe) and leads me to the centre of the dance floor. The people around us respond to his aura and give us breathing space, void of any unnecessary bumping, toe-stepping or sweaty bodies brushing up against us.

"Put in your earphones and turn to channel three," he orders, sticking one of his gold and black ear buds into his ear. I do as I am told.

I hear the bass, *da-dum dadada-dum, da-dum dadada-dum,* then the seductive sound of a Spanish guitar follows, and then..."*Maria, Mariaaaaaa...*" –I love this song!

Jade stares down at me, he isn't smiling anymore – my stomach clenches. As the intro plays, he laces one arm around my waist and clutches my body against his, the heat now burning through my dress and scalding my skin. With his free hand, he takes my arm and drapes it around his neck. Without requiring further prompting, I let my other arm follow. His height prevents my fingers from meeting, but I relax into his embrace as if it is second nature to me to be this close to him. The corner of his mouth twitches upwards; he is pleased that I am conceding without argument. He holds me a little tighter.

His heady scent is something that I can't describe as anything other than pure, undiluted Jade Washington. Combined with his Guyanese rainforest eyes, he has my pulse quivering at a rate that makes me fear for my life. Is it like this for every girl he's been with? Does his touch set them on fire as it does to me? Do they find their thoughts tangling into nonsensical ramblings when they look at him? Do they yearn to hear his voice of melted honey speak their names in the way that only he can, that makes it sound like a prayer...or is all of this just me? I am caught up in him, with no way of breaking free until he allows me to. A part of my brain urges me to take whatever shred of sense I have left and fight, but the other part of doesn't want to. All I want to do right now is yield to his every whim and dance until my feet bleed, to every song, any song, just like this; pressed up against Jade 'I'm-SO-glad-you-can't-read-my-mind-right-now-even-though-you-can-probably-see-it-all-over-my-face' Washington.

He begins with a simple salsa step: *1 2-3, 1 2-3, 1 2-3,* swinging his hips as he moves. I mirror his smooth sway, holding his tempestuous gaze as our bodies sway together as one: *1 2-3, 1 2-3, 1 2-3.* It's just a dance but it feels surreal. Firstly, because I have never gone to a night club and salsa danced with anyone - I'm 18, I'm used to tu'n back way, ben' ova, ben' ova, ben' ova, inna-inna-inna-inna-inna-inna-inna - and then it dawns on me that I'm not dealing with an 18-year-old boy. Jade is a 21-year-old MAN, and that only adds to his sex appeal. Grown and sexy is most definitely the way forward. The other reason that this dance feels so...*wow,* is because it feels like more than a dance. It is so sexual that I can lick the air between us and taste the arousal; sweet hot and sticky like melted toffee.

Carlos Santana chants in Spanish *'Ahora vengo mama chula, mama chula, ahora vengo mama chula'*, and we continue to step; *1 2-3, 1 2-3, 1 2-3.*

Jade tugs out one of my ear buds and bows his head so that I can hear him.

"I like the way you move. You think you can keep up?" he asks in his after-dark voice, awakening my other senses.

"Keep up with what?" I pant.

Jade pulls away and gives me a playful version of his 2000 watt smile. "This."

Without warning, he changes his footing and spins us 360 degrees before grabbing my hand from around his neck and spinning me out into the crowd, then quickly pulling me back into his arms as if I had been gone too long. That smouldering look is on his face again. My heart races from the exhilaration, while my head tries to stop spinning and catch up with the real world.

"Okay, colour me impressed!" I gasp just before mentally kicking myself for sounding like a nerd. Jade pauses for a beat, then laughs gently before reverting back to his usual demeanour.

"You really do look amazing in that dress. That thigh high slit just makes me want to..."he finishes the sentence with a throaty grunt and buries his face in the curve of my neck. *1 2-3, 1 2-3, 1 2-3.* I refrain from translating his guttural noise and focus on not losing my balance. My knees are already weak; if he makes another tempting remark, they will give way.

"I could do *so* many things to you right now with no one noticing, if you'd let me," he groans pressing his flushed lips against my flesh. An electric shudder shoots through me, covering my skin in goose bumps. I cling desperately to my last shred of sense and let his invitation pass without comment. If I open my mouth right now, I can't guarantee that I will refuse him, so I say nothing. *1 2-3, 1 2-3, 1 2-3.*

“You smell lovely, Rio.” He lifts his face from my neck; his previously smouldering irises have evolved into green flames. I am playing with a fire that I know will burn me in the worst way, and make me call out to Him in the darkness till my throat is sore. My back is arched, and my toes are curled, it’s a dark fantasy, but I want it. I want Jade to burn me so badly that it will scar me, ruining me for other men.

He raises my arm above my head and spins me repeatedly, making the material of my dress flare out. He yanks me back to him, perfectly aligning my back with his front (if you get my drift). *1 2-3, 1 2-3, 1 2-3.*

"Say the word and we'll leave right now - and don't say you don't want to, because I know you do," he hums, placing both hands on my thighs. I shudder as they travel up my legs - one against the georgette and the other against my bare skin - each producing enough heat to melt my insides as he travels higher and higher and higher. I say nothing. *1 2-3, 1 2-3, 1 2-3.*

He spins me back to face him, grabs both of my hands, pulls away, pulls me back, switches sides with me and pulls away again. This is such a rush; his moves were so unpredictable yet fluent. Dancing with Jade is poetry in motion; he is my brother to the night, and I am developing a love jones.

"Don't make me beg Rio, just say yes," he growls. *1 2-3, 1 2-3, 1 2-3.* "Everything I said in those texts, I meant. I will do EVERYTHING I said I would, to you. Say yes."*1 2-3, 1 2-3, 1 2-3.*

Jade pulls me back in, but not against him. He is staring at me, eyes burning, holding me firmly in place so that I can't get any closer. My body aches from withdrawal.

"Say yes."

"I can't," I croak pathetically, knowing that all I want to do was say yes, yes, yes, YEEEEEESSSSSSS!

"Rio," he purrs, easing my frame back against him. We stop moving; his arm slides down my waist, over my ass, down one of my exposed thighs. He lifts my leg up, holding it against his hip -oh dear lord!

Jade crushes himself into me so I could FEEL him; long, thick and tensed, so ready for me to...

"Say yes."

13
Special Delivery.

It was like throwing a brick into a glasshouse - all it took was one broken section to send the whole thing crashing down - that was the only way I could think to describe the devastating effect that Jade had on my defences. As he holds me in his arms, the urge to close the miniscule gap between our bodies grows stronger. His blushing mouth is dangerously inviting and I find myself going onto my tiptoes in my already high heels so that I can reach it with my own. He removes one hand from under my leg and trails his fiery fingertips from my temple to the outer edge of my lips before cupping my chin and lowering his face to mine. The delirious rush of excitement that you get when you acknowledge that you are going to kiss someone for the very first time, grips me. Time stands still; it's me, Jade, and nothing else. We are in the middle of the dance floor, so to engage in such an intimate act is definitely tacky, but I don't care one bit. All I can think about is how liberating kissing him would feel.

He skims his mouth across mine slowly and my heart lurches forward in anticipation.

"Say yes," he whispers once more.

I inhale him and sigh, ready to surrender for one exhilarating moment in time. I brush his hair back from his face tentatively, and open my mouth to reply.

"Ye_"

"RIO!"

I am jerked out of Jade's grasp and back to my senses by a surprisingly sober Carmen. Her eyes are wide and glistening with tears that have not yet fallen, and Bless is close by, stone-faced. Something is wrong.

"What happened?" I ask, all the irrational lust gone from my voice. Carmen glances at Jade unsure if she should tell me in front of him. This makes me more worried because if she is undecided about telling me in front of him, it only means that whatever is wrong is really bad. "Car, what's wrong?"

"Didn't Fontaine message you?" she asks, trying to find a way around letting Jade in on the situation. I stuff my hand down my top and fish out my iPhone; there are new messages there from some bothersome boys that I wished hadn't given my number to, and some female acquaintances just checking in on me, but none from Fontaine.

I look back up at Carmen and shake my head. "Nah she didn't. Is she okay?"

"Yeah, she's fine. It's...it's Yoshi, Ri."

I furrow my brow. "Yoshi? What happened to Yoshi?"

"You were right." Carmen stares into my eyes until what she is trying to communicate to me clicks. I gasp -Ace had happened to Yoshi.

"Oh God! Is she okay?"

Carmen shakes her head, "He's still there." I don't need to hear anymore. I knew that this would happen to her again. She foolishly tried to cover up for him when we saw the bruises the first time, but I bet she's wishing she hadn't right now. Ok that sounds spiteful, but it's true. She knows how he is and yet she's still sticking around because she thinks she loves him.

Some of the things females will accept from men just because they *love* them, baffles me sometimes. We believe that if we stick around and love him like there's no tomorrow, hopefully one day he will open his eyes and realise what he has in front of him, and make some miraculous change because he loves us too - that's hardly ever the case. Even if things improve for a while, it's highly unlikely that that person has changed; a leopard can't change its spots. It's like Maya Angelou says, "*When someone shows you who they really are, believe them.*" Sometimes we need to accept defeat and throw in the towel, but we won't because when it comes down to it I believe that we might be slightly addicted to the drama.

Jade's well thought out attempt to seduce me is over; my friend is in trouble, and I am not about to leave her hanging for anyone, no matter how unfairly gorgeous they are. I turn from Carmen and look up at him – he's trying to contain his frustration at how the situation is inconveniencing him. He had me exactly where he wanted, and now, thanks to Yoshi, he has missed his chance. For him this couldn't have happened at a worse time; for me, this couldn't have happened at a better one.

His eyes meet mine and he composes his features.

"You need to jet?" he asks taking my hand, not wanting me to leave. I can't help but feel a little flattered that he still wants me around...then I remember why – he's not being romantic Rio. I remove my hand and nod.

Jade runs his hands through his hair, flipping it to the side nonchalantly and sighs. "Okay. Well, I've got some business to handle before I leave, so I'll see if I can get Carter to drop you back. Is that cool babes?"

I stare at him. It isn't cool. 'Why would Carter drop us back when you brought us here?!' I mentally shout at him. What *'business'* can Jade possibly have to handle at a nightclub that he can't find the courtesy to return me - his date - back to her house? He is probably going to satiate his desire with one of his many groupies.

I am tempted to argue with him, but right now it doesn't really matter who takes us back; Yoshi needs us, and all that is important is that we're there to help her. I press my fingers to my temples in annoyance and take a deep breath.

With my eyes squeezed shut I reply, "Yeah. Carter. Okay, whatever."

Jade brushes the back of my hand.

"You're not mad at me are you?" he asks softly. I squeeze my eyelids tighter in fear of being swayed by his features.

"It doesn't matter. Just get Carter."

Jade sighs and puts his arm around me. "I'm sorry babes but I need_" I shrug him off and move away. I am not in the mood to be sweet-talked. I open my eyes.

"Jade, right now I couldn't care less about what you *need* to do. I need to get home so can you please quit trying to bullshit me and just get Carter!" I snap.

His eyes widen in disbelief that a girl like me would talk to a guy like him in that way. He glares back at me, no longer amused by my attitude. He is angry with me. His face twists into a look that makes me want to take back what I'd said, but instead of backing down, I jut out my chin defiantly. Jade's eyes flash and his cheeks take on heated pigments of colour that, had it been under different circumstances, would be very flattering. He closes his eyes and inhales deeply through his nose. When he reopens them, they are empty, and his mask of pompous nonchalance is back up, concealing his thoughts from me.

"Fine," he shrugs. He walks away without another word. Once he is out of sight, I exhale, breathing hard, as I had been holding my breath. I guess I'm more intimidated by him than I thought.

Bless busies himself by going to collect our belongings from the cloakroom, whilst Carmen and I stay put in the hope that Jade had actually gone to get Carter.

"What else did Fontaine say?" I enquire to fill the silence, embarrassed that my friends had witnessed Jade Washington react to me like that. Carmen retrieves her phone wordlessly and scrolls through the relevant conversation until she reaches the part she needs. She read a few lines mentally then summarises it for me.

"She said that they went to Bagel Monarch to get some food and when they came back they were arguing."

"Arguing about what?"

Carmen shrugs and looks up from her screen. "She didn't say, but it must've been something serious for him to hit her when he knew Fontaine was about."

"Maybe, guys like that are unpredictable. The smallest thing can set them off..." I reply, trailing off into my own world as flashbacks of a time when someone like Ace was involved in my life pops into my head; my dad.

My father was someone that I hardly ever speak, about and avoid thinking about as much as possible, but Yoshi's situation is bringing him to the forefront of my mind. I know how destructive and cruel abusive men like that can be, which is why it is important that Yoshi gets Ace out of her life before he has her completely under his thumb. A woman stupid in love is one thing; a woman that does stupid things in fear of her lover is another. My Dad was an unrelenting tyrant in my household up until I was 13 years old. Day after day, I was forced to sit through never-ending arguments, heavy thuds followed by ear-piercing screams, and the sound of my mother crying. My dad never put his hands on me like that, but having to witness him doing it to my mother was just as bad. He is another one of the reasons that Ty and I are so close, because whenever I couldn't take it anymore, I'd shoot off to Aunty Michelle's house and stay with Tyson until it was over. I spent a LOT of time at Tyson's house. The day my mother saw sense and finally got rid of my dad was one of the happiest moments of my life. He was a horrible man, and if I never see him again, it won't be a moment too soon.

I clear my throat and shake those thoughts out of my head before Carmen notices that something is up, and go back to repressing those memories like I always do.

"True," Carmen shrugs, "Maybe this incident will provide Yoshi with a much needed wake up call."

"I hope so."

We both divert our eyes to hide what we are really thinking from each other; Yoshi has let Ace get away with putting his hands on her before, so what makes this time any different? If she was going to leave him, then she would've done so after the first time. I think she will probably take a few more knocks before she quits him for good, after all that's the way it goes right?

After a half-assed promise from Jade that he'd check on me later, followed by a tense drive back to campus with Carter, the four of us are in the lift anxiously watching the floor numbers light up as we ascend to our flat. Carmen and I are posted by the doors with our heels in our hands, ready to charge to the rescue if needed. Carter and Bless stand close behind, ready to stop us from doing anything stupid.

The last time we checked in with Fontaine, Ace was still there and the situation had escalated. Fontaine had heard Ace laying into Yoshi from her bedroom 4 doors down - and if she can hear it from all the way down there, chances are the rest of the flat can too. She went to try and defuse the situation, but that had only resulted in making Ace angrier, hence making things worse for Yoshi. I had messaged Tyson telling him to get over there, but the little tick didn't show up by my message to let me know if he had read it, so I assumed that he had switched his phone off for the night, which was understandable as it was almost three in the morning, and he was up at Herring visiting Angelica.

The lift pings signalling that we have reached our destination, and the steel doors slide open. The first thing we hear is two voices echoing from the kitchen at the end of the hall. I am poised and ready, with my keys in my hands, so the moment there is enough space between the steel doors, I bolt out to get into our flat as quickly as possible. I am livid and ready to give Ace a piece of my mind regardless of whether it is my place to do so or not. I fling the door open, dropping my heels by the entrance, and charge down the hallway, my footsteps heavy and determined. The others are close behind, calling my name and urging me to calm down because I would probably end up making it worse. I ignore them; he has already beaten her ass, how much worse can it get?

The distinct sound of chairs scraping against the speckled linoleum floor slows my walk slightly; whoever is in the kitchen is coming out to meet me. I take off my earrings; the idea of having it out with Ace becoming more appealing the closer I get to him. I am even more annoyed because Ace is allowed to be an Unfamous. His work with Moonlight Ents means that people respect him even though he's a woman beater. He's the Unfamous Chris Brown; he beats chicks, but his work is good and he's cute so his bad traits are overlooked. I'm a freaking *saint* compared to him, and yet I'm fighting for my place. Maybe I should punch Jade in the mouth; maybe that will make them open their arms to me.

Carter rolls up beside me and puts his hand on my arm.

"Calm the fuck down," he hisses sternly.

"I am calm!" I snap, flicking his hand off. I don't want to calm down, I want to march inside of that kitchen and punch Ace in the face until his features are no longer distinguishable, then tell him to get the fuck out of my flat and stay away from my friend. Although we have only known each other for a few months, my girls have become like sisters to me, and in my book, if you mess with one of use, you mess with all of us.

Fontaine comes out of the kitchen followed by who I expected to be Ace. To my surprise, Nathaniel emerges after her. I freeze. Fontaine looks at me apologetically.

"Ace was out of control and I needed help. Nate was the only one I could get through to," she explains reading the knocked for six look on my face.

It is as if someone had flicked my anger switch to 'off'; just like that, all of my animosity towards Ace is gone and is replaced with an eclectic blend of shock, fear, happiness and anxiety for Nathaniel. He stands before me with his arms folded over his torso, donned in simple grey sweat pants and a form fitting vest top. He has never looked more effortlessly delectable, which in turn sparks a dull ache in my chest. If I missed him before, it is nowhere near as much as I miss him right now, when he is standing right in front of me and I don't even have the option of touching him; and I want to touch him, if only for a moment. To me it is better than nothing.

I mimic his stance and cross my arms, crushing my hands against my rib cage hoping that my longing to touch him will ease up a little. He appraises my apparel briefly, taking care to mask how my appearance affects him, and then his eyes flicker over to Carter -whom I had forgotten was standing by my side (everything else becomes irrelevant when Nathaniel is around, whether I like it or not). As I come to grips with reality, I get that uncomfortable feeling in my stomach because now things are quickly becoming even more awkward than they were a moment ago. Now that Carter is thrown into the already tense equation, I find myself wishing that the ground will swallow me whole so that Nathaniel will stop glaring at me as if I have disobeyed him. I'm not a child.

His jaw muscle palpitates at an unsteady pace.

"What is he doing here?" he asks stonily. I look down guiltily, knowing that Carter is one of the last people on the planet that Nathaniel wants me to be around.

Carter straightens up and juts his chin out with an antagonizing smirk.

"I dropped them back," he answers for me.

Nathaniel's head swings in Carters direction. "Fam, did I ask you anything?"

"What?" Carter steps forward with his hands rolled into fists.

Uh oh!

"Will you two give it a fucking rest already?" Fontaine shouts, stepping between the two of them before they can get close enough to start exchanging blows. "This ain't about your beef with each other, it's about Yoshi, so if you can't put your differences aside then I think it's best that you leave, because we've had more than enough drama tonight."

The boys glare at each other for a little longer, neither one wanting to back off before the other.

"Ay, you man, 'llow it," Bless huffs, hoping that his interjection will assist the situation. It does. Carter exhales and turns away from Nathaniel to face me. I look back at him hesitantly, knowing that interacting with him, no matter how harmless it may be, is sure to rub Nathaniel the wrong way.

"I'll see you later princess," he says tightly, squeezing my hand gently. I nod in reply then divert my eyes. Carter chuckles. He knows that I am being more distant from him than usual because I am wary of how Nathaniel will take it. It irritates me that he laughed, because it makes me aware that as much as I swear off Nate, and convince myself that he doesn't love me so he doesn't matter, he is still more important to me than he should be.

Carter bids everyone - except for Nathaniel – farewell, and leaves. The sick feeling from the tension eases up a little. I turn to Fontaine who is still watching me warily.

"Where's Yoshi?" I ask.

Fontaine tugs on her curls, "She's in her room," she replies quietly.

I press my lips together.

"And where's Ace?"

She tugs even harder, "In her room_"

"WHAT!" Carmen takes the words right out of my mouth, "ARE YOU FUCKING STUPID? WHY WOULD YOU LEAVE HIM ALONE WITH HER IN THERE?" she screams.

"'Cause that's what she wanted. What the fuck am I supposed to say?" Fontaine replies.

"Hmm; how about, NO!"

Fontaine rolls her eyes. "You think I didn't try that? She doesn't want to hear me."

"Well you should've made her hear you!"

"HOW?" she screams back. "Look, if you think you can get Yoshi to leave that prick alone, then be my guest. I'm going to my bed."

14
3:16AM.

We tried...and failed. She wouldn't even open the door, and the fact that Ace was in there in her ear only made matters worse, because she was churning out the regurgitated replies that he was giving her. It hurt to see my friend reduced to this level, but it was like Fontaine argued, if this was what she wanted then there wasn't much we could do. Carmen and Bless had thrown in the towel and gone to bed, leaving me alone with Nate for the first time in a long time.

Nathaniel is seated at the head of our cheap, student-standard table, with his arms outstretched in front of him and his large fingers locked together. He looks like a mafia don at a sit down with a capo that has been causing a stir within the family; the wannabe is getting too familiar within the Unfamous familia. The look in his steely grey eyes has me feeling like after this talk I will wake up with a horse's head in my bed if I don't behave myself. I had half expected him to leave after the others had retired, but part of me knew better; I had shown up with Carter, someone I knew that he'd rather I'd keep away from. He isn't happy about it. The turquoise veins under his buttery skin undulate as he discreetly flexes his finger, trying to keep from balling them up into fists. He's livid but he's trying not to let on how much I have angered him. I gather that it is for both of our benefits; he doesn't want to scare me off or seem too affected by my actions.

I busy myself washing a few left over dishes that have been sitting in the sink for days, trying to work my way through the angry tightness that Yoshi and Ace have conjured in my chest and the anxiety of having Nathaniel less than 5 feet away from me, burning holes in my back. Every time my curiosity gets the best of me, and convinces me to sneak a peek at him to see if he is still watching me, he is. The colourless shade of his eyes, make his stare more unnerving than it should be. I hate the way they follow my every move, like a predator waiting to strike. One of us isn't going to survive this encounter, which makes me apprehensive because it is usually me that gets the shitty end of the stick. I can't decipher his thoughts through the complex mixture of emotions his eyes hold. I want to know what he is thinking, but I dare not ask, in fear of the answer. Words can be like knives.

I saunter around the kitchen uneasily, too aware of his presence to relax. I would like to appear unfazed, but I just look wound up. Every step, reach and facial expression feels choreographed. The fact that I am trying to be 'Little Miss Perfect' is painfully evident, but I can't make myself stop. An outsider may have been fooled, but this is Nathaniel, my Nathaniel, the boy that can see any pretence of mine from a mile away. Even though I know that he is onto me, I still want him to watch me in the hope that somewhere between a 'casual' flip of my hair and a measured stride that makes my cocoa coloured legs slip out from under the dress through the thigh high slits, he will miss me.

After washing and drying all of the dishes, I pour myself a tall glass of water, still in silence, forbidding myself from communicating with him. It's killing me but I am sticking to my guns this time, (we've heard that before) and I mean it with every cell in my body (we've heard that too). My obsession with Nathaniel is only getting in the way of my potential Unfamousness, and as he no longer feels the way he used to about me, there was no reason to make what once was, a priority. Now it's all about me. Once I make it into that upper circle, there would be endless amounts of 'Nathaniel Gibson's' at my disposal. I steal a glance at him and retract my last thought. Yeah there are other popular pretty boys out there, but none of them will ever match up to Nate.

His eyes find mine, and the corners of his mouth turn down.

"What's wrong?" he asks gruffly, sensing the melancholy shift in my mood. I shake my head and turn from him, trying to reconstruct my tough as nails expression. I sip my glass of water and the tension in my throat eases as the cool liquid trickles down, reducing the size of the uncomfortable lump that has formed inside of it. "Rio?" His voice is softer this time.

I hear the chair scrape against the speckled linoleum floor and my body tenses -he was coming closer. I grit my teeth, fighting the part of me that wants to let him console me.

"Stay where you are?" I hiss.

"Rio_"

I spin around and glare at him. The lump in my throat re-expands. "Just say what you have to say and leave!" I can't afford to engage in anything that extends past necessary civility with him or I am sure to let myself down again.

Nathaniel straightens up and lifts his chin - a subtle way of reminding me that he is the alpha in this...whatever it is. I matched his stance. His jaw muscle flickers and he narrows his eyes at me.

"Fine; stay away from Carter."

I roll my eyes; I knew this is what he wanted to say to me. He has been itching to lecture me since I walked through the door.

"We're just...friends," I argue, finding it weird to refer to Carter as my friend out loud. It still feels foreign to think of him like that.

Nathaniel looks me up and down and comes closer.

"Nice dress! Do you dress like this for all your friends?" he asks fingering the sheer fabric just above the thigh high slit. I smack his hand away and stand my ground, not letting his proximity affect me. I have already established myself as another alpha, so now this was war. Which one of us will break first?

"No, not all of them...just Jade," I smile with a deadly sweetness.

Nathaniel's eyes widen - I have caught him off guard making him forget his Carter lecture completely.

"Jade? Jade who?"

"Jade Washington; who else?" My smile grows wider and takes on a Carter-like quality. In my head I have already won.

Nathaniel steps away from me and a look of disgust decorates his features.

"You slept with Jade Washington!" he says in disbelief, gawking at me as if I had grown three heads.

"Fuck you Nathaniel!" I exclaim feeling my irritation go through the roof. He's still the only boy that I have ever had sex with. Why does he keep assuming that I will sleep with these men that I barely know? First Carter, and now Jade; I thought he knew me better than that. Maybe it's because it's Jade...

"Oh wow! Well if you haven't yet, then you will."

Yup, it's because it's Jade.

"Carter says he likes me," I spit, throwing in Carter's name to rub salt into the wound.

Nathaniel's eyes flash.

"This is Jade, Rio. He *fucks* chicks, he doesn't *like* them."

"Well that's obviously not true because he likes me." I argue, not believing my own words. I know that it was more than likely that Nathaniel is right, but in the heat of this stupid battle that he has decided to wage with me, I need to believe that what I'm saying is true. When it is over, I will surrender to reality, but for now I will fool the both of us into thinking that Jade having more than just a physical interest in me, is a possibility.

"You keep telling yourself that," Nathaniel scoffs, distancing himself from me. I definitely have the upper hand now. He is looking at me as if I am already tainted by the touch of someone else; I know this because that is the exact face I had given him when I found out about Georgia. Even though I have (miraculously) managed to keep my legs closed, Jade's debauched reputation, to Nathaniel, means that I am as good as marked by another man. Well whatever, he's already been marked by other women.

It's strange how the whole double standards thing works when it comes to break-up aftermath. Men can go around and hump anything that walks, and apparently it's acceptable 'cause they're men and that's what men are supposed to do - the bastards! In contrast, if women go out and sleep with someone else, even if it's only one person, men treat it as if you've betrayed them. To them, you being intimate with another man, means that you are no longer theirs. To put it metaphorically; we're the trees, and they're the dogs! They cock up their legs and piss all over us - marking their territory - then eventually another dog comes along and does the same thing ruling out the first one. It's political.

I continue to smile through my annoyance, and run my hand over my dress slowly, from the side of my bust, to the dip of my waist, and the curve of my hip.

"If you're so sure that he doesn't like me, tell me why he bought me this 'nice dress'?" I smirk, quoting Nathaniel's earlier comment.

His face falls.

"He bought you that?"

"Yup. It's designer too y'know. I can't imagine how much he spent on it."

All the snide humour drains from his face; his jaw muscle is working overtime and I know in that instant, that I have gone too far. Within seconds he closes the distance between us and his large fingers coil around my wrist so tightly that the blood stops circulating to my hand.

"What the fuck is wrong with you Rio? You think you're so fucking big now don't you? You have no idea what you've gotten yourself into. I'm in this world because I can handle the heat, but you are way out of your league and you're gonna get burned. These people are not your friends, none of them! They're leeches and are only out to see just how far other people can take them before they drop you and move on to bigger and better things. You're so far up your own ass that you can't even take notice of the signs right in front of you. I keep trying to warn you, but it's like you ain't hearin' me - those who can't hear, must feel. You think you're the shit 'cause you got Jade Washington on you? Well, how about this," Nathaniel crushes his mouth to mine just as roughly as he had done the last time that he kissed me. It is short lived.

I shove him off, feeling my heart flutter against my will. I am not going to let him reopen those wounds.

"Nathaniel, what the hell?" I scream, thumping him in the chest.

He touches his hands to his lips and looks away.

"I had to do it one last time...just in case that was my last chance," he says quietly. From the way he says it, I know that a bomb more lethal than my Jade one, is about to fall. His eyes return to mine and I know for certain that I had celebrated too early; I had won the battle, but Nathaniel is about to win the war. I brace myself.

"Didn't you find it strange that Fontaine messaged Carmen instead of you, even though YOU'RE supposed to be the head of your clique? Didn't you question why, when you came through the door, I came out of the kitchen? Didn't it even cross your mind for one moment that Fontaine, your bredrin, has the means to contact ME?"

I blink slowly and hold my breath. The world slows down and I can feel the scales tipping in his favour.

"What are you saying Nathaniel?" I ask quietly, bracing myself for the answer that I have already figured out, but am hoping is wrong.

He looks me dead in the eye. "You're not the top dog anymore. The dynamics of what used to be your group has changed right in front of your eyes and now Carmen is. And d'you know what else Ri-Ri? While you were out with the guy who *likes* you, the man you love was fuckin' your so-called bredrin."

At that moment my heart breaks all over again, accompanied by the snapping of something else higher up. I want to kill him. I literally wanted to find a knife and sink it into his chest. If he is dead then he can't hurt me anymore.

"When did you become such a bastard?" I croak, the weight of his betrayal crushing me from within.

"The day you made me one."

He sweeps out of the room and doesn't look back. I stand shaking, alone in the kitchen, alone with my thoughts. The horse's head had been in my bed all along, but it's only now that I had seen it.

15
Labyrinth.

I'm back at square one; that place where I finally fall asleep after something really bad happens, and then I wake up the next day and for a few fuzzy moments everything is okay...and then I remember. What I wouldn't give to stay in that state of mental limbo. The more I try not to think about it, the more my mind replays clips of last night's events from my memory.

When I recollect everything, I sink back into that dark place where it's just me against the world. Once again, I'm in the middle of this on-going war with life itself, where it seems intent on luring me into a false sense of security, then dealing me another bad hand all over again. Is this the way things are going to be for the rest of my life? Will I always have to deal with the people who are meant to be in my corner, screwing me over?

I want to go back to sleep and live in a dream world where things just go my way without all of the excess complications. The real world is breaking me down to a point where I am questioning EVERYTHING, and I hate it. I am lost, and right now, I can see no possible solution to rectify the situation without alienating myself and making things worse. It is bad enough that Nathaniel had found a brand new way to write 'Fuck You' all over my heart, but now Fontaine - the girl that was supposed to be one of my closest friends in this place - had slept with him; how am I supposed to deal with that?

I can't figure out who I am angrier with. Instinctively, I want to place the majority of the blame on Fontaine because she is meant to be my girl and for whatever reason, as much as I hate him right now, I'm almost defending Nathaniel because...well, he's Nathaniel - but this time I'm not so sure that that weak argument is going to suffice. Georgia, Sky, Fontaine - the girls change, but the main culprit stays the same. It is stupid for me to vent my rage on these girls when it is evident that they aren't really the problem - Nathaniel is. I have already had it out in one way or another with the first two without thinking, because they were no one to me, but things are different this time because it's Fontaine. If I go out there, guns blazing, I'd lose another member of my entourage, and right now that isn't something that I can afford to let happen as Carmen has subsequently gained control of the girls without even trying.

My Jade Washington buzz has only just started circulating, so right now it isn't enough to bump me back into first place as everyone (probably including Jade) is under the impression that I am just a booty call. At this stage, if I get rid of Fontaine I am running the risk of becoming clique-less. Something like that could be the end of @RioDuran, and I'd go right back to being boring old Rio Greene.

I close my eyes, hoping that if I keep them shut long enough, sleep will return to me. It doesn't. I lie in bed trying to figure out how I am going to work my way through this fresh pile of bullshit, whilst being tormented by images of my so-called friend and my prick of an ex engaging in acts that they should have never engaged in with each other - EVER. In my head, they are kissing, touching, stripping, moaning and melting into each other over and over. No matter how hard I try, I can't stop thinking about it. I grip my head and growl lowly. I want to scream; the rage is building in my chest, bubbling and swelling inside of me like a cancerous growth. The scene loops again and I am shaking. My eyes burn; ready to send hot, angry tears streaming down my face. I blink and take a deep breath to calm myself. No such luck. I want to march straight into her room and punch her in the face just like I did to Sky, but my remaining sanity reminds me that if I am going to punch anyone, it shouldn't be Fontaine. If Nathaniel was here right now...WOW!

How can I love such a certified prick? I would never, nor could I ever, do the things he does to me, back to him; but right now, I really want to. I had considered calling Jade last night and just getting it over with just so I could rub it in Nate's face...then I remembered that I am a female, and thanks to the rules of conduct in our sexually-biased society, women don't get ratings for sleeping with someone. Nope, only men can get away with that crap.

I sit up and rub my hands over my hot and puffy face; last night's make-up smears and transfers onto my clammy palms. Fantastic! In my haste I had fallen asleep fully clothed, and now that I am awake, I realise how uncomfortable this dress really is, plus the boning in my bra digging into me. I yank the zip down, shimmy out of the dress, unclip my bra - ooooh that feels good - and fling it to the side. I trudge into my bathroom, groaning in irritation when I see my reflection. Look at my weave! I couldn't be bothered to wrap it last night, but now I am vehemently cursing myself for not doing so because it looks like a clump of stiff black tumbleweed that is unfortunately attached to my head. So not only do I feel like shit, but I look like shit as well.

Next door I can hear Yoshi and her live-in Chris Brown moving about. I roll my eyes; stupid girl. Soon enough they will all be up and I'll have to face them and pretend that I am accepting of Yoshi's decision to keep that bastard Ace around, Carmen effortlessly claiming my crown that I have worked so hard for, and that dirty stop out, Fontaine. The friends that I was so grateful for in the beginning suddenly don't seem like the right bunch I should have selected for my 'ladies in waiting' - we're only 5 months into our first year, and already they have stopped waiting on me...I CAN'T BELIEVE SHE FUCKED NATHANIEL! What the hell happened to her and Nadia? Did she cheat on her with him? I bet she did, that bitch! I should...

I catch a glimpse of my features twisted into a very unflattering and slightly frightening expression, and breathe. I need to get out of here asap before I catch a case. I need to speak to Ty; he'll know how to fix this.

I hit the shower and get dressed and ready in record time - I couldn't risk taking too long and possibly bumping into one of the others in the hallway. I had flung on a pair of jeans that were tangled up in a pile of clothes on my desk chair, to go with one of Tyson's t-shirts that I had 'borrowed' from him without him knowing, and covered my train wreck of a weave with one of his beanies that I had also 'borrowed'. He is going to cuss me when he sees me. I smile to myself and shrug, then grab my things and leave as quietly as possible.

It has just gone 2 o'clock in the afternoon and the campus is practically dead. It's always quieter on the weekends as most of the students return home to visit their families, go to work, or are having a well-deserved lie in nursing hangovers. I wave and force polite smiles at a few people, keeping my pace brisk so that they're not encouraged to hold bland, pointless conversations with me. Tyson is still up at Herring with that insufferable dwarf, so I decide to head to the bus stop and make my way to my mum's house. I was so eager to move on to campus before, but in light of recent developments in the mini-drama that is my life, home feels like the right place to be. I haven't seen my mum since we came back to Brompton two weeks ago, and I slyly missed her...plus, I'm not in the mood to cook.

I pull out my iPhone and Whatsapp Ty.

When r u comin bk? I need 2 talk 2 u

I don't have to wait that long for a reply, which means that he isn't with Angelica anymore, thank God!

I'm on da train now. Just left Rayners Lane. Sup?

It's long 2 type. I'll tell u when I c u. I'll meet you in Uxbridge

Y? I'm comin bk 2 campus

I'm goin bk 2 ends

o_O Rah! Isit dat bad?

U have no idea ☹

I might as well go down there wid u 2. I dnt feel like bein on campus either. My car's parked by the station. I'll drive us there

Kl. How cum u don't wanna b on campus either. U ok?

Not really. Me and Angie got into an argument ¬_¬

Aww what happened bitches?

It's long 2 type. I'll tell u when I c u :p

Smart ass! I smile at the screen.

Ur smiling init lol

¬_¬ Shut up, stupid boy lol

Love u 2 bitches ☺

Tyson and I are squished together in my mum's leather recliner, with my old Power Rangers fleece blanket covering us while I force him to watch 'How Stella Got Her Groove Back' - don't judge me, I know it's a bit shit, but Taye Diggs is half naked for most of it. My mum wasn't home when we came in, so we assumed that she was at Ty's house gossiping with Michelle as usual, drinking cheap bottles of wine and bitching about men like divorced housewives.

Tyson grunts and shifts in the chair.

"Keep still man!" I snap, elbowing him under the sheet.

"Bruv, I swear, if this guy says one more word in that shit Ja-fake-can accent again, I'm going to dash your DVD out the window. He's raging me."

"Is he raging you, pluddin?" I giggle pinching his cheeks.

Tyson peers down at me with a serious face, but his chocolate eyes glimmer with amusement.

"Yes bitches, yes he is. I beg you turn it off."

"But it hasn't even gotten to the good bit yet," I whine.

Tyson kisses his teeth, "You're such a tramp man!"

"How am I am tramp?"

"'Cause I know you're waiting on that shower scene. You think I'm stupid, but I know, Rio. I. Know. That's the only reason why you girls will sit through this bullshit."

I turn my head away from him and laugh. "I have no idea what you're talking about Ty. I just like the film."

"Bruv, are you really trying to gas me? Don't make me kick you out of this chair please." I laugh again. Tyson grabs the DVD remote from the arm of the chair.

"What are you doing?" I shriek, twisting in the chair to reach across him. He uses his free hand to push me back and clicks the skip scene button. "Ty stop it!" I scream, whacking him in the head.

"Move man," he laughs, shifting in the seat again so that he is sitting on top of me.

I hit him again, "Get off me!"

"Sshhh," he replies still clicking the same button. I bite his back. "Argh, 'llow it man!" he groans, leaning away from me so I can't bite him again.

"Then give me the control!"

"Fine, here you go," he surrenders, sliding off of me and dropping the control in my lap. The shower scene is playing. I roll my eyes.

"You're a dickhead!" I cuss.

"Shut up and watch the film, these times this is what you were waiting for." he chuckles. I was going to lie and say that it wasn't what I was waiting for, but the sight of Taye Diggs's sexy ass dripping wet in the shower distracts me. We both go quiet. When the scene is over, I clear my throat and turn the film off. Tyson looks at me. I look back at him. Nobody moves. It's funny how a 2-minute sex scene can change the atmosphere of the room if you're with a guy.

Tyson speaks first. "What, you don't wanna watch the rest of the film, no?" he smirks, giving me his crooked smile and lightening the mood –thank God. I thought things were going to get awkward.

I kiss my teeth, "What for? He's not gonna do that again, so what's the point?"

Tyson throws his head back and laughs loudly, "See, I told you bruv; I know."

I roll my eyes. "Yeah, yeah, yeah, whatever, we've got things to discuss. You go first. What were you and Strawberry Shortass arguing about?"

Tyson fans me off, dismissing yet another one of my insulting yet mildly entertaining nicknames for his girlfriend before his expression turns serious.

"A'ight basically yeah, me and her was jamming in her room and two two's some yout' comes and knocks on her door. I musta answered it now, and this dickhead try screw man like I don't take lives for fun!" My expression is deadpan; why is he speaking like a hoodlum? Tyson grins and continues. Twat! "So anyway now, I ask man if he's cool init, to see if he's tryna start pop off and he asks me if Angie's in, completely ignoring my question. Now Angelica's sitting on the bed and man can blatantly see her init, so I goes 'You know what fam, she ain't even here you know'."

"You said that?" I hoot.

"Yeah, standard!"

"And what did he say?"

"Man asked me if he was a dickhead. I told him straight; yes. So obviously now man's vex and ting, starts talking heroically, and I'm ready to do dis ting coz how can this prick roll up to MY chick's room unannounced, give me attitude then ask if she's in like I'm really gonna let her talk to him after he's on some disrespectful tip. Is he dumb? No Rio but really doh, is he dumb?"

"He's dumb bruv!" I mimic his manner.

Tyson grins again, glad that I'm playing along with his roadman persona. "I know bruv! Now hear this piss take; Angie gets off the bed and comes to the door and was like rah you two 'llow it init, so I goes to her 'Babes, who's dis?' Before this stupid girl just tells me who the fuck this guy is, she switches on me and goes, 'Why are you questioning me? Just go inside and come off your hype.' Ri, I'm thinkin I musta had 'Made in China' tattooed on my forehead because she is clearly tryna take me for a mug."

I burst out laughing. "Manaman said TEA CUP!" I chortle.

Tyson nudges me and flashes his crooked smile, "Stop it man, I'm tryna be in Bad Man mode!"

"A'ight, I'm sorry. Continue."

"Cool. So now I'm fully mad. How is she really gonna talk to me like that in front this sideman. Ri, swear down I almost drop kicked her in her forehead. Is she crazy?"

"Must be."

"AH DAT MI AH SEH! I closed the door in the wasteman's face, no long ting, and I asked her to repeat herself. She's like 'Why you getting upset for?'" Tyson pulls a confused face and I have to purse my lips to keep myself from laughing. "I had to look at her and ask her who she was talking to, 'cause I know it wasn't me, 'cause I *know* that she knows better. She starts gassin' to me about how he's just a friend and there was no need for me to be rude like say this guy didn't come to me on some aggy tip. I had to blast her cause she was trying to take the piss. You know me Ri, I'm a nice guy and I treat her good init?" I nod in response. "Anytime she calls me I'm there, when she wants to chat shit I pretend to listen, if she needs something I'll help her out and on top of all that I give her the top class 'Neighbours Know My Name' futtawackin, and she has the audacity to come at me like that. Don't rage me! She's tryna take my kindness for weakness and I can't stand people like that. Like I'm cool, but I'm a man. Know yourself." I put my arms around him and bury my face in his shoulder so that I could giggle silently. He's such a knob, bless him. "Now here's the bit you're gonna like. She's crying now and I'm starting to feel bad 'cause I did blast her kinda hard, init. So I try and comfort her, give her one two kiss and tell her I'm sorry; she pushes me off and tries to blast me about you!"

I perk up. "Me? What did I do?"

"I dunno. I think it's one of dem ones where she's been thinking it for a long time but just decided to drop it at that moment, init. You know how you girls are; you like to store up ammunition for the big arguments so you can win. I told you bruv, I know."

I roll my eyes.

"Whatever Ty, carry on. What did she say about me?" I ask, ready to gather some ammunition of my own.

Tyson sighs, "Long story short, she said how I treat you more like a girlfriend than I do her."

I furrow my eyebrow. "How? I don't even get to chill with you half as much as I used to 'cause she's always on your nuts."

"I know. I told her that me and you are just tight like that and that there's nothin' goin on, but she wasn't even tryna hear me. Then she try drop the bar, 'Well if you can have female friends, I can have male friends' like I ever told her she couldn't. What got me was that she knew about me and you from day dot, and she pretended like she was cool with it, which obviously isn't the case. She just wants to get male friends to spite me, and it's pissing me off. These guys ain't hanging around her 'cause they wanna be her friend and she knows that, but for the sake of the argument she's tryna deny it." He frowns.

I shake my head. This isn't the first time that we have had one of *these* conversations. Every girlfriend that Tyson has ever had, always ends up dragging my name into their arguments; it was only a matter of time before the garden gnome started doing the same thing. I sigh and stroke Tyson's hair, running my fingers through the gaps between his silken braids.

He leans his head back into my hand and exhales. "It's like she doesn't trust me Ri and I don't understand why. I have never given her reason not to. The fact that she is bringing other guys around is making me feel wary of her," he confesses quietly, all of the comedic hype gone.

I pull him closer and cuddle him.

"Don't worry Ty, I'm sure that she'll get over it and everything will be okay now that she's gotten it off of her chest," I say reassuringly even though I know that this argument is the beginning of the end for them (it always is), and I think Tyson knows it too.

He nuzzles his face in my chest and puts his other arm around me. "I hope so."

We sit like that for a few minutes, in silence; me playing with his hair, and him cuddling me like a child. This argument with his half-pint is really getting to him. He likes her a lot, and when she finally leaves it's gonna hurt him, but good riddance to bad rubbish I say. She's not right for him anyway...

Tyson lifts his head and pecks me on the cheek.

"Thanks Ri," he says softly, giving me a tamer version of his crooked smile.

I smile adoringly back at him. "For what?"

He shrugs, "I dunno; just being you I guess."

"Oh. I am pretty great aren't I," I laugh.

Tyson kisses his teeth. "All right, modest! Anyway, it's your turn to share your sob story."

I stop laughing. Up until that moment I had completely forgotten about my troubles, which is what usually happens when I am around Ty. I wonder if I have the same effect on him. I look away as those awful images of Nate and Fontaine together start up again.

Tyson frowns at my expression and sits straighter.

"Ri, what happened?" he asks concerned, bringing my face back around to meet his. The unshed tears sting my eyes. I fling my arms around him as the first one falls.

"Oh Ty, everything is falling apart and I don't know how to fix it," I sob. Tyson holds me and rubs small circles on my back, trying to get me to calm down.

"What do you mean everything's falling apart? Is this to do with your quest for popularity or are we talking about that asshole?"

"Both."

Tyson sighs, "What did Nate do this time?"

"He slept with Fontaine." Tyson's hand freezes in mid-motion.

After a heavily pregnant pause he replies, "Are you being serious? How do you know?" he asks in disbelief. I think even Ty, who has pretty much always been #TeamFuckANateGibson, can't believe that Nathaniel would stoop this low.

I pull away from him and wipe my eyes, "He told me himself."

Tyson frowns. "And what did Fontaine say?"

"I haven't spoken to her yet. I couldn't. I'm just so angry Ty, I mean, how could she do this to me? She's meant to be my friend."

"Ri at the end of the day, you don't know none of these girls from Adam init, so yeah it's a piss take that she did that to you, but she ain't the one that you should really be mad at. That dickhead Nathaniel is. That's a fuckin' violation! I don't care if you two ain't together no more, there are levels. He could have mashed any chick on campus, but yet he chose to mash your bredrin_"

"I know, but she could've said no_"

"Stop defending him!" he snaps.

"I'm not," I frown.

"Yes you are. That's what you always do."

"But he said she contacted him," I argue.

"He didn't have to give her his details."

"Okay I guess so, but then she invited him over, it's not like he just showed up."

"He didn't have to go," Tyson points out. I huff and fold my arms.

"How do we even know that he seduced her, maybe_"

"RIO!"

I shut up. I'm pathetic; a fool who is still willing to pull the wool over her own eyes for a guy that cares about her as much as spoilt child cares for one of their many toys. I bury my face in my hands.

"D'you know what else he said?"

Tyson grits his teeth "What?"

"He said that Carmen is now the head of my group. Ty, I'm just another face. I'm insignificant again. What am I gonna do?" I wail. Tyson pulls me to him and kisses my forehead; his lips linger a little longer than the last kiss.

"Don't worry Ri. You'll figure this out."

16
Vogue.

After my mum came home that evening merrier than usual (we had guessed right, she had been drinking with Michelle), Tyson went home, promising to return in the morning so that we could embark on stage one of my 'comeback' with a day of retail therapy. He showed up at 10am the next day and carted us off to Jonny's Salon in Streatham.

As it's a Sunday morning, most of Jonny's customers were still at church or preparing Sunday dinner, so we didn't have to wait too long - all my ladies know how sometimes going to the hairdressers makes you feel like you're serving a damn prison sentence 'cause they take so damn long! I got a much-needed new weave, opting for 14 inches of bouncy Roman Curls by Sleek in 1B, then, I got my nails, eyebrows and lashes done. By the time Jonny's staff were finished with me, I had fallen head over heels in love with myself. Every 5 seconds I was looking at myself in the mirror, flipping my hair and pulling 'come hither' faces. Tyson made sure to pass less than flattering remarks every time he caught me adoring myself, which he claimed was to keep me grounded.

Tyson's hair was washed and braided into a simple, yet very flattering, fan style. His stylist continuously complimented his 'good hair' and how pretty he was. Tyson smiled shyly and mumbled blushing thank yous' every time she did, which only made her love him more. I love looking at Ty when his hair is freshly done; I develop temporary crushes on him. His onyx plaits fell past his shoulders in thick glossy strands, curling at the bottom, and his soft baby hairs lay romantically against his mahogany skin, flaunting his diluted Asian ancestry. As his braids were so tight, his eyebrows had been lifted a little so he couldn't help but have that look of attractive arrogance. I feel momentarily envious of Angelica.

As we make our way back to his car, I take his hand and pretend that we are 'together'. It is foolish for me to do such a thing when this could actually be for real if it wasn't for me and my stupid issues. I enjoy the way his grip is gentle yet firm; as if he doesn't want to hold on too tightly because he knows I'm fragile, but he can't risk holding me too loosely just in case I slip away. It warms my insides. Would it have been this easy if I hadn't been so hung up on that asshole Nathaniel and just let Tyson in? I glance up at my best friend and wonder...

Tyson peers down at me and smiles a small shy version of his crooked smile.

"You cool?" he asks.

I look away embarrassed and nod. "Um yeah, yeah. I'm cool," I reply, fidgeting with my nails. His eyes linger on me, but he doesn't say anything - he knows. That is one of the downfalls of having such a hot guy as my best friend; it isn't so easy to conceal my random moments of attraction to him because he knows me so well and can identify my goo-goo eyes.

Tyson gives my hand a small squeeze.

"I should get my hair done more often, init?" he chuckles. Blushing, I yank my hand from his grip and playfully shove him away.

"Get over yourself! Where're we going now anyway?" I ask changing the subject.

Tyson smirks and reclaims my hand. Ever so lightly, he brushes his thumb across my knuckles.

"Eastpark." he replies, "You need to get a new outfit for tonight and," his full crooked smile dances across his lips, "we're gonna get you a camera, Miss Photographer," he says, throwing in a wink for good measure, because I'm obviously not drooling over him enough already.

I stop walking.

"What? Ty it's still January. The next loan payment doesn't drop 'til April. I can't afford a camera right now, the outfit yes, but not a proper 'I'm a fancy pants photographer' camera."

Tyson whirls me around, now taking both of my hands.

"See this is why you need a job you wasteman, but let's not get into that right now. I'm gathering that you didn't pick up on the 'WE'RE' part of that sentence. I'M gonna get you the camera; YOU handle the other junk."

"You're gonna buy me a camera?" I ask in disbelief.

Tyson shrugs casually. "Yeah, consider it an early birthday present."

My face lights up and I jump on him, wrapping my arms around his neck. He smells like Versace Blue Jeans and Dark & Lovely hair lotion.

"Oh my God Ty; you are the bestest bitches ever! I love you so much right now," I squeal.

Tyson laughs and hugs me back. He breathes me in too.

"Make sure you remember that when my birthday comes, bestie. The ACS Amsterdam Weekender is not gonna pay for itself."

I release him and roll my eyes. "Yeah, yeah, yeah, I know."

We continue walking. The ACS Amsterdam Weekender, hosted by Moonlight Ents (of course), is held once a year during Spring break – it's the prequel to Ayia Napa for university students, with the added bonus of legalised marijuana. Every Afro-Caribbean Society, from every university in England is involved. For roughly £139, we are carted off across the water to Holland to watch a talent show made up of acts from the universities involved, and a few UK acts that have made an impact in the world of the Unfamous (usually Sunday Slam favourites), two themed raves, and all of the weed and kinky site seeing (generally via the red light district) our hearts desired.

"You excited?" he asks, putting my hand back in his.

"About 'Dam?"

"Yeah."

I shrug. "I guess, but Aiya Napa is what I'm looking forward to the most."

"That's ages away."

"I know, but it's NAPA," I stress, visualising myself chilling out on Nissi Beach during the day, and the intense raving that I would be embarking on at night.

"Bruv, Amsterdam has drugs. We get to be high on a variety of cannabis LEGALLY for a whole weekend," he argues.

I consider his words for a moment.

"This is true. Bring on Amsterdam!"

After a productive shopping trip at Eastpark, Tyson and I are back at my mum's house with new outfits for tonight (Tyson revealed that we were going to Sunday Slam where I am to make my photographic debut), and my brand new Nikon D5000 camera, courtesy of my bitches. I bought the rest of the junk to go with it, including a flash gun, a carry case, photo editing software and an additional lens. I had to close my eyes when I handed over my debit card - I hate spending large amounts when it isn't items of clothing. I shouldn't really complain though; Ty did have to fork over roughly £500 for my camera alone. I made sure to thank him thoroughly while he punched his PIN into the reader, to soften the blow. On the way home I used my trusty iPhone to create a Facebook page for my new venture – Vanity Mode Photography - and I invited as many people as I possibly could. I instructed the girls to do the same. Seeing as I now have a 'profession', I thought it necessary to update my Twitter profile as well. I am now @VanityDuran. Tyson had promised to create my company logo and a snazzy background for my Twitter page so that it will look more official. I can't wait. I am so excited about how people will react to me now that I have a purpose among the Unfamous, that I can already taste the fame. It is electric.

Tyson is sprawled out haphazardly on my double bed, which he had literally flung himself on, dragging my blue cotton bed sheets over to one side like I didn't make it up this morning. His fingers travel ruthlessly over the touch keyboard of his iPhone screen as he Whatsapps Angelica. They are arguing again. This won't leave him in the best of moods; if he wins the argument he will probably feel bad about what he had to say to shut her up, and if she wins then he will just be vex. Either way, I will hear about it. I sit at the end of my bed and busy myself trying to figure out how to use the camera. So far I have discovered how to turn it on, take a picture, and review the photos. As far as I am concerned, that is all I need to know right now. I'll learn the complex stuff later.

Tyson growls and throws his phone down next to him – hard enough to convey that he was irritated, but not hard enough to actually damage the phone -a man after my own heart. It bounces a little then settles by his side with Thumbelina's reply glaring up at my spotlighted ceiling. I discreetly lean over to see what she said to make Ty quit. As soon as I see it I wish that I hadn't:

You're still in love with her aren't you?

Tyson rolls over onto his side and looks at me. I conveniently look away at the same time back to the LCD screen on the back of my camera, holding my breath praying that he didn't notice that I have seen anything because then we may have to talk about it, and I am pretty sure that the outcome of that won't be great for our recently rekindled friendship.

"Did you invite the girls to Slam?" he asks blandly. This conversation is a distraction from what Polly Pocket had said. I run with it.

"Yeah; I told Carmen and Yoshi."

"What about Fontaine?"

I look at him and sneer, "What about her?" Tyson cracks a smile.

"Ri, you can't *not* invite her."

"Like hell I can't!" I mumble. Why would I invite her when my rage is still red hot? I could kill her.

"I'm serious."

"So am I. Ty, I get angry just hearing her name. I don't want to be around her," I explain, prodding a random button on the back of the camera. The screen goes from colour to greyscale. I press another button and it switches back to colour (thank God).

"I know Ri, but you're not in a position to drop her just yet. For the time being you have to tolerate her, you know, kind of like I do with you," he grins. I kick him. "'Llow it man," he whines rubbing the sore spot just above his knee. "Anyway, in order to be Unfamous, you're gonna have to have a few fake friendships. It's an image ting, but it works. Do you know how many of them man don't actually like each other but they act like they do because being friends helps elevate them socially. Like Manny for example, he can't stand Ace, but Ace is doing big things with his Moonlight Ents, and people rate him, so because of that, Manny still jams with him. It's political."

He has a point.

I furrow my brow, "Really? I never would've guessed. Why doesn't he like him?"

"Shaquille told me Manny likes Yoshi," he explains, "He knows how Ace treats her so he's a bit protective of her."

"Oh? Wow!" I exclaim, "Look, I hear what you're saying, but if people knew that I kept Fontaine around even though she snaked me, alie I look like a dickhead?"

"Not even. It's all about how you handle the situation. When you see Fontaine, pull her up on it, but on a mature tip. Tell her straight, I know what you did. Don't do it again. No long ting. Don't explain yourself or allow her to explain herself, just make sure she knows that if it happens again there will be consequences. Make it so she knows that you're running tings again. She needs to fear you." I nod in agreement. I can do that. I'll drop it to her so that she knows that if she ever tries to cross me again I will DESTROY her. A little bit of fear goes a long way.

Tyson's phone jingles. Angelica had done that irritating thing people do when they sent a question mark because you haven't replied, even though it's clear you're ignoring them. I roll my eyes and grudgingly invite Fontaine to Sunday Slam while Tyson replies to his insecure imp. I don't know why he is bothering; she's obviously made up her mind. Nothing he says will convince her otherwise. After another heated typing session, he sighs and flings his phone down again. It lands face down so I am unable to satisfy my curiosity and see what his reply to her question is.

He nudges me with his foot to get my attention.

"You figured out how to use that thing yet?" he asks eyeing up the camera that I had casually dumped in my lap. I had meant to pick it back up but I had been side tracked by Twitter; the trending topic was #CertainMan. The indirects are flying out left, right and centre; it's tense on the timeline right now!

"I know all I need to know for now," I reply, smiling at a tweet Calvin made with the #CertainMan hashtag. He is so talking about D-Man.

"A'ight, well take a picture then," he says sitting up and vogue-ing.

I look him up and down. "Of what?"

"Me init. I'll be your first model."

"Not posing like that you won't."

"What's wrong with my pose?" he pouts.

"It's making me question your sexuality, dude."

Tyson scoots closer to me, snatches my iPhone out of my hand and put it next to his.

"Fine Mrs Photographer; if you think you can top my immaculate posing skills then prove it," he flings himself back onto his back. Arching his brow suggestively, he asks "How do you want me?" I bite the corner of my lip and look away. Ignore him Rio, just let it pass and take the picture, no need to react to him...oh why won't he stop looking at me like that?

Taking a deep breath to clear my head, I huff and shuffle to the top of the bed so that I'm sitting near his top half, dragging the already rumpled sheets with me. Tyson smirks at me, lying as limply as a disobedient child who is intent on making it difficult for you to pick them up. His generously lashed brown eyes twinkle with mischievous excitement as I reach across him to position his arm, which he allows to fall back into its original position once I let go. I make a face.

"If you're not gonna be serious then I won't bother," I threaten knowing that if I put an end to his newest form of entertainment that it will bother him more than it would me.

Tyson puts his arm back where I put it. "Okay, okay, okay. I'll behave."

Smiling triumphantly, I pick up the camera and point the lens at him. I cock my head to the side and look him over, trying to set my expression in a way that makes it seem as if I am forming an artistic vision of some sort. Tyson watches me watching him. I clear my throat.

"Okay, I want you to tilt your head to the left a little and look down. Try not to laugh," I admonish him quickly, seeing the right side of his mouth lift a little. He straightens his face and does as instructed. I close my left eye and press the right one to the viewfinder. I admire the way his lashes cast long shadows underneath his almost closed eyelids, the sheer volume of them blocking out the pale slit of his eye. Without the presence of his gaze I am able to appreciate the rest of his features, like his thick eyebrows that wield two slashes near the ends where they arched slightly, the straightness of his nose set between high Red Indian cheekbones, his slightly boyish jaw line that keeps his appearance from becoming too man-ish, giving him a lovable vulnerability, and his proud mouth with a cupid's bow so subtle that you really have to study his top lip to realise that it is there. I realise it is there. My hands become clammy.

I hold down the capture button; a little red light blinks, the camera beeps, followed by the all mighty glare of the flash gun. His features light up. I pull the camera away and review my very first professional photo with a sense of pride. It came out pretty good; whether this is down to my voluntary model or the quality of my camera, I am unsure, but either way, it is a stunning picture.

"Lemme see." I look over at Tyson who is still frozen in the same pose with his brown eyes now watching me curiously.

I hug the camera to my chest possessively. "You can see when I'm done. I wanna take a few more." Tyson shrugs and looks down obediently. I bring the camera back up to my face, poised to take another photo.

"So I make a good subject I take it?" he asks holding his position.

I press the capture button.

"What makes you say that?"

"'Cause you had that look on your face," he replies. I hesitate.

"What look?" I ask, still peering through the viewfinder, glad that the camera is big enough to hide most of my face so that he can't see my slightly panicked expression. He looks up at me from under the lushness of his lashes, causing the camera to start sliding from my grasp. Quickly, I take turns wiping each hand on my jeans before snapping another photo. I take longer to review it to give myself a break from directly ogling my best friend.

My tummy is starting to feel light. The picture does nothing to aid the unwanted feeling; his autumnal eyes are just as intense in the picture. It looked like he was seeing into my soul, sensing my innermost thoughts that I am trying my best to conceal from him. I swallow and look back at him; he is still in the same position with the same intense look in his eyes. My tummy flutters.

"That look," he says quietly, breaking my train of thought.

I blink uncomfortably and look away to fiddle with the camera.

"I'm just getting a bit caught up in the whole photography thing. The pictures are REALLY good," I smile convincingly. Tyson says nothing and looks down again so I can continue shooting.

I reposition myself, sitting further away so that I can get a wider shot.

"Rest your other arm on your stomach, and sit up a little for me....good. Okay, now look at me." His eyes flick up to meet mine.

Sweet Jesus!

My stomach flutters harder and the camera starts to slip again. I press the capture button before it is too late.

I clear my throat. "Okay, now try and give me a little more emotion," I direct him, trying to sound like I know what I am doing. It's clear that I've been watching too many cycles of America's Next Top Model.

Tyson laughs.

"And what emotion would that be?" he asks. I blush, embarrassed that he had noticed my sudden change in attitude.

"I dunno. The whole seductive brooding thing you're doing right now is good I guess."

"You're feelin' the sexy romance yeah?" he smiles stupidly. I kick him.

"Shut up, idiot. Anyway, I need more...umph!" I grunt, thrusting my fist at my side. Tyson snickers and shakes his head at me. I blush harder, imagining how silly I must've looked. "Just turn it up a bit okay."

"Okay."

Without warning, Tyson's hand glides up his top and rested on his abs, revealing the waistband of his boxers and one side of the deeply tempting ridge of his hip. He keeps his eyes on me. "How's this?" he asks coolly. Unintentionally, my eyes fall to the cavernous crevice and watch, disappointed, as it disappears into his underwear.

I swallow and put the camera back to my face. "That's, um...fine."

SNAP!

"And this?" His hand ascends under the light cotton of his t-shirt, revealing both ridges like an embossed arrow in his dark skin. My sexual curiosity wants to see what it's pointing to. The bottom of his six-pack undulates and tenses as he breathes - it's taunting me. I tear my eyes from his torso and look at his face. His chocolate eyes smoulder, daring me to let him continue with his mind game, which is teetering precariously along the line of innocent flirting and promising a batch of fresh regrets. How the hell did we end up here?

I lower the camera and frown at him.

"Ty, what are you doing?" I sigh.

He furrows his brow and attempts to look confused. "What do you mean? I'm doing what you told me to do; I'm turning it up a bit. Giving you more…umph." His heady grunt grips his abdomen and the muscles become more pronounced.

I put the camera down and wipe both my palms on my jeans. "Well that's a bit much don't you think?" I gesture at his immaculate midriff. Tyson rolls his eyes and yanks his top down, frustrated.

"Happy?" he snaps, more annoyed than he should be. I hadn't risen to the challenge and – judging from his reaction - he clearly wanted me to do the opposite.

"Hey, don't get snippy with me," I snap back.

He sits up and glares at me. "Why are you being dumb for? I was doing what you asked. Don't blame me if you started reading into it."

"What? Ty don't try it; you knew what you were doing."

"Rio shut up, I wasn't doing anything! What is it with you? Why do you think that every man is on you? You ain't THAT nice!" he yells.

I flinch. It isn't so much of *what* he said that stings; it's that *he* said it. I don't think that every man is on me; I know that I'm not *that* nice. If I was, I would have the one boy I wanted more than life itself.

I look Tyson up and down then get off the bed. "You can be such a dick sometimes." I turn to walk away.

Tyson growls in protest realising that he has upset me. He drags me back and wraps his arms around me. "Ri, I'm sorry; I didn't mean it. Angie pissed me off and I took it out on you. I'm sorry." He pecks me on my head.

I sigh. "It's okay. What'd she say?" I ask, choosing to forgive him now, as I know I'm going to do it eventually anyway. Tyson stiffens and loosens his hold on me. I swivel around and look up at him. "Ty?"

He brushes my curls aside and plants a kiss on my forehead. "It doesn't matter. Go get ready, we've gotta leave soon."

17
Cocaine.
Jade

I peer into the watermarked mirror and wipe my nose roughly. The bad lighting teamed with my sudden light-headedness is making it difficult to see if there are any traces of the tell-tale snowy powder left around my nostrils. I grunt and pull the tip of my nose up in a far from charming fashion and inspect the insides. Looks like I'm all clear. I take an extra hard sniff to make sure. Nothing more embarrassing than walking around with coke residue hanging out of your nose, I'll tell you that. I splash some cold water on my face, accidently catching a few loose tendrils of my hair that I had spent my time blow-drying bone straight. I glance back at my reflection; the hairs around my face have coiled themselves into loose black curls - great. I roll my eyes, tug my emergency hair band from my wrist, and pull my hair up into a messy topknot, leaving the few curling locks free to frame my face. I'm annoyed that I've messed up my hair, but the girls won't care. They'll see the curls and swoon because I have 'good hair', and somewhere along the line the 'crazy stalker bitch' inside of them will make them fantasise about having my babies...as if any of them have a shot in hell. Durex and I are Mates for life. When you look like, possess the kind of status and power, and are as well off as I am, you have to be extra careful. There are a lot of scandalous females out there that are willing to sell their soul to secure a good catch.

I adjust my red classic Obviously long sleeve shirt, tucking the front of it into the waistband of my jeans so that the Gucci emblem of my belt is visible, then I slide my Ray Bans on to hide my eyes. It isn't obvious now, but as the effects of the drugs kick in, my pupils will dilate and my eyes will take on a glassy appearance - not that anyone would notice. I'm high off something or the other 95% of the time, so unless it is weed that tinges the whites of my eyes red, I'm guessing my eyes always look the same to them - green.

I hadn't planned on doing coke tonight. I'd scored some MDMA just before Carter ran out of, which is understandable as we are still in the throes of a new term. Back to uni raves are all the rage right now. Whenever there is some serious raving going on, MDMA is always in high demand. I'd felt a bit jittery on the way here, so I scored some Coke from Carter too to straighten myself out. I'd sniffed three lines and rubbed a little on my gums too for good measure. Tonight I wanted to hit a new high; one that will light me up inside and chase my shadows away so I can to lose myself in the moment, live in it without fear or doubt of what is to come, and especially not of what has passed. Eventually I will come down and re-join the rest of reality – the thought is depressing. I wish I could stay like this; I wish I could stay happy.

My skin is getting warmer and my heart rate picks up. Euphoria is just around the corner. I can hardly wait. The door to the men's room swings open and some guy enters wearing what looks like a knock-off Ralphy polo. He looks at me and nods his greeting.

"You cool Jade?" he asks casually, walking over to the cleanest looking urinal. I grunt a semi-comprehensible reply, wondering who the hell he is. It's expected that he knows who I am – everyone does - but I have no recollection of him. I probably did know the guy, but the likelihood is that the night we met I was too far gone to remember his face the moment he was out of sight, or his name mere moments after he had disclosed it to me; that's the way it is with a lot of these people that think that they are my friends. I only remember people if I consider them worth remembering. I don't remember nobodies, let's just put it that way. This guy is a nobody.

My selective memory constantly gets me in trouble with the infinite amount of girls that I have been with, but after years of consorting with them I have discovered that if you're pretty enough, if you lay a good pipe and lay on enough charm, most girls will forgive you almost anything; that's because most girls are fickle. One moment they are fuming because of something I had done (and with good reason too), but all it takes to get back on their good side is a cheeky line, a flash of a smile and just like that, all is right with the world. After that they are back in my bed making the same mistake all over again. Fickle! I will hold up my hands and admit that I am a top class bastard! Honest to God, I am a cunt; but for whatever reason, these silly girls seem to like that aspect of my personality. They think the fact that I can make them shut up by just giving them a look is hot, because it's "manish". How stupid can you be? I'm clearly taking you for a dickhead. The thing with most girls is, you only have to be a fraction nice to them as you are rude to them for them to be really into you. Sad but true.

Of course these tactics don't work with all girls. Different girls require different strategies. Take this new girl I'm trying to get at; Rio Greene. I have been dangling some of my best bait in front of this girl, but she's not biting and it's doing my head in. I'm used to some girls playing hard to get; normally I would have cracked them by now, but this Rio chick genuinely doesn't want to like me. No matter, she will eventually. The attraction between us is painfully obvious, but she is fighting it extremely well. Just over a week ago I went out with her, my boy DJ Bless and that loud mouth girl he's been stringing along for a few months, to Malaysia Blaq one; of the most exclusive night clubs in London. I had us up in VIP sipping champagne, not to mention I bought both her and her bredrin Gianfranco Ferré dresses - I didn't pay full price as I had done some modelling for them, and the store owner likes me, so I got a discount…and some mediocre head. I am actually TRYING to get this Rio girl, but she's hell bent on refusing me.

I pulled out the big guns and salsa danced with this chick! I was swaying, twirling and dipping her around like a pro, and I almost had her...then she had to go 'cause something happened to her Asian friend that's designing Manny's new line. What's her name again? Aww I'm too gone to remember now, but yeah, the Asian chick that's going out with my bredrin Ace. No need to wonder what happened to her - it's no secret that Ace is a bit too 'hands on' with his partners. Anyway, if it wasn't for that little misdemeanour, Rio would have woken up butt naked in my bed, wondering if she should start regretting all of the illicit things we had done now or later, and unable to walk properly. Needless to say, I wasn't best pleased at having gotten so close to bedding her and having the chance snatched out from under me, so I ended up taking two other girls home to make up for all my wasted effort.

My boys don't understand why I am trying so hard to get this girl when I can clearly do much better, but I have my reasons (none of them honourable of course). The fact that she is (surprisingly) proving to be such a challenge is annoying, but it excites me because it makes my little mission more interesting. This girl isn't going to stand still and let me catch her like all the others; she is going to make me chase her. If I were her, I'd run a mile and never look back. It's very rare that I never succeed in my conquests, seeing as I am such a great catch. On a scale of one to ten, I am easily a twenty – yes, you heard me correctly. You can call me arrogant and conceited all you like, but if I decide that it is YOU that I want, then it's you that I'll have. I'll have you hollering out 'Yes' into the night until your spine curves, your head is thrown back, and your weave is beyond salvaging. Oh yes ladies, the stories you hear about me are true; I am the whole package and more. I've got the kind of status that these other heads couldn't achieve in their wildest dreams -I'm paid, powerful, very well connected, charismatic, I've got the kind of looks that make even the prettiest girl feel insecure around me, and on top of all that, I fuck like a God damn porn star. Google me!

What girl can say no to all of this...and mean it?

This is the reason nobody understands my fascination with Rio -I'm CLEARLY out of her league -but then so was Nate Gibson, and he wifed her. I'm just tryna have a little fun and then some. To be frank, Rio is average –average in the sense that if there was picture of what average looked like in the dictionary, it would be of her. There's nothing wrong with her, she's a good looking girl, but there is nothing about her that would make a man of my stature look twice unless she made an effort…like the time she wore that backless nude dress…or when she was wore the dress I bought her with the slits that ran all the way up her thick thighs. Okay, so she's a little better than average, but that's just because she's got a body. I'd give her seven out of ten.

I dry my hands under the dryer and make my way back upstairs. The sound of raucous laughter hits me the moment the door opens, followed by the sound of clinking glasses and a comedic ignorant male voice flowing through the speakers; Shaquille. I ascend the stairs, preparing myself for the hassle of getting over to the bar. I reach the top of the stairs and squeeze my way through the overflowing crowd. What should have taken me under a minute, ends up taking at least five because I am constantly having to pause and say hi to the many people (females mostly) that are happy to have made my acquaintance (and then some). Everyone wanted fist bumps or hugs and inane conversations, so by the time I actually reach the bar I am thirsty as hell.

I hail one of the bar staff and order a JD on the rocks; after all, JD goes great with coke. I take a gulp of the sticky, bitter whiskey, enjoying the way it travels down my throat and burns my chest when another acquaintance wants to be greeted; a tall lighty with big brown eyes and wild gold and copper curls that she twirls flirtatiously between her manicured fingers.

"Hey you," she smiles giving me a friendly nudge, "Remember me?" I hate when people asked me that. No I do not remember you, but you look good so I'm going to act like I do.

I furrow my brow like I am trying to recall her.

"I think so. I've definitely seen your face before; what's your name again, miss?" I ask, pulling my glasses down so I can get a better look at her...and to show off my eyes.

She smiles, "Fontaine. We met at the Benetton shoot."

So she's model. A real one that books actual jobs, not like the rest of these wannabe Instagram models around here. I think back to the Benetton shoot and realise that I do remember her after all. I had taken her number with the intention of making her another notch in my bedpost. I flash her my version of a genuine smile and pull her in for a one armed hug.

"Yeah, yeah I remember you. What's good darlin'?"

She reacts to my touch in surprise. She wasn't expecting a hug, which is exactly why I had done it. I want her to feel comfortable around me, that way breaking the ice wouldn't be so long and tedious.

Fontaine laces one arm around me to return the unexpected affection and smiles again, "I'm alright. You?" I release her and lean against the bar.

"I'm good sweetheart. I love how you ain't hollered at me though. I'm hurt," I say playfully, making sure to beat her to the punch. Girls love to drop that line like it's always the guy's fault that we haven't been in contact, as if to say their hands are broken.

Fontaine's mouth falls open and she laughs.

"I could ask you the same thing, Mr Washington," she replies, swatting me softly.

I laugh.

"Nah, don't try flip the script. Why didn't you holler at me?" I ask placing the fault back on her. I expect her to look away embarrassed, but instead she shrugs as if she doesn't care. Okay.

"I dunno." She's one of those overly confident chicks who want to pretend like they aren't fazed by me. I have to switch up the game a little and come at her a little more head on.

"See you ain't even got a good excuse," I kiss my teeth.

She smirks and folds her arms. "Well what's your excuse?" I take her hand and step a little closer. I notice her eyes widen a little; that is a good sign.

"I was waiting for you to holler first. You're an attractive woman; you've probably got loads of guys chasing you. I didn't want to look eager," I smile.

She cocks her eyebrow.

"Is that so? And there's me thinking it was because you were too interested in moving to my friend," she says removing her hand from mine.

Shit.

I tilt my head to the side and regard her. As far as I'm concerned she hasn't caught me out just yet, so I'm not confessing to anything.

"Is it? Who's your friend?" I asked casually.

"Rio."

Double shit. I can't sweet talk my way through this one because I want Rio more than I want her, and from what I know of Rio, me messing with her friend won't go down well.

I take a step back having already figured out how to remove myself from this situation.

"Oh. Well that changes things, doesn't it? What did you say your name was again babe?" She rolls her eyes. I still remembered what her name is, but as she is no longer on the menu, I can talk to her however I feel.

"It's Fontaine," she says, kicking some attitude into her tone.

"Yeah, yeah. My bad, Fontaine. You're the one that's fucking Nate behind your *friend's* back, right?" I ask brazenly, smirking and taking another gulp of JD.

Her mouth tightens and finally she looks away, embarrassed. "What did you say?"

"Do you really want me to repeat that in this environment?" I ask, gesturing to the people surrounding us that are obviously listening in on the sly.

Fontaine looks about then back to me.

"How did you know about that?" she asks quietly.

I shrug and take one final gulp from my glass.

"People talk init. As you're part of Rio's little clique I'm gonna assume that she's here too. I'll talk to you later." I throw her a cheeky wink, set my empty glass down on the counter, and make off into the crowd.

I spot Rio from the VIP booth. She is sauntering around by herself with a huge Nikon camera dangling from her neck, dressed in a pair of skin tight red skinny jeans, a black Michael Jackson Bad t-shirt, which she'd knotted at the back to accentuate her tiny waist, and silver sequined low top Converses. The girl knows how to dress, I'll give her that. It was the sort of outfit I could see myself in. Every few steps she takes, Rio pauses and sheepishly holds up her camera with a shy smile directed at the nearest group of people around her. They smile back, cluster together and strike a mediocre pose for her to take their picture. After she takes at least two shots, she shows them the photo, to which they'd either smile or frown, which determines if she took another one. After that she leans in, tells them something, and then move onto the next person.

I watch her intently for a few minutes then decided to make my move. I signal to my friends that I am off again. Carter is the only one who raises his eyebrow at me, knowing exactly where I'm going. He looks at Rio then back to me and shakes his head. Needless to say he doesn't approve of me trying to get at her. He had already warned me to keep my distance because she is a 'good girl' and doesn't need me fucking with her head. I'd told him to stop getting in my business and worry about his own shit; he didn't like that much, and if we weren't friends he probably would've taken a swing at me, or worse. Carter is currently dealing with some drama of his own, which he doesn't like people to mention. Long story short, he's gotten a friend of mine pregnant, but she had tried to pass the baby off as someone else's, because she didn't want her drug dealing ex in the child's life. Thanks to Rio, Carter had found out about her indiscretion last year at my end-of-year house party, and now my friend is stuck with him, and the baby that she no longer wants. The few times I have been to see her since then, she's been absolutely miserable; holed up at Carter's house, too embarrassed to go to back to Brompton and face everyone. I have to give it to Carter though; he is dealing with her exceptionally well given the circumstances, but he loves her like crazy, so I'm not surprised. If it had been any other girl that had done that to him, I'm afraid to know what he would have done. Carter Johnson should not be taken lightly.

I sneak up behind Rio and snake my arm around her waist, pulling her body against mine. She feels soft and warm, and as always, she smells good. I lean my head down and let my lips graze her earlobe.

"How come you haven't asked to take my picture?"

Her body stiffens in my arms as she realises who is behind her.

"Jade?"

"Miss me?" I respond, making my tone throatier. Her heartbeat quickens against my chest just before she wriggles out of my grip. That is one thing I like about Rio; she is extremely easy to read - it makes messing with her more entertaining because I know that every reaction is honest. I make her nervous and uncomfortable, but I also turn her on. There is no doubt that she wants me, but she is good at fighting temptation...when it comes to me anyway. I will soon change that.

Rio's hands immediately fly to her head, and she self-consciously runs her hands over her hair. I smile.

"You changed your hair; I like it. Curly looks good on you," I compliment her new hairstyle. Girls like it when you notice little shit like that. Finally she smiles back. She doesn't have a perfect smile; she had a slight overbite that makes her top lip protrude a little, but it is still a nice smile.

"Um, thanks. Curly suits you as well," she says nervously, pointing to the few black coils that hang limply around my face. I find it sweet that that is the best compliment she could come up with. I laugh and thank her.

"So, you're a photographer now, huh?" I ask fingering the camera.

She straightens up a little with pride. "Yeah, I'm doing event photography. It's called Vanity Mode Photography." I roll my eyes inwardly. Just what we need, another event photographer that's never gonna get anywhere; and what a stupid name: Vanity Mode. Give me a break.

"Cool name. How long you been doing this for?" I feign interest.

"Today is my first day actually."

"Really? The way you've been working the crowd I thought you'd been doing this for a while," I lie. She looks like a beginner, but I'm not gonna tell her that. The more I fluff her ego, the better my chances are. Girls like Rio receive compliments, but not as often as they'd like, and not always from the kind of guys that they like, so I know that she appreciates hearing it come from me.

"You're just saying that," she blushes "It's obvious that I'm a beginner, but I think I'm actually doing all right. Wanna see some of the pictures I took?" No.

"Sure!"

She grins excitedly and steps closer to me so I can see. I take her by the hand and pull her back to my front so she can show me without having to take the camera off. She hesitates and looks around, embarrassed to be back in this position with me again in front of everyone. A few girls throw her dirty looks and mutter bitchy comments to their friends.

"Look at you, making girls jealous," I tease giving her a squeeze. She giggles nervously and starts showing me the pictures, deciding not to take any notice of her haters. Truth be told, her pictures are a little better than she had made them out to be; she's allowed the right amount of frame space for each shot, chosen the right angles to shoot from, and it is evident that she is aware of the lighting. I feel my respect for her go up a level and the name 'Vanity Mode' becomes a little less ridiculous. "You're quite handy with a camera aren't you," I gush. I lower my voice, "You're much better than the resident photographer I'll tell you that."

She giggles again, "I'm guessing that was meant to be a compliment, but given his photographic standards it kind of takes the shine off of it." Now it's my turn to laugh. It is universally known that the guy Ace hires to do the photography for Sunday Slam is pants, but not many people have the balls to say it as he is Ace's cousin, which is definitely the only reason Ace kept him.

The act that was performing comes off the stage with momentous applause. I glance up to see Sean the Poet exiting the stage. Shaquille replaces him and announces that it is time for an intermission, and just like that the air becomes thicker, and the available space more sparse as everyone begins moving around either to go to the bar, go to the bathroom, or to go and have a chat with friends. If there wasn't enough attention on me and Rio before, there definitely is now.

Bless throws on some Drake and I watch amused as the crowd let the song excite them into hitting up the bar and flirting. Rio, still in my arms, bubbles gently to the song and bobs her head while she lip syncs the lyrics. I smile to myself; although she is no angel, there is naive innocence about her that makes me feel a little protective of her. Hmm.

She wriggles out of my arms, less panicked this time, and smiles softly.

"I'm gonna go take some more pictures. I'll see you later?" she half says, half asks.

I nod. "Definitely."

After the intermission I find myself back in the men's room trying to get myself to calm down. Having all those people crowding me when I am so doped up, doesn't always have a positive effect on me. My heart feels like it is beating at 1000 beats per minute, and I am burning up. My skin literally feels like it is on fire.

I lean over the sink and rest my head against the mirror. The coolness of the glass feels good against my face. Slowly, I turn my head so that the rest of my face is on the mirror, and began taking slow deep breaths to try and calm myself down. I have taken too much, but I know from experience that panicking isn't going to help anything. I tug off my Ray Bans and let them fall noisily onto the wet counter top. My pupils are the size of tiny black beads, sitting in a sea of jade green; it looks creepy. After standing like that for about 2 minutes, I decide to turn my head over to cool down the other side of my face again –no such luck. The blood vessels in my neck have constricted, and I find myself unable to move. Damn it! I hate it when this happens. It hurts like hell if I try to adjust my head in the slightest, and even worse, it is ruining my high.

So here I am; Jade Washington, 21 years old, doped up in the men's room with my face pressed up against a dirty mirror, unable to move. If only the people who worship me could see me now. I rest one hand against the mirror to make sure that I don't make any sudden movements, and use the other to massage my neck. Hopefully I'll be okay before anyone comes in and sees me.

With my ear pressed against the glass I can hear the muffled sounds of a conversation being held on the other side of the wall. I'm not going anywhere soon, so I strain my ears to listen while I wait. It's a boy and girl having an argument...about...damn I didn't catch that. Anyway, they are arguing about something and whatever it is, it's bad, because as every word is exchanged between them, their voices become louder and more irate.

I lift my body slowly, trying with all my might not to move my neck. Short stabs of pain shoot through my neck muscles and spread all the way to my temples. If this doesn't go away soon I am going to end up with a splitting headache.

I shuffle myself closer to the door and press my ear against the tiny gap between the doorframe and the door. I really hope no one comes in. The voices are now crystal clear.

"What are you so worried about Fontaine?" the male voice asks.

"Jade Washington knows about us Nathaniel, which means that That other people probably do too. Rio's gonna hate me."

Oh snap, it's Fontaine and Nate Gibson! I am listening in on the RIGHT conversation boy!

I hear Nate scoff, "Oh so NOW you're worrying about how Rio feels. You weren't so worried the other night though, were you?"

"Well I never thought she'd find out, did I? She still thinks I'm with Nadia!"

"What, is that supposed to make it okay or something?"

"Of course not, but at least she wouldn't be hurt. Nathaniel, she's my friend and you're like her...everything. What happened between us should have never happened."

Nathaniel growls. "You're saying it like it was some sort of mistake. Fontaine, me and Rio are over. I like you_"

"Nathaniel, I like you too but she's my friend_"

"I don't care!"

The conversation is silenced for a few moments, and then as if the situation couldn't get any better...

"Rio!" Fontaine gasps.

It's as if someone up there wants to play her right into my hands. This is too perfect. I want to open the door so I can watch how the argument pans out visually, but I have to time my entrance.... that and my neck is still stiff.

"Well isn't this sweet. Oh please, don't stop on my account," Rio sneers.

"Ri, it's not what it looks like I swear," Fontaine says already sounding hysterical, as if Rio is going to do something to her. That would be fascinating; I never got to see her slap Sky.

"Well from where I was standing it looked like you two were kissing."

"That's because we were," Nathaniel replies coldly. I can detect the seething anger in his voice. He wasn't this angry before when he was arguing with Fontaine. I guess Rio really gets to him.

"Nathaniel!" Fontaine gasps, "You're not helping anything!"

"Oh what, and you are by trying to play it off as if it's nothing? Yes Rio, we were kissing; so what?" he hisses.

After a moments silence Rio's voice sounds, but it has lost all of its harshness and is now pained.

"Why are you doing this to me?"

"No one's doing anything to you Rio. This is about me and Fontaine. This has NOTHING to do with you." Nate replies.

"You're supposed to be my friend," she says to Fontaine.

"Ri, I know and I'm sorry but_"

"But what, Fontaine?" she almost screams, her voice breaking in places.

"I like him Ri. I'm sorry but I do."

I step back from the door and slowly straighten my head. I am going have to go out there soon if I want this to work. My neck is still a bit stiff, but the pain is tolerable. I grab my Ray Bans from the counter and wipe the water droplets off of them with my jeans, then placed them back on my face. I place my hand on the door handle, awaiting my cue.

"Both of you fuck off," Rio hisses venomously.

"Rio_" I hear a smacking sound. Did she box her? Oh my days!

"I SAID FUCK OFF!"

Fontaine sighs in defeat and I hear her and Nathaniel make their way back upstairs.

I pull the door open slowly to see Rio standing tight lipped in the middle of the foyer staring angrily at the wall with hot tears gathering around the brim of her eyes. Her eyes shift to the men's room door and widen when she sees me coming towards her. She rolls them up towards the heaven as if to say 'why'.

"As if that wasn't embarrassing enough..." she croaks gesturing limply at me. I say nothing and put my arms around her, rubbing her back gently. I feel her take a sharp intake of breath then shudder as the tears finally come down. "I feel so freakin' stupid," she sobs. I hush her and continue to rub her back. I'm not going to say anything pointless like 'it's okay' when it clearly isn't, or gas her up and say 'you deserve better'. Girls don't want to hear that mess when they're sad, because they know you're only saying it to make them feel better. They just want to have someone to hold them when they're crying; so that's what I did. I stood there, in the middle of the Plan X foyer, and held Rio as she cried.

I have her exactly where I want her.

18
Nostalgia Ultra.

April 2011

A rush of cool air breaches the covers and whistles down my exposed spine, leaving a trail of fresh goose-bumps in its wake. I am naked. Rolling over onto my back, I open my eyes and rub the sleep out of them before flinging my arm out lethargically to retrieve my phone from Nathaniel's cluttered bedside table. It's 7am; the lazy late autumn sun barely shines through the fine slits in his wooden shutters. I have only been asleep for 4 hours, which is nowhere near enough sleep for me, so why on earth am I awake? I return my phone to the debris of rolling papers, screwed up squares of cling film, cigarette butts and empty condom wrappers, and rotate back onto my side.

Nathaniel is fast asleep next to me, breathing deeply with his plush pink lips slightly ajar and his thick lashes resting on the upper curve of his cheekbones. Even in the overcast lighting, his golden skin retains its perpetual after-sex glow, made even more entrancing by the fact that he too is naked. I smile to myself and shift closer to him, wanting to snuggle up to him, but restraining myself in case I disturb his sleep. After what we had engaged in a mere 4 hours ago, he has earned his rest.

Tentatively, I caress the side of his face; he stirs a little and releases a mellifluous groan. I snatch my hand away and let it rest in the space between us, with a half guilty expression. After a few moments Nathaniel groans again and reaches forward to take my hand.

"That felt nice," he gutturalizes, his raspy voice huskier than usual, thick with sleep. He pulls my hand back up to his face and I happily resume stroking it.

"I thought you were asleep."

"I was." he grunts.

"Sorry." I apologise, not sounding the least bit remorseful. Nathaniel chuckles.

"It's okay baby; I was dreaming about you anyway. Why dream when I can have the real thing?" he smiles lazily, taking my hand again and pressing the base of my palm against his mouth to kiss it. A second set of goose-bumps flourish across my skin –they have nothing to do with the chill in the air. If it was any other guy, I would have rolled my eyes at the banality of that line, but Nathaniel just randomly say things like that with such uncomplicated sincerity, that it stops me from questioning him. Every day he shows me that the luxury of true romance isn't restricted to the dog-eared pages of my Mills & Boons harlequins.

"You should stay over more often," he continues as his feather-light kisses decorate my wrist, "I like waking up to you."

"Even though I wake you up at 7am?" I giggle.

"Even though you wake me up at 7am," he repeats.

"Even though my hair looks like a bird's nest in the morning?" Nathaniel reaches up slowly, and touches my mass of dry, bushy, tangled hair that is sticking out at curious angles. I frown and swat his hand away before attempting to smooth down my bedraggled tresses to no avail; the moment my determined hands pass over it the rebellious tufts spring back up as if I hadn't even tried to tame them.

"I like bird's nests," he smiles against my skin. "If I had my own way I'd wake up to you every day for the rest of my life Ri."

"Ha! You say that n_" I pause in mid-sentence – he's finally decided to open his eyes and he is staring at me with a look filled with impassioned admiration. My heart stutters, stops, and restarts. By and by I find myself becoming lightheaded; I have forgotten how to breathe again. He's so intense.

"I'll say it forever. Yes, you will probably annoy the hell out of me one day; but I'd still rather you were there than not. I don't ever want you to go away Ri; I mean it." He draws me into him and wraps his illustrated arms around me. The slow, gentle reverberation of his heartbeat nudges lovingly against my skin like a constant reminder that it's there and that it beats for me. He kisses my forehead. "I love you Rio; you are my heart. What would I be without my heart?" he purrs as our bodies began to react to the close, intimate contact.

"You'd be heartless," I joke awkwardly. Nate shakes his head, smiles adoringly at my failed attempt at humour, and kisses my forehead again.

"Exactly."

Present Day

I know I should stay put; that little voice in my head is screaming at me not to follow them, but I do it anyway. As I lower myself onto the first step, my determination fizzles out and that sick feeling bubbles up in my stomach. Nothing good will come from me facing Nate and Fontaine head on, I know that, but I can't bear to stand around trying to force being okay, while they're down there alone doing God knows what. I'm already dangling off of the cusp of sanity; continuing down this path will be like flinging myself into a darkness that I know full well I am not mentally strong enough to deal with, still I grit my teeth and take another step down…then another…then another.

Already the music is quieter and I can just about pick up two voices – male and female. It's them. My last spot of inner-light grows dimmer. I keep walking, rounding the curve halfway between the flights, treading lightly, not yet ready for them to notice me because the moment they do I will have no choice but to confront them. The idea scares me too much at this point; I need to find my courage first. Nathaniel and Fontaine are partially in my sight, and their voices are as clear as day. My heart jolts with adrenaline laced fear - if I turn back now I can continue to live in bittersweet partial ignorance, only having to endure the pain of what my overactive imagination conjures. If I keep going, I will have to face what I pessimistically assume will be the end of me. I take one more step and observe the cause of my ultimate undoing.

He is touching her; not in a sexual way - he only has his hand resting on her arm - but the sight of their two bodies in direct contact make my blood boil and my heart freeze over. Fontaine hangs her head, hiding her eyes beneath her curls, and half murmurs something. I don't hear what she says, but it doesn't go down well with Nathaniel. His eyes tighten and he drops his hand from her arm – I breathe a little easier.

"Oh, so NOW you're worrying about how Rio feels? You weren't so worried the other night though, were you?" he says unpleasantly. My chest tightens.

Fontaine frowns and folds her arms. "Well I didn't think she'd find out, did I?" I grit my teeth.

"What, is that supposed to make it okay or something?" he chuckles.

"Of course not, but at least she wouldn't be hurt. Nathaniel, she's my friend and you're like her...everything. What happened between us should have never happened." I pause. She's admitting that what they did was wrong, and she actually gives a damn about how I feel about it. I'm still mad, but it soothes me a little...just a little.

Nathaniel growls in frustration, "You're saying it like it was some sort of mistake. Fontaine, me and Rio are over! I like you_"

"Nathaniel, I like you too but she's my friend_"

"I don't care!" he bellows.

A sharp pang in my chest sends my adrenaline level skyrocketing to the point where I begin to quake. My initial fear subsides, and anger takes over - how can he not CARE? How the hell is he able to push his feelings for me to one side and be so willing to act as if I don't even matter to him? How can the person you claimed was your 'heart' not matter? He used to be so lovely... he used to love me...but now... I sigh inwardly. After all of the shit he put me through and how much time it took for those old wounds to heal, begging me for my forgiveness, convincing me that he is sorry and that he'll never hurt me again, all he does is create fresh ones, each additional laceration cutting deeper than the last. Times like this, I regret ever loving him.

He stares at her, devouring her with his magnificent eyes. She stares back at him, yielding to his spectacular ocular consumption. The attraction between them is sickeningly obvious, and what makes it worse is that she has the same thing over me that Georgia did; she looks like the kind of girl that belongs with a guy like him. They look perfect together. If they become a couple, no one will question it like they did when he was with me.

They stand like that for a few moments, staring intensely at each other, and then he leans in. I hold my breath, hoping that she will back up her preaching about being my friend and not wanting to hurt me, and pull away from him. She doesn't; instead, she succumbs to his welcoming mouth, and they kiss, strong and slow. An uncomfortable lump forms in my throat and it aches. I try to swallow it but it won't budge. I thought that my imagination was bad, but to see them together like this, right in front of my eyes, is more than I can take. I would take my bitter-sweet partial ignorance over this any day because my reality is sheer torture.

Unable to support my own weight on my quivering knees any longer, I slump against the wall noisily. They jump and spring apart, astonished to see me watching them, seething.

"Rio!" Fontaine gasps - her eyes wide and guilty. She moves further away from Nathaniel who is looking back at me stonily.

"Well isn't this sweet! Oh, please, don't stop on my account," I sneer.

Fontaine raises her hands in front of her and walks towards me cautiously.

"Ri! It's not what it looks like, I swear."

I cock my head to the side and narrow my eyes at her. "Well from where I'm standing it looked like you two were kissing."

"That's because we were." Nathaniel interjects icily. My eyes snap to him and I form a tight fist.

"Nathaniel!" Fontaine gasps, "You're not helping anything."

"Oh what, and you are by trying to play it off as if it's nothing? Yes Rio, we were kissing; so what?" he hisses. His eyes are ablaze with a steely fire that overpowers my own. He's so angry. I've seen him mad before, but never like this; this time it's different. The way he's looking at me…it's almost like he HATES me. Briefly I wonder if he had seen Jade and I hugged up earlier, but even if he had, that is *nothing* compared to what he is doing with my friend, so why is he being like this? What does he have to be so mad about? No one is ripping his heart to shreds with no remorse.

"Why are you doing this to me?" I ask, my voice wavering and breaking.

His expression doesn't change.

"No one's doing anything to you, Rio. This is about me and Fontaine. This has NOTHING to do with you!" he snarls.

At this moment I feel like less than nothing. The last time I felt this way was in college, before Nathaniel had come into my life and saved me, and now the person I need saving from is him. What do you do when your hero turns into the villain? As difficult as it is to confront them, I need answers, but I'm so afraid of what answers Nathaniel will give me.

Unable to withstand his glare any longer, I turn to Fontaine. "You're supposed to be my friend!"

"Ri, I know, and I'm sorry but_"

"But what, Fontaine?" I scream, feeling my eyes start to burn with tears as the lump in my throat dissolves.

She runs her hands through her curls and looks away.

Quietly she replies, "I like him Ri. I'm sorry, but I do."

To rub salt in the wound, Nathaniel takes her by the hand and pulls her in close. He fixes his hurricane eyes on me and kisses Fontaine on her forehead. I see red. I storm over to them with both of my fists clenched so tightly that my nails dig into my palms.

"Both of you fuck off," I hiss, wanting to deliver multiple blows to their pretty faces. Nathaniel looks down at me and laughs spitefully. He's enjoying this.

Before I can stop myself_

"Rio!" Fontaine cries as my fist connects with Nathaniel's face so hard that the flat side of my knuckles create a deep slapping sound as they collide with his flesh. Nathaniel's head snaps to the side by the magnitude of force behind my punch.

"I SAID FUCK OFF!"

Nathaniel's eyes flash dangerously with a look that I had seen more times than I care to remember…from my father. I watch with wide eyes as the world slows down while the boy I love rears back and raises his hand to hit me back. My heart stalls and I brace myself for the blow, but Fontaine grabs his arm just in time.

"Nathaniel, don't!" she whispers shakily, clutching his huge fist against her chest, "Don't."

Nathaniel pauses. He looks from Fontaine, to his clenched fist, and finally to me. Suddenly he exhales heavily, breathing in short, crippling bursts as if he has been holding his breath, stepping away from me with astonished grey eyes. He drops his hand immediately.

"Rio? I'm sorry…I didn't…I wouldn't…I_" he babbles, desperately grasping at apologetic sentences, pleading with me in a flustered fashion that further illustrates how out of control he is. Nathaniel almost always kept it together, but not this time. For a few brief moments, he had really snapped.

I don't say anything; I continue to stare at him blankly while I reflect on that wild look that had contorted his features.

"C'mon. You need some air," Fontaine suggests softly, pulling him further away from me. She manoeuvres around me, making sure that she is between us at all times, and then leads him up the stairs and out of sight. Guiltily, Nathaniel drops his gaze and follows her, still muttering unfinished sentences; he doesn't look back. I hadn't realized till now, but I too had been holding my breath. Once he is out of my sight I exhale and finally unclench my fists to find that my hand is swelling up from the impact of my enraged attack. What have I done? The gathering of tears in my eyes increase, and any moment now they will rain down on my face. My adrenaline is subsiding and I have no choice but to acknowledge what had just gone down. I had hit Nathaniel, and he was ready to hit me back. He lost control for only a moment and turned into one of the people I hated most, and it was my fault. He pushed me, so I pushed him, and now look.

We really are no good for each other.

To my surprise and dismay, the door to the men's room creaks open behind me and out comes the last person on earth that I would want to see at a time like this; Jade Washington. I roll my eyes towards the heavens and mentally asked God why he is fucking with me today. First Ty, then Nate, and now I have to be caught crying in front of Jade fucking Washington, and if he was in the men's room he probably heard the whole thing. WHY ME?

"As if that wasn't embarrassing enough..." I croak gesturing at him. Jade watches me curiously as he walks over to me. I wait for him to make some snarky comment, but instead he says nothing. He put his arms around me. I want to push him off and try to save what little face I have left, but I can't, the adrenaline rush has dissipated completely. I surrender to his comfort, collapsing against him and sobbing my eyes out. "I feel so frigging stupid," I cry angrily. Jade hushes me, rubs my back and lets me cry.

What I'm doing in the men's room with Jade 'suddenly-sympathetic' Washington I do not know, but I can't bear to venture back upstairs with my puffy eyes and face everyone yet, especially with the unlikely chance that Nathaniel and Fontaine are still hanging around, so oddly this is the safest place to be. Although I'm with someone I can't trust as far as I could throw them, at least Jade is the only one around to judge me right now. Surprisingly the men's room appears to look a lot cleaner than the women's, but I can't stomach the pungent smell of urine, which is most likely splashed in places that it has no business being; the ragged breaths I take through my mouth as I cry don't help much. The air leaves a faint undesirable taste on my tongue.

Jade wipes down the counter with a large wad of tissue, before picking me up and perching me on top of it, between two of the sinks. He stands in front of me, sweetly dabbing tears off my face in silence. Never in a million years could I have imagined that Jade would be someone who would comfort me, and yet here he is doing just that. It confuses me a little.

"People like that aren't worth your tears," he says disapprovingly. I don't reply. I don't really know what to say to him; I'm not entirely comfortable with discussing my personal affairs with the likes of Jade. "People do shitty things all the time - I should know, I'm one of those people – but you can't let it get to you; not if you want to run with the 'elite' crowd." He chuckles briefly then instantly reverts back to his disapproving tone "Snakes are everywhere, Rio."

"What makes you think I want to run with the elite crowd?" I frown, going for curious but sounding defensive. It's embarrassing that even Jade knows that I want to be an Unfamous; I thought Carter was just being an ass when he said that they all knew I wanted in. Am I really that obvious?

Standing stock still, he stares at me, and even though his eyes are hidden behind his Ray Bans, the force of them presses down on me like a ton of bricks…very sexy bricks. I shift and swipe self-consciously at another tear, feeling too highly strung to show weakness in front of him when I can feel him trying to dominate me with so little effort. I jut out my chin; one corner of his lips lift.

"You're *very* easy to read, so there's no point in denying it. Plus, I've been about for a hot minute; I KNOW when someone wants…in." he purrs. The way he says 'in' makes me drop my chin and lower my eyes. I automatically flip back into being self-conscious and start fiddling with the edge of my t-shirt, too inconveniently flushed to say something smart. "You could do it you know, if you toughened up a little." The edge of his thumb glides underneath my lower lash line, tidying my smudged eyeliner. "I hear your name here and there. You've caught our attention. You've made us curious." He extracts my nervous fingers from my clothing and lifts my head, forcing me to look at him. My spine stiffens.

"Who's 'us'?" I ask quietly.

"Me; I'm curious."

I frown at him.

"Yeah…why is that? I'm not interesting, glamorous or as beautiful as those other girls, so why me?"

Jade releases my face and rests his hands on either side of me on the counter, trapping me. He leans in, too close for comfort, peering at me inquisitively.

"Why do you think they're better than you?"

I lean away from him, turning my head in time to hide a fresh tear from his probing view.

"Because they keep winning!" I snap as Fontaine, Sky and Georgia come to mind, "They always win."

Jade cocks his head to the side. "What are they winning exactly?" Another tear rolls down my face. I swipe at it angrily.

"…Everything." I croak, feeling my heart cave in and crumble the more I dwell on it.

Jade dabs sweetly at my tears again, but his mouth is set in a frustrated grimace as if my sadness is starting to annoy him. He probably regrets coming to my aid now. I'm an emotional mess.

"Nathaniel is not everything." he scolds.

"Then why is it that every time I lose him I feel like I have nothing?" I cry pathetically, my shoulders sagging as I curl into myself.

Jade huffs and pulls me to him, wrapping his arms around me awkwardly as I sob harder into his chest.

"Hey, hey, stop all that! Everything is okay." he consoles me lazily.

I shove him off. If he doesn't want to comfort me then I'd rather he didn't bother as his attitude is only making me feel worse.

"No, it's not! It hurts…" I scream, quickly losing my momentum and trailing off with morbid realization that yes, it really is a bad as I think it is. Jade stares at me but says nothing, sensing that more of his dismissive manner is not what the doctor ordered. Crestfallen, I look down into my lap and continue talking, more to myself than to him. "He's a bastard and I hate him, but worse than that, I still love him, which makes me hate him even more because I wish I didn't. It hurts so much, and I don't know how to make it stop!"

"Do you want it to stop?" His tone is gentler and full of promise for a resolution.

I glance up at him. "More than anything."

With the back of his hand, Jade gently strokes the side of my face, down to the hollow of my neck. Suddenly, I can't breathe.

"Just say the word, and I'll make it all go away. You'll never have to feel like this again; I promise."

I furrow my brow. "What word?"

He lifts his glasses and fixes his hypnotic orbs on me. Despite my current mood, I feel the tug of his alluring aura beckoning my inhibitions to come undone.

"You know what word, Rio." he says sternly. His sexual dominance washes over me and with the curl of his lip, Jade transports us from the dingy Plan X men's room, to the lustful lavishness of Malaysia Blaq. My stomach tightens; I know what I have to say.

"Yes." I squeak. His smile widens.

"Good girl. Close your eyes." he orders.

I blink at him. "What? Why should_"

"You ask too many questions. I said I would make it stop, and I will, but first you have to close your eyes. I'm not going to hurt you, I swear. You're safe with me Rio," he purrs in a way that foolishly makes me want to believe him. "Just close your eyes."

Alarm bells sound in my head. My instincts warn me that trusting Jade is probably a bad idea, but I reason that after the night I've had, I doubt anything Jade will do to me can top what Nathaniel has done. I'm already at rock bottom; the only way is up, so if simply closing my eyes can help me get over this, I'm all for it. I study Jade for a few more seconds, still conducting a last minute debate in my head about whether to accept his help or not. The whole time, he stands there patiently, waiting for me to accept his offer. I close my eyes.

A quiet rustling sound makes my ears prick up and the alarm bells ring louder, but before I have the opportunity to come to my senses and protest, Jade's heated mouth crashes against mine. His hands grasp my waist, yanking me forward and pressing my body against his in the most cavalier manner, so close that my centre moulds around his. I whimper pathetically in half-hearted protest, knowing that I should be gathering my morals to fend him off; but his kisses are liberating. I don't want to push him away. All of the pent up sexual tension between us explodes and thrives with such heady intensity that I'm almost tempted to continue kissing him even after his tongue briefly invades my mouth, leaving a small pill in its wake.

He withdraws his lips from mine, but keeps our centres connected. I'm staring at him, open mouthed and panting; too overwhelmed to react to his impulsive behaviour. He flexes his hips against me, only once. Once is enough for me to gasp and shudder.

"Swallow it." he demands huskily, his eyes glittering with a dark excitement.

"What is it?" I ask in the most unbecoming fashion, trying to balance the pill on my tongue and talk at the same time.

"The answer to your problems." he purrs, sliding his fingers down my back until the tips of them graze the strip of exposed brown skin between the hem of my top and the waistband of my jeans. I shift against him.

"What will it do to me?"

"It will make it stop. Just swallow it, darlin'. What have you got to lose?" I had lost the only person - outside of my family (Ty included) - that mattered most to me already, so when he put it like that I realised that I really had nothing left to lose. I swallow it.

"So what happens now?" I ask in a hushed tone, knowing that I've just done something that I shouldn't have; paranoid that any moment someone could come bursting in and overhear our conversation.

Jade eases away from me, replaces his Ray Bans, and shrugs coolly like we hadn't just been wrapped around each other.

"Whatever you want, babe. The world is yours!" He glances at his watch, "I've gotta run. I'll see you around."

With one last fiery kiss on my lips, he walks out of the men's room leaving me alone on top of the sink, hot and flustered with an unknown substance flowing through my veins.

19 Blurred Lines.

It's been an hour since I'd taken the unknown substance Jade had delivered through his kiss, and my high is almost at its vantage point. I had been high many times before, but that was from weed. This high is different; the level of psychedelic surrealism makes everything burn brighter, sounds more ethereal, smells more pronounced. I'm walking on air, filled with an electrical force that's impossible to contain. I've never been so aware of myself; it's empowering. I feel like…a *woman.* The drug has given me a sense of sensuality and joy that I've never tapped into before. Jade was right about one of the side effects of this drug - it had made my sadness stop. All of the drama with Nathaniel just didn't seem to matter anymore. I'm slinking around Plan X like the world is mine and I can possess anything in it; all it takes is a suggestive look, a subtle arch in my back, or the slightest touch of my hand, and any boy I want is at my mercy. A few girls continue to give me dirty looks and mutter bitchy things, but for the first time in my life, I don't care. I love it.

I'm in the DJ booth with Yoshi, Carmen, Ace and Bless, having the time of my life. Every song Bless drops unleashes a new rush of excitement and I am dancing like no one is watching. The girls are baffled by my behaviour but eventually they assume that I'd simply treated myself to a few too many drinks. If only they knew. If this small piece of heaven is all it takes to deal with all the bullshit that comes with being an Unfamous, then I want in until it has numbed every ounce of anguish left inside of me. I feel indestructible, something I've wanted for so long, and know I know the secret to having it…sort of. I need to find out what this little miracle is.

In the middle of the latest track by some alternative Hip Hop/RnB sensation, Tyson appears, seeming a little stressed out, but completely doable, just as he had when we'd first left the salon…and during our little test shot incident earlier. I have half the mind to tell him so, but I think better of it. Instead I ask, "You okay?"

He shrugs. "Not really, Angie's still moaning." I refrain from rolling my eyes. "I'm ready to bounce you know. You comin'?"

I nod, say goodbye to everyone, collect my stuff, and then we're off.

Due to his mood, I expected the drive back to campus to be an awkward one, filled with long silences and skirted issues, but my high allows me to converse so well that after 20 minutes of driving, Tyson and I are talking our regular rubbish. He vaguely explains to me what the munchkin is fussing about; unsurprisingly it's over his feelings for me, and Tyson being the type of person he is, feels guilty about it. He drones on about how upset she is, and I know that I should offer some friendly advice, but I can't seem to pay attention long enough to keep up. My mind keeps wandering back to Jade, and the feel of his troublesome mouth finally conquering my own. The only problem is, Jade isn't here, Tyson is, and I'm extremely turned on, craving to quench my thirst for lust. I sit with my thighs pressed tightly together, trying to focus on what Ty is saying for more than 5 seconds, fighting the urge to substitute my longing for Jade with him. Every time we stop at a red light I want to lean across the gearstick and kiss him.

It's normal for me to be aroused when I'm high, but because of the way that Jade had decided to give me the drug, I was hot and flustered before the high had even kicked in, and now that it has, those feelings are severely amplified.

45 minutes later Tyson pulls into the Brompton student parking lot in front of his building. I had talked him in to letting me stay the night in his dorm room, which he agreed to causally, seeing as it isn't something out of the ordinary for us to do, but my heightened libido had concocted other plans that would make this sleep over differ from the others. I keep trying to tell myself that what I'm doing is wrong and will inevitably put me in a sticky situation once it's over and I have come down, but the high has a hunger that demands to be appeased. I now want Tyson in the worst way, and this time, it's not because I'm feeling sorry for myself, but because the attraction the high is giving me is making me crave his body like an addict craves their fix. It's clear that sex

is the main objective of this mystery substance. Maybe this drug is the cause of Jade's notorious playboy ways; a need this strong cannot go unfulfilled.

We're now in Tyson's wreck of a room and I'm about to explode. The feeling has festered to the point where simply looking at him, hearing him, smelling him, adds to the slow build-up of the lethal arousal that aches so mercilessly in my lower region. I'm certain that if he so much as grazes my skin with his fingertips, my body will combust. I'm concentrating so hard on NOT surrendering to the strong pulsations that resonate through me, that I have to keep reminding myself to breathe and sit as still as possible. I can FEEL everything. My sense of touch is so intensified that I am able to distinguish the weight of my clothes on every part of my body, to the way that Tyson's body heat keeps on spontaneously reaching out and licking waves of warmth against my skin. Each time he shifts, his delectable scent wafts into the air, temporarily becoming more potent, more inebriating. I want to lean in, press my nose to the hollow at the base of his throat, and just breathe him in until I'm giddy. His voice is low and unintentionally enticing, like the sound of the bass when you're standing outside of a nightclub. It excites me to hear him speak; imagining how much more beguiling his voice would sound if I were to successfully push the boundaries of our friendship.

I close my eyes for a moment then look back at Tyson. He is lounging on the bed with his head rested against the wall adjacent to it, his braids fanned out across his broad shoulders. As he breathes and speaks, his 6 pack undulates underneath the black cotton material of his vest top. I want to stroke them, to feel them harden beneath my touch as he tries to impress me with his prestigious physique. I smile coyly to myself and shift on the bed, tucking my hands between my thighs to refrain from touching him. Tyson, oblivious to my war within myself, continues to speak. I squeeze my eyes shut again; attempting to lock onto his voice to figure out what the hell he is talking about now.

Eventually I'm focused enough to catch the end of his sentence; "...I know it's hurting her, but I don't know to shake you, Ri." My eyes snap open in surprise; how did the conversation make it to this point? And why has he chosen to go into this now when I'm less than lackadaisically trying to behave myself? I risk looking directly at him, trying to form a cohesive reply, to see his honey brown eyes already fixated on me, filled with boyish trepidation. I hold my breath. All I can think of now is the divine pressure of Tyson's body crushed up against mine. The thoughts are so vivid that my body is overcome with flashes of heat, as if my longing is already in motion.

There is a moment of stunned silence before I deliver my most honest reply to date.

"I don't want you to shake me. I want you to want me...'cause I want you." I say plainly.

Tyson freezes, completely thrown off by my response.

"What? But earlier on...when we were doing the test shots...you_"

"I wanted you." I confirm.

He furrows his brow, "Then why did you stop me?"

I shrug then lay back on his bed, sticking my legs in the air and twirling my ankles. "Because it was the right thing to do."

"Okaaaay..." he slides further down onto the bed, watching me curiously, "And now?" I turn my head to look at him.

"It would still be the right thing to do; but the difference is that right now," I drop my legs and roll onto my side, propping my head up with my hand, the spirit of my indestructible vixen seductively unveiling herself to him, "I don't care."

Tyson matches my position, his head sitting a little higher than mine due to his height advantage.

"And what if I care?" he asks quietly.

I smirk at him, "Do you?"

"I don't know."

He reaches out cautiously, battling with his principles, and places his hand on the curve of my waist. His eyes drop as he pulls us closer together. His warmth is all over me, his face a few mere inches from mine, and that's when the first shudder rips through me, exposing my desire in the most violent of fashions. It's so strong that my breath catches in my chest, and a loud, shaky gasp slips out. He hasn't even done anything yet.

"Should I stop?" he laughs nervously.

"I don't know."

My eyes dart across his handsome features, taking every detail in greedily. I want him in the worst way. I'd love to blame the urge on solely my high and Jade's illicit provocation, but I know that these feelings didn't just pop up randomly; I have always wanted Ty. I'd convinced myself that it was nothing more than a (recurring) passing fancy and that he deserves more, but right now I'm too uninhibited to act like I know better. I place my hand on top of his, running my fingers over the contours of his arms.

"Tyson..." I breathe, biting down on my lower lip and leaning in a little closer, wishing that he would summon the kind of reckless nerve that Jade possessed and just take me.

His eyes flit to my suggestive lips, then a glimmer of realisation that I really am allowing him to go through with this, flashes across his face. His whole stance goes from cautious, to the effortless seducer he had become when we were taking test shots in my bedroom earlier on. His liquid chocolate eyes meet mine again. Our underlying sexual tension is laid bare, hanging hot and heavy in the air, pressing down on the both of us, completely un-ignorable. Another uncontrollable wave of arousal shimmies up my spine. I blush, embarrassed of what he may be translating my reactions towards him into, as my body curls and convulses, practically screaming at him to take control.

Tyson smiles the carnal version of his signature crooked smile at me. "Yeah?"

I trace the cursive tattoo on his forearm, delighting in the way his face remains so controlled, yet as I stroke his dark skin, his prominent veins dance under my touch. I smirk arrogantly, gazing up at him from under my lashes with my best 'come hither' look. He leans in closer.

The tips of our noses touch just before his lips graze mine. I shudder again and swallow the air I had forgotten to exhale. We stay frozen in this compromising position, waiting to see who is going to push the other over the edge, our skin hot, and our breath ragged.

Tyson takes the reigns, skim his mouth across mine, catching my top lip between his slightly parted ones...then breaks the connection. He is teasing me - I want him even more. I stop tracing his tattoo and run my hand up his arms, revelling in the way the dimensions of his muscles feel as my palm glides over them. The strap of his vest top interrupts the skin on skin sensation for a second - I make a mental note to remove it as soon as possible. I reach the sweep of his neck, resting my hand where his pulse resides. Applying a little pressure, I coax him into coming closer still. Without hesitation he obliges, brushing his off limit lips against mine again.

Further illustrating my desire, I release a breathy moan; "Kiss me."

Tyson's hand creeps up the outside of my thigh, to the waistband of my jeans. His fingertips tease the small strip of skin between my top and the top of my jeans, just like Jade's did in the men's room at Sunday Slam. My flashback provoked shudder is all it takes for him to stop with the teasing and give in to me. He tugs my top over my head and kisses me with passionate ferocity. I moan as his tongue moves expertly against mine, and sigh as he nips at my desire-swollen lips. Every bite is aided by gentle sucking, accompanied by hands that tend to every inch of my flushed flesh accessible, until his fingertips dance along the edges of my black lace bra. His hands ascend, skimming across the textured material, and then with carefully applied pressure, he caresses me in soft circular motions. I sigh into his mouth, pressing my chest further into his practiced hands.

He kisses me harder. I moan louder. He goes a step further, yanking my bra down, allowing me to truly revel in his heated touch. I gasp and fling my head back, breaking the kiss; arching my back and panting like a lioness in heat. Tyson's talent, mixed with my high, is already overwhelming…and we'd only just begun. I'm delirious and almost unable to form coherent sentences.

"Don't...stop," I breathe, reaching to touch him below his waistline. I prod him gently at first, before slowly stroking my fingers along his length through his jogging bottoms. To my delight, Tyson sucks in a breath and drags me back to him, raining another selection of luxurious kisses from my swollen lips down to my neck while his hands continue to unhinge me. I apply more pressure and he groans, burying his face in the curve of my neck, no longer kissing me, but breathing heavily.

He rolls onto his back, taking me with him, then wraps his arms around my waist, crushing my body against his, and presses his lips against my neck once more. I discard my bra and am now resting on him in just my skin-tight jeans. Tyson admires my exposed flesh, first with his eyes, then with his mouth.

My breathy moans became vocalized, and once I start, I can't stop. I roll my hips to a steady rhythm, increasing the pressure and speed as the heightened sexual euphoria does away with my remaining inhibitions. My body is grinding against his body so vigorously that his bed is adlibbing my cries of exhilaration. Tyson groans again and bites down on my nipple. He grabs my hips, melding himself into my centre, encouraging an impromptu orgasm cry to tear through what in comparison, were mediocre moans.

I call out, clutching Tyson for dear life, trying my best to stabilise myself against wave after wave of climatic feedback. He watches me unravel on top of him, waiting for me to stop shaking before gently pushing damp stands of hair out of my dew-covered face. He leans up and kisses me softly, holding me tight as I relax into his embrace. Within the next 20 seconds we are both naked on his bed; me on my back with his hands creeping between my legs. He slides two fingers inside of me, reaching all the way up until he locates my g-spot. The sensation of his touch collides with the aftershock from my previous orgasm and robs me of my breath. Tyson smiles that sexual crooked smile of his down at me as he works his fingers inside of me, and just like that, I climax again.

He watches me jerk and writhe beneath him, pressing harder on my spot every time I show signs of regaining my sanity. The orgasm is never-ending, and I'm sure that if he doesn't allow my body to calm, that I will pass out in a blissful haze. I scream a vehement cocktail of religious words and profanity before Tyson takes mercy on me.

He moves away from the bed and stares down at me in all his glory, his soft baby hairs slick with sweat, his braids and lick-able six-pack quivering with every ragged breath he inhales, with his proud mouth erotically distorted into that damn smile. He looks like a mahogany God; so unequivocally beautiful that even though I have just experienced the biggest orgasm of my life, I become insatiable all over again. I reach out and run my fingers between the centre crevices of his abs, all the way down...

He grabs my wrist before I reach my desired destination, and pulls me to my feet. With his cocoa eyes locked onto mine, he skims his lips across the back of my hand then around to the sensitive part on the inside of my wrist where my veins criss-cross over each other. I shiver. He makes me feel wanted, desirable and powerful all at the same time. Yes, he's my best friend, and yes, on any other day I would not condone this sort of behaviour, but right now, I have a severely bruised ego, a broken heart and I'm currently experiencing an epic high, so I do the most selfish thing I have ever done to him. I know I will feel guilty about it in the morning, but right now I need to hear it...

"Do you love me?"

Tyson freezes caught off guard by my enquiry, then frowns at me. "How can you ask me that?"

I take him into my hands and work dexterously along his manhood. I ask him again, "Tyson; do you love me?"

He bites down on his lip and groans, "Rio…stop it."

I move my hand faster, tugging him forward so I can kiss his chest and paint transparent erogenous artwork over his abs with my tongue. My kisses trickle down to the base of his length, and then stop. I keep my lips connected to his flesh, tilting my face upwards to stare at him from under my lashes.

I ask one more time, "Do you love me?"

Tyson curses and throws his head back to break my gaze, trying to collect himself as best as he can under the current circumstances.

"You know I do!" he growls in frustration. I dip my head and smile to myself, satisfied with his response. I reward his admission with my mouth. Tyson curses and pants, tangling his fingers in my curls to guide me to please him the way he wants me to.

Before he is too far gone, he pulls out and takes a moment to collect himself again. I never imagined that Ty and I finally being intimate with each other would turn out to be so surprisingly well matched - maybe it's the drugs. There is a blue rawness between us that leaves me perpetually trembling with exaggerated anticipation.

Tyson exhales then pulls me to my feet, greeting me with a heady kiss on my mouth. He laces my arms around his neck, pressing himself firmly against me; skin to hard, hot, pulsating skin. To feel of his body pressing into mine with no fabric separating our natures makes me swoon with rhapsody. Tyson tightens his hold around my waist to keep me steady. His readjusted embrace allows him the first taste of my liquid excitement. He sucks in a breath and digs his fingers into the small of my back. The sting of his nails compliments my arousal, and makes me curious to see what he'll do if I push him a little farther.

I spread my thighs partially, shifting so that his key grazes the entrance of my lock. Steadily, I rock my hips against it. Tyson's voice box strikes a deep guttural chord. He buries his face in my neck and bites down -I sing the harmony.

I tilt and roll my hips so that with each calculated curl of my waist, the tip of his head almost slips inside of me -almost. The teasing transmits waves of pleasurable spasms through me and I wonder what this feels like to him. Does he think I feel as good as he does to me? Is he surprised at how effortlessly we are coming together too?

I rock forward again, taking a little more of him in than intended. A tell-tell sigh flows readily from between my parted lips. Tyson summons the will to pull back.

"Hold up a minute." he growls, holding me at arm's length. His teeth are firmly lodged into his lower lip and his eyelids shut so tightly that his lashes look tangled.

I slap his hand away and launch myself back to him, now hungrier for him than ever before. The small hit I'd been treated to has abolished my control. I grind on him, uttering soft broken pleads of desperation against his lips. Every time his rigidness grazes my centre, my knees buckle. The ache is back tenfold, screaming for a remedy.

"Rio, wait!" he grunts unevenly.

"I can't." I breathe, sinking my teeth into his bottom lip.

He growls at me and forcefully pushes me down onto the bed. "I need to get a condom, now stop making shit difficult!"

"Oh," I blush apologetically, "My bad!"

Tyson laughs adoringly and smiles his lopsided smile at me. I cross my legs.

"It's okay. I like that you want me so bad." he smirks leaning in for a kiss. I grab the back of his head and kiss him back; hard.

"Hurry!" Ty's smile spreads to the other side of his face and now both of his dimples are showing. I stare at him. "Seriously; hurry!"

While Tyson roots around for a rubber, I half stumble off of the bed and open his wardrobe door that houses his full length mirror to check my appearance - I want to look as ravishing as possible for our consummation. I smooth down my hair and fan the ebony curls out over my shoulders so that they spiral rebelliously down onto my bust, and poke my ass out a little. Tilting my head to the side, I make bedroom eyes at my reflection. I'd felt sexy at Sunday Slam, but now I feel like sex itself, moulded into dangerous chocolate curves, wearing nothing but an indulgently suggestive smile.

Tyson slides up behind me and rests his hand on the thickest part of my hips. He closes his eyes, kisses my neck and begins to explore me. Mesmerised by the amatory reflection, I observe my best friend undo me. I'm captivated by the sight of his hands travelling over my skin, squeezing my breasts, then disappearing between my legs. I gasp.

Watching Tyson touch me so intimately has my head reeling; I can't believe that this is really us reflecting back at me, chocolate on chocolate, melting and sighing, writhing and cursing. It's surreal. Every now and then his carnal eyes flit open to witness my reaction, and I respond more animatedly, aroused even further by watching him watch me like that.

"Tyson..." I breathe as I melt onto him.

Needing no more prompting, he turns my body 90 degrees so that my reflection is now in profile. I brace myself against the cool laminate wood of the other cupboard door, trembling with anticipation of his sweet torture. Taking me by surprise, Tyson grabs the back of my hair with one hand and my hips with the other, creating a deep arch in my back. He regards us appreciatively in the mirror, lines himself up, and enters me with breath-taking speed.

Maybe it's the thrill of Tyson (of all people) crashing into me over and over, or that I'm watching him do it that causes my mouth to hang open with absolutely no sound escaping. He groans, riding me faster and harder. I slam back into him to make the sensation travel deeper. In the short amount of time that we have been going for, I am already ready to let the demanding sensation transport me to that sexual limbo.

My insides tighten around him; as it squeezes, he curses. He releases my hair and reaches down the front of me, stroking up and down whilst pushing and pulling himself in and out of me with perfect synchronicity.

I can't breathe. My head spins and I'm biting down on my lip so hard that I can taste blood. My whole body is on fire.

"Tyson!" I cry.

The sound of my strangled pleas provokes him to fuck me harder. I clutch at the edges of the cupboard door. "Ty..." He exchanges the strokes for small, deep circles. "Ty-son... I can't...oh God!"

The orgasm summons every ounce of energy I possess, drawing the power from every available source; like a sex bomb filling up with extremely powerful orgasmic electricity. He slows, pulls all the way out of me, then delivers one earth shattering thrust that initiates the end of me. I tremble uncontrollably, screaming until my lungs are empty. Rampant rolls of heat sing in my veins. I can't stand, I can't move; I can't do anything but feel the vastness of my galvanized ecstasy. The more he sexes me, the faster I relapse into erotic euphoria.

It's not long before I hear him shout my name; reality is submerged in blinding white light.

20 Keep Calm and Carry On.

It's morning and I haven't slept a wink. All night I tossed and turned, watched TV, read Ty's text book on graphic design, went on Instagram, posted utter nonsense on Twitter, cleaned Tyson's room, had a long, hot shower, listened to music, woke Tyson up and had sex with him again, went back on Twitter once he conked out…this drug will not let me rest. I'm exhausted, but no matter how hard I try, I can't seem to fall asleep.

Tyson is attached to me; one leg entwined with one of my own, one arm curled over my chest. I trace my index along his sleeping face then gently press my lips to his forehead. No matter how bad things get, Tyson always makes an effort to protect me, even during times when I least deserve it; even when by protecting me, he is leaving himself open to be hurt…by me.

Memories of last night cling to me; the way we'd kissed, touched and fallen into each other without resignation after a lifetime of denying ourselves from that very experience. It felt so good, almost right even…except he's in a relationship and I'm a self-absorbed mess. Given my track record with his more intimate feelings, it was a foolish thing for us to do. As much as I won't mean to and don't want to, I'm so afraid that I'm going to hurt him. I scowl inwardly at myself, remembering how I had selfishly asked him if he loved me just so I could hear it from someone, just to soothe my ego. I hadn't said it back and he'd never even asked to hear it because he knew better.

I nuzzle closer to him and take his hand, pressing my lips to his knuckles before returning our intertwined fingers to my chest. I close my eyes.

"You're still awake." he states gruffly in his morning voice.

"Couldn't sleep."

"Me either. I was drifting in and out of it." Sighing he eases his upper half off the mattress, and the duvet tumbles into his lap. I readjust myself to suit his new position. "You stayed." He says quietly, stroking his hand along my back tenderly.

"You sound surprised."

He laughs, "To be honest, I am. I thought that you'd have snuck out and already be in the process of avoiding me until I came to hunt you down so we can talk." I stare blankly at the mounds of bunched up quilting before me, trying to think up a delicate way of nipping this conversation in the bud before it gets awkward.

"There's nothing to talk about." He stops stroking me.

"Rio, we had sex."

I roll onto my back and look up at him. "I'm aware of that." I laugh.

Tyson frowns. "Well are you aware that I cheated on my girlfriend with you; twice?"

Here comes the awkward part that I'd hoped to avoid.

I clamber into a sitting position then lean over the side of the bed to locate my jeans with the crushed packet of cigarettes that I'm prone to buying on social occasions in case I get bored so that I have an excuse to be somewhere else without looking like a loner. I stuff my hand into the back pocket and pull out the box. There are four cigarettes left in the box, and a cheap orange lighter crammed in there with them. After several attempts of trying to get the sparks to catch the gas, I spark one up and take a long drag.

"You've made it sound so sordid." I pout.

"Facts are facts Ri."

"Okay; well now that you've pointed out the facts, what happens now?" His hand scrubs his face with growing distress. Last night it was easy to pretend that there would be no consequences, but now faced with them in the bright daylight of mid-March, reality demanded to be dealt with.

"I have to tell her." He plucks the cigarette from between my fingers and takes a drag. Tyson isn't a fan of cigarettes. He'll smoke weed until his eyes turn red, but straight tobacco is usually a no-no for him. It's his misconstrued stoner logic that weed is less harmful than cigarettes because it's 'natural'.

"If you tell her, she'll hate you." I point out, watching him as he puffs away at my irregular nicotine fix.

"What else can I do? It's better she hears it from me that from someone else."

"You don't have to tell her anything. I'm the only other person that knows about this. You're my boy; I'm not gonna talk." Tyson pauses; he looks down at me with furrowed brows, studying me while he processes my response. I wait patiently for him to reply, but he doesn't. Instead he looks away and laughs bitterly, shaking his head. "What?" I ask.

"Nothing."

"It's not, *nothing*. Tell me what you're thinking."

Tyson takes another drag; this one is deeper, harder, like he's purposely trying to suck the tar out. Lungs filled to the brim with smoke get exhaled into the air, the thick ash clouds billowing out of his mouth into a never-ending stream of grey.

"What time is it?" he asks.

"Coming up to 8, last time I checked." He gestures to an empty cup covered with greasy fingerprints on the window sill. I pass it to him and he stubs the cigarette out then drops it inside it. The glow of the orange embers fade, as the remains of whatever small amount of liquid that was left in the cup, get soaked up by the ash.

"Don't you have a lesson to go to?"

I raise my eyebrow. "Are you mad at me?" He doesn't look at me. Throwing back the covers, he slips out of the bed and tugs on his joggers. "Ty?" I snap. He's ignoring me and I don't like it.

"What?" he snaps.

"You're being weird. Am I missing something?" I ask, confused.

"I guess not." He shakes his head again, "Look, I'm about to jump in the shower, I've got basketball practice. Let yourself out." I contemplate badgering him further but his abrupt shift in attitude has derailed my good mood and I can't wait to get out of there.

"Fine!"

I spring out of the bed and tug on my clothes in the same manner he had. All I've done is assured him that I won't tell anyone about us; something like this getting out would damage his relationship. She already suspects his feelings for me, so confirming it won't do him any favours. As far as I'm concerned, what she doesn't know won't hurt her and he gets to keep his girl. I'm just doing what any good friend would do. I move to tell him this but he's already stepped into his boxy en suite student bathroom and closed the door behind him. "I guess I'll see you later then?"

"Yeah. Later." He switches the shower on. I reach into my back pocket for another cigarette and slam the door behind me.

I head to my dorm in last night's outfit, puffing on a cigarette with the grace of a crack fiend and my hair looking like it had seen better days. It is still fairly early, so luckily there aren't many students milling around to throw me judgemental glances. Now that I'm away from my personal safety bubble (Tyson) and as pepped up as ever, my mind gradually shifts towards the one thing I had been trying to avoid thinking about; my ex-boyfriend and my ex-girlfriend. I'm not sure how composed I will be when I finally see Fontaine, which is part of the reason I wanted to stay with Tyson – I don't want to see her - but unfortunately, we live in the same flat so I can't dodge her forever. I'm dreading the awkwardness and unavoidable confrontation that will take place when I do. What is bothering me the most is that there is no way to predict exactly how much I'll have to fight to keep myself together when I see Nathaniel. I could easily break down and let it all out with the usual tears or a tantrum, but I don't want to.

I have a flashback of him kissing Fontaine in near enough the same fashion that he used to kiss me. It's one thing to have knowledge of your ex being intimate with someone else, but it's another thing altogether to actually witness it. I had already had to endure the Georgia saga, and believe me that had burned enough; it had made me feel like shit. Nathaniel being with Georgia made me angry because of the way that they had come to be, coupled with the fact that it was her who had tormented me endlessly; the bitch! Now, the prick is repeating the entire ordeal with a girl who is meant to be my friend. It's a double betrayal - at least Georgia was my enemy. The worst part is that both of them are perfect examples of the kind of girl a demi-god like Nathaniel Gibson belongs with in society's eyes; tall, light-skinned model types, with long hair and looks for days…and then there is me. If I had felt inadequate before, that was nothing compared to how I felt now that'd he'd moved his focus onto Fontaine. I can't stand it. I can't stand him.

I decide that I'm going to skip my lesson. I'm not ready to face Nathaniel yet, especially after going as far as to punch him in the face. I shiver, recalling him ready and willing to swing back. If Fontaine hadn't stopped him, Nathaniel would have hit me. As the revelation dawns on me again, I slow my walk; look at what we've done to each other. I hate admitting it, but Nathaniel is right; we are not good for each other. We possess too much power over one another other, which for a stable ex-couple would be fine, except Nathaniel and I are far from stable. Instead of forgiving and letting go, we cling to memories of what used to be, which prevents us from moving on, and then we use our connection to manipulate and control one another, both of our miseries loving company so much that we weren't willing to let each other be happy without the other, yet we're so fucked up that we can't even be happy together.

Even as I rationally analyse our pathetic situation, I still don't want to accept him being with Fontaine...or anyone else for that matter. He is mine and she's supposed to be my friend. She can't have him, even if I don't want him anymore. I really don't want him anymore. I want to be at least halfway okay again. I want to have power over the masses, not this one boy. I want to be loved and feared, in equal measure because I had successfully become a 'Boss Bitch', in charge of my clique and able to command unwavering attention from the best of them. Being hung up on my ex is only hindering that. I had forgotten how excited I had been to attend uni, and how mature and empowered it would make me feel. I have foolishly allowed Nate to distract me from my main focus -me. When you're in love, you sometimes allow the other person's existence to consume a lot of your time. They become part of you, that's why it's so hard when it's over because you notice their absence so much, it's like a piece of you is missing. Sad isn't it? It's not until they're gone that you realise how much of your life you have not been living because you're too concerned with being with them, and not concerned enough about yourself.

From my memory bank, Jade's nonchalant voice echoes reminding me that if I wanted to run with the 'elite crowd', that I can actually do it. I just have to toughen up and let bullshit slide. I'm always the victim, always the one who needs saving and I'm tired of it. It's about time that I force myself to be strong enough to save myself. I can do this; if I really focus I can finally move past this crap and be the Rio that I came to be. Fuck Nathaniel!

With a wave of renewed determination, I take a deep pull of my cigarette and quicken my pace, smiling wickedly, glad that I had hit him. It's not like me to revel in harming someone, but after everything Nate has put me through, I feel I deserve to revel…just a little.

21
Scandal.

I decide to spend my self-enforced free period in the campus café, opting to be indirectly alone; surrounded by people but essentially by myself. The girls were just starting to move about in their rooms when I got in, so I quickly jumped in the shower then out the door before I'd be forced into interacting. I order a coffee, accompanied by what tastes like a day old pastry, then take a seat by the window. As I pick at my snack whilst trying to concentrate on remembering to forget about Nate, I hear my name called. I peer up from my plate to see Yoshi bouncing towards me, dressed in her usual urban-oriental street style. I sigh inwardly as she smiles brightly and plonks herself down in the seat next to me.

"Hey Ri!" she says in her soft voice, air kissing both of my cheeks. I attempt to mirror her heartfelt grin, but it doesn't reach my eyes.

"Hey Yosh, what are you doing here?" I ask in the most cheerful tone I can muster. I sound like I've just come off of anti-depressants.

"I'm meeting Manny."

"Oh?" I don't mask my surprise, "You guys doing more clothing stuff?"

Yoshi shakes her head, "Nope, we're just…hanging out." She drops her head a little, hiding her obvious blush behind a curtain of dip dyed hair.

"I wasn't aware that you and Manny just…hung out. I wasn't aware that you hung out with any other guy but Ace."

Yoshi's blush deepens into a shameful scarlet hue at the mention of her boyfriend's name. She leans towards me conspiratorially.

"It's a new thing I'm trying. No one knows about it…well aside from you now, obviously," she whispers, paranoid that the rest of the café is dying to hear our conversation. I don't blame her; the way gossip travels in enclosed communities (in our case, university), speaking a little too loudly in public spaces could result in a whole lot of drama you hadn't anticipated. In Yoshi's case, it's completely understandable as to why she is being so cautious. The consequences should people start running their mouths about her and another guy 'hanging out' could be fatal.

"How long's this been going on?" I enquire, matching her volume.

"Today's the first time. Manny's wanted to hang out for a while, but I always said no cause of…well…you know…" she trails off not needing to elaborate any further. I nod. She hasn't hung out with Manny before because of Ace and his volatile temperament. I'm surprised that she's telling me this; Yoshi has always been very adamant about her privacy. Sipping at my too hot coffee gives me a reason to keep quiet in the hope that she will continue. "He's just a cool guy; easy to talk to, laid back, funny_"

"Hella cute!" I interject with a wicked grin.

Yoshi blushes again, "Yeah, I guess he is." I set my coffee down.

"You like him, don't you?"

"Don't say that!" she gasps, eyes wide and shooting around guiltily to see if anyone had heard my scandalous assumption.

"Oh my God you do! Aww, that's so cute. He likes you too you know," I smile, nudging her playfully.

Still looking around warily, Yoshi's smile flattens into a hard line, "Well it doesn't matter; I'm with Ace." I roll my eyes and the bubbly atmosphere dissipates back to the way it was when I was sitting here alone.

"Fuck Ace!"

"Rio, don't start," she sighs. I tear of a piece of my stale pastry and crumple it into my mouth, then take another small sip of coffee too soften it up so that I can chew without straining my jaw. I don't care to discuss him. "Look, I know what you think of him, but he's getting better. He's really working on his temper." she says in his defence.

"Mmm hmm." I'd heard it all before; 'he's changed, he promised it would never happen again, he loves me'…it's all bullshit! Growing up I had heard my mother spout the same nonsense to Aunty Michelle about my dad. He would promise to be better and she'd naïvely choose to believe him because she loved him. Things never got better. Each time he'd mess up and decide that he'd want to make things right. For a short period of time, there would be the routine honeymoon period in which my dad would treat my mother extra nice. He'd compliment her, buy her things, and take her out; but eventually something would arise and he'd flip the switch and become worse than he was before.

I look over at my foolish friend, trying to contain my annoyance at her familiar naivety, then speaking in a quiet, controlled tone of voice, I ask, "How is he 'better', Yosh?"

"He's more patient with me. We go out, we talk about our problems…he's apologised for everything he put me through, he buys me gifts and the sex_" I hold up my hand. I've heard enough.

"How many times have you gone through this 'make-up' routine?"

Yoshi frowns, "He's really trying this time, Ri."

"No, he's recycling the cycle. Ace is a bastard, Ace will always be a bastard and you deserve better!" I snap. The door of the café swings open and in strolls Manny, smiling to himself , bobbing his buzz cut coolly to the conscious rap music from his Dre Beats headphones. I cock my eyebrow and gesture in his direction with my head. "Better -just walked through the door." Yoshi turns to look at him. The moment their eyes meet, their faces light up like Christmas. "Ace doesn't make you smile like that," I point out. Yoshi's doll like face returns to mine and I see her struggle to play down the childlike happiness that Manny had inspired.

"That's his friend Rio, which means he's just my friend," she tells me seriously. "Yes Ace has his flaws, but he has never been unfaithful, and when we're good, we're really good. You of all people should know how hard it is to find a faithful guy these days." I narrow my eyes at her. "Ace isn't perfect, but I know he's mine, and I won't jeopardise that."

Manny is now within earshot so I decide to hold my tongue for the time being. In truth, I don't really need to respond; she only took a shot at me to make herself feel better. Yoshi is more aware of the true state of her relationship than any of us, but she is my friend - I don't want to have to stand by and watch her crumble because she is too disillusioned to know when enough is enough. Manny is clearly the better option! Yes, Ace is Mr Unfamous Event Guy, so being his girlfriend has its perks. Yoshi is granted instant respect from our peers, she can get into pretty much any Unfamous run event for free, he keeps her suited and booted in designer labels, takes her pretty much anywhere her heart desires, and despite his huge personality flaw, he is all about her. Those are the pros, but in my opinion, they will never outweigh the cons. If she'd stop being so fixated on the perks and take a rational look at her relationship, she'd realise that there are loads of other guys milling about who are capable of giving her all of those things without laying their hands on her; but that's the problem with our generation: impatience. We all want instant gratification for whatever, or whoever, we invest in because society has trained us into rushing through our adolescence. The moment we experience our first liberating taste of independence, we run wild with it, flinging aside the simple innocence's of childhood and moulding ourselves into premature adults -most of the time with the wrong mind set especially when it comes to relationships.

Every girl wants to meet Mr Magnificent; the magical man who appears to have his shit together, who adorns us with all he has to give mentally, emotionally, physically, financially and more if he has it (in Unfamous terms; status because we'd all love to be part of a power couple). Instead of us holding out, and waiting to find a man who encompasses all of these things, we latch onto those with some of the above and rely on the rest of it to come together through the potential that we see in them, even if they don't see it in themselves. What we need to realise is that even though some men have the *potential* to be better, they may not *want* to be better. If they can skate through life being a bastard, that's what they'll do. The only reason they continue with any unsavoury behaviour, is because we allow them to. We bamboozle ourselves into accepting their bullshit, because we'd like to think that we're Wonder Woman – the exception to the rule, that can save them with our love, nurture them with patience, loyalty and understanding, and help them grow into the potential we've dreamed up in our heads of who they could be. We're still little girls who really don't know any better either. Some of us try so hard to save our partners when we should be saving ourselves instead.

Manny is still smiling when he reaches us.

"What are you two gossiping about?" he asks in his easy tone.

"You," I reply before Yoshi can tell him otherwise. She scowls at me while I cheerfully drain the contents of my cup.

"Oh really?" he blinks. Every drop of blood in Yoshi's body now resides in her cheeks, burning brightly while her slender leg twitches as if she'd love nothing more than to swing her white spiked Creepers into my shin. Amused and charmed by her discomfort, Manny laughs "All good things I hope."

"Of course!" she giggles nervously, dropping her head so that her vibrant tipped hair hides her coy expression from him. Manny unconsciously bites down on the corner of his lip and shifts closer to her in a way that I can't clearly distinguish as predatory or protective. It made me think; is Yoshi's obvious vulnerability the thing that draws guys in? - the way that she strikes people as someone who needs protection? If her height, petite frame and almost childlike features weren't enough, her timid nature only amplified her fragility. It makes sense; men love a damsel in distress because then they can save them and be their hero. This analogy makes me think of Tyson and the sad fact that I don't want to be saved.

Yoshi tilts her head slightly to peer up at Manny from under her long lashes, and says in her softest, most sugary voice, "I'm just gonna finish up with Ri quickly, then I'll be right over, k."

Manny smiles at the thought of having her all to himself.

"A'ight. I'm gonna jump in the queue; do you want anything?" he asks gesturing to the counter.

Smiling sweetly, Yoshi shakes her head.

"Manny, you don't have to get me anything." she giggles. His responsive smile warms my heart; the man is besotted. He clearly adores her, even if he doesn't say it directly, it's as plain as day. You could bottle up his energy towards her and sell it as a love potion; it's that powerful. This is the guy she's meant to be with; I'm sure of it.

"I know, but I don't mind. What do you want?"

Yoshi sticks the tip of her pinkie finger in her rosebud mouth and squints at the menu lining the back wall, then shrugs.

"I dunno; surprise me! Get me something sweet."

Manny eyes her suggestively as if he is offering up himself. Yoshi doesn't miss it. She blushes again and goes back into bashfully hiding behind her hair. Manny smirks and strolls off coolly to join the queue.

"You so like him!" I tease.

Yoshi sighs and address me with a serious look on her face, "Look Ri, I know you mean well but I'd prefer if you stuck to your own love life instead of meddling in mine. I don't want Manny to get the wrong idea and now thanks to you, he has." I want to tell her that I wasn't the one that had arranged to meet up with him in secret and had been all cutesy with him a moment ago, but I decide to keep that to myself too.

"Good. You two look cuter together anyway," Yoshi fights the smile threatening to break out across her face because she so badly wants to be stern with me right now. She narrows her eyes at me.

"You're just saying that 'cause we're both Asian." The smile breaks through anyway.

"Amongst other things," I laugh. "Yosh, all I'm saying is that Manny is already sprung on you and you haven't even slept with him yet; that's a huge achievement in this day and age, plus, he can offer you everything that Ace does…minus the 'you-know-what'."

She frowns at me. "Rio, I appreciate your concern, but I can take care of myself. I love Ace okay! Of course I don't like it when he acts out, but I know that he'll take care of me before anything or anyone else."

I furrow my brow. "That doesn't sound like love; sounds like dependency."

Yoshi snaps, growling in frustration and throwing her hands in the air. She glares at me, completely fed up with my opinions.

"D'you know what? It doesn't matter what you think of MY relationship because it has nothing to do with YOU, and to be perfectly honest, I think that the only reason you're so up in my business is because right now you can't bear to handle your own!" she hisses jabbing her finger at me. "We all have our vices Ri. The same way you'll never understand why I love Ace is the same way I'll never understand why you love Nathaniel."

I'm slightly taken aback by her outburst. Yoshi is the meek one, but today I'm seeing a whole other side of her that I never knew she had in her. Not only did she give me a good telling off (despite the fact that I'm right), she's also having secret hang out time with Manny. Maybe she is finally growing a backbone.

Undeterred, I place my hand on hers and speak softly in an attempt to diffuse the situation; I don't want to upset my soft spoken friend any further.

"I hear you Yosh, and I'm sorry for getting in your business like this, but it's only because I care. I've seen how bad an abusive relationship can get. I just don't want you to get hurt."

"Fair enough, but doesn't seeing that hurt even more?" she points towards the window where Nathaniel is casually strolling by with his arm laced around Fontaine's shoulder. They are chattering away, smiling and laughing as if being together is second nature to them. As if it's okay.

Yoshi watches me cautiously, waiting for me to snap. I keep my expression neutral. Seeing them together hurts as much as it did the first time; it angers me. I want to look away and pretend that it isn't happening, but envious curiosity spurs me to look on until I can't take it any longer. Their relationship is developing right in front of me. I wonder if Nathaniel replacing me with one of my own so-called 'friends' bothers him at all. Does his conscience occasionally nip at him and bring forth any guilt? I mean, how could it not? Fontaine didn't spring up out of nowhere; he had met her through me, so wouldn't that connection always be there? Would he look at her and think of me at all? And if he did, would it take away some of the joy of the moments they shared because she served as a constant reminder of the lovesick girl he had thrown to the wayside? I hope it does.

As they walk along the almost pristine cosmopolitan Brompton campus, dragging their feet contentedly across the red brick walk way that runs in front of the café, Fontaine loops her beaded arm through Nathaniel's leather clad one, and rests her curly head against his broad shoulders as she speaks fondly to him. He tilts his head down and smiles affectionately as if she had said something adorable, then they both laugh. My chest tightens. How can they be happy together knowing what they did to me - what they are still doing to me? It isn't as if I'm some irrelevant part of their lives, especially not his, so how come it seems so easy to act as if my feelings don't matter? Or maybe they're not acting. Maybe blocking me out comes naturally to them because it's easier to be together that way.

I understand that everyone has the right to be with whom they choose and to be happy, but when happiness comes at the expense of someone else's, as a friend or a former lover, out of respect, loyalty even, wouldn't you think twice about doing something so hurtful? They are selfish; him even more so than her. Nathaniel is one of the most sought after boys on campus, he can have practically any girl he wants, so why Fontaine? Why my friend? It isn't as if I'm overrun with so many friends that I won't notice losing one - and I will lose her…not that I particularly want her around anymore. Eventually, she will stop apologising and trying to make me believe that she regrets her decision, and she will choose him completely. That's just the way it goes with some females; they are so relationship-orientated that losing a partner will always leave a bigger void than losing a good friend. God forbid they feel unwanted.

Yoshi's petite hand squeezes my shoulder sympathetically.

"Forget about them Ri; if this is what they will do to you so willingly, then you don't need either of them. The people that truly love you don't hurt you on purpose, and if by chance they do, they do what they can to make it right."

I try to smile at her, but my face won't cooperate. Instead, my mouth presses into an awkward line that conveys no distinguishable pleasant emotion. I turn my head back to the window, feeling the weight of Yoshi's pity call to the part of me that I vowed would stay hidden from now on. To my displeasure, Nathaniel notices me. Fontaine is still nattering away happily, oblivious to my presence, but Nathaniel's knowing eyes watch me cautiously. He knows it stings, but obviously that isn't enough of a reason to stop. I notice the corner of his lip turn down and his proud shoulders sag a little.

My phone jingles and vibrates briefly from a compartment inside my bag, notifying me that I have a message. Quickly, I reach for it, welcoming the distraction. I read the words on the screen with a blushing smile knowing that Nathaniel is still watching me and that as much as he would like to act like I don't matter all that much anymore, it will still irritate him to some extent to know another man is able to push away the sadness he brought me. A curtain of long, dip-dyed black hair tickles my face as Yoshi tries to peer into my hand

"Who's got you smiling so hard?"

I turn the phone so she can see before looking up at Nathaniel as her mouth falls open with a thrilled gasp, and say very clearly, making sure my lips formed the name as flawlessly as the appearance of its owner; "Jade."

Nathaniel stops looking at me, and the muscle in his jaw flickers.

In her excitement, Yoshi snatches my phone out of my hands, staring at the message with awe.

"Honestly, I don't even know why you care about stupid Nathaniel when his upgrade times a million, is hot on your tail."

I giggle triumphantly and take my phone back. "I'd hardly say he's 'hot on my tail' Yosh."

"Um, hello? THE Jade Washington is messaging you during daylight hours. Not many girls have that privilege."

I shrug. "I guess not, but I don't want to read into it too much."

"Okay, well read into that beautiful dress he bought you, and that date to Malaysia Blaq he took you on, and of course, those messages he sends you that you *won't* show us." Yoshi grins, nudging me and accompanying it with a cheeky wink when she mentions the latter.

I smile to myself and read his message again for a temporary ego boost:

I wanna c u.

It would be nice to enjoy the fantasy with her, but sadly, at the tender age of 18, I am already too jaded to revel in things that seem too good to be true because they usually are. Jade is far too cavalier in his dealings with women for me to even entertain the notion that he wants anything more than to get between my legs again - but next time without the crying and clothing involved.

"Yosh, Jade's a notorious playboy who's loaded, so splashing a bit of cash in the pursuit of pussy is hardly him going out of his way. I'm not reading into anything." I say firmly.

I message him back:

Why?

"I hear you, and given your current situation I can see why you'd think that way, but Ri, what if he wants more than that?" she asks picking up her bag, getting ready to join Manny who had been sitting at a table on the other side of the café anxiously looking up at her every few seconds; bless him.

"He doesn't. He's Jade 'womanising' Washington." I reply, instantly disposing the foolish notion that Jade could possibly want anything else from me.

"That's my point though. If Jade REALLY wanted to get you into bed, from what I've heard of him, he would have done it already."

"Not likely." I snort.

"Have you seen him?" she quips.

"Have you spoken to him? The guy's a self-important ass!" I argue.

"He's beautiful!" I roll my eyes at her. "All I'm saying is that if Jade wanted you, he would have had you and there'd be nothing you could do about it."

My phone jingles again:

I feel like it. I'm comin 2 get u in 20.

I'm tired. I couldn't sleep a wink.

Lol, Pills are a bitch aren't they? Ur not going 2 sleep netime soon.

I just remembered, I have a seminar.

Skip it.

I roll my eyes and drop my phone back in my bag.

Yoshi stands.

"You gonna see him?" she asks with a knowing smile.

I kiss my teeth, "He's not giving me a choice."

Her smile grows. "Told you! That's kinda hot."

"It's annoying."

"Annoyingly **hot**! Don't act like you're not even a little intrigued. Look, just give the guy a chance; he might turn out to be just what the doctor ordered." Her slanted Lolita eyes travel over to Manny. He smiles at her sweetly and her cheeks turn rosy.

"I think you just like to see the good in everyone Yosh." I pick up my things and pull her in for a hug.

"Everyone's got good in 'em Ri, some people just need someone to be brave enough to find it. Give him a chance."

22
The Breakfast Club.

At 10:30 I step out of the elevator. My heels click clack off beat against the linoleum floor in the lobby to my flat as I struggle to keep my pace steady. I'm coming down; tiredness is setting in and I can't wait to crawl into bed. Sleep, how I've missed you.

"I don't like to be kept waiting. You'd do well to remember that, miss."

I jump and clutch my chest.

"How on earth did you get in here?" Jade kicks himself off the wall he is leant up against, scowling at me.

"One of your flat mates let me in." He swaggers towards me, pushing his silky hair off of his face with effortless vogue attitude. His eyes travel over me, and the scowl fades. "I must say, you look very fuckable in those shorts, miss. You all set to go?"

I roll my eyes and readjust my bag on my shoulder haughtily. "I told you I have a seminar Jade," I snap, side-stepping him. He matches my movement.

"And I told you to skip it." His voice is cool but his eyes betray him, boring into mine, warning me not to dispute with him any further if I know what's good for me.

"I don't have to do what you tell me," I challenge grouchily, glaring up at him, trying my hardest to match his intimidating stare from more than a foot beneath him. He smirks approvingly.

"You will though."

I arch my brow, "And who's gonna make me?"

I go from vertical to horizontal in an instant as Jade picks me up and flings me over his shoulder. My legs flail feebly in front of his chest as I try to kick myself free, and my head dangles over his back giving me a great view of his pert ass, that is being hugged by a pair of black cotton Ralph Lauren boxers and chinos held up by a red Hermes belt.

"PUT ME DOWN!" I yell swinging my heels near his face in the hope that he'd get spooked that I'd vandalise his pretty face. He laughs then locks one tattooed arm across the back of my knees. "I MEAN IT JADE. PUT ME DOWN THIS INSTANT!" I opt to use my hands and smack his back, my ascending tiredness putting me in no mood to mess around. A moment later I release a surprised yelp as he spanks me back on my bottom.

"Keep still."

I yell all the way to the car, drawing attention from the entire campus. Jade doesn't even bat an eyelash as hoards of students stare at us in disbelief, although I'm not sure if it's down to the predicament that I'm in, or that I happen to be in that predicament with Jade '*bratty*-man' Washington of all people. He fishes a spliff out of his jacket, lights it and smokes as I scream, occasionally subjecting me to another swift spank whenever he felt I had gotten too many hits in.

Eventually he slides me off his shoulder, putting me down next to his Lexus and pulls the passenger door open. He takes a pull of his spliff, closing his eyes as the drug seeps into his system.

"Get in." I raise my eyebrow and take a step back. Jade, in turn, props the spliff between his lips and raises his hand in front of his face, studying it with a sadistic grin. "I quite enjoyed spanking you. Give me a reason; I'd be glad to do it again."

"You wouldn't dare!" I hiss rubbing my bottom absentmindedly.

Jade pulls me to him and runs his hand slowly down the curve of my spine, and over the firm curve of my ass. I tense up, poising my hand, ready to whack him again. He catches it and pins it behind my back, then lowered his lips to my ear.

"I'll put you across my knee if you like." I freeze, determined not to let a shudder run through me, then jerk myself out of his grip. He is staring at me again, his rainforest eyes hot and heady. "Rio, get in the car, please."

I narrow my eyes at him to save myself from looking completely captivated by the collaboration of his appearance and smooth manner.

"Do I have a choice?"

"Not really." he chuckles softly.

I surrender and step into the vehicle. He closes the door after me with a victoriously smug smile. I fold my arms across my chest and pout. Maybe Yoshi was right; it hadn't taken much but a sultry look and some manners and I was like putty in his hands. Had he been holding back in his attempts to bed me? I think back to that night at Malaysia Blaq; the lavish setting, how immaculate we both looked, the extravagantly seductive manner in which we had danced, his body hot, longing and crushed against mine as he whispered 'Say yes…', then again to the way he had handled me the night before in the men's room at Sunday Slam when I stupidly spoke that little word which has probably landed me in something I'm too inexperienced to handle -"Yes." He hadn't held back. He'd known I was going to say yes; low and behold, I had. With that being said, he knew the effect that the drug would have on me; an inexcusable horniness, yet he chose to distance himself from me after I'd taken it. Am I really fighting against sleeping with Jade, or is Jade simply biding his time until he's ready?

He pulls out of the student parking lot and flicks on his state of the art sound system. Kelela fills the car.

"You look beat." he comments annoyingly.

"I told you I was tired, you know I haven't slept. What exactly did you expect?" I snarl through gritted teeth.

He throws me an amused glance as his Lexus weaves expertly through the midday London traffic.

"Okay, moany!"

"Whatever."

"You hungry?"

"No."

"Well I am. I could do with some Bagel Monarch; you know you could too."

"I'm fine, thanks."

He rolls his eyes and passes me the spliff. When I don't reach for it he presses the roach to my lips.

"Don't be boring! I hate boring people. Smoke this and we'll go get some food for your munchies, have a quick road trip and then you can sleep. Sound good?"

It didn't, but I don't want him to call me boring again. The word sounded like such an insult coming from someone as interestingly eccentric as Jade 'peer-pressure' Washington. I accept the spliff and take a quick hit.

"Sleep where?"

"At my place."

"I'm not going all the way to Herring with you."

"I've got a studio loft in Earls Court. It's where I stay when I want to get away."

"Get away from what?"

"Stuff." he snaps, annoyed by my questions. "So you on it yeah?" he says softly. He's so mercurial, the way he jumps from one emotion to the next. I'm beginning to notice a trend with him; a majority of the time he's his usual charmingly arrogant self, then if prodded he snaps, but it never lasts long, it's merely his grip on his self-control slipping from his firm grasp. Whenever his temper reveals itself, he quickly covers it up again. I find it fascinating.

"We've already established that I don't have any choice in the matter, so yeah, whatever." I pout.

He flashes me a wicked grin and presses harder on the gas, sending us flying down the road just before the red light catches us. "That's the spirit!"

By the time we reach Bagel Monarch, I'm lit, my stomach is growling like I haven't fed it all day and my mouth is parched. Jade tells me I can get whatever I want; it's on him. We walk back to the car with enough food to feed an army; bagels with varied fillings ranging from smoked salmon and cream cheese to chicken and sweet corn, patty and coco bread, Jamaican bun and cheese, apple crumble and custard, plantain and two cans of KA each. I devour my food the minute I'm back in the passenger seat while Jade drives to the next unknown location. He mumbles that he needs to pick something up from his friend quickly. I don't respond. I'm eating what tastes like the best food on the planet; I don't care where we're going.

The Lexus pulls up in a suburban cul-de-sac in front of an impressive 2-storey detached house. There is a woman in a Hollister jogging suit in the front yard, bent over a flower patch that ran along the front of the house. She looks up when she hears the car and smiles. With a heaped spoonful of apple crumble custard on its way to my greedy gob, I freeze. The woman is the last person I'd expected to see.

The woman is Georgia Daniels.

23

Breaking Bad.

I drop my spoon into the Tupperware.

"What the fuck are you playing at?" I hiss at him, watching a heavily pregnant Georgia waddling down the curved pathway that snakes itself through the freshly cut grass from the front door to the pavement. Even as a mother to be, she still manages to intimidate me; her beauty still manages to overshadow mine, those piercing green eyes still see right through everything.

Jade's jaw tenses briefly as she continues to smile at him.

"I didn't know she was going to be here," he says quietly. There is an edge to his voice that leads me to believe that he is as 'happy' to see her as I am.

Georgia comes to a halt at the end of the pathway. I sink further into my seat, anticipating her tirade of snide comments about my presence.

"Well aren't you a sight for sore eyes, Mr Washington!" she beams. Jade mimics her grin.

"Hello beautiful; you good?"

"Yeah, I'm all right babe! Carter's inside, I'll let him know you guys are here. Hello Rio!"

I raise a suspicious eyebrow. Georgia has never greeted me before…EVER, so I'm unsure of what the natural reaction for your arch nemesis being courteous is. I settle with an awkward 'thumbs up' and a tight smile that isn't fooling anyone. Jade glances at my response and stifles a snort.

He turns back to Georgia, "Okay darlin'; we'll be in, in a sec." Georgia smiles again and waddles back up the path, into the house.

I whack Jade in the chest. "Excuse me? WE are not going anywhere! I don't like Georgia, YOU do! Why the hell did you bring me here? And what is she playing at, about *'Hello Rio!'* -fake ass bitch!" I fume.

"Didn't I just say I didn't know she was going to be here?"

"Well now you know. I'm not going in!"

"It's Carter's house; he's your friend, is he not?"

"Depends on how you look at it." I reply stubbornly.

Jade rolls his eyes at me and gets out of the car. Instead of heading to the house, he comes around to my side and opens the door.

"Get out of the car, Rio." he orders in a controlled voice.

"What for?"

"Because I want you to."

"Didn't anyone ever tell you that you can't always get what you want?"

Jade kisses his teeth, reaches into the car, and pulls me out so hard that I shriek and stumble into him. He secures his arm around my waist to keep me from falling, then pins me up against the car, pressing his solid frame against me.

His incautious green eyes bore into mine; "No." Without warning, he bites down on my lower lip, tugging gently at the flesh as he pulls away. "And for the last time; stop hitting me." He releases me and stalks over to the house whilst I remain frozen against the car trying to remember how to breathe. "Hurry up and close the door so I can lock it." he yells over his shoulder. I do as I'm told.

Carter glowers at the two of us when we walk through his front door. I already feel out of place in his home because Georgia is here, so Carter not being happy to see me only adds to my discomfort. Jade is unfazed; he ignores the glowering and reaches out his hand to slap his friend's own. Carter accepts the gesture stonily. I don't know what to do, so I stand awkwardly behind Jade, wishing to be anywhere but here.

"I see you two are getting better acquainted." is the first thing to come out of Carter's mouth. Jade smirks at him.

"I see I still don't have your blessing." He turns to me, "Mr Johnson doesn't want you getting involved with me. He thinks I'm bad news."

"That's 'cause you are, you cocky bastard!" Carter growls.

Jade laughs, shrugging apathetically, "Better to be a cocky bastard than a cock-blocker mate. Stop looking so serious and let's prepare for tonight's festivities. I'm sure the girls can keep each other company." He throws a sardonic smirk my way. My expression now matches Carter's.

Georgia smiles at me. "Sure. Would you like a drink Rio?"

"No, I'm good. I'm gonna go wait outside."

I turn to walk back out when Jade pulls me back. He leans in close to my ear and asks me in a hushed tone, "How do you expect her to respect you if she knows you're still scared of her?"

I pause briefly, mulling over his words. He's right; I have to withstand being alone with the she-devil, no matter how much the prospect of it makes my stomach churn. I'd wanted the opportunity to really prove that 'College Rio' and 'Uni Rio' are two completely different people - now is my chance. Conceding to the latter option, I sigh and roll my eyes.

"Fine!"

The boys are downstairs in Carter's basement, and Georgia has disappeared off into the kitchen while I sit rigidly on the cream leather sofa in the lounge, trying my hardest not to project the full extent of my nerves. My stomach is in knots and my palms are slick with sweat. Had the TV not been on, the sound of my vociferous heartbeat would probably be audible too. I haven't seen Georgia since the end of last term, when I had destroyed her fabricated family plans with Nathaniel at Jade's house party, and now here I am sitting in her baby father's lounge while she waddles about fixing a drink for me that probably has poison in it...well, her saliva at least. It's a complicated fix to be in; I mean, how exactly do you handle consorting with the enemy? Are we meant to make conversation, sit in silence, or rip into each other? I'd prefer the latter option, but my mother had taught me better than to enter someone else's home and be the cause of any trouble. I cross one leg over the other and fiddle with the hem of my shorts; I can be polite...I guess.

Georgia waddles in with two cups in her hands; she hands one to me. I thank her starchily and set it down on top of a coaster on the coffee table without taking so much as a sip. I'm not putting the poison notion past her. She fixes her eyes on me and takes a long gulp with a small smile on her face, as if she can read my thoughts.

"Not thirsty?"

"No."

She snorts in amusement at my mistrust and sits down at the opposite end of the sofa, fluffing some pillows and placing them behind her before she leant back. Her belly pokes out even more in this position; it's surreal to see her like this. Georgia had always had an enviable figure, which is now subsequently disfigured because in a few months she would be someone's mum - poor child.

"Well, I must say I'm amazed at your physical improvement; you look fantastic!" she exclaims. I furrow my brow – did Georgia Daniels just pay *me* a compliment? Never in a million years did I think I'd see the day. She's freaking me out. I have the urge to march downstairs and ask Carter where the real Georgia is and what he has done with her. She continues, "At a glance you could almost pass as one of us…almost." Ah, there's the Georgia we all know and love!

"I was wondering how long you were going to keep up your little nice girl act," I chuckle. Georgia keeps smiling.

"I think I'm being very nice, *Rio*!" she sneers my name. "I could tell you that your weave looks cheap, that your crappy make up is doing nothing to hide those disgusting blemishes, and that your thighs are so humungous that those shorts – which by the way, you might as well burn – look like they are cutting off your blood supply; but that would be mean. I'm in a better place now." she smiles.

You can't hit pregnant women, Rio…at least not below the neck. I fight not to show it, but her words touch a nerve. I can feel my college insecurities beginning to resurface and I hate it. This is what she used to do to me all the time when I was with Nate. Back then I was too much of a coward to put a stop to it - I'm not a coward anymore.

"Oh! Well I suppose being a pregnant 18 year old university drop out, stuck with the baby father you don't want must have it perks!" I reply snidely. Georgia's catlike eyes glare at me.

"Carter loves me Rio, who loves you? From what I hear, it's certainly not dear old Nathaniel. He's too busy loving the lighties behind your back as usual. Weren't this one meant to be your friend; that lippy hippy chick right?" Dammit! How did she find out when she's not even around anymore? I sigh inwardly; Rio, you know how the Unfamous scene is; everyone knows something about somebody, so eventually everyone knows something about everybody!

I keep my expression controlled and feign nonchalance.

"Nathaniel's not my problem anymore and he shouldn't be yours either, so stop fasting in his business; it's pathetic! You're lying here knocked up for Carter and your mind is still on the boy who was never willing to have you as anything more than a part-time side chick when I wasn't available." For the first time, Georgia looks slightly stunned, and I have to admit, so am I. Who knew I had it in me? Standing up to her properly, feels awesome! Not one to let a good thing go to waste, I continue. "You actually have some nerve, you know! Even after doing such a disgusting thing to Carter and him taking you back in spite of it, you'd still rather be Nathaniel's whore, wouldn't you? I've told Carter he deserves better_"

"I AM 'BETTER'!" she screams! She's now sitting upright, shaking, with her fists clenched so tightly that her French tips dig into her palms. Looks like I pushed a button. I settle back into the sofa and smirk triumphantly, openly revelling in my victory.

"You're a conniving, spiteful, ungrateful little bitch who deserves nothing but misery."

Georgia blinks and for the first time ever, I see tears in her eyes. Maybe it's her hormones – you know how emotional pregnant women can be.

"Well thanks to you, misery is all I've got! You sit there feeling sorry for Carter, looking down on me like I'm the bad one, when you don't even know what he's really like. People aren't afraid of him for nothing Rio. Why do you think that I was so desperate to pin this baby on someone else? Now I can never get away from him, and it's all your fault!"

"Well the 'someone else' you tried to pin the baby on belonged to me, and now I can never get him back, and that's all YOUR fault, so excuse me if I don't give a fuck! Your life is what you made it; deal with it!" Georgia looks away as the truth hits home. After a moment she starts up again, unwilling to back down and let me come out on top because she's still convinced that I'm beneath her.

"You and I both know that Nathaniel should never have belonged to you in the first place! You're not one of us, and you will never BE one of us. This is MY world, these are MY friends, and believe you me; they will chew you up and spit you out without a moment's hesitation. Sooner or later, we can all spot a faker." She leans in closer, "When we're through with you, you're not even gonna know what hit you. You're gonna be so irrelevant they're gonna have to make a new word for it. I'm more than happy to do the honours, bitch!"

"Is there a problem, ladies?" Georgia stiffens. Carter looms in the doorway watching us –when did he get there – with Jade stood behind him looking highly amused; at least someone thinks this is funny!

"Yes there is; your baby mum is a heinous bitch. I'm ready to go - have you lot finished whatever it is you're doing?" I ask haughtily, getting to my feet. Carter frowns.

"Yeah, we're done. Gee, you look a bit tense, everything okay?" he asks. Georgia composes her expression and smiles at him.

"I'm fine babe!"

"Maybe you should go upstairs and lie down."

"No. Honestly, I'm fine."

"Georgia, go and lie down please. All this stress isn't good for our baby." He says it kindly enough, but I can detect an underlying warning in there somewhere…or maybe I'm overthinking it because of what Georgia said about me not really knowing what he is like.

She gives him a tight smile. "Yeah, you're right. I'm gonna go lie down." She hoists herself out of the sofa and waddles up the stairs out of sight. Now Carter's attention is on me. I shift my footing.

"What were you two arguing about?" he asks.

"The usual."

"Answer the question, princess."

"I just did." I scowl. Despite the obvious tension in the air, he smiles his Cheshire cat smile. I shiver; I don't think it will ever stop creeping me out.

"I suppose you did." He looks up the stairs in the direction Georgia had gone and runs his tongue contemplatively along the top row of his teeth.

"Maybe leaving them alone together wasn't the brightest idea." Jade chimes in, still entertained. I roll my eyes at him.

"No shit, Sherlock! Can we go now?" I huff.

Carter raises his eyebrow in amusement and peeks at Jade; Jade isn't so entertained anymore. He walks over to me slowly, purposefully, his grave gaze fixated on my mouth. Carefully, he takes my face in his hands and rubs his thumb across my lips. I jerk my head to shake him off but he tightens his hold.

"You and that mouth…hmmm," he groans thoughtfully. The throaty sound pulls me back to a few minutes earlier when he had me pinned up against the car. Absentmindedly, I bite down on my lip. Jade's eyes darken, making my stomach flip –he never fails to beguile me at random intervals, luxuriating in his custom made dysfunctional erotic niche, spurred on by being challenged. I have yet to figure out if he enjoys the challenge because being Jade 'submit-to-me' Washington, he rarely has to come across it, or because he likes using sex as a weapon to regain dominance. All I know is that whenever I step out of line, he always reels me back in by doing something that shakes me to the core and robs me of oxygen.

"Carter, we'll see you at The Spot later on." he says, still staring at my mouth.

"You're bringing her with you?" Carter asks, not masking his surprise.

Jade pulls my lip free from my teeth.

"I am now."

24
Loft Music.

I'm panting, I can't walk straight and my energy levels are so depleted that I could possibly drop dead at any given moment. Why does Jade have to live on the top floor of this six storey building with no elevator? As I lean forward with my hands on my knees struggling to catch my breath, all I can think is 'It must have been hell trying to move his furniture in.'

Jade stands regally by his front door, his breathing perfectly normal and un-humiliating, watching me with a bored expression.

"You're being dramatic." I still have enough energy to lift my head high enough to glare at him.

"You just made me trudge up six flights of stairs. I'm lucky I'm not dead!" He rolls his eyes and slips his key into the lock.

"You need to work out more." He turns his head enough that I can see a quarter of his profile and the corner of his mouth curls up into a downplayed mischievous grin, "I can fix that." Pushing the door open he steps aside and spreads his arm out to welcome me in. I straighten up and continue glaring at him.

"I don't need you to fix anything." I snap stomping past him into the flat.

"Maybe you don't; I can picture you being more of a D.I.Y girl." he chuckles closing the door behind me making me blush furiously. What a cringe-y thing to say to someone. I want to deny it, but I feel he will read into my denial and assume that it confirms his embarrassing comment. Before I can take another step, he pulls me back gently so that we are standing face to face. He lets go of me but he doesn't move back; I have the urge to. I can't function well when he is this close. "But," he continues, leaning in a little closer, "I think you'd enjoy hiring a professional to do the job." I swallow a mouth full of air, doing my already parched throat absolutely no favours.

"I don't think I will." I am lying through my teeth and he knows it, but I jut out my chin anyway to make it seem as if my fib is almost true. Jade reaches behind me and flips the light switch. A contemporary arrangement of clustered spotlights hangs from the centre of the high ceiling bursts brilliantly to life. Jade keeps his hand pressed against the wall behind me and I get the feeling of being closed in on.

"Suit yourself," he shrugs "Take of your shoes please, miss."

He stalks gracefully across the large room, pulls off his jacket and flings it onto a chair by the wall. The flat is almost empty but filled with eccentric character. Exposed brick walls adorned with a few pieces of contemporary artwork, wooden flooring, mismatched renaissance furniture, a vintage record player posted on a small distressed chest of drawers, a small dining table set down the far end near a simple blacktop kitchenette and an open futon for a bed with the sheets unmade. Tucked away in the corner behind a large stack of vinyl records I notice a guitar propped up on a stand.

"You play?" I ask pleasantly surprised as I kick off my ankle boots.

Jade moves to the kitchenette and pulls a bottle of vodka from one of the cupboard units.

"Yes." He grabs a glass then a bottle of lemonade from his fridge.

"You any good?"

He shrugs in a non-committal way as he pours himself a drink. It's 1:30 in the afternoon.

"I think so."

"You think so?" I edge further into the room, not quite sure where to place myself. It feels strange to be in Jade Washington's house. Who'd have thought that we'd ever reach this point? Certainly not me! When Jade first spoke to me I assumed it would be one of those empty fleeting affairs of nothing more than a polite greeting because I am Carter's friend, and that I'd spend the rest of my life never getting another chance to encounter him up close again because I'm so irrelevant that he'd forget who I am; and yet, here we are, alone together in his studio flat.

"I only have my opinion to go by. I don't play for anyone but myself."

"Oh, well that's a shame. I'd have liked to hear you play a little something." He raises his glass to his lips, staring at me from over the rim.

"Not gonna happen." he says with abrupt finality. He downs the vodka and lemonade in one go, then turns his back on me and pours himself another. I feel a twinge of disappointment.

"You can grab a t-shirt from the bottom drawer. I'll be quiet."

I furrow my brow, "Huh?"

"I don't like outside clothes in my bed. Wear a t-shirt. You're tired, are you not?"

"Oh, um, yeah." In getting swept up in the surroundings and present company, I'd forgotten about my tiredness and now I'm not sure that I am even tired anymore. I can't sleep in Jade Washington's bed; I feel so out of place.

I set my bag down a toddle over to the chest of drawers. Once I find a t-shirt that I think will be long enough to cover me up as decently as possible, I hold it carefully, afraid that should I hold it carelessly , he'll find fault in it.

"Um, where I am I supposed to get changed?"

"You can use the bathroom if you feel uncomfortable." He knocks back another drink.

"Okay." I scurry off at an embarrassing speed.

When I return I'm even more awkward, continuously tugging the hem of the t-shirt down to cover my granny panties and hoping that Jade won't notice the slight stubble on my legs from where my hair had already started to grow back after being shaved the previous day. I wish I could embody sexy super vixen Rio again like I did last night. Here in Jade's flat I am a nervous bumbling better preened version of my college self. Jade is sat at his dining room table rolling up several blunts, drinking more vodka and lemonade whilst listening to Van Hunt at a volume slightly loud enough to cut through the silence. He doesn't look up. Quickly I slip into his bed, feeling a little less self-conscious using the duvet to shield my indecency.

I lie down and close my eyes praying that the need for sleep will overrule my nerves and settle my heartbeat, but it doesn't. The smell of Jade 'someone-should-totally-bottle-his-scent' Washington is all over me and it only unsettles me further. I readjust myself several times in the hope that the right position will aid my mission, but it doesn't.

I sit up.

"What's The Spot?"

"I thought you were tired?" he asks with gentle amusement peering at me over his shoulder mid roll. He lifts the partially perfectly crafted blunt to his mouth and sticks his tongue out then drags it along the sticky line to seal it up. I shift in the bed.

"I am, but sleep seems to be evading me right now." I giggle anxiously.

"I'll put you to sleep." He replies casually without intentionally trying to make it sound sexual, but it's Jade, so it does. I think he's incapable of turning it off.

He pops the just rolled blunt in his mouth, picks up another and tucks it behind his ear, then grabs his glass. He's had a few drinks already and yet he's seems so in control of his body. He doesn't sway, stagger or misplace his footing once, he just glides in his fluid rebellious male model catwalk fashion, then lies next to me on his futon; on top of the covers. I notice then that he's changed into a worn pair of dark denim jeans and a plain grey hoody. Even dialled down, he can't help but look like he belongs on the cover of Nylon magazine.

He takes the blunt perched behind his ear and passes it to me before taking a swig of his drink (not backing the whole thing this time) and lighting his own.

"It's a very exclusive party, and one of our best kept secrets, so if anybody asks you about what you were doing tonight, just tell them you were chilling with me and that's all." he instructs.

I try to control my expression when I come to the realisation that the silly rumours aren't actually so silly. Word on the street is that the Unfamous hold secret gatherings and that if you aren't a part of the top circle, you can't attend…not that it would be possible even if you wanted to; no one ever knew when or where these parties were, and now here I am being taken to one by Jade Washington. Does that mean that I have obtained some kind of status; I must have! These invitations aren't warranted to just anybody. I press my lips together to suppress my excitement because the more I think about it, the more irritatingly giddy I get.

I take the lighter from Jade to light my blunt, using smoking as a distraction. The smoke hits the back of my throat harshly; this is some serious stuff. I don't want to look like an amateur and risk becoming a hot spluttering mess

"Oooookay! What do people do at *The Spot*?"

"Whatever we want, darlin'! The only rule of The Spot is that you do not make it common knowledge. It's for us and us only,"

"By 'us', you mean the Unfamous?" I blurt out.

Jade raises his eyebrow, "The who?"

For crying out loud Rio, why on earth would you reveal to Jade 'king-of-all-kings' Washington, your stupid name for the social cult that he practically runs! I need to put this weed down before I say something else that makes me want to die a thousand social deaths.

"That's my name for the 'elite' bunch; Unfamous – underground celebrities," I explain awkwardly making sure to avoid eye contact that I don't have to see the judgement on his face. You can't buy this kind of embarrassment!

Jade takes a pregnant pause then bursts out laughing. "You're weird; you know that right?"

I blush and fiddle with the hem of his t-shirt. Jade 'too-cool-for-school' Washington thinks I'm weird! I frown; I've blown it now, haven't I?

Jade reaches over and smiles; lifting my head up with the tips of his fiery fingers. It's the first time he's touched me since we got here.

"Don't be embarrassed miss, I like weird." he winks.

I blush and pull back, opting to use my original distraction tactic of smoking the too strong blunt. I can handle spliffs just fine, but blunts are bigger and have no tobacco in them to dilute the weed, hence the effects are more powerful and hit you a lot quicker. The fat head glows brightly as I timidly inhale blueberry flavoured blunt paper and kush, taking small puffs to stay on the safe side while Jade takes long lazy drags, washed down with yet more vodka and lemonade.

"It's a bit early to be drinking." I comment, the drugs making me a bit more forward as the high ascends.

"Says who?" he replies disinterestedly.

I shrug "I dunno; it's like one of those rules –no hard drinking before five." He makes a face.

"That's not one of my rules."

"Do you even have any rules?" I snort. I've never seen or heard of Jade behaving in a way that resembled any moral limitations. He pretty much just does what he wants and gets away with it.

"I do. One."

"And what might that be?"

"Don't get attached." He blows a smoke ring into the air. It floats upwards, expanding as it goes, before disappearing into nothing.

"Makes sense; I never figured you for the relationship type." I'd meant it to come out as a passing comment, but I detected a hint of bitterness which was odd because I don't even want to be with Jade, he's a dog. He's one of those gorgeous young men who are the epitome of the eligible bachelor, but you can never really have them. Maybe that's the thing that draws me to him; the fact that I can't have him. People have a habit of wanting things that we can't have. Jade is like a presidential hotel suite; you can live in its lap of luxury for a few nights, but eventually you have to check out so that the next guest can have their time. He belongs to no one and I doubt that, that will change anytime soon.

He gives me the dreaded eye roll.

"What is it with you women and your fixation with relationships? When I say that my rule is not to get attached, I mean in general. I don't get attached to people, ideas or things, period."

I perk up a little –this isn't a direction I'd expected him to go in.

"Why?"

"Getting attached to something is like setting yourself up for disappointment because nothing stays the same; change is constant. Life is better when you just go with it."

I blink at him.

"Um, yeah, I guess that makes sense…"

"You don't sound too convinced."

"I'm trying not to get attached to the idea." I joke. Jade smiles warmly, appreciating my lame attempt at humour.

He turns towards me and takes the blunt away from me without asking then sticks it in his mouth alongside his one and takes a boastful drag before setting them both down in the ashtray that rests between us. I open my mouth to point out that I hadn't said I was finished only to have my words get tangled in streams of marijuana smoke when he grabs me and presses his mouth to mine, blowing everything he had just inhaled into my system. His technique lacks the gentle, sensually consensual etiquette of a blowback. It's a dominant force without a hint of romance, that makes me want to fight against him…and submit at the same time. The effects hit me instantly, sending my high into overdrive.

"Just go with it." he murmurs against my lips. He releases me and goes back to smoking his blunt as if nothing had happened while I sit there stunned and seriously high.

"What the fuck?" I slur, clutching my head as I begin to sway.

"It's time for you to go to sleep. At the rate you were smoking at, by the time you got your head down there wouldn't be much sleep to be had. You're welcome." he smirks.

"No I'm not welcome!" I moan as the room starts to spin, "I'm high…like really high. Oh my God, I don't like it. Why did you do this? Make it stop!" I panic.

"Calm down; you're fine. Whatever you think is wrong with you is all in your head." he says in a soothing tone.

"Is that meant to help? 'Cause it's not!"

"You just need to focus on something, that's all. Take a deep breath, lie down on your front, and close your eyes." I raise my head briefly to throw him a 'do you think I'm an idiot' look.

"I bet you'd love that!" I sneer. "I'm not having sex with you, Jade."

"I know," he replies unfazed, "I've decided that you're not allowed to."

I furrow my brow in confusion, "What?"

He reaches across me and takes my left arm, pulling it over to my right so that my body (which is too tripped out to fight against him) follows, and I flop into the position he had instructed me to…be it in a less than elegant fashion. He lies alongside me, still not coming under the covers with me and places his hand on my back. He begins to run his palm over it in the shape of the infinity symbol. By and by the panicked feeling subsides. I close my eyes and focus on his touch.

"I'm not going to fuck you," he continues in the same soothing tone, "Not until you beg."

I frown, "Beg? Never in a million, billion…*gazillion* years will I *beg* you to have sex with me."

He continues rubbing the tranquil pattern onto my back.

"You will."

"C'mon, it's time to go."

My deeply comfortable sleep is disturbed as I'm shaken awake by the headliner of my dream. Normally when I wake after dreaming of Jade I merely shake my head and force the lurid visions of us into the little black box at the back of my mind where I store everything I don't want to think about, and get on with my day. Engulfed in his scent, with his hand stirring me from my slumber, and the knowledge that he has banned me from sleeping with him until I beg him stops the usual dismissal of my thoughts of him from vanishing. In my dream he had pulled out his guitar and played for me in nothing but a pair of ripped jeans that hung low on his hips. The song was foreign to me and I have no recollection of how it went now that I am conscious, but it was transcendent; it spoke to me, the collection of hyper-melodic notes convincing me into stripping for him while he watched me unwaveringly as his deft fingers plucked at the nylon strings of his instrument. I was fascinated with the way he clutched the beautiful instrument, touching it in poetically articulate ways that caused it to cry out it's appreciation to him. In the end my body replaced the guitar and he was strumming at my anatomy making me sing the same desire surrendering melody.

As you can imagine, it's no easy task to wake up to someone when mere moments ago you had been imagining yourself wrapped around them, but now that you're awake, reality delivers the harsh reminder that your dream is just that; a dream.

I grumble and tug the duvet over my head to hide my 'morning' face from him. I discreetly rub around my eyes, nose and mouth hoping to rid those areas of any unbecoming gunk. The task is laborious; I'm still dog tired and a little high so I can't function effectively.

Impatient as ever, Jade kisses his teeth and rips the covers off of me. I curled up in the foetal position with his t-shirt hitched up around my waist and my granny panties and stubbly legs on full display. I shriek and yank the t-shirt down, bringing my legs up towards my chest and tucking them in under it as well.

"What's your problem?" I snap grouchily, glaring up at him with smeared panda eyes courtesy of my mascara and eyeliner.

"Oh good, you're up! Put your clothes on, we've gotta move." He drops the duvet at the foot of the bed out of my reach then saunters over to the table where he is rolling up more blunts accompanied by another glass of vodka and lemonade. Is this all he's been doing while I've been conked out?

Once he's seated with his back to me, I hoist myself out of the bed grabbing my clothing from on top of the chest drawers that I'd taken his now over stretched t-shirt from, and zip into the bathroom. When I emerge with my visual sins removed/hidden, Jade is bouncing around his loft with his hair in a top knot, a black bandana tied round his head Tupac style, and his Ray Bans on, playing air guitar like a pro and singing along at the top of his lungs to none other than Duran, Duran 'Her Name Is Rio'. He knows it word for word.

My mouth falls open.

"Is this really happening right now?" I whisper to myself. Stunned by his song choice, vibrant display of hip thrusting, cool strutting and spinning, I can't help but admire him. He is clearly very intoxicated; his energy is electric, he is free, alive in a way I've never witnessed face to face. I envy him a little. He's changed his outfit to a black Guns 'N' Roses t-shirt with the sleeves ripped off, an acid wash denim waistcoat, black skinny leather trousers with a thick silver link chain hanging from two belt loops, and tan Timberland boots. He looks like a rock star, and I in turn feel like his number one groupie.

He spots me in the corner and runs over to me like an excited little boy, grabbing my hands and tugging me into the centre of the loft. I squeal as I stumble after him, wondering how this man can be so off his head but still move so gracefully when I have problems putting one foot in front of the other while sober.

"What are you doing?" I giggle gaily as he takes me in his arm and dips me.

"What does it look like?"

"Like we're dancing to Duran, Duran in the middle of your loft."

"Then that's what we're doing."

"Yes, but why?" He spins me three times then dips me again. I squeal again, laughing as he lifts me back up and wrap my arms around his neck.

"How do you feel right now?"

I shrug, feeling too awkward about my answer to verbalise it.

"I dunno."

"Don't get all shy on me now miss, I've had you in much more compromising positions than this." he reminds me with a cheeky grin, "Are you having fun?"

"Yes." I admit sheepishly.

"Then that's why." he smiles.

"But it's so random."

"For once in your life, stop finding issues where there aren't any and just go with it. You gotta get out of your head and live in the moment babe. Don't overthink this; enjoy it!"

Without warning he grabs both of my hands and suddenly we're spinning around and around, faster and faster, screaming and laughing until we collapse dizzily onto the bed in a breathless heap with Jade on top of me. As our laughter subsides it's replaced with a hard-hitting electrical current that crackles and sparks between us. Jade removes his Ray Bans and stares down at me with smouldering green eyes and a roguish smile on his permanently puckered lips. My breath hitches in my throat.

"I wanna kiss you," he tells me, leaning in a little closer, "I've been wanting to do it all day, but right now especially." His mouth hovers over mine and my heart rate increases dramatically. I want to tell him that I've been thinking the same thing, but my bashfulness won't allow it.

I close my eyes and tilt my face up, offering my mouth to him. I feel the slightest tickle of Cupid's bow, and then suddenly he's not there anymore. Confused, my eyes snap open –he's over by the record player, stopping the decks from rotating and lifting the needle to be the record back.

"Get your stuff babe. We've gotta shoot back to Brompton so you can get ready. The location is a bit of a drive."

I frown at him. "What was that about?"

"What was what about babe?" he glances at me with a knowing smile on his face.

"Why didn't you kiss me?"

"Did you want me to?" he asks feigning ignorance.

"Well duh!" I snap getting to my feet. I stomp over to the chair pushed against the wall and drag my bag up onto my shoulder with sexual frustration, muttering angrily to myself internally for allowing myself to fall for another one of his erotic mind games.

"Come here then." His voice has changed to the honey-dipped baritone that makes me weak at the knees. I turn to look at him; he's leant against his dining table, beckoning me to him with his index finger. I'm still annoyed. I don't move.

"No."

"Why are you being childish, babe?"

"I don't like being toyed with." I pout.

"I'm not going to toy with you, I'm gonna kiss you. Come." He extends his hand and bites down on his lip. I would have run to him, but I didn't want to look too eager. I take slow measured steps, with my eyes to the ground, not lifting them until I reach him. He produces a small blue pill, holding it between his index finger and his thumb then sticks it on his tongue and swallows it.

"Want one?"

I furrow my brow, "Is that that Molly stuff again?"

"Yes ma'am." He produces another out of thin air and offers it to me. I eye it sceptically.

"I dunno…"

"Oh don't start all this again. It's a harmless little party drug and we're going to a party like you've never seen before. It's the perfect combination!"

"I'd hardly say it's harmless." I frown.

"Did anything terrible happen to you while you were on it?" I shagged my best friend, but I'm not gonna tell Jade that.

"Well no but_"

"Then what's the problem? It's not like its cocaine babe. It's just one tiny little Molly to get you in the best frame of mind for tonight's festivities. Didn't you feel amazing last night?"

"I felt hot and slightly dizzy." I cross my arms.

"And after that passed," his arm snakes around my waist and pulls me to him, closing the gap between us. With his free hand, he reaches behind my neck, wrapping my hair around his fist and pulling downwards in a diagonal direction, exposing my profile to him. His heated lips find the hollow behind my earlobe and his kisses it slowly. "How did it make you feel baby?" he purrs against my skin. It made me feel sort of like how he's making me feel now; desirable, confident, but to the power of 10 with a shot of indestructability, and I had loved every minute of it.

"Amazing." I breathe.

"Exactly," he kisses me underneath my jawline, "Once you've experienced Oz, what's the point in going back to Kansas?"

"How poetic!" I scoff.

He raises the hand that has a hold of my hair so that I'm forced to look into his hypnotic eyes.

"How true."

He puts the second pill on his tongue and leans in.

25
The Vapours.

It's a little chilly outside but Jade is driving with all the windows down in order to counteract our drug provoked body temperature. The last of the evening sky is visible when we set out; burnt oranges, reds, pinks and purples bleed into each other as Londoners retire to their homes. That's the thing about Monday's, the urge to go out is overshadowed by the promise of relaxation after having to kiss the weekend goodbye the previous night and drag yourself out of bed to go back to robotic normality, which is generally the case for most people in this hustling, bustling city, but for not us.

We enter my flat and instantly hear the girls chatting and squealing excitedly in the communal kitchen at the end of the hall –Fontaine is with them. Had I been sober I would have probably snuck into my room without a peep, but I am high, Jade 'VIP' Washington is with me, and soon we'll be heading out to a secret Unfamous soiree that the girls and I had assumed was hearsay. I'm feeling kinda bossy right now and I want to flaunt it so that they can see that **I'm** still the queen of this castle.

I grab Jade by the hand, "Come say hi to the girls with me." He looks down at my hand grasping his, but says nothing and lets me drag him down the hall. I let go of it just before we step through the doorway into the kitchen, assuming that maybe I'm being a bit too forward, in the intimate sense. We're not together –I'm not sure what it is that we are doing exactly, I'm not sure that whatever this thing that we're doing even has a label. Our generation has made the dating game so misconstrued that it's more acceptable to have sex with someone than to hold their hand, or in some cases, kiss them, because those things are considered *real* intimacy; not sex. To hold someone's hand, kiss them on the mouth, or cuddle with them holds a hell of a lot more weight than sex because there is the implication of romance, and in a society where romance has become a luxury, we reserve simple gestures like that for people who mean more to us than a call at 2am asking to 'come and *chill'*.

"Hey Car, hey Yosh!" I beam, purposely not acknowledging Fontaine's existence. The girls look up and the tension thickens the air instantly. Carmen and Yoshi glance between me and Fontaine, who is frowning at me, offended that I never greeted her. What did she expect?

"Hey Ri, can I talk to_"

"You guys remember Jade right?" I cut Fontaine off as he steps through the door at just the right moment.

"Evening ladies." he smiles, exuding his effortlessly sexual charm. Smugly, I register the looks of surprise and adoration on each of their faces.

"So that's where you disappeared to." Carmen grins, clearly impressed by my guest. He takes my hand of his own accord and their eyes bulge further. My smile widens.

"Yeah, sorry about that. I kidnapped her for the day. I don't intend in giving her back yet either." He rubs his thumb back and forth slowly across the back of my hand. The girls don't miss a beat.

"Oh, and why's that?" Carmen asks looking at his simple display of affection.

"We're going out." I reply casually, not wanting to make a big deal of it as it's supposed to be a secret. I want to show Jade that I'm cool enough to hang with the big boys.

"Aww, you guys are so cute!" Yoshi squeals girlishly. Carmen nods in agreement.

"Well, have fun! Ri, I want *full* details when you come back." she winks.

Jade glances down at me, his expression morphing from charming to smouldering.

"I haven't decided if I'm going to give her back yet." he smirks, talking to them but staring at me. I want to look away, but he's unleashing the full force of his emerald orbs on me, holding me under his spell. The atmosphere of the kitchen shifts dramatically and everyone falls silent. Jade and I are the main attraction.

"Can you lot go and eye fuck each other somewhere else please?" Carmen teases, but I can detect the envy hidden in her tone, and I love it! Yes, I love that I'm making my friend jealous – does that make me a bitch?

Without breaking his gaze, Jade releases my hand and places it on the small of my back, adding pressure to navigate me back out of the kitchen. "Let's go to your room." The way he speaks in his guttural tone makes that simple sentence hold so much weight.

"But Rio, I still need to talk to you!" Fontaine pipes up again. I don't bother wasting my time looking at her when I respond -looking at Jade is a lot more fun.

"And I still don't want to hear it. Now if you'll excuse me."

I react to Jade's gentle prodding and walk out of the kitchen. I don't want to hear what she has to say. I'm with Jade Washington and great times are ahead. Everything else is irrelevant.

At around 11pm Jade and I are zipping across town, high off of more Molly and Mary Jane, blazing the Disclosure's hit 'White Noise' with all the windows down. I'm alive again, even more so from experiencing this awesome high with Jade; he is freedom!

...That's probably the drugs talking.

We've been driving for over an hour and I'm getting a little antsy from being trapped in the car for so long. I can't wait until we reach our destination so that I can stretch my legs and get '*turnt up*' with the Unfamous. I've been toying with the possibilities of what it will be like -a party this exclusive has to be phenomenal for it to be kept so under wraps. I have to make sure to be my 'best self' tonight, I can't go embarrassing myself like I did at Jade's party last term -that's what they all remember me by. Tonight is my chance to rebrand myself as one of their equals and I'm determined not to mess it up.

With Jade's impeccable talent for putting outfits together, I'm rocking my simplest, but hottest smart casual look to date. I'm in all black; cat suit, leather jacket and Timberland, with my gold Cuban link chain, plenty of rings and door knocker earrings glitzing it up. My curls are pinned on one side and wild on the other, and my makeup is simple; cat eyes achieved by my liquid liner, false lashes and plum coloured lipstick. After giving me the once over to make sure that I had executed his suggestions correctly, Jade demonstrated his approval with a quick make out session on my bed. I had to redo my hair and lipstick afterwards.

Jade takes a turning off of the main road and the street lights become fewer and farther between. Up ahead I can see the coastline. He pulls over and switches off the engine.

"Open the glove compartment," he instructs me firmly. I open it; inside is a black satin blindfold and nothing else.

I raise my eyebrow at him, "What's this for?"

"It's for you. I told you, the spot is a secret. You're a first timer, tonight will determine if you are invited back again. Just in case they don't want you back, they don't want you to be able to find it." I frown. Is there no end to the self-importance of the Unfamous? It's bad enough that this soiree is a secret thing, but now I have to be blindfolded so that I can't return until I have been given their approval. How bloody pretentious!

"Seems a bit excessive."

"Maybe," he agrees, "But we're not exactly a crowd known to do things by halves. A little excess speaks volumes," he reasons. "Plus," he pulls the blindfold from between my fingers slowly so that the smooth material tickles my palms, "I like the idea of blindfolding you. This gives me the opportunity to kill two birds with one stone." he jokes darkly. I squirm in my seat. Under the dim street lights, Jade's eyes glitter with excitement. "Turn around and close your eyes." he orders me in a crushed velvet tone.

I narrow my eyes at him; I don't want to let him blindfold me, I don't trust him enough. "Is this really necessa_"

"Rio!" he warns, his green eyes flashing as his careful mask of complete composure drops for a moment. "Stop overthinking this and just go with it. It's the only way you are getting into that party. If you refuse I will call you a cab and you can go back to your uni."

"You've got to be kidding me!" I guffaw. Jade watches me laugh in silence, waiting with irritated patience while I get it out of my system. My hysterics quieten down when I realise that it's not a joke; if I don't let him blindfold me he *will* send me back and I *will* miss out on the one experience that could potentially boost my social status so dramatically that I will never be referred to as Nathaniel's desperate, loser, ex-girlfriend ever again. "Oh, all right!" I huff, shifting in my seat so that my back is to him. I let him blindfold me, which he does with a deliberate slowness.

"What can you see?" he asks once the blindfold is secure. I feel air swirling in front of my face; I'm guessing that he is waving his hands to check that the blindfold is doing its job.

"Nothing." I reply tautly, still a little sore about having to surrender to this ridiculousness.

"Are you sure?" His voice is closer and his warm breath tickles my face. Suddenly I'm on red alert, not because I'm afraid that he'll do something, but because I'm afraid that if he does something, I will like it. I swallow and nod, not trusting my vocal chords not to make my reply tremor. With my sight eliminated from my sensory equations I now have to rely on my other senses to let me know what's going on. Under normal (sober) circumstances, this would make me anxious. Under the circumstances of Molly and painstakingly potent marijuana, I'm slightly terrified and hyper-aware. My heart is racing, my breathing is shallow and sharp, the music is obstructing me from hearing Jade's movements, my palms are sweaty, and all I can smell is him. Why is he so close? It's driving me mad. He hasn't done anything but tie a blindfold over my eyes, but the lack of action doesn't hinder the charge of carnal electricity from crackling around us. "How sure?" he presses.

"Very sure!" I snap.

"I don't believe you. You're positive that you can't see anything?"

I fling my hands in the air. "Oh for fuck's sake, I just told you that I can't see so will you_" My ranting is cut short by his surprising mouth crashing against mine. I jump, stunned by the contact, and instinctively reach up to push him off. He grabs my arms before I can attack him and pins them to my side and slips his warm tongue between my gradually surrendering lips. I whimper and melt into the kiss, but he doesn't loosen his hold on my arms. His dangerously high body heat pulsates against my already flustered skin, making me writhe in my seat. I nip at his lower lip and he groans, then to my disappointment, he pulls away.

"We'd better keep going, otherwise we'll never reach that party and I will miss out on hearing you begging me to fuck you." he laughs. I roll my eyes behind the blindfold but I don't reply. I can't; I've had the wind kissed out of me. Catching my breath seems more important than wasting it reminding him that I will *never* beg him.

He restarts the engine and we're off again.

"How much further?" I ask, fed up once more of being trapped in the car. The urge to move is now stronger than before since Jade decided to unsettle me.

"About five minutes." He pauses momentarily before following up with, "You excited?" The way he says it makes it sound like a loaded question -I'm not sure whether he's asking me about the party, or the tense, fluttering feeling in my stomach. Either way the answer is…

"Yes." He makes that stupid amused sound that he and Carter have in common.

"Just a heads up; Nathaniel normally turns up to these things." I press my lips into a flat line.

"Well isn't that fantastic!" Of course Nathaniel's gonna bloody be there; he's one of them, his presence is to be expected a hell of a lot more than mine, but that doesn't make it any less frustrating that in an attempt to lose myself and forget about him, I'm going to be trapped in the middle of God knows where with him. Quite frankly, the thought of it is ruining my high.

"What are you thinking?" Jade asks.

"Do you really want to know?"

"I'm not sure yet. Tell me." I can hear him smirking.

"I'm thinking about how I'm going to manage to avoid letting Nate completely ruin my night."

"Darling, that's on you, not him. If you want to enjoy yourself, you will. Nathaniel doesn't have the power to control how you feel, you do." he says matter-of-factly.

I shake my head; clearly he doesn't get it. It's easy for him to simplify the way I react to Nathaniel because he's probably never loved anyone but himself. It's never that easy. You don't get to be in control of your feelings when you love someone because love is insanity; it's irrational, intense and unpredictable. Sure, I can *pretend* that Nathaniel doesn't bother me and maybe one day I'll truly believe it, but right now, that's as far as it goes – pretence. Rage fuelled pretence.

"You're shaking your head. Am I wrong?"

"That's a matter of perspective." I say fairly.

He pauses and I wonder if he's considering my response, or if he's rolling his eyes at me. "I'd like to hear your perspective."

"I just don't believe that things are that simple when you love someone."

"Hmm, I suppose they aren't." The car begins to slow, and then reverse. "That's why I do don't do relationships." It moves forward then reverses again. I hear Jade mutter "Ahh fuck it!" under his breath. He toggles the gear stick, turns the engine off and yanks the keys out of the ignition. "Some things are too complicated; like parallel parking for instance."

"But they're worth it."

"How?" he scoffs. "Please explain to me how a relationship is worth all of the unnecessary complexities that being single is free of." He reaches over and unties my blindfold. It takes a moment for my eyes to refocus. It's dark outside. The only thing I can see clearly is how hazardously Jade has parked among a moderately impressive line-up of cars; someone could easily drive past and crash into the front end of his Lexus, which is sticking out from the line up like a sore thumb.

"Security, for one." I say gesturing at his…unique spin on parallel parking.

"Oh please!" he rolls his eyes and lights a blunt. "Security is an illusion. Your safety, physically, mentally or emotionally is never guaranteed no matter the circumstances. Look at all the shit you had to go through with Nate; the cheating, the rejection, him almost getting another girl pregnant, sleeping with Sky and now dating Fontaine, not to mention the fact that he was going to slap the shit out of you just the other day. Half of the shit he did when you were both single, he done when you guys were together. What's so fucking secure about that? Are you really telling me that, *that* relationship was worth it?"

I frown at him. How can he boil our whole relationship down to a pile of indiscretions as if there was nothing else to us? Nathaniel is still currently public enemy number one but that doesn't mean that I will disregard all of the good times just because he's a colossal jack ass. I know our love was worth it because it mattered, and I know it mattered because it hurt like hell when it was over and it still does.

"Yes. I know it doesn't sound like it, especially when you put it like that, but yes it was. If you ever loved anyone, you'd understand that love is fucking hard sometimes!" I hiss.

Jade peers at me out of the corner of his eye. "Love isn't hard darlin', love just *is*. Relationships are hard, and that's because once you get past all the quirks and initial niceties, people are generally pretty shit!" He climbs out of the car and comes around to open the passenger door for me like a gentleman. "Don't put your faith in anyone but yourself. You don't need anyone to be happy, you have to just be, and if you can't just be, then there are drugs to assist you." he laughs, but it is an empty laugh -he's not joking.

He holds his hand out for me to take it. I do so, awkwardly of course; I wasn't aware that guys still did things like this since us females decided that we were the poster children for independence. I guess chivalry isn't dead after all.

We begin to make our way down the road towards the coastline; me gazing at the sky and Jade finishing off his blunt.

"Is that why you're high all the time, because you can't just be?" I ask absentmindedly.

"What?"

I draw my eyes away from the tiny twinkling lights and look at him. He is frowning.

"You're always high. Is it because you don't know how to be happy?" I repeat with innocent trepidation, fearing that my question may have offended him. He blinks at me and his mask of coolness flickers. He opens his mouth to say something, then just s he's about to speak he snaps it shut again and shoves the last of the blunt in his mouth. His drag is long and deep. He flicks the roach out into the darkness then slips his arm around my waist, tugs me against him and crushes his lips to mine, forcefully exhaling the mind-altering substance into me so that I have no option but to take it all in, just like he did back at his loft. I cough and splutter vehemently, trying to rid my lungs of the large mass of smoke that I'm not used to taking all at once. Jade laughs and lets me go and I curl over trying to stabilise my breathing pattern, not finding this funny in the least.

"Don't be silly love, I'm just bored. Now stop being so dramatic and come on, we've got a wild night ahead of us."

He grabs my hand and pulls me along after him.

26
Burning Man.

Toto, I don't think were in Kansas anymore!
Jade and I are so far away from the city that I can see the stars in their entirety; millions of them occupying the inky darkness of the night sky like a generous fistful of glitter dashed onto a black velvet sheet. The moon is full and beneath it just a few yards ahead of us people are howling up at it. I'm about to enter the wolves secret lair; it's a good thing I'm running with their pack master.

"Are you okay?" he asks, brushing his fingertips lightly across the back of my hand. An explosion of butterflies erupt inside my stomach when I think he may actually hold it again…but he doesn't, and I can't help but feel a little disappointed -not because I particularly want him to hold my hand, but because if we entered the party and he was doing *that*, it would definitely not go unnoticed by anyone.

"I feel like I'm going to float away or sink into the ground." I murmur musically as my head lolls forward, the weight of my skull too heavy for my neck while I'm in this trippy state.

"Just try and keep your shit together, okay."

"I am trying but everything is just…it's too much." I wail, "It's dark, I can't see, they are really loud and I don't like it. I just want to sleep but I can't because I'm wide awake. Oh my God, my legs feel like spaghetti. I can't walk…I'm going to collapse. Go on without me!"

Jade rolls his eyes, "Darling, stop being so melodramatic, you're going to be fine. I told you that when you feel like this you have to focus on something to help you relax."

We're in the middle of nowhere walking -or in my case **stumbling** -towards the best kept secret of London's Unfamous, which doesn't exactly put me in a relaxed state. All I can focus on is trying to stay vertical and that's only making me panic, which is causing me to sway even more. I need something solid to tether me to this reality instead of the hyper-surreal circus that my mind is projecting, like when Jade was stroking my back -that worked wonders. That's it! I need physical contact, and I know exactly the kind I want that will keep me focused and make the impact I desire. I grab Jade's hand. He peers down at me and raises his eyebrow.

"What is it with you and this hand holding thing?"

"You told me to focus on something, so I'm going to focus on what your hand feels like until I can sit down and not worry about crumbling to the floor." I say providing him with only half the truth. I doubt he'd go along with it if I told him that this was also necessary so that the Unfamous would think that there is more to us than there really is. It's not often you see a guy like Jade Washington holding a girl's hand, especially not a girl like me.

"If you wanted to know what my hand felt like, all you had to do was beg a little." he teases, unsmilingly. I blush.

"Shut up!"

We make it down to the edge of the coastline; the hooting and chatter has now reached deafening volumes, colliding with the one of those hard to come by house songs that don't get played in raves that only true house music connoisseurs would have knowledge of and be able to appreciate. It's all noise to me. I can't see the party-goers yet, only the vibrant glow that is being emitted from behind the curve of a rocky cliff that rises and falls along the length of the pebbled shore. When we round the corner I grip Jade's hand that little bit tighter to curb my excitement –if I had an event this dope I'd want to keep it a secret too!

Approximately one hundred people are writhing, lounging, drinking, getting high, making out and chattering amongst a brilliant British rendition of an urban hipster chic beach party. There are several large metal trash cans filled with broken pieces of old furniture that have been set on fire, transforming them into edgy bonfire lanterns, and ice boxes lodged into the ground full of bottles upon bottles of alcohol and chasers. The music blazes triumphantly from a powerful portable stereo system in the shape of a retro boom box, playing that repetitive house music that drags on for ages and sounds like every other house track ever made that I can't stand. A large picnic table is lined up along one of the rocky walls of the cove, covered in food, cutlery and illegal party favours. The walls of the cove are artfully spruced up with soft pearlescent white fairy lights, and seating is a quirky collection of rustic wooden stools, white washed lawn chairs, stripy deck chairs, or simply a blanket or a rug lying on the gravelly ground. There aren't enough seats for everyone, but nobody seems that bothered. It isn't what I was expecting to find at all; I expected more glamour because that's how I'm used to seeing the Unfamous, as glamorous people, but this has taken me by surprise. It literally looks like they grabbed all of the most fitting supplies they could find to accommodate their guests, got some mood lighting, food, drink, music and drugs, and it just happened to come out spectacularly. The atmosphere is nothing like the haughtiness I'm used to seeing them display at regular events. The Unfamous amongst only the Unfamous are relaxed and care free –maybe it's because they have no one to exclude or put on a show for.

"How is this even possible?" I gawk, watching people cut shapes around the trash can lanterns.

"You approve?" Jade asks with a wry smile on his gorgeous face.

"This. Is SICKKKKK!" I sing, accompanying it with an enthusiastic hand gesture that throws the two of us off balance a little.

"Chill." he orders me sternly as a few people look over and scrunch their noses up at us. By and by, more heads turn our way until it feels like the whole party is staring at us –some faces I recognise, some I don't, and some I don't want to –Nathaniel is here. Ignore him, Rio!

"Sorry; it's just so cool!" I grin up at Jade, pretending that I am unfazed by Nathaniel's presence, and shying away from the Unfamous's looks of astonishment and disapproval. Without thinking, I bury my face into the crevice of his arm, humming a little tune and holding onto him, stroking his bicep absentmindedly to calm my nerves as we resume walking. It's ironic how the boy, who once had me on edge every time he acknowledged me, is now my sanctuary. His body tenses as I nuzzle him, but he doesn't stop me from doing it, he simply looks down at me with amused curiosity. Eventually he relaxes, accepting that I am latched onto him and returns to his coolly indifferent demeanour. A chorus of greetings begin as soon as King Jade is within earshot of his subjects; a few people even say hi to me. Jade nods absentmindedly at them while I smile and wave at back, over the moon that they are acknowledging me first. I know that it's down to Jade 'All mighty' Washington turning up here with me wrapped around him; he's their God, so to see him carrying on with me, lil ol' Rio Greene, like this, counts for something major among them.

Nathaniel's steely eyes glare at me as we get closer to the area where he is standing with the majority of Brompton's Unfamous -Calvin, D-Man, Bless, Shaquille, Tanya Woods and Sky -all of whom are the most surprised to see me here. The muscle in Nate's jaw starts working overtime when I pretend not to notice him as Jade and I stop to exchange fist bumps, hugs and air kisses with the Brompton lot. He shouldn't feel that bad about it, I'm ignoring Sky and Tanya too. At least Jade has the courtesy/nerve to greet him. Needless to say it isn't the most comfortable encounter; Jade is arrogant, doing more smirking than smiling at Nathaniel as he fist bumps him, whilst Nathaniel grits his teeth and tries to keep his expression as calm as possible.

"There you are handsome," Tanya smiles holding her arms out to embrace Jade and peck him on the cheek, "I was worried you weren't going to show."

Jade breaks Nate's pending glare to smile at Tanya.

"Did you miss me?"

"You know I did," she purrs, fluttering her stupid eyelashes at him like I'm not standing right here. "I haven't seen you in a minute, where have you been hiding?"

"I've been busy. You know Rio right?" he laces his arm around my waist. I notice his eyes flick over to Nathaniel again and I wish he would let sleeping dogs lie. I elbow him.

Tanya's expression sours, "Mmm," she replies stiffly.

"Well aren't you gonna say hi?" he asks. Tanya raises her eyebrow at him -it's common knowledge that we don't get along due to her being one of Georgia's cronies.

"Rio and I aren't friends." she replies plainly, folding her arms.

"I didn't ask if you were friends. I asked if you were going to say hi." he says evenly. Tanya shifts uncomfortably and purses her lips. She doesn't want to greet me and I couldn't care less because I don't want her to either.

I look up at him. "Jade, it's fine."

"No, it's not." he says tightly, keeping his eyes locked on Tanya.

She rolls her eyes and mutters a forced greeting, "Hello Rio."

"Sky?" Jade shifts his gaze to my former friend.

"Hi." She greets me without hesitation, throwing a plastic smile in for good measure, more for Jade's benefit than my own.

I don't respond to either of them. Instead, I rest my head on his shoulder and slur languidly, "I need a drink." He smiles down at me, amused by my casual dismissal of their forced greetings.

"What would you like, miss?"

"A white wine, please."

"Tanya, fetch Rio a glass of wine." he orders her. We all take a pregnant pause, eyeing Jade as if he's lost his mind.

"Are you joking?" Tanya scoffs.

Jade frowns, "Why would I be joking? Rio wants a drink and I want you to get it for her. Is that a problem?" Tanya's lips press into a thin line, but she does as she is told without further argument.

I watch her as she walks, amazed that she is getting me a drink even though she can't stand me, just because Jade told her to. It's then that I realise that I haven't the faintest idea of how powerful Jade really is. Tanya Woods is pretty important in the Unfamous social scene, not only because she is Georgia Daniels's best friend, but she owns her own PR company and has connections to some of the strongest platforms in urban media so the fact that she is begrudgingly stepping off of her high horse because of Jade, tells me that if I want to survive I their world, I'd better stay in his good graces.

"Come." he ushers me away from my friends.

"But what about my wine?" I whine.

"I'll get you some."

"Then why did you send Tanya to get it?"

He shrugs, "Because I felt like it.." He tells the guys he'll see them later and as we walk away I can feel Nathaniel's eyes burning holes into my back.

We head over to the area where Carter, and a bunch of Herring's Unfamous are gathered. I notice a few eyebrows raise, followed by curious murmurs as we come closer.

"You made it," Carter says, speaking to me but eyeing Jade. His tone is casual but his expression says otherwise –he's not happy with Jade for bringing me here.

Cocky as ever, Jade slaps his friend on the back and grins.

"Lighten up Mr Johnson. I've been on my best behaviour," he takes the seat next to Carter and pulls me into his lap, nuzzling his face into my neck, "haven't I darling?"

"No," I giggle, "Nate looked like he wanted to knock you out."

"Did he? I didn't notice." he shrugs.

"Yes you did, you just don't care." Carter interjects dryly "Nate doesn't like me around Rio, and we're just friends, so I am positive that he sure as hell doesn't want her around the likes of you, pretty boy."

"Me? I'm harmless!" Jade quips cheekily.

"You're about as harmless as a fucking hurricane mate. What did you give her?" he asks in a serious tone, jabbing his finger at me.

"Calm down Johnson, it's only a bit of weed and MD. She's fine," he slips his hand onto my thigh "Aren't you, gorgeous?" I'm not, but the feel of his warm hand sliding slowly up my leg prompts me to nod and sink further into him. He smiles at Carter, "See, she's fine. She's a big girl, Johnson; you don't need to worry about her."

"Jade my darling, who's this?" a beautiful blonde girl dressed in a sheer white tank top with no bra underneath asks curiously.

"This is Rio," Jade replies. "Rio, this is Persia. You already know Leon, Carter's boy. That's my boy Andre, his girlfriend Robin." he says languidly, pointing to the rest of the Herring lot. Leon and Fontaine dated for a while last term; I wave at him and he nods. I recognise Andre and Robin from a few coach parties, but I've never seen Persia before.

"Rio? Why does that name sound familiar?" Persia asks.

"She's Nate Gibson's ex," Robin replies knowingly. I shift in Jade's lap. I don't know these people and yet they know my business.

"Ahhh yes! He's here tonight isn't he? And here you are snuggled up with our Jade; how scandalous!" Persia gushes dramatically pulling a gold compact case out of her Vera Wang clutch. She opens it up and pulls a pink Parisian brand of cigarettes from it.

"Persia, please!" Jade sighs. "Ignore her." he says to me.

"Are you trying to make him jealous?" she asks, ignoring him.

"Persia!"

"What? It's just if she is, she's doing a fabulous job of it, after all you're so bloody stunning darling, you'd make any man feel inadequate!" she smiles at him.

Jade rolls his eyes.

"Flattery will get you nowhere, my dear."

"Oh please!" she scoffs flipping her hair and placing the pretty cigarette between her nude lips, "You and I both know that's not true. Anyway, it's a pleasure to meet you Rio. Now, who wants party favours?"

An hour and a half later Carter and Leon have disappeared, Persia is telling a story about a rich Arab she is currently dating and all of the money he has spent on her so far, whilst Robin, Andre, Jade and I listen patiently, too spaced out from Persia's party favours to bother doing anything else. I'd gotten to know the Herring lot a little better and they seem like a cool bunch. Leon is still as charming and flashy as ever. He asks about Fontaine, but I just shrug and tell him that I don't know how she is; no need to go into detail and tell him that she went back to her ex-girlfriend, and then walked out on her for my ex-boyfriend. Andre is Jade's best friend. He and Robin (who used to date Ace) have been together for about 5 months and are madly in love. As for Persia…Persia is a gold digger, but she's cool.

"I'm hot." I huff, fanning myself. I don't know how much more of this temperature alteration I can take. I'm starting to sweat.

"Me too -wanna go for a swim?" Jade asks, grazing his lips over my temple.

"I don't have a costume."

"Me neither," he murmurs against my burning skin. A rush of heat, not induced by the drugs this time, shoots through me.

"Or I could just get another drink."

"I like my idea better." he nips at my earlobe.

"I'm sure you do." I giggle, getting to my feet. "I'm going to get a drink. Do you want anything?" Jade's eyes darken and he looks me up and down with a slow, sexy smile that makes my skin flush.

"Yes." he replies simply, making my insides tie themselves up into sexually frustrated knots. Jesus Christ, how does he do that? Blushing, I mumble an incoherent reply and stagger away from him in search of another bottle of white wine.

By the time I reach the third icebox I find one, unfortunately it's situated near the Brompton lot -near Nathaniel who has been paying more attention to me tonight than I had anticipated. Out of the corner of my eye I see him say something to Calvin before heading in my direction. Shit! Quickly, I stoop down and pull the bottle out, ready to make a dash for it when it's yanked out of my hands.

"That's enough!" he hisses.

I straighten up, swaying as I do so; glowering at him with all of the contempt that I can muster. "Give it back!"

"No."

"Fine," I shrug, turning my back on him, "I'll go look elsewhere."

Before I can take another step, Nathaniel grabs onto my arm and spins me back around. "No you won't. You're a mess and I'm taking you home!"

"Like hell you are!" I growl, trying to shove him off. He holds on tighter.

"I'm not giving you a choice. What the fuck do you think you're playing at, turning up here with Jade?"

"Moving on!"

"Not with him you're not."

"Oh, and why not?"

"Ri, look at the state he's got you in." he admonishes me, gesturing at my swaying figure. I plant my heels deeper into the pebbles to steady myself.

"It's no worse than the states you've had me in," I scowl. "Anyway, you've got Fontaine now, and you made it perfectly clear how you feel about me, so why does it even matter?"

"Because it does!" he snaps, his eyes flashing indignantly, revealing the thunder storm taking place behind them. In that moment I see the glimmer of love that he'd told me didn't exist anymore.

I go rigid, trapped between emotional relief and stubbornness. I'd sworn never to let him affect me in that way again, yet something about that look causes me to betray myself as it tugs at something deep in my chest.

Sighing, Nathaniel releases me and shoves his hands into the pockets of his black Armani jeans. He diverts his tell-tell gaze to a nearby trashcan lantern, his silvery eyes sparkle as the light from the flames dance in their reflection.

"I broke up with Fontaine," he confesses quietly.

I feel the tugging sensation grow stronger but I grit my teeth to keep it at bay. *So what if he left her, he shouldn't have been with her in the first place so this doesn't change anything*, I remind myself.

Just like clockwork, his eyes flit up to mine and he takes my hand, gently this time, to illustrate his sincerity.

"I should have never done that to you Ri. I'm not trying to make excuses, but after the Georgia thing I was pretty screwed up and I took it out on you, and I'm sorry." I frown at him; it's the same manipulative routine that he's run on me before; the dramatic explosion, the big 'I'm sorry' speech, followed by longing looks and lingering touches that he knows are a sure fire way to bring my defences down. Not this time. Too much has happened for me to cave in.

I pull my hand out of his apologetic grip, shaking my head as I distance myself from him.

"We're not doing this again Nathaniel. It's too late for apologies so you might as well go back to Fontaine because I'm done with you."

His jaw tightens. "This is because of Jade, isn't it?"

"What?"

"The reason you won't hear me out, it's because you have him now, right?" he asks sourly.

I shake my head and laugh emptily, "Are you being serious? Are you really trying to make *Jade* the issue here?"

"Well what else is it? I've told you I'm sorry, I broke up with Fontaine and I admitted that I was wrong. Isn't this what you wanted?" A ball of anger swells up inside of me; is that all he thinks it will take to fix us, another bullshit apology?

"No Nathaniel! I wanted us to be together, happy and in love, the way we used to be before all of this bullshit started, but not anymore. It's not because of Jade or anyone else, it's because of you, you selfish git!" I snarl, jabbing him in the chest. "We're only allowed to be in a good place when it suits you, and it's not fair! You have this fucked up saviour complex where you feel the need to swoop in and rescue me from any man who isn't you, just so you can have the pleasure of being the only one to screw me and screw me over! In your head, you still think that I belong to you, and I don't! The moment you see someone else showing real interest is the exact moment that you decide that you want me back, but not this time. I'm not some toy that you can pick up and drop whenever it suits you!"

Nathaniel frowns at me, "Is that what you really think? You think that this is all some stupid ego trip? After everything, you actually think that I've come back because I don't want anyone else to have you?"

"What else am I supposed to think? You told me you didn't love me and now here you are trying to get back in the picture because Jade is about."

"Jade is no good for you!" he growls.

"You have no place to criticise whether Jade or anybody else is good for me because *you* are *not* the good guy. You are the worst thing that has ever happened to me!" I scream, launching myself at him to shove him away from me and missing. He catches me before I fall flat on my face and hoists me upright.

"That's it, you're coming with me." He tightens his grip on me and pulls my stumbling, screaming frame away from the party. Everyone is looking at us, shaking their heads and muttering 'Here we go again,' as they watch yet another dramatic episode of the Rio and Nathaniel show. This is exactly what I *didn't* want to happen, but as usual I let this stupid boy get the best of me.

"Let go of me!" I hiss trying to struggle against him as discreetly as possible so as not to make things look worse than they already are.

"No! Regardless of what you think of me, I care about you and I'm not leaving you here like this. I don't want you associating with Jade anymore. I'm taking you back to Brompton and Tyson can deal with you."

At the mention of my best friend's name, I start snickering. Nathaniel raises his eyebrow at me.

"What's so funny?"

"You carting me off to Tyson. It's ironic."

"Yeah well, as much as I can't stand him, he seems to be the only person who can ever really get through to you."

"Oh no, that's not what I meant," I giggle nastily. I know I promised Ty that I wasn't going to say anything, but my spiteful side is flaring up and now I finally have the chance to make Nathaniel truly understand what he put me through. It would be hard enough hearing that I'd slept with Jade or Carter, but for Nate to know that I'd slept with the only boy he always felt he had to compete with for my attention, would break him, the same way every woman he laid with broke me -but all at once. "Here's the thing; you're worried about me getting too close to Jade, so to put a stop to it, your solution is to take me to the one person you really should be worried about."

Nathaniel stops walking and looks down at me.

"Why should I be worried about Tyson?" he asks slowly.

"Because I had sex with him last night!" I grin.

"You did what?"

I stop laughing and watch as the realisation of my words begin to sink in and take effect. It takes a while, but he gets there eventually. His face hardens, and then splinters around the edges creating a violent butterfly effect until the cracks in his ego become painfully visible.

"Hurts, doesn't it?" I sneer, "That weight that suddenly lands on your chest, crushing your lungs, making it harder and harder to breathe as the images of the one you love making love to someone else coils around your fucking heart and strangles it to death. That uncomfortable lump developing in your throat, the burning behind your eyes, that sick feeling in the pit of your stomach, and the angry pulsations at your temple; it feels like shit doesn't it?" I step closer and put my lips to his ear, "Every time you fucked me over, *this* is what I went through. *This* is what it feels like to break." I snatch my arm out of his rapidly loosening grasp, leering at him triumphantly as I back away "I'm going back to Jade now. You can leave if you want. I'll understand."

Nathaniel stares at me with dull eyes, as if he's seeing me clearly for the first time. His fists clench and unclench by his sides but the muscle in his jaw is slack –we're finally even. Without saying another word he takes off towards the main road and doesn't look back. Once he disappears around the corner of the cove I exhale and turn around to re-join the party with a sense of renewed liberation -I'm finally free of him. This is the closure I needed all along; to witness Nathaniel truly understanding how much he hurt me, and now he does and I couldn't be happier.

I'm almost halfway back to Jade when an ear piercing screech followed by a thunderous boom and the groan of heavy metal rings out over the party. Time grinds to a climatic halt as we all stop in our tracks, fearing that our suspicion of what could've made that blood curdling sound is true.

Panicking, Sky, D-Man and Shaquille run to the edge of the cove to see what happened.

Sky screams, "OH MY GOD, NATHANIEL!" and just like that everything starts moving in hyper speed. Suddenly, everyone but me is running towards the main road, dialling 999, clutching their mouths in disbelief, yelling and crying. I'm stood stock still amidst the chaos with my heart seizing up in my chest, and my breath trapped inside my lungs. Just as I think things can't possibly get any worse, a deafening explosion breaks the sound barrier, and the air is thick with smoke. The screams get louder.

"No!"

Acknowledgements

It took a while to get here but #TeamUnfamous we finally did it *whoop whoop!*

I'd like to start off by thanking my family, especially my parents and my brothers Jordan and Leon; you guys have been so supportive and patient with me and I am so blessed to have a bunch of people as weird, (tolerant) and awesome as you guys. I love you.

To my Peppergrain familia, Deb (world's best manager!), Monica and Joel, you guys have helped me in more ways than you know, not only professionally, but mentally too. Because of you guys I have developed a better outlook on life and have grown so much during my time with you. May we keep prospering and spreading good vibes yo!

To my girls, Dianne, Mel and Delia, you all requested shout outs like the hoodlums you are, so here it is lol. You are all amazing women and if I didn't have you guys I'd go mad(der).

To Selina, thank you so much for coming on board with this project, it was fate! I have had so much fun working with you, you are a dope director and I can't wait to see what we achieve next.

To the Unfamous web series cast, crew cameos and extras, it was a struggle and a half but we created something totally worthwhile in the end and I want to thank you all for being a part of this journey. I wish each and every one of you the best.

As always I have to big up the Flourish Drama Company, if it wasn't for you guys showing me that Unfamous could be more than a Facebook story, I probably would have never taken it beyond that. Thank you for believing in my work and for being such amazing, talented individuals. I wish you every success.

Love to Media Sharks, Shakira Hussain, Aiden Boyle, Corey Johnson and Kai Smith for giving the Unfamous brand the sexy revamp. It's perfect!

Lastly, gotta send more love to my fans. Guys, none of this would have been possible without you. I appreciate all of your support so much. I owe you everything. Thank you.

Keep showing love for more Unfamous ;)

Lightning Source UK Ltd.
Milton Keynes UK
UKOW05f0639080114

224160UK00001B/42/P

9 781628 905533